# Praise for *The Spider and the Sparrow*

*A. L. Sowards has done it again!* The Spider and the Sparrow *is sure to keep you reading and guessing long into the night.*

—Rebecca Belliston, author of the Citizens of Logan Pond series

*You can almost smell the gunpowder, mustard gas, and mud. This is a captivating novel that takes the reader on a roller coaster of emotions, from despair and desperation to love and hope. A great read!*

—KR Machado, former A-10 pilot, U.S. Air Force

*More interesting than your high school history class (and probably more informative), this look into the Great War aptly shows the conflict from both sides of the trenches and the cost for soldiers and civilians.*

—M. Grant, MA in military history

# THE SPIDER AND THE SPARROW

# A. L. Sowards

# THE SPIDER AND THE SPARROW

A WWI NOVEL

Covenant Communications, Inc.

Cover image: *Cutting out His Eyes—Aerial Combat in WWI, 1919* (colourlitho), Davis, George Horace (1881–1960) (after) / Private Collection / Peter Newark Military Pictures / Bridgeman Images

Cover design copyright © 2016 by Covenant Communications, Inc.

Published by Covenant Communications, Inc.
American Fork, Utah

Printed in the United States of America
First Printing: February 2016

22 21 20 19 18 17 16    10 9 8 7 6 5 4 3 2 1

ISBN 978-1-68047-938-6

This story both begins and ends in the rain, so I thought it
fitting to dedicate this novel to some of my cousins: Lela, Danielle, Shaina,
and Vanessa. We grew up on opposite ends of the country, but I have fond
memories of exploring Nauvoo, Patriot's Point, and Washington, D.C., with
them, all in the rain. These women are
fearless in a rainstorm, and more importantly, they have met
their lives' battles with courage, faith, and kindness.

# The Western

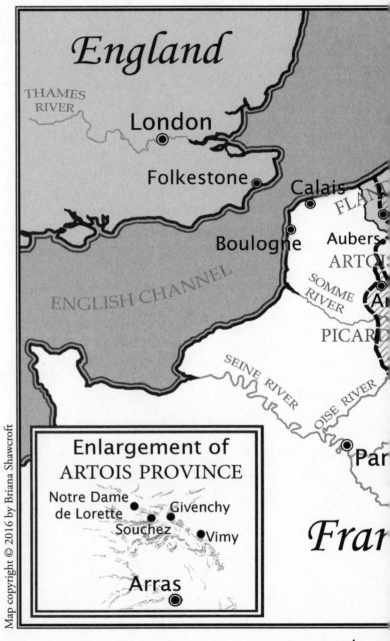

England

THAMES
RIVER

London

Folkestone

Calais

FLAN

Boulogne

Aubers

ARTO

SOMME
RIVER

A

ENGLISH CHANNEL

PICARD

SEINE RIVER

OISE RIVER

Par

**Enlargement of**
**ARTOIS PROVINCE**

Notre Dame
de Lorette

Givenchy

Souchez

Vimy

Fran

Arras

------ Area

terdam

Netherlands

The Hague

Rotterdam

Recklinghausen

RUHR Essen

Antwerp

Düsseldorf

Belgium

Aachen Cologne

Brussels

Bonn

MEUSE RIVER

ai

Germany

Lux.

Sedan

RHINE RIVER

LORRAINE

NE RIVER Verdun

MPAGNE

ALSACE

SEINE RIVER

N

100 Miles

200 Kilometers

Switzerland

ench Warfare

# Useful Terms

ALTHOUGH I'VE TRIED TO MAKE all terms understandable through context, the following are terms or expressions modern readers may find unfamiliar.

**Archie**: Short for Archibald, common slang for anti-aircraft artillery

**Boche**: Derogatory term for German

**Chasseur**: Infantry or cavalry soldier trained for rapid movement

**Deuxième Bureau**: French Army Intelligence

**Hun**: Derogatory term for German

**Jasta**: Abbreviation of jagdstaffel, term for a German squadron of fighter planes

**Kepi**: Round military cap with a visor

**Marraine de guerre**: A godmother for a French soldier

**Poilu**: Literally "hairy one," term for a French infantryman

**Rationer**: Soldier responsible for rations

# Chapter 1

*May 1915, Artois Province, France*

THE SKY RAINED WATER DROPLETS and artillery shell fragments through the loud, misty morning. The water left puddles under the duckboards at the bottom of the French trenches and turned Julian Olivier's horizon-blue uniform into a muddy mess. The artillery, most of it fired from French 75mm Soixante-Quinze guns, landed largely on the Germans and, thus, troubled Julian little.

Amid the shrill whines and distant booms of the guns, Julian huddled under a rain block fashioned from broken rifles and a tattered greatcoat. Water dripped from the edges and leaked through in three spots along the center, but the shelter was sufficient to protect his paper from rain damage as he finished a letter to his parents.

*Spring has skipped the trenches. I don't suppose it can compete with the artillery. Has spring come to Calais? I miss the blossoming trees and the new green grass filling the meadows. Is the Channel clear? When I picture home, I imagine the harbor full of shipping from England. We'll take all the men, horses, and ammunition they can send.*

*I wish I was home to help with the extra work this time of year always brings, yet I am also glad to sacrifice for France. Our existence here is rough, but Lieutenant Roux tells us we will be relieved within the week. I would do much for a bath and a real bed. Mother, you would be horrified by how filthy I look and smell, but since everyone else has been unwashed just as long, we grow used to it.*

Julian paused, his pen hovering above the paper. He decided to spare his mother the description of trench rats. She despised rodents, and he didn't want her to worry. Maybe he'd already said too much in complaining about the smell, but the scent of unwashed men was minor compared to the stench of decomposing bodies. He scratched the hair on the back of his neck. When washed, it was chestnut brown, but for now it was like everything else: the color of mud. He decided to omit the mention of lice from his letter as well. Nor would he tell her about the German shells that frequently pounded his position, but his father would want to know about French weapons.

*Our current artillery barrage is strong, thus my friends predict we shall soon see action. I hope to make you proud when we drive the enemy from our soil.*
*Today it rains, but I am well. Please pray for me, as I ever pray for you.*
*Your loving son,*
*Julian*

He added the date to the top of the sheet: *May 6, 1915.*

After the ink dried, Julian folded the letter and stuck it in his breast pocket for safekeeping. He would post it tomorrow after he'd had time to reread it and make sure he hadn't said anything he wasn't allowed to discuss. During their last period away from the line, he'd written that the cramped barn they were stationed in was covered in more manure than straw. A censor had refused to mail the letter and had given Julian extra work duty as punishment for his complaint.

He left the shelter and stepped into the rain, climbing onto the firing step next to his friend to peer through a hole in the sandbagged breastwork across no-man's land. How long before they'd be asked to go over the top? And when they went, what would they find, other than more mud and bullets? "They're awfully quiet over there."

Maximo Durand turned from his study of the German positions. He removed his kepi and wiped at his brow before replacing the visored cap. He gestured behind the line, where the artillery batteries were set. "At the rate our field guns are firing, there won't be anyone left to attack."

"Someone will survive. And they'll be expecting us." Only a fool wouldn't recognize that a major attack was coming, and for all their faults, the Germans were no fools. Julian checked his rifle for the fourth time that morning to ensure it was loaded and clean, but he didn't think they'd attack in this weather. *Soon*, he thought. He hoped he would be ready.

* * *

The next day was too foggy for an assault. Nor did the battle come the day after. When dawn broke on May 9, Julian read for the fourth time the letter he'd received the day before, a report from his father about the family dairy outside Calais. Julian cared little about the status of the garden, the weather summary, and the detailed chronicle on each of the cows, but he studied each word closely, knowing who had penned each line. The phrases were simple and the spacing uneven, as if written by an unsteady hand. Was his father getting old, or had the table become more rickety during Julian's absence?

"Any news?" Maximo asked.

Julian fought back a yawn as he folded the letter. The artillery bombardment hadn't entirely ceased for days, but its intensity had jumped early that morning. Even though the shells weren't aimed at him, they'd disturbed his already uneasy sleep. "Nothing much."

"Three pages, and nothing much?" Maximo raised a dark eyebrow and twisted his mustached lips to the side.

Julian scraped some of the mud off his left boot with his right one. He could barely remember the last time either of his feet had been dry, but he supposed everyone had their troubles. "My father still works from dawn to dusk, my mother is still ill, and my brother is still dead."

Maximo looked away. "Sorry."

Julian regretted his sharp reply. The strange mix of boredom with their tasks, danger from German snipers, and anxiety for the upcoming battle left him on edge, but he shouldn't take it out on Maximo. Julian was lucky to have someone write to him so frequently. Maximo's wife was barely literate. She usually found someone to write a letter for her once a month, but Julian suspected the stretch between letters was agony for his friend. "No, I'm sorry. Would you like to read it?"

Julian passed the letter to Maximo. The two had known each other since beginning their compulsory military service at age twenty. A new law had stretched their two years' active duty into three, and then the war had extended it indefinitely. When they were new enlistees, Maximo had tried to match his friend with his younger sister, but Mademoiselle Durand had married someone else after exchanging only two letters with Julian. She was lovely in her pictures but dull in her letters, so Julian had experienced only slight disappointment.

Maximo handed the letter back when he finished. "I'm sorry about your mother. Send her my wishes when you write her again, will you?"

Julian nodded, scratching his neck.

"Fleas?"

"I caught them from you, I'm sure." The itching moved into his hair, and Julian took his brimmed cap off for a few seconds, letting the breeze cool his head as he searched for the irritation's source.

"Why bother? They'll still be there no matter how hard you scratch. Unless a shell scratches it for you."

Julian slammed his kepi back on. He was sick of living in mud. Their unit was past due for a break, a trip behind the lines where they might have hot food and maybe even baths. "I miss the ocean. If I were home, I'd go swimming and drown the vermin."

"Remember the time I came to visit?" Maximo was the only member of the section who had met Julian's German mother and French father.

"How could I forget?" Before Julian could tease Maximo about his inability to milk a cow or the way his jaw had dropped when Julian had pointed out the White Cliffs of Dover, Lieutenant Roux squeezed along the narrow trench, gathering his soldiers.

Roux was about Julian's age, in his midtwenties. He walked with the discipline and precision of a chasseur officer. Even in the trenches, his uniform was pressed and his face clean-shaven. It was a contrast to most of the men, who were now called poilus—the hairy ones.

Everyone was silent as Roux instructed them. "Today we drive the Boche invaders out of the Noyon salient and clear Vimy Ridge and Notre Dame de Lorette. Once we manage that, we'll reach the Douai plains and cut off German rail lines. Tenth Army will attack along a broad front. Our section's goal is to take the area between Souchez and Givenchy. The timing is perfect. The Germans are still busy up in Ypres, and the British have given them new problems over at Aubers Ridge. We'll go as far as we can, then consolidate before the German counterattack. Follow the nearest NCO. Don't bunch up, but work as a unit. Any questions?"

No one spoke. Julian glanced around at his comrades. Some of them looked at Roux; some of them gazed toward the German lines. None of them smiled.

"We go over the top at ten. Check your equipment and get ready." Roux moved on to brief more of his men.

"Souchez and Givenchy." Maximo said the words as if describing something from the underworld. He cleared his throat and shook his head. "Well, I've long thought the Boches were a little too close to Paris."

"Our artillery has already killed most of them, remember?" Julian tried to lighten the mood, but they both knew it took only a few survivors to man the machine guns positioned to sweep all of no-man's land. Maybe the barrage had at least taken out the Boche artillery. He would rather be killed by a bullet than a shell fragment. He'd seen his share of corpses in the past months. Those hit by bullets were usually still recognizable as human; the same couldn't always be said of those struck by artillery. "Corporal Bernard said the Russians need a little help. Maybe this will take some of the pressure off them."

"Sure. Take the pressure off them by drawing more Boches to France. I hope the only thing we find alive over there is the rats," Maximo said.

"Don't we have enough rats for you here? You want more?"

Maximo's face broke into a smile. "During the Hundred Years' War, wasn't Calais under siege and its inhabitants so desperate for food that rats became a common staple?"

"And you country peasants turn to rats every time a crop fails. Several times a decade, right? I'll wager your wife can cook up a fine rat stew."

Maximo laughed, but his grin faded as the whine of a falling artillery shell grew louder. "You remember our agreement?"

Julian nodded. "If anything happens to you, I'll visit your wife on my next leave. And if something happens to me . . ."

"I shall visit your parents."

Julian peeked over the top of the trench. He could see Vimy Ridge in the distance, partially obscured by artillery smoke. It wasn't very high, but the slight elevation gave the German gunners an edge. *An edge we'll take from them today or die trying.*

Corporal Bernard milled around the men, tugging on straps and looking along rifle sights. The lanky noncommissioned officer with a roman nose liked things orderly, but there was always reason behind his discipline, never a show of power. Unlike the commissioned officers, Bernard spent his time in the mud with the men, sharing their hardships equally, explaining rumors honestly.

The time to advance came quickly. The guns fell silent for a few minutes, and when it was likely the Boches had emerged from their cover to man what was left of their positions, the French artillery showered them with sixteen-pound shells for another thunderous ten minutes. Julian almost felt sorry for his enemy. He'd lived through artillery barrages, and he hated them—the terror of being buried alive by a close hit, the fear of being decapitated by a closer hit, the noise, the uncertainty, and the way the whole earth shook as if hungry for fresh corpses. But no one had invited the Germans into Artois. It was their own fault.

"Ready!" Lieutenant Roux's voice carried along the trench as clear as a bugle.

Julian held his breath as he waited for the order to advance.

"Forward!"

Julian crawled from the trench on a ladder, Maximo right behind him. On Roux's orders, Corporal Bernard led their group through the gate in the French barbed wire and into no-man's land. Julian took a few deep breaths and kept hunched over as he ran toward the Boche line. It felt like he'd left something in the trenches—his stomach, perhaps. Everyone did their best to ignore the hail of bullets flying all around them. *Keep moving*, Julian told himself. Going back was both cowardly and treacherous. The only temporary safety lay ahead of them; the only permanent safety lay in victory.

Julian had studied no-man's land before, but it looked different now that he was in the middle of it, exposed to enemy fire. The earth seemed more desolate, each crater forming a nearly impassable hurdle. They dashed across twenty meters of ground and followed Bernard into a group of shell holes. Most of the soil had dried from the week's earlier rainstorms, but the bottom of Julian's hole was marked with puddles, and he splashed into one as he tried to protect his head from a persistent German machine gun.

He aimed his Lebel rifle toward the bullets' source. He couldn't see the soldiers shooting at them, but when Bernard gave the order, he would fire, along with everyone else. Ideally, they'd distract the gunners long enough for another group of Roux's men to move forward.

"Let's get that Boche, eh?" Maximo said from Julian's elbow.

"I can't see him."

Maximo fired, and the machine gun fell silent. "I could."

When the other half of their group arrived, Bernard called out to them. "Prepare to advance."

On Bernard's instruction, they fired as a group, then rushed from their shelters. One of the other soldiers spun around and cried out in pain. "Keep moving," Bernard ordered. Julian looked back. Bernard dragged the wounded man into a ditch, where he would be protected from German bullets, and then sprinted forward to lead his men again.

The noise was incessant. High-explosive shells, shrapnel shells, machine gun bullets, rifle bullets. Julian kept moving despite the artillery bursting around him, staying next to Maximo. His friend was the faster runner, but there was strength in numbers, so Julian forced himself to keep up. Bernard's section leapfrogged with a sergeant's group all the way across no-man's land. Julian heard the whine of a particularly noisy shell, and he didn't like the way the sound accelerated as if coming directly toward him.

"Get down!" Julian grabbed Maximo's elbow and yanked him down to the naked soil. The shell hit only fifteen meters away. Plumes of dirt shot skyward, and the blast's force barreled over him like a cavalry charge. German artillerymen must have sighted their guns to the area long ago because the salvo was devastatingly accurate. A dozen comrades surrounded Julian and Maximo on the ground, some of them wounded, some of them killed, and some of them obliterated.

Maximo glanced at the casualties on either side of him and then at Julian. "I would have got it if you hadn't pulled me down."

Julian swallowed back the urge to vomit as he caught sight of Pierre Bonnett's body. At least, he thought it was Bonnett. It was difficult to tell because most of the head was missing.

Corporal Bernard gathered the remnants of his group. Of the sixty men who had comprised their section, Julian could see fewer than half.

As they neared the German trenches, they were greeted by increased machine gun fire and a mass of barbed wire. The French shells had cut some of the wire, but enough remained to slow them down. Several men cried out and fell, some of them tumbling to the ground and others getting caught in the barbs.

Julian climbed over a mound of dirt and jumped into the trench. It was empty except for the German corpses littering the ground. The first trench had taken a beating, with huge sections completely collapsed. Maximo scrutinized the neatly sandbagged sides of a preserved section. They were different from the French trenches—more orderly, wider.

"They're tidy. I'll give them that." Maximo kicked the side of the trench and followed it around a corner.

"Maximo, wait." Julian ran after him, hoping no German soldiers lingered just out of sight.

Maximo grinned at him as Julian caught up. "Nothing here."

Corporal Bernard's voice bellowed over the battle. "Let's not dawdle. We've made good time. Keep the momentum before the Boches reorganize."

They were advancing again, this time from a German trench. They repeated the process of taking and securing the German reserve trenches, each a few hundred meters farther east. All morning they ran forward for an incredible gain of over four kilometers. By noon they could see the Douai Plain.

"Unbelievable," Maximo said as they sheltered in a ditch at the side of a road. "I didn't think an army could move this fast anymore. I feel like I'm part of Napoleon's Grande Armée."

Julian watched a rat nibble on a French corpse. "Sure, and Givenchy will turn into another Austerlitz." But Julian had a sinking feeling that if the other sections had fared the same as Roux's, the French Army had lost far too many troops for a victory as glorious as Austerlitz.

Roux gathered them in a slight depression behind a minuscule ridge that, in theory, would protect them from enemy fire. "Time to consolidate. Our flanks haven't advanced as far as we have, so the Boche can shoot at us from three sides. We need reinforcements before we move on." Roux glanced at his men. "Archambault."

"Yes, sir?" A soldier with a muddy kepi and a thick beard crawled forward.

"Find our reserves. Tell them our location and that we need them at once." Roux pointed to another group of soldiers. "You six provide cover fire. The rest of you dig in."

"Yes, sir."

Archambault climbed from the shelter and headed back the way the section had come. He'd made it only ten meters when the crack of a rifle sounded. Archambault jerked to a stop, his back arching, and dropped to the ground.

Roux swore under his breath. "Olivier."

Julian's hands tightened on the shovel he'd just removed from his pack. "Yes, sir?"

"We need those reserves."

Julian put his shovel away. He tried not to picture what had happened to Archambault, tried to convince himself that the man's death had been a fluke. But that wasn't true. Around the trenches, dead runners were almost as common as rats. He wasn't exactly safe where he was, but out in the open, things would be far worse. He had a lot of ground to cover, and enemy machine gun nests and snipers had plenty of light with which to see him.

"I'll go instead." Maximo grabbed Julian's arm and looked to Roux for permission.

Roux shrugged. "One of you go, now."

"Your legs are too short for you to be a runner." Maximo gave Julian a forced smile. "You'll never outrun their bullets."

"You're married," Julian said. "I'll go."

"Julian, I owe you my life. Let me repay my debt."

Julian forced a laugh. "Our artillery killed all the snipers, remember?"

Maximo didn't loosen his grip. "Julian . . ."

"I'll see you in a few hours. If not, write to my parents." Julian pulled away from his friend and scrambled from the ditch, dashing into a shell hole where he could pause long enough to locate another shelter. French rifles discharged as Julian's squad provided cover fire.

Inside the crater, Julian took a deep breath. His friends depended on him, so he had to stay alive until he delivered his message, and he had to move quickly. *Time to return across the chaos you just conquered.*

# Chapter 2

*May 1915, Artois Province, France*

WARREN FLYNN EXAMINED THE WINGS of his B.E.2 biplane, checking the repaired canvas and inhaling the scent of castor oil and petrol. Around him, the aerodrome roared to life as mechanics spun propellers and men shouted over the noise in preparation for takeoff.

"Ready for your dose of hate, Canada?" Captain Jimmy Prior asked.

Warren wasn't the only Canadian in this squadron of the Royal Flying Corps, but the nickname had stuck, even though he'd left his father's farm in Cardston, Alberta, almost five years ago. "Of course, sir. And Boyle is ready to dish it back out to any Hun unlucky enough to fly within range. That is, if Boyle's willing to come up again. We had a rather thin time of it this morning with that Albatross."

"I'm always happy to fly, sir." Tommy Boyle looked up from the ground with a wide grin as he put away his wrench and other tools.

Prior studied the repairs. "Flynn, do you remember the village we ate in last Wednesday?"

"Yes."

"I'm meeting a mademoiselle there this evening." Prior winked. "Should I see if she has a friend?"

"No. Thanks though." Warren enjoyed the attention his uniform generated with women as much as the next man, but he wasn't on the hunt for a lady friend.

"That's right. You've got that Yankee girl. In Paris, isn't she?"

Warren smiled. "Yes, but I don't think Americans from the South refer to themselves as Yankees, even when they move to France."

He owed Claire a letter. He'd received one from her the day before, written in flawless handwriting and smelling slightly of lavender. He would try to write back soon, but first he had to worry about the patrol.

"Carry on, then." Prior nodded at the two of them before gathering his own observer and striding to his own plane.

Boyle stood and used a rag to wipe the oil from his hands. "Do you speak French, Lieutenant?"

"Badly."

"I wish I did, even badly. Hard to talk to the women when you don't speak the language."

"Have you seen one you fancy?" Warren finished inspecting Boyle's repairs. They looked perfect, as usual. Boyle was a competent gunner and a top-notch mechanic.

"I'd fancy a walk with just about any of them, sir, but someone has to keep this troublesome old plane flying."

Warren didn't mind the mismatched fabric patches or the scratched fuselage as long as the battered biplane continued to function. "I should have checked with you earlier about going up again, but I knew you'd say yes. You're almost as addicted as I am."

Boyle helped mount the twenty-eight-pound machine gun onto the plane. "I don't suppose it's likely that a tanner's son could ever be a pilot, but I would like to fly someday, sir."

"Your eyesight is sharp—probably better than mine. You have that in your favor."

"Perhaps, but my birth puts me at a bit of a disadvantage."

"I was born on a small farm in Western Canada. I'm lucky enough to have a rich English grandmother, but I imagine our boyhoods weren't so different. You watch, this war isn't going to end quickly. Soon a man's abilities will be of greater worth to the Royal Flying Corps than a man's birth, and I'll be the first to recommend you for pilot's training." Most men would tell Warren not to encourage the lad, but Warren felt the hope he gave was real.

Boyle's lips curved up in surprised joy. "Thank you, sir."

"I'm just not sure where I'll find another mechanic as good as you."

"You'll find someone, sir. I'll train him myself if needed." Boyle's eyes glimmered with anticipation. Warren recognized the yearning there, the deep desire to soar through the sky, because he'd had the same hunger since the moment he first witnessed flight. He could still picture the plane in the black-and-white newsreel, striking him with awe and inspiring a thirst for audacity.

Warren made his last preflight check, reaching into his pocket to make sure his good-luck charm, the broken handle of a teacup, was still there. He'd dropped his china cup the last time he'd had tea with Claire and her English grandmother in London, the day after Britain had entered the war. Claire had picked the piece up and tossed it to him, saying, "I trust this cup is the only thing you'll be breaking during the war, Mr. Flynn. I would hate for this to be our last meeting. Do take care as you fly your plane off into glory."

Off into glory . . . Warren had quickly discovered that war wasn't glorious, but flying was, regardless of the circumstances that allowed him up in the air day after day.

The men climbed into the plane, Boyle in the forward observer's seat and Warren in the rear pilot's seat. They adjusted their goggles and safety straps, then Warren signaled for one of the mechanics to spin the propeller. Soon the Renault engine thrummed steadily.

Warren loved the feel of the airplane's vibrations as it sped along the ground, seeming as eager to be airborne as he was. Even more, he loved the sensation of the plane leaving the ground and climbing ever higher, no longer bound by the rules that had held men to the earth for centuries. There was freedom in flight, marred only by the carnage below.

And the ground below was covered in carnage, even if all he saw from eight thousand feet was a colorless muddle of gray and brown sliced with trenches and pocked by high-explosive shells. Yesterday the British Expedition-ary Force had attacked Auber's Ridge in conjunction with a nearby French attack. Warren had spotted for the artillery before the men had charged across no-man's land. Today the front line looked unchanged. The poor devils on the ground had advanced but a little, and they'd given up their meager gains the night before under persistent pressure from the Germans. The effort had been a waste of blood and munitions.

"There they are." Over the roar of the engine, Warren could just hear Boyle's shout from the observer's seat. "Hun field guns."

"Signal in the coordinates. Let our artillery know where to hit."

Boyle pulled out his signal lamp and sent the initial flashes.

A series of shells streaked skyward from behind the German lines. "Here comes Archie." Warren wasn't sure who had started referring to the antiaircraft shells as Archibald, but he sent the plane into a dive to avoid the latest explosions. After his evasion, Warren pulled the nose of his plane up to regain the altitude he'd lost.

"How short was that?" Boyle asked as a British salvo hit the German lines. "Sixty yards? Seventy?"

"Fifty, I'd say. You'd best signal again." Warren's ability to judge distances from above was improving, but artillery spotting was still just trial and error.

He glanced behind him, squinting at three dark specs that grew into three biplanes. "On second thought, time to trade in that signal-lamp for the Lewis gun," Warren shouted. He couldn't yet make out the type of planes, but his gut told him they weren't friendly.

Boyle made the switch in an instant. "You think we'll be needing it?"

"Three aircraft, five o'clock high." As they drew closer, he added, "Rumplers."

"Do you think they'll attack?"

Warren didn't answer immediately, turning west and getting a better view of the German scout planes that adjusted their courses to match his. "If I had planes like that, I'd attack. They've got the advantage in numbers, and they can hit more than ninety miles per hour."

"So can we, sir, in a dive with a tail wind."

Warren forced a laugh as they crossed into British-held territory. He wasn't opposed to scrapes with enemy aircraft, but when his machine was outnumbered and outmatched, he preferred to fight over his own lines in case he had to make an emergency landing. The Rumplers were faster than his B.E.2, but it would take them a while to catch up. He considered diving to increase his speed, but the Rumpler pack was already above him, and he didn't want to increase their altitude advantage.

The next few minutes stretched out, each second slower than normal, as if time were caught in a roll of barbed wire and was having difficulty extracting itself. It was three against one, and the enemy had the better planes. But perhaps their pilots were poor or their gunners nearsighted. As the Rumplers grew progressively closer, a desperate plan formed in Warren's head. It might backfire, but there weren't many alternatives.

When the first Rumpler was about sixty yards away, nearly within firing range, Warren pulled his plane into a loop-the-loop. When he'd first learned to steer his plane through a vertical circle, he'd thought of it as a stunt, not a tactic, but that had been before the war had started.

Two of the enemy planes followed him as he returned to a level course, but the third was now ahead of him in perfect range for Boyle's Lewis gun. The .303 caliber cartridges tore into the Rumpler, the rhythmic thumps of the bullets barely audible over the engine's drone. Warren gave Boyle a few good seconds to shoot, then dove sharply to the left to lose the airplanes still on his tail. He heard the double sound of Rumpler guns but didn't feel anything crash into his plane. He'd flown beneath the stream of bullets.

Warren sped through a cloud and leveled off. The plane Boyle had shot turned back to the German lines, smoke trailing from its engine. Warren's dive had increased the distance between the two remaining Rumplers and him, but they would soon catch the B.E.2 again.

It took the Hun planes less than two minutes to return to firing range. Warren dove again, this time to the right, but his plane simply wasn't fast enough. German bullets tore through the canvas wings and across the observer's seat. Wires snapped, Boyle slumped forward, and the propeller splintered. The plane dropped.

"Boyle?" Warren switched off the engine to keep it from igniting. He tested the stick. The plane still responded to his commands, although its movements were no longer smooth.

"Boyle? Are you all right?" Boyle didn't answer, but in case the lad could hear him, and because things seemed less dire if he spoke aloud, Warren continued. "We'll glide down. We're over our lines now—or the French lines. No hardship to make it back to our aerodrome once we land."

The vast majority of pilots would recognize that Warren's B.E.2 was going down and leave the damaged plane to its dismal chance of a successful landing, but one of the Rumplers came back for another pass. With a broken engine and an unresponsive gunner, Warren was as easy a target as the French troops had been charging across Alsace in bright red trousers the previous autumn. The bullets didn't hit Warren, but the smooth glide he'd managed to coax his plane into disintegrated to a spin as bullets struck the fuselage and tail.

Warren fought with the stick and the rudder, trying to regain some measure of control. Between the clouds, the smoke, and the rotation of the plane, he could no longer see the Rumplers. He hoped they'd gone away. He was suddenly grateful for all the practice in coming out of spins that his flight instructor had insisted on. He'd lost track of his altitude, but the ground was coming up fast. He wrestled the plane into a straighter course and coaxed it past the rows of trenches.

Only feet above the earth, he braced himself for a crash landing.

# Chapter 3

TWENTY-FOUR HOURS HAD PASSED since Julian's return to Lieutenant Roux and the rest of his section. He'd brought no reinforcements because when he'd arrived at battalion headquarters, he'd been told all the reserves were several miles away, out of German artillery range, too distant to be of immediate use. His comrades' disappointment still weighed him down like an overfilled pack. The subsequent hours had brought no improvement as the desperate men fought off a series of German counterattacks.

Four hours ago, the reserves had finally made it forward to bolster the front line. They were a day late, and by then Maximo and Julian were among the wounded.

Julian tried to ignore the pounding in his head and the sharp pain in his side. He repositioned Maximo's left arm. It was slung across Julian's shoulders so his friend could use him as a crutch, and it was trickier than it sounded because Julian didn't want to aggravate the shrapnel wounds in his friend's upper right arm. A slightly smaller piece of shrapnel was lodged in Maximo's right thigh. Despite Julian's best attempt to be gentle, Maximo winced.

"Sorry." Julian glanced from the ground in front of him to his friend. As he looked up, he stumbled and barely caught himself in time to keep the two of them upright.

"Sorry?" Maximo laughed softly. "Yes, why haven't you conjured up a cart for me yet? Preferably one with a mattress in the back. Or a bathtub."

Julian led them around the edge of a shell hole. The French and German armies were still exchanging artillery salvos, but at least the two soldiers were out of range for accurate small-arms fire. "I've yet to see a cart that wouldn't get stuck within minutes out here. But you could certainly use a bath."

Maximo chuckled again. "So could you."

"So could the entire section."

The humor in Maximo's voice vanished. "Most of the section is in need of a coffin, not a bathtub." Of their sixty-man unit, only twelve had survived to welcome the reserve troops.

A shrill whine sounded in Julian's ears, but he was experienced enough to know it was their own French 75mm guns. Maximo stumbled, and Julian struggled again to keep his balance in the uneven dirt. "Are you all right?"

Maximo nodded. "Your head is bleeding again."

With his free hand, Julian felt the trickle of blood escaping the bandage wrapped around his forehead where a shard of shrapnel had burrowed into his skin, stopping at the bone. "It's nothing."

"Sure. And your face isn't turning white either."

"My face is covered in mud. You can't tell what color it is."

"I can guess." Maximo grimaced as Julian tripped a third time and jerked them both to keep from falling. "You're so dirty your own mother wouldn't recognize you. Do you suppose my wife would recognize me?"

"No, and you wouldn't want her to." Julian glanced at Maximo. Grit and blood coated him from the top of his kepi to the bottom of his boots. "I'm your best friend, and I barely recognized you when I came back yesterday."

"If you were smart, you wouldn't have come back. You would have developed a sudden case of trench fever or managed to sprain your ankle."

"If I hadn't come back, who would drag you to the aid station?"

Maximo gave the faintest of laughs. "Yes, without you, I'd still be lying in that shallow ditch, praying the Germans weren't mounting another counter-attack." Maximo coughed and moaned as the movement jarred his injuries. "Thank you for coming back. When you left, I was sure you'd be picked off by some Boche sniper."

Julian didn't answer. He'd thought the same thing. They'd all had close calls during their initial push through the German lines yesterday morning. To make it back to headquarters, then to return to his unit—crossing the same ground three times that day without dying—was nothing short of a miracle.

Maximo groaned again as Julian jostled him around a mound of dirt.

"Let's rest." Julian eased his friend to the ground under a tree that had lost most of its branches and all of its leaves. Julian felt the cut along his ribs, put there by a Boche bayonet during one of the German counterattacks. It was shallow, but it hurt. He sat next to Maximo and tried to ignore the pain.

"Is it bad?" Maximo asked.

Julian shrugged. He glanced around, wishing a stretcher-bearer would materialize. The entire landscape was unnatural. Summer would soon arrive, but the absence of vegetation was like winter, and the pockmarked mud was like nothing Julian had ever seen before. A crashed plane caught his eye. He assumed it had been there a while until he noticed a thin tendril of smoke rising from the wreckage.

"I'm going to see if anyone survived." Julian glanced at Maximo, who stared at the wreck.

"Probably all dead. But be careful."

Julian struggled to his feet, trying to ignore a bit of nausea. He approached the airplane cautiously, not sure who he would find inside. It didn't look like a French plane. If a German pilot was inside, would the Boche shoot? But what kind of man would Julian be if he left him to die?

One of the airmen lifted his head and fumbled with his goggles as Julian approached. By the time Julian reached the plane, the man had crawled forward and was trying to pull out a second airman. He tugged a few times but had no success. Julian was slim and among the shortest in his section, but he offered his assistance anyway. "Can I help you?"

The man turned his head. "Yes. He's wounded and not responding. Shot through the arm, and I think he smashed his face up a bit when we landed. I need to get him to a doctor." The man's French accent was horrid, but he seemed otherwise fluent. And he was British, not German.

With two men, the impossible became merely difficult. They each grabbed a shoulder and manhandled the unconscious airman from his seat to the ground. When they finished, the cut in Julian's side burned. As Julian breathed through the pain, the British man bandaged the second man's wounds with a scarf and a handkerchief. He finished and pulled off his flying cap, revealing brown hair a shade darker than his eyes.

"Is he all right?" Julian asked.

"He's breathing, but other than that, I'm not sure."

Julian frowned. "The aid station is that direction, I think." He gestured west. "I was heading there myself, with a comrade."

The man followed Julian's hand as he pointed to Maximo. "Can your mate walk?"

"Not by himself."

He swallowed and bent over his comrade again. "Boyle? Can you hear me?"

Boyle didn't move.

"You're a pilot?"

"Yes. Got jumped by three Hun planes while on reconnaissance. The name's Flynn. Warren Flynn. From Canada originally."

"Olivier. Julian. From Calais."

"Good to meet you, Julian Olivier. Thank you for your help."

Julian shook Flynn's offered hand. "Can you carry him?" The Canadian was taller and more muscular than Julian, but so was Boyle.

"I can try."

Julian went back to help Maximo, and the four of them continued west. Flynn carried Boyle on his back. Everyone but the British gunner was soon breathing hard from the exertion, and their conversation dried up accordingly. They were accompanied instead by the crack of small arms and the whistle of artillery shells.

The pounding in Julian's head and the stabbing in his side grew worse. He felt a wave of dizziness wash over him. Through the ringing in his ears, he heard Flynn's voice.

"Shall we take a break?"

Julian grunted his agreement and helped Maximo to the ground, then joined him as his legs gave out. A few lone trees stood nearby, but nothing with sufficient branches for shade. He took out his canteen and sipped at the foul water before passing it around to the others.

"They say you made good progress yesterday and today. Better than we did at Aubers Ridge." Flynn gazed north, toward the British lines, then at the poilus.

"Yes, but the reserves weren't quick enough to exploit it. So many dead . . . and I don't know why." Julian heard his voice slur.

Maximo nodded at the bandage on Julian's head. "The bleeding's worse."

Julian felt his forehead. He didn't need to probe his side to know that it too was bleeding.

"You should rest." The pilot pushed himself to his feet. "I'll get help and be back as soon as I can."

After the Canadian pilot left, Julian drifted in and out of consciousness, watching the sunlight disappear and the stars move about their celestial course. Maximo and Boyle remained alive but still, and the sounds of distant battle faded to a murmur.

* * *

Julian didn't remember being put on a stretcher, but sometime the next day he woke to find himself in a long row of wounded poilus. His head felt as though it was on fire, and so did his side.

He drifted off again, and as the daylight grew dim once more, he awoke in a makeshift hospital. Two men spoke quietly in French. With effort, Julian turned his head toward them as they inspected the man next to him.

"This one will never fight again," one of the orderlies whispered. "We'll have to amputate the entire arm."

Julian looked more closely at the wounded man—Maximo. Given the choice, would Maximo trade his arm if it meant he could go home?

The other orderly grunted. "Put him outside. We'll tend to him if we have time later."

Julian's throat was dry. He tried to grab one of the orderlies to stop them before they discarded Maximo like a spent shell casing, but they paid no attention to what Julian tried to say, even as they moved on to him and studied his wounds.

"He's got a fever, but he'll go back to the lines if we take care of him. Move him to the table."

It was all wrong. Why should his care be more urgent than Maximo's? And he didn't want to go back to the trenches. But the jolt of pain that went through him as he was lifted from the ground ended in darkness, cutting off his thoughts again.

* * *

When Julian woke he was in pain. His head felt unsteady, and the agony in his side told him the bayonet wound was worse than he'd originally thought. He caught a passing orderly's attention. "I need to find my friend."

"You're not leaving your bed anytime soon."

"Will you find him for me?"

The orderly huffed. "Do you see how full we are? I don't have time to look for one man who may or may not be here."

"His name is Maximo Durand. He was brought in at the same time I was, with injuries to his right arm and right thigh. I overheard talk of amputating the arm."

"I don't have time."

"I'll pay you." Julian still wore his dirty uniform. He felt in his pockets, but they were empty save for two sous. His other money was in his pack, abandoned along with his Lebel rifle when Maximo had needed help walking. Julian grabbed a ring from his finger and pressed it and the coins into the orderly's hand. "Please."

The man looked at the ring. Julian's mother and father had given it to him when he'd completed his third year of military service. It wasn't expensive enough to impress a wealthy man, but his parents had saved for several months for the gift. The orderly slid the ring into his pocket. "I'll see what I can do."

Later that day, the same orderly shook Julian awake.

"The man beside you won't last much longer. When he dies, I'll have your friend moved to that bed. But don't expect much. He isn't doing so well either. And we've got too many new casualties for the doctors to spend time on someone vomiting up blood the way he is."

The man was gone before Julian could ask more about Maximo's condition, but his prediction proved prophetic—the poilu beside Julian did indeed die only a few hours later. Julian felt sorry for the poilu, but he was more concerned for Maximo. Was his condition as dire as the orderly had said it was? Within minutes of the neighboring soldier's death, Maximo took his place.

His friend groaned and turned his head toward Julian as the orderlies left. He looked awful, his eyes dull and his arm still wrapped in the same filthy bandage from the trenches. No one had amputated the arm, but Julian didn't think anyone had tried to save it either.

"I was wondering what happened to you." Maximo coughed with alarming force. With his good arm, he reached into his pocket and pulled out a band of copper. "I made my wife a bracelet out of a shell casing. Will you take it to her?"

Julian handled the delicately carved circle. Julian almost told Maximo he'd be able to deliver the gift himself, but that would be a lie, and the two of them were past lying. As he studied his friend's ghostlike skin and listened to the rattle in his breath, Julian had the feeling it was time to say good-bye.

# Chapter 4

WARREN'S NEXT FURLOUGH WAS SEVERAL months after the plane crash. He usually spent leave in London and stayed with his grandmother. She had never approved of Warren's father, but she'd been generous in supporting her oldest grandson through Oxford, and she'd seemed to understand his drive to become a pilot. He thought she would also understand if he took advantage of an invitation to spend his leave in Paris.

Warren visited Boyle in hospital outside the French capital on his way to the city. Boyle was in good spirits, and Warren made them even better by bringing chocolate and news of the squadron's recent successes. Then Warren posted a letter to his grandmother and sought out Claire Donovan's address.

The Donovan estate was located in a promising section of Paris. Thick ivy filled the wrought-iron fence, and the home's architecture eschewed simple elegance and instead called out for attention. The home was large, but the oversized gilded lions would have been better suited to a building the size of the Paris Opera House, and two stories weren't enough to do the Gothic lines justice.

The home was a sharp contrast to Claire's understated fashion. The home was probably Mr. Donovan's choice, like the heavy, gold cuff links Warren had noticed when he'd met Claire's father in London last winter. Mr. Donovan was still trying to impress his late wife's family. Warren's father had been like that for a time, if Warren's grandmother was to be believed, but he'd long ago given up and moved across the Atlantic.

Warren hesitated before ringing the bell. When they'd met, Mr. Donovan had invited him to spend his next leave with them in Paris. He had meant it, hadn't he?

A uniformed butler answered the door and showed Warren into a parlor with windows overlooking the street. Warren heard low murmurs coming from a room on the other side of the front entrance, and before long, Mr. Donovan followed the butler across the entryway and into the parlor.

"Mr. Donovan, sir?" Warren stood as the tall, broad American entered the room.

"Ah, welcome, Mr. Flynn." Mr. Donovan stretched out his hand, and Warren took it, trying to adjust to *Mr.* instead of *Lieutenant.* "We wondered if you would ever take us up on our offer. Are you here for leave?"

"Yes, sir. If the timing is convenient."

"Quite convenient. Please stay as long as you can. I apologize that I'll be the only one available to keep you company today. Claire's gone to London to visit her grandmother."

Warren swallowed back his disappointment. Perhaps if he stayed one day with Mr. Donovan, he could catch the good ship *Victoria* from Boulogne to Folkestone tomorrow and still have most of his leave in London. "Yes, I really ought to visit my own grandmother for most of my leave." His Grandma Beatrice's friendship with Claire's grandmother Huntley was at least twice as old as Warren. Surely he'd see Claire's grandmother and Claire if he went to London.

Mr. Donovan looked him over from head to foot. "Oh, and when do you plan to leave for England?"

"Perhaps as early as tomorrow, sir."

Mr. Donovan laughed. "In that case, Claire will be sorry she missed you. She's scheduled to return tomorrow."

Warren tried to think of a way to extricate himself from the knot he'd gotten himself tied up in. "Well, sir, perhaps I could arrange to stay in Paris a bit longer. I would hate to disappoint your daughter."

Mr. Donovan chuckled again and slapped Warren on the back. "Mr. Flynn, I was young once. I am not so vain as to suspect you've come to visit me. I have some business to finish, but Franke can show you the house. I'll see you for supper at seven." Mr. Donovan went back to his office on the other side of the entry, and Mr. Franke, the butler, showed Warren the dining hall, ballroom, library, gardens, and an enormous, elaborately decorated guest suite.

Supper was served precisely at seven, and the smells floating into the dining hall were infinitely superior to anything Warren had smelled at the aerodrome. Warren and Mr. Donovan sat alone at a table that could have seated two dozen. "Tell me, Lieutenant, how are things up your way? Ready to beat the Huns yet? I have a few countrymen placing bets on the various sides, and they keep pestering me for inside information."

Warren's first three spoonfuls of soup had been delicious, but the fourth was suddenly repugnant. Betting over the war as if it was a horse race? Warren set his spoon down, taking care not to show his discomfort. Mr. Donovan owned several munitions factories back in the U.S., but in Paris, all he saw were soldiers on leave, politicians stumping with patriotic fervor, and procurement officers bargaining for better shell prices. He couldn't know how awful it was on the front line. "It's turning into a contest of roughly equal sides, sir. I have my hopes that one more offensive will break through the lines, but that's what the Germans did at Ypres with gas and what the French did at Artois with a massive artillery barrage. Neither side could get replacements up fast enough to exploit their success."

"Perhaps if things were on a larger scale."

"Perhaps." Warren glanced at the soup—it was some type of tomato bisque—and the color reminded him of torn flesh. Maybe an attack on a larger scale would work better, but if it didn't, wouldn't it just result in casualties on a larger scale?

"Is something wrong with your soup?"

"Oh, no, sir." Warren picked up his spoon again. He wanted to be on Mr. Donovan's good side, and snubbing the first course was unlikely to help him with that goal. He'd endured far worse things than luxurious food, so he would eat and force his mind to think of something else. "It's much better than what we humble airmen usually eat."

* * *

From his room the next afternoon, Warren heard someone playing a spirited rendition of Haydn's *Surprise Symphony*. He found Claire sitting in front of the grand piano in the library. Her back was toward him as he watched from the doorway and admired the way her fingers danced along the keys with a grace that came from a different world than the gore of the battlefields. Her auburn hair shone in the sunlight streaming through the windows, and her curls swayed in time with her hands. When she finished, she reached for another piece of music.

"Playing music written by an Austrian, Miss Donovan? Not very patriotic of you," he said.

She swung around on the piano bench until she was facing him with an amused expression. "I'm an American, Mr. Flynn. We are officially neutral. And I shan't hold a composer who died over a hundred years ago responsible for Europe's current disaster." Her Southern drawl was just noticeable enough to be interesting.

"Who would you hold responsible?"

"I suppose there is enough blame to spread across the leaders of most of Europe's empires. But not much for Canadians pilots, so I shan't hold it against you."

Warren walked to the chair nearest the piano and picked up Claire's wide-brimmed hat. He kept hold of it as he took its place on the chair.

She studied his hatless head and unbuttoned jacket. "How long have you been here?"

"I walked in about thirty seconds after you began playing."

One side of her mouth pulled up, making the freckles on her left cheek more prominent. "Not the room, silly. The house."

"Yesterday. And you? I suppose you walked in and came straight to the piano?" He held up her hat. She hadn't even paused to put it on the rack.

"Yes. I suppose that's why no one told me you were here. I haven't seen my father or Franke, and Granny was so tired when we arrived that she went straight to her rooms." Claire turned back to the glossy black piano and straightened her music.

"How is your grandmother, other than fatigued from your voyage?"

Claire's blue eyes met his for an instant before she concentrated on her music again. "She is well, thank you. She asked if I'd seen you recently. She'll no doubt find it a pleasant surprise that you're in Paris. I think she's rather fond of you."

"As is my grandmother of you."

"I had tea with your grandmother just yesterday. She expressed some sadness that your letters are frequent but shallow."

"Do you think I should write to her less, then?"

Claire gave him an exaggerated smirk. "Of course not. But she wants to know more about what you're doing, how you're feeling."

Warren leaned back in the chair, placing Claire's hat on his knee. "She may not know it, but she doesn't really want to hear about war."

"Then tell her about things other than war."

"Fine. I shall write to her about you. Even though she already knows all about you and approves of you in spite of it. I still wonder how the granddaughter of a Yankee carpetbagger and the daughter of the scoundrel who stole her best friend's only heir became one of her favorites."

Claire's smile turned impish. "It's my piano playing. And my genteel Southern manners. Not that you should talk. The son of a man who stole your grandmother's daughter and took her to another continent to join some strange religion. How many wives has your father had?"

"Three."

Claire's eyes widened. "Three? Oh dear, that was supposed to be a joke. I didn't know there was any truth to it."

"He's had them one at a time. The first died giving birth to my oldest sister. Then he found my mother, and they found religion and decided to immigrate to Canada. She died of cholera twelve years later. Now a third woman is happily married to him—no doubt happier since I left."

"You don't get along with your stepmother?"

"I don't suppose I'll ever get along with a woman who wishes to control me. I had absolute freedom from age eleven to fourteen. Then she came along and expected me to tell her where I was every second of every day, and I had to wash my ears nightly and suffer punishments of the most vexing nature for putting holes through the knees of my trousers."

Claire took his chin and turned his head to either side. "Your ears appear clean now. Apparently her admonitions stuck."

He could still feel the warmth from her soft fingers as she released his jaw. "Cleaning is fine when it's a choice rather than a chore."

"Good. Because I would hate to have a dirty Royal Flying Corps officer take me on a stroll through the Paris streets. Whatever would people think? It's still an hour until tea time. I don't suppose you'd go on a walk with me now?"

Warren handed Claire her hat and offered her his arm. "My pleasure, Miss Donovan. If you can bear to be parted from your piano so soon after returning to it."

She slid her arm through his. "It's only a temporary separation."

When they were outside, he slowed his pace to match hers.

"So, Mr. Flynn, what is it about war that you don't want your grand-mother to know?"

"I'd rather not talk about war during leave. Especially around someone with such genteel manners."

Claire laughed softly. "You know as well as I do that my manners are far from genteel. I speak my mind much too often."

"And I never complain when you do."

"Not aloud anyway. A trait you perhaps inherited from your grandmother. She's rather indulgent with my outspoken nature. But I would very much like to hear your thoughts on occasion. When you're quiet, I find myself forced to talk about trivial things in order to keep up the conversation."

"And what bits of trivia do you have stored up for today should I fail to keep up the conversation?"

Claire's lips turned down as she glanced sideways at him. "I was hoping it wouldn't come to that."

"But what if I'm in the mood for trivial conversation?"

She slowed and lifted one foot until her boot was sticking out from underneath her skirt. "I might could tell you about my shoes."

"Please do."

"They're new. I didn't mean to go shopping in London, but I only brought one pair of boots with me, and the laces broke. So I went to purchase new laces, and the cobbler suggested I buy these. It seemed silly to get a new pair of shoes when all I needed were laces, but the poor man said his oldest son lied about his age and enlisted, and he let him because he has nine other children to feed. Ten children total, all of them living. Can you imagine? Oh, but I mentioned the war. I'm sorry."

"Never feel like you have to apologize to me, Miss Donovan." Warren released her arm and took a few steps away to admire her new shoes. "Are they comfortable?"

Claire frowned again, making a dimple appear on her left cheek. "I'm hoping they will be after a few days. But no. Right now they're something awful."

"Let me take you home, then. You can change shoes, and we'll go on another stroll after teatime."

Claire wove her hand through the crook of his arm again. "My grandmother says you are practical to a fault, but today I think that's an admirable trait."

"And what of yesterday? Was it a good trait to have yesterday?"

"You assume you were on my mind yesterday."

"Perhaps I assume too much."

With her free hand, she tucked a loose curl behind her ear. "I was having tea with your grandmother. Of course you were on my mind."

Claire had always been pleasant company, ever since he'd met her four years ago. Then one summer, he'd seen her again after she'd been in Charleston for eighteen months, and he'd realized she was not only pleasant but beautiful too. Now it seemed like she was also a good distraction. Claire was about as opposite from the war as Warren could get.

* * *

Warren didn't make it to London during his week of leave. His stay with the Donovans soon fell into an easy pattern. In the mornings, he took Claire on a stroll, or they went into the garden to play croquet. They had a light midday meal together and usually spent the time between luncheon and tea in the library under the watchful eye of Claire's Grandma Huntley. But Grandma Huntley had returned to London the day before, leaving them largely to themselves the last day of Warren's furlough.

Claire finished another khaki sock and placed her knitting basket on the floor. While in London, she'd decided to "knit her bit," and she'd made visible progress learning the new skill over the past week, even with Warren as a distraction. But as she sat at the piano and started to play, it was obvious her passion was for the piano keys, not the knitting needles.

"I've noticed you play only classical pieces when your father is home." Warren ran his hand along Claire's latest yarn creation. "But if you know he's away, you pull out the ragtime."

Claire smiled mischievously. "My father prefers traditional music."

"And do you avoid playing ragtime when your father can hear because it's forbidden or out of respect for his taste?"

"I don't think he's ever heard me play it, so he can't forbid it." She straightened her music. "Most respectable young women play something else."

Warren chuckled. "Has my grandmother ever heard you play? This type of music, I mean?"

"Your grandmother is the biggest fan of ragtime I've met in all my born days."

"What?" Other than her acceptance of Warren's flying career, his grandmother had conservative taste in everything.

"Who do you think purchased this song for me?"

"Really?"

"Her butler did the actual shopping."

Warren and his grandmother always found plenty to talk about when together, and he'd spent years living in her home, but he'd never heard her compliment anything newer than Wagner. "She had absolutely no interest in ragtime when the war began."

"A lot can change in a year. Perhaps if you spent more time with her, you'd know of her new music interests."

"So on my next leave, I suppose I should go to London."

Claire's fingers hesitated on the piano keys. "Your grandmother would be happy to see you, I'm sure."

"And you wouldn't have to occupy your days entertaining me."

Claire frowned. "I have plenty of days without visitors. If you do decide to go to London instead of Paris, I might could arrange a visit to London at the same time because I very much enjoy entertaining you."

Later, after their evening meal, Warren and the Donovans retired to the library, as they'd done all week. Mr. Donovan got out his pipe and settled into his favorite armchair by the coal stove. Warren didn't use tobacco. For the most part, he'd left his religion in Alberta, but he imagined his mother, if she still existed in some type of afterlife, would cringe to see him flout the rules she'd so diligently taught him. Claire never stayed longer than it took to hear about her father's day and find a way to make him laugh. When she left, Warren did his best to satisfy Mr. Donovan's curiosity about the war.

When the questions lulled, Warren plucked up a three-week-old New York City newspaper from a nearby table. One article struck him so strongly that he read part of it aloud.

"'This past July, a member of the German embassy fell asleep on the New York subway and neglected to collect his briefcase upon arrival at his destination. The item was collected by the American Secret Service, who yesterday disclosed some of its contents. It appears German diplomats have contracted with several Irish and German-American lowlifes to stir up labor unrest, sabotage munitions before they are shipped to Europe, and even recruit groups of willing Americans to invade Canada. Could such schemes cause our northern neighbor to hold back men for border defense and send fewer troops to Great Britain?'" Warren lowered the newspaper. "The United States invade Canada?"

"It wouldn't be the first time." Mr. Donovan added tobacco to his pipe.

"It would be the first time in one hundred years. Do you think the idea will catch?"

"There are plenty of Americans who dislike the British. But, no, I don't think German agents could muster a real invasion force. Even if they did, the U.S. Army might do a thing or two to prevent anything serious from happening."

"Sabotage is a little more likely to succeed though." Warren folded the paper and put it aside. "Like the men trying to blow up the Welland Canal between Lake Erie and Lake Ontario. And the British Army is already short on shells. A few strikes at munitions factories, a bit of arson in the wrong places . . ."

"Are you so uncertain of victory? Do you think a few Canadian divisions held back to defend the border and a few less shiploads of shells will tip the scales?"

Warren wanted to project confidence. But he also wanted to be honest. "I don't think it would take much to tip the scales, sir."

Mr. Donovan leaned back in his seat, chewing on his pipe. "A few saboteurs here, a few saboteurs there. A shortage in the wrong area leading to a breakthrough." He shook his head and puffed on his pipe. "Frightening stuff."

Warren couldn't agree more.

# Chapter 5

*September 1915, Picardy Province, France*

THE WALK FROM THE TRAIN station to Maximo's home took fifteen minutes, although Julian probably could have done it in ten. He had to keep his promise, but he wasn't looking forward to the visit with Maximo's widow.

The little village was spread out, with wide streets and gardens around most of the homes. In the trenches, everything had been muddy, brown, and lifeless. The only other color had been blood. Here in Maximo's village, color was everywhere: in the blue sky, in the green grass, in the vibrant flowers and the golden fields.

Four months had passed since Maximo's death, four months since the wretchedness of Artois. Julian had spent most of that time in a schoolhouse converted into a hospital, fighting infections and slowly regaining his strength. To his shame, he'd envied those who wouldn't make a full recovery. Their war was over, and they were going home. Julian had been granted a week at the family dairy as part of his final convalescence. His family lived outside Calais, where the most common smells were the ocean and the cows. It had been pleasant but far too brief. After his visit with Maximo's widow, he was going back to the trenches, where the most common smells were cordite and rotting corpses.

Maximo had described his home in such detail that Julian knew it immediately. Yet he was hesitant to knock. What would he say? Tapping on the door was different than going over the top into no-man's land, but both required copious amounts of courage. His knock echoed in the house, with no audible response. He panicked for an instant—he still wasn't sure what he'd say, but he wanted to keep his promise. He doubted he would live long enough to earn another leave, so this was likely his only chance.

Slowly the door creaked open, though Julian hadn't heard footsteps. He recognized Maximo's widow from the picture his friend had carried. She wore black, and the mirthful expression from her picture was replaced with a sober expression that couldn't quite disguise the grief.

"Madame Durand?"

"Yes?" Her voice was a whisper.

Julian struggled to find the right words. "I knew Maximo. He asked me to come see you if he was unable to come himself."

She stared at him for several long seconds. "You're Julian?"

"Yes."

Madame Durand stepped back, clearing the doorway. "He wrote about you in his letters. Please come in."

Julian followed her inside, and as his eyes adjusted to the reduced light, he picked out things he would have expected to see. Maximo's parents were dead, but his maternal grandmother, a woman of nearly ninety years, was exactly as Maximo had described her, from the wrinkled hands to the white hair. She sat in a rocking chair, knitting. The home's furniture was of good quality. Like most men in his village, Maximo had been primarily a farmer, but in the winter, he'd taken on woodcarving.

"Please sit down."

Julian waited for Madame Durand to sink into a chair before he complied. Maximo's grandmother glanced up from her knitting, but according to Maximo, she had been mostly deaf for a decade.

He forced his hands to stop their fidgeting. "I'm sorry for your loss. Your husband was my best friend. I can't tell you how much I wish he was still alive."

She sniffed softly.

Julian reached into his pocket and retrieved the bracelet Maximo had fashioned from a shell's copper driving band. "He wanted me to give you this. It was the last thing he ever said."

She accepted her husband's gift, turning it around to examine each of the marks Maximo had made before putting the bracelet on her lap. He had been good with his hands. She sniffed again and wiped at her tears.

"You should know that whenever we were pulled back for rest, he always behaved himself. Sometimes the other men didn't, even the married ones, but Maximo never did anything to make you ashamed."

She lifted her eyes to meet his. Maximo had called them the color of honey. The color remained, but the surrounding whites showed a redness that came with too much weeping. "How did he die?" she asked.

"Pieces of artillery in his arm and leg. Then infection." Julian left out the part about the doctors ignoring him because they were busy with men who could make a more complete recovery.

"Was he in pain?"

Julian looked away. "He handled it well."

She inhaled deeply, her breath ragged. "Why did he die?"

Julian studied her face, wondering what she meant. He'd died from infection and neglect, but if she was searching for a deeper meaning to the war, a worthwhile reason for the massive casualties, Julian couldn't give her one. He decided on a strategic explanation. "We were in Artois, advancing into the Noyon Salient, trying to push back the German lines. We captured all the Boche trenches and advanced four kilometers before noon. But no one expected us to move that quickly, and the reserves were too far away. I was sent back to get them. Maximo offered to go in my place—we both thought the courier had the more dangerous task. That's the type of friend your husband was."

Madame Durand wrung the soggy handkerchief with her hands. "We'd only been married six months when the war started." She put aside the cloth and picked up the copper bracelet. "He said he wanted to stay, but I could tell he was eager to go. So afraid the Boches would be defeated before he had a chance to fight them. And now he's dead." She ended with a sob.

"We all thought things would be different last August."

Her lips quivered, and she dipped her chin.

"Will you be all right? Maximo said your parents would help you if something happened to him."

"I'll have enough to eat. But I want my Maximo back." She buried her face in her hands and sobbed.

The rest of the visit with her was painful. Julian had expected as much. Why had he and Maximo made their deal in the first place? It wasn't as if a visit from a comrade could make up for the loss of a family member. His little acts, even those done with the best of intentions, would never be anything other than insignificant.

As soon as Maximo's widow dried her tears and calmed her breathing, Julian excused himself. He couldn't do anything for her, for anyone. He was destined for the trenches. The trenches and death. He liked to think dying for his country would mean something for those who survived the war, but in reality, his body would be just one more corpse decomposing in the sun or freezing in the chill. Perhaps he'd turn into a temporary battlefield landmark. *Advance as far as that poilu with his head blown off, then move to the north.* That was the most useful role he could look forward to.

Julian stepped from Maximo's house, feeling like a man walking to his execution. He believed in an afterlife, and he hadn't done anything horrible enough to condemn himself to eternal damnation, so why was he terrified of death? He kicked a loose stone with his boot. Regardless of the reason, he was scared to go back and wasn't sure how or if he'd ever get over it.

He passed several streets on his way to the train station, trying to let the warm breeze and fragrant wildflowers cheer him. Maybe he'd live. Italy wasn't fully mobilized, but he'd overheard businessmen on the train contending that if Italy distracted Austrian troops from the eastern front, then maybe the Germans would have to move men from France to Russia to make up the difference. His mind raced with possibilities, all of them unlikely, until an argument across the street drew his attention.

"But if you take my horse, how will I move my mother?" The woman who spoke was young and petite, with delicate facial features and brown hair tied at the nape of her neck. A large bruise marred her temple, and her hands clung to the bridle of an old bay stallion loaded with a set of chairs and bundles wrapped in cloth. She stared up at a burly French sergeant who gripped the horse's reins.

"How will I move an army without horses?"

"Can't the army wait an hour?"

The sergeant huffed. "The army can't wait for old women."

"No, the army just widows them and conscripts their only sons." The woman stood her ground. "The horse wasn't Gaspard's to sell."

The sergeant drew a paper from his pocket. "I have a certificate of sale right here."

"This horse belongs to my brother, not to my half brother, and my brother left it in my care."

"Take it up with Gaspard, then. But I saw him at the market, and he already spent the proceeds."

The woman didn't relax her grip on the bridle. "It wasn't his horse to sell, but you can come back for it this evening."

The sergeant was twice as big as she. He moved closer, making their disparity in height and weight more noticeable. "Look, mademoiselle, there's a war on, and we need this horse, even if he is old. Either you get out of my way, or I'll be forced to arrest you as a traitor."

The woman's hands dropped. "But how will I move my mother's things without a horse?"

The sergeant began untying packages from the back of the animal. "That's not my concern. I have bigger things to worry about, like making sure the Boches don't overrun our lines." One of the bundles fell to the ground, and something shattered.

"Please, sir, these things are all my mother has left." The woman's voice shook as she pleaded.

The sergeant didn't apologize, but he lowered the next item to the ground without breaking anything.

Julian had seen and heard enough. "Excuse me, Sergeant."

The sergeant glanced at him before turning back to the ropes that fastened the chairs to the horse. "What?"

"Is this horse to be placed on the afternoon train?"

"Yes. Why?"

"I'm catching that same train. It doesn't leave for an hour. What if I helped the mademoiselle move her things, then brought the horse back with me?"

The sergeant gave Julian a closer look. For the first time, Julian wished he was an officer. Then he wouldn't have to ask; he could demand. He did his best to imitate his former lieutenant's calm composure and air of authority.

"You're willing to help her and make sure the horse gets to the train on time?"

"Yes."

"Why?"

Julian reached up to brush his fingers along the horse's forelock. "Because if my mother was widowed, I would want someone to help her." Remembering his mother, Julian frowned. He'd never seen her as frail as she'd been during his week at home.

The sergeant considered the offer, then handed over the reins. "Have him there early so I can load him properly. If you aren't to the station on time, your punishment will be more severe than anything the Boches can hand out."

Julian bit the inside of his cheek to keep from speaking. He didn't want to antagonize the man, but the sergeant's threat was empty. There wasn't anything worse than returning to the trenches.

With a curt nod, the sergeant strode away. Julian turned to the woman. She blinked rapidly as tears pooled in her vivid green eyes. Julian fastened the chair back onto the horse's back. "How far are you moving?" He probably should have asked that first. If it was too far to make before the train left, perhaps he could hire someone with a cart.

"A kilometer," she said. "Thank you for your help. I don't know what I would have done otherwise."

Julian nodded toward the first bundle the sergeant had dropped. "Is there anything worth saving inside?"

She knelt and untied the package. Inside were the remnants of a crockery set. He watched her trembling hands sort through the broken shards to find a few salvageable pieces.

"I'm sorry," he said. "He should have been more considerate. Sometimes when you're fighting a war, everything else seems unimportant."

She glanced at him for an instant, then turned back to examine a cracked plate. "Have you been in the army long?"

"About four years."

She tied a few of the pieces back into a bundle. "Like my brother." She tucked the bundle under her arm and patted the horse. "My brother, who had his horse sold today but will see no money for it."

"And your half brother sold it?"

"Yes." She fastened the bundle back onto the horse, and Julian did the same with the second pack the sergeant had removed.

"Will you straighten it out with him? Gaspard, is that his name?"

"That's his name. But, no, I don't expect I'll be able to straighten anything out with him." She pursed her lips briefly. "It doesn't matter. I'm leaving as soon as I can. Once my mother is settled, there won't be any reason for me to stay." She took the horse by the reins and guided it down the street.

"Where are you moving your mother?"

"To my sister's home. Her husband was called up, and she wants my mother's help with the children. It's a tiny house, but it will be better than living with her stepson."

"Her stepson—Gaspard?"

The woman nodded. "Gaspard and I share a father, but he's dead now. Part of the Territorial Reserves. Killed by a stray German shell. My mother and I are only a burden to his heir, but when my mother is with my sister, I'll be able to leave my half brother's home without worrying about her."

"Where will you go?"

"Paris."

"Ah, Paris. Every girl's dream."

A soft smile spread across her lips. Something about her expression made the day seem a little brighter. "It wasn't my dream. I like the village. But if I get a job at a factory in Paris, I'll be able to take care of myself. My cousin said they pay factory workers a hundred sous a day."

"That much?" Julian wondered if the cousin had given the woman false information, either deliberately or by accident.

"Maybe not to women, but still, a hundred sous a day! With money like that, I could live anywhere I wished." She spread her arms like a bird as if she could picture herself flying away.

Julian grinned at the gesture and at the woman. There was something infinitely appealing about her face and the soft tones of her voice. He hesitated to give her reason to doubt her cousin, but he didn't want her to have unrealistic expectations. "Do you know how much a poilu is paid?"

"No." She turned her head toward him, her dark eyebrows lifted into delicate arches.

"Five sous."

Her mouth opened in astonishment. "Five sous? Is that all?"

"That's all. It used to be less."

"My cousin was sure of her information." She frowned. "But if a factory worker is paid a hundred sous a day and a soldier is paid only five, something is very wrong."

"Pay discrepancies are the least of what's wrong with the world." He thought back to the trenches and the way the earth shook with each shell burst, the constant fear of being shredded by shrapnel, the rats, the lice, the rotting feet, and the endless mud. *And you're going back, back to the trenches.* He held in a shudder.

The woman led the horse around a corner onto a smaller path. "The world may be falling apart, but that doesn't mean factory workers should be paid twenty times what a soldier is paid. My brother's in the army. It's not an easy life."

Julian glanced at her again, focusing on the dark purple bruise on her left temple. "Is life easy for you?"

Her expression grew guarded, and she turned away.

"How did you get that bruise?"

"I fell." She wouldn't look him in the face, and he knew she was lying.

They continued a few more paces, the silence awkward. "But you have hope life will be better working in a factory?"

She nodded.

"Perhaps there aren't as many places to fall in a factory?"

She paused, her eyes meeting his, pleading with him to keep up the pretense that her bruise was the result of an accident. Eventually her gaze fell. "No, I don't think there will be as many places to fall."

"And how soon can you escape to the factory?"

Her voice was soft when she spoke again. "My brother has been sending me money. I think I'll have enough to leave by the end of the year."

She didn't deny she was trying to escape something, and Julian didn't press her as she halted the horse in front of a small farmhouse. He untied the bundles, and she took them inside. He followed with the first of the chairs. It was a one-room house, old and worn. A curtain partially concealed the home's sole sleeping place, a pallet, probably made of straw. There was scarcely enough room for the mother, and no place at all for the woman with the bruise. Through a back window, he could see a pair of women, one young and one middle-aged, working in the fields, and several small children running through the surrounding barley crop.

They unloaded the rest of the belongings, and she followed him when he returned to the horse. Julian reached into his pocket and pulled out his money. *Back to the trenches.* He wished there was a way he could escape his fate. Perhaps he could at least help someone else escape hers. He kept enough for his train fare back to his post and handed her the rest. "Here, take this. For your train ticket."

She glanced at his hand, then his face. "Oh, no. I couldn't take your money. You've already been generous with your time." She took a step back, retreating toward the house.

"Yes, you can." He gently took her wrist, and she winced in pain. Confused, Julian reached for her elbow and pushed up her sleeve. A mass of purple and yellow splotches covered her forearm, matching the bruise on her temple. "From your fall?"

She easily pulled away from his grip. "A different one." She was a mystery. Despite her lies, he sensed she was honest at heart. And despite the stoicism she had about her abuse, she was searching for a way out. There was iron underneath the fair skin and bright green eyes.

"I might not be alive long enough to spend this. Let me at least know I've helped you get away from whoever it is that's hurting you."

"But I . . . I'm not a charity case." Her voice wavered, and slight lines formed around her mouth as she set it in determination.

"And I am not a philanthropist." Julian was far too poor for that. "But I am a soldier about to return to the ugliness of war. Let me help you so I can have one beautiful memory to take back with me."

She hesitated, and he could read a swirl of emotions on her face: hope, uncertainty, fear.

A train whistle sounded. Julian turned toward the noise. Was the train early, or had he lost track of time? "I've got to get this horse to the station." He took the woman's hand and put the money in her palm. "Godspeed, mademoiselle."

Her lips parted, but no words came out. Instead, a few tears escaped down her cheeks, and the breeze blew a few stray strands of brunette hair across her neck. Julian used the fence to climb on the horse's back and urged it into a trot toward the train station. He looked back at her as he turned the corner, wondering if he would ever forget those green eyes and that perfect mouth. He felt like he'd just set a bird free, and more than anything, he wished he could linger to watch it soar into the sky.

# Chapter 6

EVETTE TOUNY CREPT UP THE staircase leading to the upper floor of her late father's home. She walked along the edge of each step because the middle was more likely to creak and stepped with the outside of her foot first, slowly rolling inward in the hope that her half brother wouldn't hear her as he read the newspaper downstairs.

All she needed was five minutes. Five minutes alone in the room she had shared with her mother since the day they'd heard her father was dead and Gaspard had taken the downstairs bedroom for himself. After she gathered her clothes and collected her letters, she could leave.

Her brother Emile's words crossed her mind. *Never accept money from strange men; they always expect something in return.* But the soldier she'd met yesterday hadn't demanded anything in exchange, had even ignored her lie about the bruises. No stranger had ever been so kind to her, and she hadn't even said thank you. She should have become his marraine de guerre, joining other Frenchwomen in adopting a soldier and sending him letters, woolen socks, and extra food parcels. At the very least, she should have asked his name. Or did the man have a wife? Evette scowled. But why should the thought of him married to another woman make her feel so twisted up inside? She should be happy for him. Someone who possessed kindness in such abundance, to say nothing of his warm brown eyes and pleasant smile, surely deserved a blissful marriage.

Evette took her letters from a scratched wooden chest in the bedroom and paused. If she left, she would miss some of her brother's letters. But Emile would understand. Even though Gaspard had never raised a hand against Emile—their half brother preferred to pick on people who couldn't fight back—Emile had seen the bruises during his last leave and guessed where they had come from. With the money from Emile and the gift from the handsome stranger, Evette would have enough to leave. As long as she found a job within a week or two and managed her funds wisely when it came to lodging and food, she would make it. At least she hoped she would. Food might be more expensive in Paris.

She banished her doubts. The village was small enough that a train only stopped once a day, and she hadn't been able to make yesterday's departure with the kind poilu. Sufficient money or not, she was leaving today.

Evette gathered and folded her extra stockings, underthings, blouses, and skirts. Everything fit easily into a potato sack. She tucked her letters and her money into the bag and tiptoed from the room. Once downstairs, she went into the kitchen and added herbs to the soup, hoping the aroma would entice Gaspard to eat before he pursued her. Even if he wasn't hungry, he wouldn't begin his search at the train station. He'd probably assume she was working in the field as usual. If he did look for her, he would start at her sister Veronique's house.

She was about to leave when she heard the familiar step-drag of his walk coming from the hallway. His left foot had been mangled in an accident several years before. The French Army was not yet desperate enough to call up crippled reserves, so he always exaggerated his limp while in public. His footsteps sounded different over the smooth wooden floor, not as dramatic as over paving stones, but they filled her with terror all the same. Gaspard had never been kind to his four younger half-siblings, but his resentment had festered after the accident, and Evette, the youngest by three years, seemed to receive the brunt of his frustrations.

Gaspard turned into the kitchen before Evette could escape out the door. He was a head and a half taller than her, and today his eyes brimmed with virile irritation. "What are you doing inside, you lazy girl? Stealing more food? You're supposed to be weeding the south field."

"I'm sorry, sir. I'll do it now."

He grabbed her arm and propelled her toward the door. She had to step quickly to keep from falling over, and the potato sack swung out in an arc. Gaspard focused on the bag. "What have you got in there?"

Evette felt her voice catch in her throat. If she told him the truth, he would beat her and take the money. She couldn't escape without it, and she had no way of replacing it. "Some of my mother's things. I was going to bring them to her. I'll do the weeding first."

"That old hag took enough with her when she left. You'll not be pilfering anything else to her." Gaspard jerked the bag from her grasp and shoved her away when she reached for it. He wasn't interested in the clothing, but then his hands paused, and a frown etched itself onto his face. "You little thief!" He spat the words as he brought out her money. He flipped through it, counting the notes, then dropped the money and the bag to the floor. "You little thief! After all I've done for you, you've gone and stolen from me!"

"It's from Emile, sir. He sent it to me. I promise I haven't taken anything of yours."

Gaspard struck her across the face, sending her to the ground. "You're a thief and a liar. You'll pay for this." Next came a swift kick that landed in her ribs. A cry of pain escaped her lips. "I should throw you in prison for robbery, but the local gendarmerie is always a little soft when it comes to women. I'll take care of this myself." He swung his good leg at her again, and she scrambled across the floor to avoid it, only partially succeeding.

"Please, sir. Emile sent the money to me. I was going to leave. Then you won't have to feed me anymore, and you can have the entire house to yourself."

Gaspard's pink face turned purple. He reached down and pulled her to her feet, then drove her shoulders into the wall. "You thought you would just leave, did you?"

"Yes, sir. I don't want to be a burden anymore."

He relaxed his grip on her for an instant before smashing her into the wall again. "You stupid idiot. You think I want to hire someone to cook for me? Hire someone to wash my clothes and tend my fields? You're not going anywhere." He punched her in the face, engulfing her head in pain. She probably would have fallen, but his other hand was clamped around her arm in a viselike grip, keeping her upright.

He pummeled her again with his fist, each blow building on the mounting pain. She'd long ago learned that Gaspard took satisfaction in making his victims whimper, so she didn't attempt to stop her cries. "Please, Gaspard. Please stop. I've learned my lesson." She could taste the pooling blood in her mouth.

Her half brother's breathing came in deep gasps, and sweat tricked down his forehead. He paused long enough to stare at her.

"Please, Gaspard," she whispered.

His grip on her arm relaxed, and she guessed he was finished. Then he saw the potato sack again and glared in anger. His hand moved to her hair, and he dragged her to the stove. "I'm just getting started, you ungrateful thief. You and your sisters have been nothing but trouble to me. Dishonorable, scandalous wenches, the lot of you."

Evette didn't argue, even though he was being unfair. Rosemonde had been dishonorable, had caused a scandal that had affected the entire family. But Veronique's only crime was being born poor and marrying poor, and Evette had done nothing to sully Gaspard's reputation.

But she wasn't worried about his words, especially when he reached for the poker. He'd always used his hands and feet before. A metal stick took the ritual to an entirely new level of fear.

She glanced around the kitchen. She was smaller than Gaspard, but if she didn't fight back, he would cause permanent damage. He'd once beaten her unconscious with far less provocation. The cauldron of soup hung over the fire. She swung the hook out, gripped the handle, and threw the simmering liquid onto him. It wasn't until he yelped in pain that she felt the burning on her hands. She bashed the pot into his face. As he stumbled back, she scooped her money into her potato sack and ran.

She didn't stop running until she could see the train station. She checked behind her, but either her half brother hadn't chased her, or she'd outrun him. She took a handkerchief from her pocket and wiped it across her face. The swollen spots were tender, but the cloth was still white when she examined it again, so she assumed her face wasn't bleeding. An angry pink line marred the palms of her hands where the pot's handle had burned them. They throbbed, and she knew it would cause her pain for several days, but it was a small price to pay for freedom—if she was really free.

After she'd caught her breath and smoothed her hair, she forced a normal pace to the station so as not to attract suspicion, but she was terrified. The station was crowded with military police and gendarmerie, and although they mainly scrutinized leave passes for the soldiers boarding the train, they could easily detain her. Gaspard might press charges. What would her punishment be for assaulting her legal guardian? She was sure he would have maimed her, possibly killed her, but if she told the authorities that, whom would they believe? An eighteen-year-old girl or a landowner who often shared drinks with the mayor? No one would believe a stranger had given her money, and Emile's low rank couldn't account for all her savings. Or would Gaspard come for her himself, wanting to keep his revenge private? That was perhaps the most frightening of the options.

Her hands trembled as she purchased her ticket, trembled as she clung to her potato sack and boarded the afternoon train, trembled as she found an empty seat. She sat near a window so she'd have warning if Gaspard or a gendarmerie came to chase her. It wasn't until the train started moving that she felt the shaking begin to stop.

She was leaving her mother, sister, two nieces, and nephew. She could write them but wouldn't be able to tell them where she lived lest Gaspard learn her new location from the postal workers. Her family would have to send news to her through Emile. She studied the burns on her hands again, thinking of Emile and the French soldier who had given her this bittersweet chance.

As her village disappeared from view, she wondered if she'd done the right thing. She had never stood up to Gaspard before, but right or wrong, she felt no regret for her actions, only uncertainty about whether they were justified. She finally concluded that sinful or not, she would do the same thing should similar circumstances arise. Never again would she meekly submit to a beating.

# Chapter 7

*September 1915, Artois Province, France*

As soon as the propellers stopped, Warren bounded from his new Airco DH.2 single-seat biplane and checked the wings. Archie had been vicious. He was lucky to have landed with all the damage the antiaircraft fire had caused his upper left wing—one of the wires frayed in his hand as he inspected it. The DH.2 was a new type, and he'd been lucky to get one. He groaned as he realized how badly it had been mauled.

Captain Prior clapped a hand on his shoulder. "Well done, Flynn. Number three, isn't it?"

Warren turned from his plane. "I hit that Fokker, but it's unconfirmed. He may have been diving away to evade."

"Wrong, Canada. I saw him hit the ground. You are the first pilot in our squadron to shoot down a Fokker Eindecker. In fact, you may be the first man in the entire Royal Flying Corps to take down a plane like that."

A confirmed victory banished some of Warren's exhaustion. "Wish I could have forced it down on our side of the lines. The pilot was an idiot, but I'd love to give his plane a spin. Why give a beautiful machine like that to someone who can barely fly it?"

"Don't be modest, Flynn. You had the perfect setup—diving out of the sun from above. Textbook maneuver. If you're not careful, they'll pull you from France and make you an instructor."

"Me, an instructor?" Warren doubted that. He wasn't spit-and-polish enough for duty back in England. "I certainly hope not."

"We'll have a proper celebration after supper. And if they try to drag you back to England for longer than a week, we'll threaten mutiny."

Warren laughed. His eyes scanned the field and stopped on a solitary figure in a British Army uniform meandering toward him. "McDougall, you old devil. Come to celebrate with me, have you?"

As he approached, Lieutenant Howard McDougall examined the planes set along the side of the landing strip. "What are we celebrating?" he asked in his distinctive Scottish brogue. "The fact that you haven't yet gotten yourself killed in one of these contraptions?"

"No, my third kill."

"And not just any kill," Prior broke in. "A Fokker Eindecker. Only the best plane in the air right now."

"Captain Prior exaggerates."

"Only on rare occasions, and only with women. The Fokker scourge is real enough."

Warren grinned. He had shot down a Fokker Eindecker, and even if the pilot had executed only mediocre maneuvers, it was still a victory. "Only with women?"

"When the situation calls for it," Prior said.

"Speaking of women, McDougall, how has your luck been with French women? Better than with the British ones, I hope."

McDougall's lips curved upward, but the smile didn't reach his eyes.

"I suspect there's a story behind that." Prior glanced at McDougall, who gestured for Warren to tell the story.

"We were on leave last winter, waiting to see a play in London, and a cute little English girl walked up to him and put a white feather in his buttonhole. I was in uniform, or she probably would have had a feather for me too. I told the little hussy that Lieutenant McDougall's uniform was at the cleaner's having a thick layer of Flanders mud removed, and I stuck the feather in her hat and sent her on her way."

Prior laughed. "Not your most chivalrous moment, Flynn."

"Brainless woman. Don't know how she thinks embarrassing men not in uniform will help beat the Huns."

"I like the brainless ones. They don't argue with you. Nor do they question exaggerations."

Warren wondered if Prior's words were a slight against Claire's outspokenness. For better or worse, Warren never had to guess what she was feeling, and he preferred that to the type of woman who obscured her opinions or failed to develop them at all.

Despite the joking, McDougall still hadn't even chuckled. Maybe he was still touchy about white feathers and the woman's insinuation that he was a coward.

"You seem in need of a little cheering up," Warren said.

Prior excused himself. "I'll be off. I have an engine to tweak and a new Vickers gun to test. Then I'll report your latest kill. Well done, Flynn."

"Thank you, sir." When Captain Prior left, Warren turned to McDougall. "Normally you intelligence chaps are too busy for trips to aerodromes unless we're handing over reconnaissance photos. What have they got you working on?"

"Almost nothing."

"So that's your trouble. You're bored."

"No, frustrated. Before the war, I knew the wife of one of the German military attachés assigned to London. Her father is Dutch; her mother is English. She loves her German husband but once mentioned her sympathies in the arms race were squarely with Great Britain. I am better acquainted with her brother than with her. He studied at Oxford while we were there. Hendriks. Do you remember him?"

"Yes. His Greek was almost as good as yours."

McDougall nodded. Ancient languages and cultures were his prewar passions. "I received a letter from him two weeks ago. Said his brother-in-law is off at the front, but his sister is influential in Essen, and she's willing to help us. She passed on some rather informative data about the Krupp Works."

"The Krupp factory—that's where they make all those guns that try to blow my plane from the sky, isn't it?"

"Aye. My friend's sister claims she can secure a place for the right person, but no one seems to believe her except me. I was told if I could find someone fitting and discover a way to get him into Germany, I could run with it. But I am on my own. I don't know anyone who can pretend to be German. Nor do I know how to smuggle them into Essen. An opportunity like this doesn't come along often, and my superiors are squandering it."

"Find the right person, and I'll fly him in for you."

"Fly him in?" McDougall pursed his lips while he considered it.

"Why not?" Warren and McDougall didn't officially work together, but Warren wasn't one to turn down a flying opportunity, no matter how unusual it was. "Pick a moonlit night with calm weather and load the plane up with extra fuel. I'll find a clearing behind the German lines, land for a few minutes, be back before dawn. Your man can walk to the nearest train station and get to Essen from there. You just have to get the right paperwork and find a competent spy."

"The military attaché's wife said she could help with papers. But finding someone who can act German . . ."

"Ask French intelligence," Warren suggested. "They've been spying on the Hun for decades, haven't they? Maybe they can loan you someone."

"I doubt they would loan someone of that caliber."

"Ask. You have a way to get said agent into Essen with a cover story that the city's leading citizens will accept. Check with any French officers you know too. The worst they can say is no."

McDougall watched a plane come in and land. "That is what I like about you, Flynn. You make the nearly impossible seem manageable."

Warren smiled. It was a day for doing and planning nearly impossible things, like shooting down a Fokker Eindecker and smuggling spies into Germany.

# Chapter 8

As JULIAN PICKED UP HIS allotted ammunition, he cursed the Boche. The war wasn't entirely their fault. There had been that rouge Serb assassin in Sarajevo and Austria's ridiculous ultimatum that bore some of the blame, but it was the German Army that had invaded his country and come close to annihilating his army. Perhaps the French Army was still destined for annihilation, but it would be a slow death by attrition rather than the speedy military victory the Germans had planned for. Julian worried about the future but doubted he'd be around to see much of it.

That was what really bothered him: the Boches hadn't stolen his life—yet—but they would. He'd end up as an unrecognizable lump of flesh lying on a battlefield for the flies and worms to feast upon. And what of the peasant girl he'd given money to for a train ticket, the girl he couldn't forget? Without the war to interrupt, might he have returned and asked her for another walk? Learned her name? Defended her from whoever was beating her? Courted her? The Boches had taken all that from him and sentenced him to a short, miserable life of mud and artillery shells.

Julian didn't recognize anyone in his new unit. As he followed his sergeant toward the trenches, a French officer and a guard marched a group of twelve German prisoners past his group. One of the Boche prisoners stumbled and fell. The French officer shouted at him in French. The German boy yelled back in German.

Julian translated since the two of them obviously weren't understanding each other. "He says he twisted his ankle yesterday and he just twisted it again."

"Tell him to get up anyway."

Julian repeated the instructions, adding a request for one of the nearby prisoners to assist his comrade.

The French officer eyed him. "That's not exactly what I told you to say, is it?"

"Sorry, sir. I assumed your goal was to get them in cages. I was only trying to help you accomplish that as quickly as possible."

"So the extra message wasn't a translation error?"

"No, sir." Julian hoped the officer wasn't going to make a big deal out of something so small. There were officers like that, of course. Julian didn't like them, but they couldn't do much worse than send him back to the front, where he was headed anyway.

"Hmm. Follow me."

"Me, sir?" Julian asked.

"Yes." The officer motioned for the prisoners to be on their way, and Julian too.

Julian glanced at his sergeant, who raised a shoulder in sympathy. "Off you go."

Taking a deep breath and blowing it out slowly, Julian followed the French officer and his captives, wondering if he was now one of the prisoners. Imprisonment couldn't be any worse than an artillery barrage, but he didn't like being in trouble.

The march continued past green replacements, piles of equipment, and supply troops leading heavily laden packhorses forward. Was the horse that belonged to the girl from Maximo's village among the animals? He remembered the letter he had penned his father that morning. *Dear Papa, I met a woman when I went to visit Maximo's widow. I didn't learn her name, but I can't stop thinking about her.* Now Julian thought of a postscript. *I'm being punished for not following orders as directly as I should have. It seems it is not enough to follow an officer out of the trenches and across the battlefield. A good soldier must also refrain from any independent thought and certainly from any effort to help an officer do his job more efficiently than he is doing it by himself.*

The officer came back to walk beside him. "I'd like your help interrogating these men. You'll translate."

Julian hadn't exactly been frightened of the officer's discipline, but he breathed a little easier and allowed his shoulders to relax. They reached their destination, and Julian translated for the officer as he questioned the prisoners one by one, asking them about the state of their reserves, whether they planned to use gas shells, where they came from, and dozens of other questions.

As the last Boche was led away, the officer turned to Julian. "How did a poilu like you learn German?"

Julian didn't want anyone to question his loyalty. But their suspicions couldn't make anything worse than it already was. "My mother is Alsatian. She moved to Calais when she was a teenager, but German was her first language. It's what she speaks at home."

"And where do your mother's loyalties lie?"

"Certainly not with the Kaiser. Her father was a civil servant in 1870. When the Germans won the war, he lost his job. They stayed for a few years—my grandmother was German—but my mother blames the change in government for interrupting her education and reducing her family to poverty."

"Very well. Good work today."

"Thank you, sir." Julian hesitated before voicing a new thought. "Is there often a need for translators? I'd happily accept new duties if I can be of service to your mission."

The officer tilted his head to the side and reached up to rub his chin. "How good is your German?"

"Fluent, but I have an accent."

"How long have you been in the army?"

"Four years, sir. I was wounded at Artois and I'm just now rejoining my unit."

"And I suppose you would do nearly anything to keep from going back to the trenches?"

When the officer put it that way, it sounded cowardly. But Julian didn't think he was a coward. He might prefer an alternate assignment, but he would obey orders when they were given. "Yes, sir. The time I spent there was enough to last me an eternity."

The officer studied Julian for several long seconds. "I have no permanent need for a translator."

Julian felt disappointment creeping in the way chlorine gas flows into a trench.

"But if you can pretend to be a German who grew up in Alsace, I know someone who might be able to use you."

* * *

Julian sat on an empty artillery crate in a stifling canvas tent and waited, wondering what was in store. He'd been waiting for a day, but that was one day less in the trenches, and he'd been given food, so he had no complaints. But he did have worries. The French officer interrogating captured Germans had asked if Julian could pass as a native Alsatian, and though Julian had come up with a few other possibilities, the scenario that seemed most likely was that French intelligence needed a spy.

Spies were loathsome. Dishonest. Unscrupulous. Julian was no saint, but he tried to be a good person. Could he stoop that low? The alternative was a return to the trenches, so he hadn't yet rejected the possibility, but neither had he embraced it. He wasn't sure what to do. Either way, he was unlikely to survive the war. He could die in the trenches or be executed for espionage. Neither sounded significantly worse than the other, but what of his soul? He expected to see the next life soon and didn't want to do anything that would risk his status there.

"Bonjour." A British officer pushed aside the tent flap and strode inside. A French officer followed him.

Julian stood at attention, but the officer waved him back to his seat.

"I understand you speak fluent German," the man said in appalling French.

"Yes, sir, but with an Alsatian accent."

Both officers took seats on empty crates. "When were you born?" the British one asked.

"1890."

The man mulled over the answer. "So when you were born, Alsace was part of the German Empire. Do you know enough about Alsace that you could convince someone in the Ruhr that you grew up there?"

Julian remembered the stories his mother had told. They had all taken place long before his birth, but there had been so many tales, memories of the past, insights into the customs and the people. "I think so."

"I will be very direct because I have limited time. I am looking for someone to go into Germany, pose as a German national, gather information, and send it back to me. I need to know, first of all, if you are capable of such a job and, second, if you are willing."

Julian dodged a direct answer. "How would I get the information back to you?"

"We can go over that later."

"What of my age, sir? Are you expecting me to join the German Army? Surely they've called up as many men as we have. I don't imagine there are many men between age twenty and forty left at home."

The British officer smiled. "Good, you are already thinking like a spy. Your cover story will explain you were invalided out of the army. The Germans generally send Alsatians to the Eastern Front, so you were wounded by the Russians."

"I know nothing of the Eastern Front."

"Should you accept the assignment, I shall give you time to study as many newspapers as you like. French and German."

Julian hesitated for an instant, then went ahead, even if it was bold. "Most newspapers don't report the war accurately."

"Oh, how so?"

"They minimize our casualties, depict the Boches as inept, and pretend all our soldiers are eager to die for France."

The officer sat back and crossed his arms. "I imagine German newspapers do the same. You have enough experience with war that you'll be able to sift the facts from the fiction, should you agree to do this."

Julian still wasn't ready to decide, despite the officer's second request for commitment. Going back to the trenches would be like returning to hell, but it would end eventually. Becoming a spy might postpone hell, but then he'd be stuck there for eternity. "I would like the advice of a clergyman before I decide."

The man's eyes widened, and the muscles in his jaw hardened. The French officer, who had been silent up to that point, let out a huff. "A clergyman?"

"Yes, sir. I would do almost anything to keep out of the trenches, but I won't risk my soul for it."

"You think becoming a spy might place your soul in jeopardy?"

The answer was obvious, so Julian didn't bother answering.

The British officer was silent for a few long seconds; then he turned to the French officer. "Do you know any clergyman?"

"I would like to find one myself." Julian didn't want the French officer ordering a chaplain to tell Julian what the British man wanted him to hear. He needed to speak with a neutral priest.

The French officer looked ready to chasten Julian, but the British officer chuckled. "I like that. You want an unbiased source. That disposition will serve you well should you accept the mission. Go find your clergyman. We will arrange a day's leave for you. But think of this—men are dying in the trenches every day, and nothing we have tried so far is making much of a difference. Oh, the generals all have their grand plans, but frankly, this war is turning into a test of endurance. Breakthroughs will remain elusive unless we gain the advantage, and we won't gain the advantage on the battlefield. Your work can help with the war effort far more than a rush across no-man's land can. Will you condemn more men to more time in the trenches when you have the background we need to gather vital information? Consider that as you make your decision."

\* \* \*

Julian would do anything to stay out of the trenches. Anything except put his soul at risk. Yet the British officer had brought up a point Julian hadn't before considered. Could his efforts help shorten the misery of the poilus still condemned to the front line? If he could help them, becoming involved in espionage seemed less repulsive.

The small village church he found had been damaged by an artillery shell, but the roof was patched. Another shell had blasted a crater in the surrounding cemetery, but the dead had been reburied and the tombstones straightened.

Julian had cleaned his uniform as best he could, but he still paused at the church door. He had gone to Mass and confession with his father in Calais, despite his memories of Artois, but having his father by his side had made it easier to walk onto consecrated ground. Alone, he hesitated.

"Can I help you, my son?" The priest's black robes contrasted starkly with his snowy hair. Wrinkles lined his face, but far more noticeable was the man's aura of peace. No one else along the Western Front had the calm this man did, and Julian was envious.

"I wish to ask your advice."

"If you are thinking of deserting, I can offer you my sympathy for what you have been called to suffer, but I cannot condone your actions."

"I'm not planning to desert, Father."

The priest's face, if possible, changed to portray even more of the serenity Julian craved. "Follow me." They walked to a small chapel, and there, under the crucifix, the priest motioned for Julian to sit. "Tell me what is on your mind."

Julian swallowed. Neither the British nor the French officer had told him what he could and could not say about their previous meeting, though Julian knew such things were best left unspoken. Yet this was a man who had devoted his life to serving his fellow men, and he was French. "I've been asked to be a spy."

"By whom?"

"A British officer cooperating with a French officer. They want me to go to Germany, gather information for them. My mother is Alsatian, so I speak the language. But it will involve lying, Father. Every day. I think I might be able to help the other soldiers, the ones still stuck in the trenches, but I fear what I might become in the process."

"You want to serve your country, but you do not wish to lose your soul."

"Yes." Julian was impressed by the man's astute summary.

The priest thought for a while, his arms folded, staring up at the Christ. "This morning I was reading in the scriptures of the night when our Lord told Peter that before the cock crowed that morning, Peter would deny Him. I've read the Gospel of John many times, but I had a new thought today. Was the Lord prophesying? Or was He commanding Peter to save himself, even by deception?"

The priest relaxed his arms and turned to Julian. "All morning I've wondered where that thought came from. But now I see. I still do not know what Jesus meant when He said those words to Peter, but I believe God is mindful of you, and He has sent you a message through me. Go your way, my son. If you are lying for the right reasons, the Lord will not hold it against your soul."

# Chapter 9

JULIAN ACCEPTED HIS ASSIGNMENT THAT afternoon. He still worried about his ability to blend in, about whether he would be effective, and about whether he would be caught, but he no longer agonized over his soul.

"Glad to have you," Lieutenant McDougall, the British officer, said. "We are sending you to Essen, in the center of the Ruhr. We are interested in any intelligence you can give us, but I expect you will have the most luck gathering information about the Krupp factory. If the Germans are developing secret weapons, any warning we have will improve our response and decrease our losses. I recommend forming friendships with factory workers and courting them for information."

"How will I blend in?"

McDougall pulled a few documents from his leather satchel. "I have had some paperwork forged for you. Your new name is Becker. Hans Becker. You served in the Polish areas of the Russian Empire with a distant nephew of Herr and Frau Von Hayek. The nephew doesn't exist, so you can make up his name and how he died. Pick something you can easily remember. Frau Von Hayek will introduce you to a local family, and you'll be one of their servants. I hope that won't be too large of an inconvenience. Workers are less suspicious."

"That's fine." He could tolerate being a servant if it would help the poilus in the trenches. He wasn't scared of hard work—he'd been brought up on a dairy, and cows had to be cared for no matter the weather and regardless of holidays. As for a dead friend, he would describe him as a Teutonic version of Maximo. "So I'm Hans Becker from Alsace. Invalided out of the army after an injury in Russia. Assuming I survive long enough to learn anything, how do I report it?" Julian hesitated for a moment, then decided to mention the one idea he'd come up with. "I can write backward. It was a game my father and I used to play. But it would look suspicious, and it's easy to read with a mirror."

McDougall pulled a small jar from his satchel. "Invisible ink. Call it aftershave if anyone asks. Use it as you would normal ink, but use a smooth pen so you don't leave scratches on your paper—or find rough paper. Write an ordinary letter in ordinary ink, then put this between the lines. If you write backward as well, you'll buy yourself time should something happen."

"How does it get from me to you?"

"You'll mail it to someone near the Dutch border. Either I will sneak in to collect it, or I'll have an associate smuggle it to me. I am still setting up the details."

"Still setting up the details?" Julian preferred a tried-and-tested method, not one currently being thrown together.

"It will be in working order before you go in."

"And when will that be?"

McDougall shrugged. "About a week. It depends on the weather."

Julian had one week of life left, perhaps more if he could successfully become Hans Becker. He'd already been told he would get no additional leave, but at least he had time to write to his parents. He couldn't tell them what he was doing, but he wanted them to know they wouldn't hear from him for a while, if ever again. He bowed his head in sorrow; even if he survived, he doubted he would see his mother again in this life. Her health had been fading anyway, but the decline had accelerated when her sons had gone to war, then taken a permanent turn for the worse when Julian's brother had been killed.

He spent the next five days training. An officer from the French Deuxième Bureau briefed him on what to expect, and McDougall spent hours every day drilling him on his cover story. Most afternoons he studied hand-to-hand combat with a retired British sergeant. The man's techniques were unconventional—perhaps unchivalrous—but he seemed eager to teach Julian the tricks he'd learned in the jungles of India. Julian spent his remaining time studying maps of the Essen area, reading newspaper accounts of the war in the east, and practicing with invisible ink. He wrote a dozen normal letters to his mother and father, and McDougall agreed to mail them at two-week intervals. Julian had a feeling the war would outlast his letters, but he doubted he would. The Germans, the French, the British—everyone executed spies.

* * *

On a crisp autumn morning a week after Julian was asked to go into Germany, McDougall told him it was time to leave. A pilot in a Royal Flying Corps uniform accompanied McDougall to the final briefing that evening, held in the tent where most of Julian's training had been conducted. It took Julian a few seconds of staring at the familiar-looking man for the memory to surface.

"You look different when you aren't covered in oil," he told Warren Flynn, the British-Canadian pilot he'd met while taking Maximo to the aid station.

"You look different when you aren't dipped in mud and speckled with blood."

"You've met?" McDougall asked.

"Yes, Olivier helped me pull my wounded gunner from a wrecked plane this spring."

"Did he survive?" Julian asked.

"Yes. Boyle made a full recovery, and his injuries don't seem to have tamed his thirst for flying. Last week he shipped home for pilot's training. I'll miss having him as my mechanic, but I'm flying a single-seat plane now, so I don't need a gunner anymore. And your friend? How is he?"

Julian looked away. "He didn't make it."

"I'm sorry."

Julian turned the conversation back to their assignment. "I don't suppose you're using a single-seat plane tonight?"

"No, a two-seater reconnaissance aircraft. I flew it around this morning for a test. It's slow, but that's why we're going in by moonlight."

An orderly came into the tent and handed McDougall a bundle of cloth. Julian knew it instantly by the color—a German uniform. At his current age, it was more plausible for him to dress like a member of the military until he was established in Essen. *If I live that long.*

"Let's go over everything one final time," McDougall began. "After Lieutenant Flynn drops you off, he will fly to the Netherlands to refuel."

"You're sure the fuel will be waiting for me? And no Dutch officials protesting an invasion of their neutrality?"

"Land on the correct field and you'll have no trouble. Now, Olivier, let's review your instructions. After you leave the aircraft . . ."

"I go to the nearest train station and purchase a ticket to Essen. I avoid all unnecessary conversation and go directly to Frau Von Hayek's home. She'll supply me with the remaining papers I need and find me work. When I have news, I write a mild, completely unsuspicious letter, put my report in the lines between with invisible ink, and mail it to the Düsseldorf address you gave me. I learn what I can, report often, and stay out of trouble."

"Good. And I've added a code name: Arachne. Use that if you need to communicate through a different method—a telegram requesting withdrawal, for example. In the ancient Greek myth, Arachne claimed she was a better weaver than even the goddess Athena. The goddess challenged her to a contest and won. In despair, Arachne hung herself, but the goddess took pity on her and turned her into a spider. That is what you shall be—a spider in a German family's home. Seeing all and arousing no suspicion."

"You can't give him a code name for a woman," Flynn said.

McDougall's head snapped from Julian to Flynn. "Why not? It fits the mission." "No, it doesn't."

"It most certainly does. All about changed identity and gathering information as something ordinary."

The pilot folded his arms across his chest. "I'm currently disenchanted with King Constantine and the rest of the Greeks. His code name is Spider."

McDougall cleared his throat. "Last I checked, you were not in charge of this mission."

"No, I'm just the transportation, and I don't transport male agents who have been given feminine code names. And please don't give me a code name. I don't want to be Icarus."

Red crept onto McDougall's temples, but eventually his face relaxed. "Fine." He looked at Julian. "Spider."

Julian didn't care what his code name was; he hoped he'd never have to use it. But he had found the conversation amusing. McDougall handed him the German uniform, and Julian turned around to put it on.

While he was changing, the other men continued. "Do you speak any German, Flynn? If something happens, I want you to be able to get out."

"Kann der Kaiser in der Hölle verrötten."

Julian chuckled.

"What was that?" McDougall asked.

Flynn didn't answer, so McDougall turned to Julian. "A translation, please."

"'May the Kaiser rot in hell.'"

McDougall glared at Flynn. "Maybe this isn't such a good idea."

"I know when to keep my mouth shut," Flynn said.

"Except around me."

"Yes, except around you."

# Chapter 10

*October 1915, Artois Province, France*

SEVERAL HOURS BEFORE SUNRISE THE next morning, Warren ran through his preflight checklist. He had timed the flight so he would land in Holland shortly after dawn, thus having only one nighttime landing. Olivier and McDougall spoke a few yards away, probably repeating the same things McDougall had been drilling into his spy for hours on end.

When the plane was ready, Warren motioned the others over.

McDougall held his hand out to the Frenchman, who shook it. "I hope to hear from you soon." He turned to Warren. "I will stop by your aerodrome this evening to see how everything went."

"Fine."

"And, Flynn?"

"Yes?"

"No insulting the Kaiser within earshot of anyone German, eh?"

If all went well, Warren wouldn't be speaking to anyone in Germany, and the only person he would communicate with in Holland would be the farmer on whose field he planned to land and refuel. Warren checked his pockets. The gold promised to the Dutch farmer was still inside, as was his lucky teacup handle.

Warren made sure Olivier was seated properly in the observer's seat of the B.E.2. It was a tight fit with his luggage shoved in between his legs. "I don't suppose you've ever flown before?"

"No."

"Just sit back and relax." As Warren sat in his own seat, he grimaced at the inane words he'd said. He was flying Olivier at night into enemy territory so he could pretend to be someone who didn't exist. The Germans executed spies—even female spies—so the chances of the Frenchman relaxing were slim.

Warren had practiced nighttime flights before—only a dozen times, but the darkness was less of a concern than the destination. The nearly full moon lit the field he would take off from. One of the mechanics from his aerodrome had come along, and when Warren gave him the signal, he spun the propeller.

Warren brought the reconnaissance plane up to speed and felt it lift off the ground. He hoped he'd find an equally useful field to use near Essen and that the moon would stay clear of clouds.

The plane didn't handle as smoothly as usual—probably because of the extra petrol tank fitted on the previous evening. With a map strapped to his leg, Warren navigated toward his enemy's country. He'd planned an indirect flight path that offered frequent checks over obvious landmarks to confirm he was heading in the right direction. The first check was the line of trenches. Even in the dark they looked sinister from above. They were different from their daytime appearance, now quiet and motionless. He supposed it was sleep that had overcome the infantrymen below, but a shiver went up his spine. Death too brought silent stillness.

His passenger didn't talk during the trip. The engines made conversation impossible unless the men shouted, and Warren's French needed work. Olivier seemed content to watch the landscape below while Warren flew.

Warren piloted the plane over a railroad junction and past a river—the Ruhr, if his calculations were correct. Then he passed another train junction and began hunting for a decent place to land. He decided against one field because there were too many homes nearby, then a second for the same reason. Another area appeared ideal, other than its proximity to a stream. He didn't want to land on soggy ground and get stuck. If he couldn't fly out, he wouldn't last long. His German was limited entirely to *ja, nein, guten morgen, danke,* and predictions of where the Kaiser might spend the afterlife.

After another ten minutes of searching, he circled back to the third field he'd spotted and decided it was worth trying. He brought the machine down and felt it bounce lightly along the uneven ground. He turned at the end of the field, where he'd have more room for takeoff, and slowly came to a stop.

Armed with a pistol, he stepped from the plane and looked around. He didn't see or hear anything suspicious, so he motioned Olivier out of the plane. "We flew over a train track. I would guess a half mile back, mostly to the south. It will lead to a station eventually."

Olivier nodded and grabbed his gear. Just one canvas kit bag, as one would expect to see a soldier carry. One bag to see him through the war.

"Are you scared?" Warren asked. It wasn't really any of his business, but Olivier seemed so calm.

"What's the worst they can do to me?"

Warren hesitated, hating to appear blunt, but Olivier already knew the risks. "If they catch you, they'll shoot you."

"The French sent me to the trenches. Trust me, that's far worse."

"Do you have food and money?"

"Yes." Olivier hauled the bag to his shoulder. "Lieutenant McDougall ensured I have enough for a few days. I've survived on less in the trenches, and here I'll have the benefit of not being a target. Not yet anyway."

Warren watched him for a few moments. Olivier appeared to have in abundance what he would most need: courage.

Olivier stretched out his hand, and Warren grasped it in his own. "Thanks for the ride."

"Let me know when you need a ride home."

Olivier's lips pulled into a slight smile. "We both know I'm unlikely to return to France."

Warren wanted to protest, but anything he said would seem trite. Besides, Warren didn't believe in miracles anymore. Everyone spoke of "The Miracle on the Marne" the previous fall, but that hadn't been a miracle, not really. The Germans had simply made a few tactical errors, reconnaissance aircraft had seen their weaknesses, and a determined counterattack had prevented the capture of Paris. Warren had grown up with people who believed in miracles, and he supposed at one time he'd believed in them too. But none of the earnest faith he'd grown up surrounded by in Cardston had done anything for his mother when she'd been sick.

"Let me know when to spin the propeller."

"Thank you." Warren climbed back into his plane, feeling as though he'd delivered a man to his death. "Spider?"

"Hmm?"

"*Bon courage.*"

# Chapter 11

*October 1915, Essen, Germany*

JULIAN SPENT A SLEEPLESS NIGHT hiking through the countryside and a long morning asking for directions. He inhaled deeply as he turned up the path to a respectable home in a quiet neighborhood. It was conveniently close to the train station and disconcertingly close to an army recruiting center. Julian swallowed and rapped on the door, hoping Lieutenant McDougall was right, that Frau Von Hayek was truly sympathetic to Great Britain and France despite her husband and her current residence. She had been in correspondence with McDougall through a mutual contact in the Netherlands, but what if it was a trap? The thought was both terrifying and amusing. If they were planning to trap him, they were going to be disappointed when all they caught was a lowly poilu, not even a corporal.

A maid answered the door.

"I'd like to see Frau Von Hayek, please."

The servant eyed his uniform. "Your name?"

"Hans Becker. I'm a friend of her nephew."

She raised one eyebrow and gestured him inside. "You may wait here."

While the woman hurried away, Julian took in the tall entryway lit by a rectangular window over the door. Portraits, perhaps of the inhabitants' ancestors, hung from two of the walls. Peering into the hallway, Julian saw a staircase with an elaborately carved handrail and thick rugs over a polished wooden floor. The mounted candlesticks were unlit but looked as though they would easily illuminate a space twice as large.

The maid returned before long. "I'm sorry. Frau Von Hayek is having luncheon, and I don't wish to disturb her. Could you come back tomorrow?"

"Perhaps I might see her when she finishes?" Julian didn't want to postpone the meeting. He preferred to stay off the streets, where people might question his purpose and his accent. "I don't mind waiting." He might not have the courage to come back again the next day.

The maid pursed her lips and nodded with a great show of reluctance.

Julian was left alone in the entryway with nowhere to sit and only the echo of a clock to keep him company. Some noise drifted his way from the other rooms, but the house seemed empty, as if designed to host far more than its current occupants. As the time ticked by, he wondered again if McDougall was wrong. Perhaps Frau Von Hayek wasn't eager to help after all.

Two hours later, if the clock in the hallway was correct, the maid returned. "Frau Von Hayek will see you now."

Julian followed the maid past several rooms into a cozy parlor.

"Ah, Herr Becker, I'm so glad you came." A middle-aged woman dressed in high-quality clothes stood and walked toward him. "My nephew wrote of your loyalty in the most glowing of terms. So good of you to call on me."

Julian swallowed back surprise at Frau Von Hayek's acting abilities. "Thank you, ma'am. He always spoke well of you."

"I hope you weren't kept waiting long."

"Um . . ." Julian caught sight of a guilty look on the maid's face. Rather than make an enemy of the help, he sputtered out, "No, not long."

Frau Von Hayek, perhaps noticing his hesitation, turned to the maid. "How long did you wait before telling me my nephew's dear friend was waiting to see me?"

"Is your nephew really friends with an enlisted man?"

"Look at him, Ulla. He's not old enough to have obtained a commission before the war started. How long?"

"A bit over an hour, ma'am." Ulla's eyes stayed fixed on the floor.

Frau Von Hayek made a low noise that expressed displeasure but left it at that. She turned to Julian. "Have you eaten?"

"I'm a soldier, ma'am. I am used to going without."

"I suppose that means no. Ulla, go put together a meal for Herr Becker." Red spots showed on the maid's cheeks. "Yes, ma'am."

"Had I known you were here, I would have invited you to dine with me. Perhaps you can join me for supper?"

Julian saw Ulla pause, waiting for his reply. "If it won't be an inconvenience, that would be most agreeable." He hoped the maid wouldn't resent his acceptance.

"It will be no inconvenience at all." Frau Von Hayek took a seat and, with a wave of her hand, suggested he do the same. "My nephew's letter was unfortunately very short. I suppose you were called up by the German Army last summer?"

"Yes, ma'am. And like most Alsatians, I was sent east."

"Yes, I did notice your Alsatian accent."

Julian smiled. Without saying anything that would make the staff suspicious, Frau Von Hayek had told him that, yes, he had a noticeable accent and it was a good thing he had a cover for it. "I was wounded earlier this year in Galicia. I've spent time convalescing, but unfortunately my injuries are such that I am no longer fit to be a soldier. I'm looking for work, and your nephew said you might be able to suggest something."

Frau Von Hayek clasped her hands together, keeping them in her lap. "I think I have just the thing for you. Give me a few days to sort it all out."

\* \* \*

Julian spent two days with Frau Von Hayek, and on his third day in Germany, she found employment for him at the home of Herr Sauer as a replacement for the gardener and the caretaker, both of whom had joined the army. Three days into his assignment, he still hadn't met Herr Sauer, but he finally knew his way around the large home with the steeply sloped roof. The manor reminded him of a hunting lodge, and its architecture and décor constantly reminded him that he was no longer in France.

Dorothea Kallweit, Herr Sauer's daughter, burst through the room where Julian was replacing a broken shelf in a cabinet. "Have you seen Willi and Franz?" Dorothea didn't pause for Julian's answer, going straight to the window to look into the enormous yard behind the house.

"They were outside when I cut this wood twenty minutes ago. Do you see them?"

"No." Dorothea brushed back a loose strand of brown hair sprinkled with gray and opened the window. "Willi! Franz!" No one answered her. She slammed the window shut—Julian hoped the motion wouldn't knock the trim loose, because the home already needed enough repairs to keep him busy for a year. "Those two. I spent years wishing they would stop fighting with each other, and now they spend all their time together conspiring on how they can best avoid chores."

"Mama?" The youngest of the four Kallweit children, Gerta, followed her mother into the room. "May I have a snack?"

Julian guessed the four-year-old was about to shoot up several centimeters. She had clear preferences about which foods she would and would not eat, but in the past few days, she'd eaten as much as Julian or her brothers.

"Not now, Gerta. We'll eat at noon. And we'll have a special supper tonight when your grandfather gets back from Berlin."

Julian opened his mouth, then shut it again. The ancient cook hadn't told him about Herr Sauer's scheduled return, nor asked him to help in the preparations. Though he hadn't been hired as a cook, Mathilde had quickly started ordering him around. She was skilled in her profession but preferred to have someone else chop potatoes and fetch things from the basement. He would have to check the kitchen to make sure the eighty-year-old woman hadn't forgotten her master's homecoming. Julian hoped a pleasant meal would encourage Sauer to share information about his trip to Berlin. According to Frau Von Hayek, Herr Sauer had once been a rich businessman. He'd spent years coordinating Krupp's industrial espionage efforts and still had connections with some of the Kaiser's advisors. Little things like the dilapidated state of the manor and rumors of a son's gambling debts suggested that Sauer's finances were no longer healthy, but perhaps he still had useful information.

"Would you like me to find the boys?" Julian asked.

"Yes, please." Dorothea turned from Julian to Gerta, who was pulling on her mother's long skirt.

"I'm hungry, Mama."

"Wait thirty minutes."

Julian tested the shelf and shut the cabinet door. "Gerta, would you like to come with me?" Maybe searching for her brothers would distract her from her hunger.

Dorothea gave him a smile of gratitude as Gerta scurried toward Julian and took his outstretched hand. "Tell Franz that if he doesn't clean up the mess he left in the dining room, he'll get none of Mathilde's butterkuchen."

Gerta's eyes lit up. "Butterkuchen?"

Dorothea's face softened. "You poor thing. Your grandfather used to have treats all the time, but since the war started, it's been difficult to get enough butter and sugar. It must feel like ages since we had any. Keep your dress clean and you shall have some after supper."

Gerta skipped alongside Julian as they went outside, her two blonde braids swinging with each step. She carefully avoided the mud puddles as they walked to the copse of trees that bordered the Sauer property. Julian liked the Kallweit family. Gerta was a ray of sunshine, and Willi and Franz, though mischievous, were good-natured. Dorothea was strict but fair, and despite their difference in social status, she always asked for Julian's help, even though it was her right to order. He'd yet to meet the oldest son, who was away with the German Army, or the father, away with the German Navy.

"Willi? Franz?"

"I'm here."

Julian turned to the side, where Willi sat with his back against a tree and a book open in his lap. "Your mother is looking for you."

Willi frowned. "More chores, I'm sure. I wish Grandpapa hadn't let the maid go."

"Better the maid than Mathilde. Mama always burns things." Gerta whispered the last part.

Willi pushed himself to his feet. At seventeen, he was already taller than Julian. "In Prussia we had both. I don't know why we had to leave. The Russians didn't make it past Tannenburg."

The Kallweit family and their cook had come to Essen early in the war when the Russian Army had first moved west. Fear that the front lines could shift again kept them in the Ruhr, but Willi seemed to think the Russians would never again threaten Prussia.

A whooping sounded from the grove of trees. Julian guessed it was nine-year-old Franz and his friend Max. It had rained that morning, and the boys had left the dining room in a state of siege. He would almost think they were French the way they threw up barricades and hoisted makeshift banners. As soon as the rain had stopped, they'd escaped outside, no doubt to conduct a war of movement.

"Franz?"

The noise grew louder, closer, more intense. Two mud-speckled boys ran among the trees at full speed, sticks in their hands and an upside-down pot on the shorter one's head. Julian laughed to see their spindly limbs charging him. Their childhood was so different from his own—one of leisure and making up games to entertain themselves. From the time he was Gerta's age, most of Julian's time had been spent working on the family dairy, with breaks only for school.

"Stop!" Gerta yelled. She ducked behind Julian to keep herself clean as Franz and his friend skittered toward her.

"Yes, you mustn't get any mud on Gerta's dress," Julian said. "Your mother told her if she keeps her dress clean, she can have butterkuchen."

Franz's lips formed a small circle of delight. He straightened his suspenders and pushed the pot back on his forehead. "Butterkuchen?" Franz tossed his stick to the side and headed for the house, Max right beside him.

"Wait, Franz," Willi said. "Be careful which door you use so Mama doesn't see your muddy clothes."

Franz nodded to his brother and then inhaled deeply. "I can smell it!"

Willi and Gerta grinned as they jogged over to their brother.

"Your mother said you won't get any if you don't tidy up your messes," Julian told them.

"Haven't you ever had butterkuchen?" Franz asked. "It's worth stealing. I'd rather take a beating than not have any."

"I've not had Mathilde's," Julian answered honestly. The truth was, he had no idea what butterkuchen was, but something inside the house smelled divine.

* * *

Julian carried the last of the dessert plates into the kitchen. Few of them had so much as a crumb of butterkuchen remaining. "Mathilde, you've been on your feet all day. Why don't you head to bed? I'll finish cleaning."

Mathilde looked around the kitchen, her mouth pulled into a straight line.

"I know you like the kitchen just so. If I'm not sure where something goes, I'll leave it on the counter after I've cleaned it, and you can put it away in the morning."

Mathilde nodded and patted his arm on her way out. "Thank you, Herr Becker. These legs of mine are exhausted, and Herr Sauer likes his breakfast early."

Julian still knew very little of his employer. Herr Sauer had arrived only a few hours before supper, while Julian was helping Mathilde. The meal had been an elaborate, drawn-out affair, with Dorothea and the children taking most of Herr Sauer's attention. Frau Von Hayek had filled in the basics: he was a widower with five sons, all of them in the army, and one daughter, who had disappointed him by marrying a Prussian naval officer.

Herr Sauer had brought a guest back with him, a sturdy, middle-aged man with a droopy left eye. Julian went to see if the adults, who had moved to the drawing room, needed their coffee refilled. He suspected the men would soon want something stronger to drink.

"Can I get anyone more refreshments?"

Dorothea shook her head, and the man from Berlin ignored the query.

Herr Sauer looked over at Julian. "Herr Lohr, I don't think I mentioned it before, but the newest member of our staff has something in common with you. He's from Alsace."

"I'm from Lorraine, not Alsace." Herr Lohr gave Julian a cursory glance. "Not in the army?"

"I was, sir. Wounded on the eastern front."

"Becker, Herr Lohr will be staying with us for a few days. Please give him the same courtesy you would give my daughter or me. If you would make sure the guest room by the library is ready for his stay? And bring his things in from the car."

"Yes, sir." Julian slipped from the room. Herr Sauer was the first person he knew who owned an automobile.

"You hired someone new?" Lohr's voice followed Julian into the hallway.

"He was recommended by one of Essen's top families. How is he?"

Julian heard Dorothea next. "Fine, Papa. The children love him, and he stays busy fixing things without my asking."

"I used to do all the upkeep myself, back in my younger days," Herr Sauer said. Julian didn't hear the rest of the conversation, more concerned with preparing Lohr's room before Dorothea retired. That was the real reason he'd volunteered to do Mathilde's work—he wanted to listen to the men as soon as they were alone.

When Lohr's luggage was unloaded and his room prepared, Julian returned to the drawing room. Dorothea had gone. "Will there be anything else, sir?"

"No, thank you. I'll see you in the morning."

"Good night, sir. Good night, Herr Lohr."

Julian left the room but lingered after a few paces.

"Do you think the idea's crazy?" Sauer asked.

"No, brilliant. We aren't beating them on the battlefield, and they've got our navy bottled up in port. You may be insulated, but the average citizen can tell the British blockade is working by the rising price of food. We have to try something. I can pass as French, so I'll start in Paris. It will be like before the war when I kept Krupp apprised of what its competitors were doing."

"Yes, but you're working for Germany now, not just Krupp. And we were never allowed to blow up French foundries before. You think you can do it now?"

One of the men began pacing. "Yes. I'll target munitions factories first. Look what the shell crisis did in England—scandal, disunity, lower morale. I'll give the French a shell shortage too. I haven't worked out the details. I'll have to get there first, but a factory full of munitions—it can't be too hard to blow up."

"They'll have security," Herr Sauer said.

"I've spent decades getting around security. Give me enough money, and I'll bribe or hire the help I need. Set a dozen French factories on fire and give Germany an edge in this war."

"We need information too."

"My sources from before the war will still be greedy. Give me a few months, and I'll set up a thriving spy ring."

Julian had information for his first report, but it was the type of thing he wished he'd never heard.

# Chapter 12

*April 1916, Paris, France*

IT HAD BEEN EIGHT MONTHS since she'd begun work at the Renault factory at Boulogne-Billancourt, just west of Paris, and Evette still wasn't used to the crowds. There was always someone rushing from here to there wearing what looked like their Sunday best. The serge dress that had served her so well in the village felt conspicuously rural in Paris. Her work clothes were better, allowing her to blend in with all the other factory workers. Some of her female coworkers even wore trousers, but Evette wasn't ready to try that yet.

"Have you heard from Jean?" Evette asked Anne-Marie as they changed back into their fireproof work clothing after their meal break.

"I got a letter yesterday. He might have furlough soon."

Evette wondered what it would be like to be in love and married and to worry about the man getting slaughtered at Verdun. There were other places to be killed, of course, but Evette had shared Anne-Marie's relief when Jean's unit had been rotated out. Evette's brother Emile had been to Verdun too. He had a talent with words, and even though he'd given her few details, the tone of his letters had managed to convey the gloom and the despair. She wasn't sure how much longer the French Army could hold out, but after so much sacrifice, the thought of withdrawal was practically treasonous.

"Cut the chatter, ladies," the foreman yelled.

"We're back early, and we can't say two words to each other?" Anne-Marie muttered under her breath when he walked away. "He never complains when the men talk."

"Or if they're a few minutes late."

Evette went back to her lathe. The machinery was designed for a man, but she was used to that. She had often tilled fields with a plow designed for someone taller, and every time she'd hit a rock, the handle had smacked her in the chin. In the factory, she simply had to reach higher than most workers. Her arms and shoulders ached by the end of the day, but the war couldn't go on without munition workers.

She tried not to think about how many people might die from each shell she worked on, tried only to think of how completing as many as she could with the highest possible quality might make a difference to Emile and Jean and all the other men struggling in the trenches. Maybe the poilu who had given her money for the train ticket too. Eight months later and she still thought of him every day. It was ridiculous to remember him so often, and yet she'd never had a stranger notice her before, let alone show her kindness.

One of the other factory workers walked by, a man who had lost his foot in the war. He gave her a friendly smile, and she realized she was staring his direction. *Focus, Evette. Stop daydreaming about a man who's probably dead.*

Another long afternoon passed, but Evette was used to putting in long hours. She'd done it in her village since she was old enough to pull weeds, and she was grateful for the work. Food and lodging were more expensive than she'd expected—and prices kept rising. She found herself in a strange position. She wanted the war to end, but when peace came, she would lose her job and possibly her independence.

The truth was the end of the war seemed a long way off. She could read the desperation, the depression, and the resignation in Emile's letters, could see it in the haunted eyes of soldiers on leave in Paris. Sometimes she worried France was losing.

"You know the picric acid in the shells will turn your skin yellow?"

Evette glanced over her shoulder at the foreman. He was a tall, skinny man who ignored most of the women unless they were making mistakes. Why was he talking to her? "We all have to sacrifice something. The army can't win without artillery shells," she said. Besides, she wasn't measuring out the powder, so her exposure to picric acid was minor.

"I don't know that they can win, even with artillery shells."

Evette studied him as he walked to another worker. She felt the same way about the army's prospects, but why would the foreman try to discourage her? The smell of oil and cordite was potent enough to mask all but the strongest smells of alcohol, but she didn't think he was drunk. His steps were too steady for that, and his eyes had been clear.

She watched the foreman over the next three hours. He spoke with a few workers and assisted some of the women when they had to lift a heavy object or tighten a lever the last little bit. Most of his attention was directed to other things: the warehouse structure, the stacks of shells in various stages of production, the security guards.

As she finished her shift, Evette dawdled, timing her exit from the factory to coincide with the foreman's. On the street outside the factory, he bought a paper from one of the paperboys selling the news Emile always made fun of for its lack of accuracy. Then the foreman hung back, watching the workers depart. Two blocks from the factory, he ducked into an alley.

Hesitant, Evette approached the side street's entrance and peered around the corner. Far inside the alley, the foreman spoke with a tall man in a suit and top hat. The man in the top hat handed the foreman an envelope and then walked farther into the alley, away from Evette.

She turned her back to the foreman and picked up a two-day-old newspaper from the gutter as he approached. She unfolded it and pretended she was fascinated by the contents until she had given him enough time to walk past her. She tried to locate him again, but there were still crowds of factory workers leaving, and she couldn't pick him out. She had waited too long to follow him again that night, but she set her mouth in determination. He was up to something, and she intended to find out what.

# Chapter 13

JULIAN TRIMMED THE BUSHES UNDER the open window to Herr Sauer's study, something he did far more often than was needed, because it was a convenient spot from which to overhear conversations between Herr Sauer and his guests.

"I'm certain they're losing more men than we are. Isn't that enough?"

"How many more?" Herr Sauer asked in a gruff voice. "Falkenhayn's strategy will ruin us nearly as quickly as it ruins the French."

"No, it will ruin the French first, and then we will have won."

"The French will fight till the last man. And by the time we've whittled their army down that far, we'll have only a few divisions left. Is that the type of victory you want? One with only a handful of survivors?"

"Well, what do you want us to do?" Herr Meyer from Berlin roared. "Last year proved that breakthroughs are no longer possible on the Western Front. Not unless that factory up the road is coming up with a new superweapon."

"Gas and flame throwers didn't prove decisive. What makes you think anything else will?" Julian heard a creak of wood and assumed Herr Sauer was moving his chair. "I think we ought to concentrate on the Russians and the British. We've made good progress in the east, and if we focus there, we can make progress again. End the war with Russia, then transfer more men west. Trying to knock the French out of the war is pointless for now. Where would they go? We're on land they claim as their own. But if we turn our energies against the British, perhaps they'll decide the war is too costly."

"They're getting desperate. They finally started conscription."

"So I heard. Better to finish them off now before all those newly drafted soldiers are trained and firing on our men."

"What about your other project?" Herr Meyer asked.

"Hmm?"

"Your saboteur?"

"I haven't heard from him in a while."

Julian almost dropped his clippers. Lohr came to see Sauer every few months, and his last visit had ended only the day before. Julian had learned enough about Lohr's recent progress to send in a long report; he only wished Lohr and Sauer had been more specific with the targets and contacts they'd discussed. French ports and French factories were at risk, but Julian couldn't warn McDougall about which ones. He wasn't even sure his report would arrive in France before Lohr did.

"Herr Becker, are you trimming those bushes again?" Willi's voice sounded from the garden.

"I'm thinking." Julian walked over to Willi so Sauer and Meyer were less likely to notice him. "They're nice bushes, and this side of the house is the first thing people see when they come to visit your grandfather. But it gets good light. I'm wondering if we should pull them out and plant something else there."

Willi considered it. People in Germany were getting enough to eat but not in the quantity or quality they were used to. Julian had convinced Herr Sauer to let him convert most of the yard into a vegetable garden, and Willi had turned into a good worker over the past few months. Julian had also talked the family into raising chickens. Every morning, little Gerta ran out first thing to check for eggs. Julian's suggestion to buy a milk cow hadn't been rejected, but more cows than usual had been slaughtered during the previous year's fodder shortage, so those who still owned them were reluctant to part with them. "Let's plant something we can eat. Carrots or lettuce."

"I'll check with your mother to see that she doesn't mind. Shall we look for mushrooms this evening?"

Willi's face lit up. The monotony of their meals seemed to wear on him more than it did on the adults. "Yes, please."

Julian went inside and paused outside the study. Sauer and Meyer were discussing the relative merits of the various coffee substitutes. British Intelligence might possibly be interested in such information and its effect on morale, but Julian didn't think the potential usefulness outweighed the risk of being caught.

Julian found Dorothea in Franz's room. Gerta stood on a pile of thick books while her mother fitted a half-finished dress made from a tablecloth to her. Franz sorted through a pile of hand-me-down shirts from his older brothers. Most material was in short supply, and Franz was rough on his clothing. Whenever he went outside to play, he came back looking as if a shell had shredded his shirt and trousers.

"Frau Kallweit?"

"Yes?" Dorothea said around the pins she held in her mouth to keep her hands free.

"Would you mind if Willi and I pulled out the bushes near the study window? We were thinking we could plant more vegetables there."

"That's fine. Have Franz help you as soon as he finds something with a decent collar."

\* \* \*

Herr Meyer left for Berlin that afternoon while Julian and the two boys tore up the bushes and planted the patch of ground with radishes and carrots. Julian caught snatches of Meyer's parting words with Sauer.

"You're right. Verdun won't be enough. The Kaiser wants to win a war, like his German grandfather. And he wants to be loved, like his English grandmother. If you and your friends don't manage something soon, he'll achieve neither goal and we'll all pay the price of his failure."

Long after their unsatisfying supper had ended and everyone else had gone to bed, Julian crept along the hallway to Herr Sauer's study. At least once a week he came in the dead of night to read the man's diary and go over the correspondence he sometimes received from the Krupp factory. Although officially retired, Sauer's opinion was still welcome at the all-important munition works, and with the monetary strain his son's gambling indiscretions had caused, Sauer seemed eager for the work.

When he'd examined everything, Julian went back to his tiny room in the basement. Several months ago, he had discovered it was easier to write his cover letter if it was addressed to a real person. The current letter was addressed to his father, even though he knew his father would never read it. Still, the process gave him some connection to his home, to his family, to the life he'd left behind. The connection was comforting but also bitter because he doubted he'd ever have those parts of his life again.

After he finished the note to his father, he began the report in invisible ink. If someone suspected the letter, how long would it take them to read his secret message? They would have to reveal the hidden words first, but with his current ink, they would only need to apply heat. Once the words were visible, he doubted it would take them long to figure out he'd written backward, and it would take them even less time to find a translator who could read French. He gripped the pen a little more firmly and hoped no one would think the letter unusual.

In his report, he included Herr Sauer's lack of trust in Herr Meyer, wondering if it was significant. Julian suggested a few possible reasons. Perhaps lower expectations would make any success, even a minor one, seem like a victory. Or maybe Sauer and Lohr were operating without the Kaiser's approval. Whatever the purpose behind the secrecy, if things proceeded as planned, Sauer and Lohr's schemes were about to come to fruition.

# Chapter 14

*May 1916, Paris, France*

"You don't have to be the last one to leave every day to prove you're dedicated to your job," Anne-Marie told Evette.

"I know. I just . . ." Evette let her response trail off. She feared what Anne-Marie would say if Evette told her the truth, that she followed the foreman after every shift. She knew where he slept, where he drank, which newspapers he favored. But she hadn't seen the tall man with the top hat for weeks. Maybe he wasn't important anyway. Or perhaps she had seen him but had failed to recognize him from her brief glimpse of him in the shaded alley.

"You just what?"

"I can't lose this job. I don't have anywhere to go, no family that can help me."

"What of your brother?"

"Emile? I've already depended on his charity, and he's sending part of his wages to my mother. I don't think he could support us both. And he might not survive Verdun." Evette hated to talk about Emile's odds of survival, but she knew it would change the subject.

"I'm still amazed Jean survived. He might have to go back. I have nightmares about it, and I haven't even been there."

Evette nodded her sympathy. Because conditions were so horrible at Verdun, units were rotated in and out fairly quickly. But there were only so many French troops, so some men had to return. In his last letter, Emile had told her there were no longer trenches at Verdun, just overlapping shell craters. She knew he kept the worst of the details from her, but what he did reveal was awful.

"Are you coming?" Anne-Marie asked.

Evette hesitated. Was she crazy to stalk the foreman, or was her instinct right? In a moment, she sided with her instinct. "Soon. I need to finish something, but I'll see you tomorrow."

Anne-Marie rolled her eyes. "Fine, but don't work too late, or you'll make the rest of us look like laggards."

Evette smiled her good-bye, then began cleaning the floor around her lathe. As the foreman finished his rounds, Evette stepped outside, then loitered near the entrance, waiting for him to leave. As usual, he walked out and didn't glance back. Evette tailed him, careful to keep him at a distance but still within sight.

Half a block into Evette's stalking, another man joined the foreman, and the two of them struck up a conversation. That wasn't entirely unusual, nor was it unusual that the man was similar in build to what she remembered from the alley. She crept closer. The tall man turned back. His left eyelid drooped dramatically. He saw her, no doubt, but there were dozens of other people on the street too.

She followed them as they circled the factory. When the two stopped walking, she paused behind a pile of empty crates. The tall man didn't wear a top hat anymore, but something told Evette it was the same person. They started back the way they'd come, and she crept cautiously toward them as they examined a crate waiting to be brought inside.

They moved on after a few minutes, and then they disappeared. Evette's stomach churned. Where had they gone? Should she try to find them or go back to scrutinize the crate they'd looked at? She took a few additional steps, then screamed when a hand grabbed her arm and yanked her around to face the man who'd met the foreman in the alley a month ago. His glare was icy.

"What are you doing here, Mademoiselle Touny?" the foreman asked. "Your shift ended an hour ago."

Evette swallowed back her fear and made something up. "I forgot my scarf. I came back to see if I could find it."

The other man's droopy eye squinted in disbelief. "It's May. You still wear a scarf?"

"It was chilly this morning, and it would be difficult to replace."

"Humph."

The foreman jerked his head toward the factory entrance. "Go get it."

Evette rushed away the second the tall man released her arm, but she paused as soon as she turned a corner and was out of sight. She listened to the men over the sounds of the night shift.

"Want me to take care of her?" The voice belonged to the stranger. "I noticed her following us earlier."

"You think she's up to something? She's just a worker, from the country, no less."

"Do you want to risk our plans? Weeks of preparation, and if she says something, I'll have to start over completely, and you'll go to prison."

"Go ahead, then. Take care of her when she comes out again."

Goose bumps spread up Evette's arms and crept across her shoulders. Their plans had to include something serious if it could result in the foreman's arrest. She wasn't sure exactly what they meant when they spoke of "taking care of her," but she could guess.

She ducked into the factory, searching for the night-shift foreman. A sickening thought crossed her mind: what if the men outside had accomplices on this shift? Or what if no one believed her? She didn't even know what she was trying to prevent.

"This area is closed to the public, mademoiselle."

Evette turned around. The man who had spoken was tall and broad. She usually preferred smaller men, based on the idea that smaller men couldn't hurt her as badly if they decided to hit her, but in this case, a large man was perfect. "I work the day shift. One of the men I work with has been acting strangely, and he's threatening me. Can you help?"

The man's expression changed from stern disapproval to righteous indignation. "Someone's bothering you?"

"Yes, and I think . . ." Evette hesitated before revealing her best guess of the foreman's intentions. "I think he might be planning some type of sabotage."

"Stay with me," the man said. "I'll send someone for the gendarmes."

Running and hiding behind the first person taller than the man with the slanted eye hadn't been her plan, but for the moment, it seemed better than waiting around alone. She followed the tall man as he sent another worker for the police.

"There's one other thing," Evette said.

"Yes?"

"He was with a second man, and they were examining a crate. I didn't see what was inside, but should we look at it now in case the gendarmes are delayed?"

The man motioned with his arm, and another worker joined him. Then he grabbed a large pry bar. Evette hoped the man wouldn't need it as a weapon. "Show us where."

Evette led the men outside to the loading area. She was cautious, peeking around each corner before stepping around it, but she didn't see the foreman or his friend with the droopy eyelid. "It was this one, I think."

The large man pried off the top of the crate. The box was over a meter high, and both men were in front of her, so Evette couldn't see inside at first, but their reaction made it clear they'd discovered something important.

"This could blow out a row of workers and their machines."

"Start the whole factory on fire, and there's plenty of fuel inside if something got started."

Evette walked to the other side of the crate and stood on her tiptoes, trying to see the contents.

"Fire bombs," the tall man explained. "They didn't come from this factory."

"Look at this," the other man said as he lifted one of the shells. "That writing's not French."

The bombs were surrounded by bunches of rags and were packed in straw. Evette inhaled and recognized the scent of kerosene.

"Hey, get away from there!"

The two factory workers dropped the lid in surprise. Evette made eye contact with her foreman, and his jaw dropped. He backed away and then turned to run.

"Is he the one behind this?" one of the men asked.

"Yes."

Both men took off after the foreman. Evette stayed where she was, scanning the street for the foreman's accomplice and wondering what she'd do if he appeared.

* * *

When the gendarmes arrived, they asked Evette question after question. She wished she knew more of the answers. They questioned the captured foreman too and walked around the factory to confiscate all the combustible materials he'd hidden away over the last month. The man with a droopy eye had disappeared.

"Another investigator would like to speak to you," one of the gendarmes told her. "He's with the British Army. Says he's been investigating sabotage rings."

Evette held back a yawn and nodded. She'd lost track of how many men had interrogated her that night.

"A moment of your time, mademoi—" As soon as the British officer glanced at her, he stopped talking. His French was poor, so she thought he was trying to remember the correct word, but he stared at her with an intensity that made her think her skin must have turned canary yellow. "Mademoiselle, I am Lieutenant McDougall with British Army Intelligence. May I ask you a few questions about what happened?"

"Yes."

The officer took out a pen and paper. "I best start with your name."

"Evette Touny."

"How long have you worked at the factory?"

"Almost nine months, since September."

"And when did you first notice something odd about your foreman?"

"Roughly a month ago, sir."

McDougall looked up at her again and seemed to turn back to his paper with reluctance. "The other man. Have you ever seen him before tonight?"

"Once. The night I first followed the foreman. They met in the alley, and the other man handed the foreman an envelope."

"How big of an envelope?"

"Letter-sized, but thicker."

"Can you describe him, the man your foreman met?"

"Tall, and his left eyelid is slanted. He wore a top hat then. A derby hat tonight."

He paused again. "Slanted eyelid . . . How tall would you say he is?"

"Above average. Probably 180 centimeters."

"Hair color?"

"Brown."

"Build?"

"Muscular."

McDougall tapped his pen on the paper. "I wonder . . ."

When he didn't complete his thought, Evette leaned in. "What, sir?"

He put his pen away. "Your description matches one given me by another source. It seems a man named Lohr was planning to sabotage French factories and ports, among other things. The foreman called him something different, but I don't suppose he would be foolish enough to give out his real name."

Evette folded her arms and pulled them next to her chest. Knowing Lohr had plans to destroy not just the Renault factory but others as well made him seem even more dangerous. "I wish they would have caught him."

"The search will go on," he promised. "How often did you follow the foreman?"

"Most days."

"And he never noticed you?"

"No. But Lohr noticed me tonight. I guess I wasn't discreet enough. He was planning to take care of me."

He looked up again, concerned. "How did you get away?"

"I lied. Said I needed to go back to the factory to find a lost scarf. The fore-man didn't suspect me, so he let me go. I suppose Lohr planned to deal with me when I came back, tie me up or—"

"Or kill you."

"Yes."

"Can I be direct, mademoiselle?"

She nodded, wondering how he defined direct if their conversation up to that point wasn't included.

"You have a talent for counterintelligence."

"For what?"

"For tracking down spies and saboteurs. Have you received training?"

Evette shook her head. "No, I just noticed a few things and made some assumptions."

"Most people notice a few things and make assumptions, but you managed to make correct assumptions. Not many people can do that."

Evette tried to hide her confusion. Surely anyone who paid attention would have noticed the foreman . . . except no one other than her had. Was it her years of watching Gaspard to gauge his mood that had taught her how to read men? Her practice sneaking through the house undetected that had allowed her to successfully follow the foreman?

"Surely you have some type of background in this."

Evette hesitated, but Monsieur McDougall was with the army. She didn't want to get in trouble for lying—wartime regulations gave the military more power than usual. "I often had reason to avoid my half brother. He was my legal guardian before I came to work at the factory, and he was prone to violence. I learned to walk quietly and judge his mood from a distance." The man's eyes went from the paper to her face, then back again, but he spent longer looking at her than at what he'd written. "Do you enjoy your work in the factory?"

"Yes." She didn't like how her arms ached each night, and she didn't like the crowds, but she enjoyed being self-reliant. She couldn't go back to her village, and she doubted anyone rich enough to hire domestic help would be interested in an unrefined peasant girl.

"Do you love it so much that you never wish to leave, or would you consider a change in employment?"

"I am open to other work, sir, but I want to help the war effort."

"I would like to offer you a job."

"Doing what, sir?"

"Counterintelligence. You would still be helping the war effort, probably more than you are now. Making shells every day is worthwhile, to be sure. But preventing a saboteur from blowing up a few thousand shells . . . a wee bit more worthwhile, am I right?"

Evette thought about it for a moment, Emile's advice about not taking anything from a strange man crossing her mind. But this one was up-front about what he wanted—counterintelligence work. "You want me to follow people around and see if they're planning to blow up factories? How would I know who to follow?"

"I have leads. A multitude of them. But I do not blend in here in Paris. Even if I remove my uniform, I do not sound French. You, on the other hand, look like just another lass going to and from the factory. From a distance, you look average. From up close, you sound average. And you appear to have a knack for what I need. I can match whatever the factory pays you."

"Does the British Army often hire French women?"

"I have permission to hire whomever I deem useful. While operating in Paris, French agents seem the most practical for this sort of thing."

Working to catch spies and saboteurs sounded scary but exciting. Assuming the lieutenant kept his promise, she could continue to support herself without all the discomforts of factory work. And if the officer was right, it would mean doing something that could really make a difference. Her country was hurting. Could catching a few spies help prevent further harm? "Thank you, sir. I accept."

# Chapter 15

*September 1916, Champagne Province, France*

WARREN FLEW HIS AIRCO DH.2 biplane at its maximum altitude of fourteen thousand feet, waiting for an unlucky German reconnaissance plane to stumble across his path. The DH.2 had a bad reputation because so many new pilots crashed it, but Warren liked De Havilland's design. The controls were sensitive, hence the accidents and the plane's nickname of the *flying incinerator*, but that sensitivity gave experienced pilots an edge. When handled correctly, the plane was responsive and quick.

Flying on a clear day in a good plane made it easy to forget everything else. The speed, the control, the freedom—Warren loved it more than anything. He flew over a cloud and watched his shadow on its fluffy surface, seeming to keep pace with him in a contest of aerial speed. War might be awful, but to fly was to reach up and touch the heavens. Maybe that was why the Royal Flying Corps had chosen as its motto *per ardua ad astra*—through adversity to the stars.

So far Warren had three victories that week, with leave scheduled to begin the next day in Paris with Claire. He wondered if he could get one more victory before furlough. One more story with which to regale Mr. Donovan.

It was about time for him to turn back when he spotted a small speck a few thousand feet below him. It flew over the British trenches, probably photographing them. Warren brought his plane around and opted for an out-of-the-sun attack from above and behind. When he neared the target, he dove, feeling the rush of air howl past him as his altitude decreased. The Hun observer spotted him and swung his machine gun around but started firing before Warren was in range.

It was easier to aim the plane than to aim the Lewis gun, so Warren waited until he could see the frown on the observer's lips and adjusted his DH.2. He squeezed the trigger, and a line of bullets bit into the Aviatik C.1's right wing. The trajectory was perfect, moving toward the fuselage, sure to down the plane, but Warren's gun stopped firing. He released the trigger and squeezed again, but the gun was jammed. Warren cursed and steered away from the German reconnaissance plane, not wanting to get shot while he fiddled with his weapon.

As any sane pilot would do, the German flier turned east and headed for his own lines. Warren followed, trying to fix the Lewis gun and tail the plane from just out of machine gun range, but he was low on fuel. He grabbed the hammer he always flew with and tried to knock the stuck bullet loose. It didn't work. He pried a few bullets from the Lewis gun's drum magazine and tried it again. No luck.

Running out of fuel on the German side of the trenches would put an end to his flying career. He tried to clear the gun once more, but it stayed jammed. The status of his petrol tank finally convinced him to give up the chase. Warren saluted the lucky Aviatik and turned back to his aerodrome. Not long after, he landed and parked his plane off to the side of the landing strip.

"Welcome back, sir," one of the mechanics greeted him.

"Thanks, Jonesy." Warren took his goggles off and remembered that the young mechanic was married and expecting news of his first child any day. "Hear anything about that baby?"

"Nothing yet, sir."

Warren detached the Lewis gun and climbed down from his plane. He was tempted to throw the weapon in the rubbish bin, but a replacement might be equally fickle. He put his fingers on either side of his temples, hoping the counterpressure would ease the pain in his skull. The downside of flying at high altitudes was the headache that came with it. It would probably last the rest of the day. Sighing, he left his DH.2 in Jonesy's capable hands and took the Lewis gun to the hanger. He took it apart, wiped everything spotless, cleaned out the bore, and oiled each piece before reassembling it. Next he hauled it over to the firing range for a test.

"Canada!"

Warren turned to meet Captain Prior.

"Well, how was it?"

"I missed. A nice slow Aviatik, and my gun jammed."

"Rotten luck. Happens to everyone from time to time."

Warren nodded. Bad luck, but at least it hadn't killed him. "Better the Lewis gun than the engine, I suppose."

"When you've had a chance to make your report, that Scottish lieutenant is waiting to see you. Take care. Those intelligence chaps can cause all sorts of mischief. Might send you off to Berlin on some fool's errand."

Warren laughed, glad Prior didn't know about his trip to Essen last winter. The squadron's commanding officer, Major Cook, had approved Warren's work with British intelligence, but no one else knew the details of his journey. Even the mechanic who had seen him off hadn't known Warren's destination. "I met McDougall during my initial year at Oxford. He's clever, but I know when he's manipulating me."

An hour later, Warren strolled along the aerodrome with McDougall. "I haven't seen you this distracted since just after Mons."

McDougall shook his head. His older brother had died at Mons in the British Expeditionary Force's first battle of the war. "As if competing with a taller, smarter brother wasn't bad enough. Now I have to compete with a martyr, and telling my father about any of my accomplishments would be treason."

Warren shoved his hands in his pockets. He had brothers, but none of them close to his age, so he couldn't relate to his friend, could only imagine what it would be like to grow up in the shadow of someone his parents thought was perfect.

"Bah. Enough about Henry. Where are you spending your leave?"

"Paris."

"Staying with the Donovans again?"

"Yes."

"Not visiting your grandmother?"

"She suggested Paris." Warren's and Claire's grandmothers were normally subtle with their matchmaking intentions, but his grandmother's last letter had been slightly more overt.

"Good. The Donovan home is such a convenient location . . ."

"Ah, you wish me to finagle an invitation for you." Warren wondered if Mr. Donovan would mind an extra guest. "Don't you have a room in Paris?"

"I am seeking a room for someone else."

"Who?"

"The enchanting young lass who is helping me track down German saboteurs."

"You want her to stay with the Donovans?"

"The location is perfect. And she is a refugee from a rather unfortunate domestic situation, and her vicious half brother is unlikely to look for her in the home of an American munitions manufacturer."

Warren didn't answer right away. One of McDougall's agents living with the Donovans? With a violent estranged family member searching for her?

"Sounds dangerous. I would hate for Claire to get mixed up in tracking saboteurs."

McDougall dismissed Warren's concern with a flap of his hand. "There would be no risk to Miss Donovan. My agent had a room in Boulogne-Billancourt, but most of her work is in Paris proper, and it's better for people in that line of work to move from time to time."

"So it is dangerous?"

"For my agent, not for Miss Donovan or her father. Come now, Flynn. The Donovan home is large enough to host an extended houseguest. She could help when the housekeeper's arthritis flares."

"How do you know about the housekeeper's arthritis?" Claire had told Warren about the housekeeper's condition, but Warren had never mentioned it to McDougall.

"I'm in intelligence, remember? I did a bit of investigating."

"It's that important, is it?"

"Yes. Nearly single-handedly, this young woman managed to prevent the destruction of the Renault factory."

"She did?" Warren was impressed. So, it seemed, was his friend. "About this enchanting young woman . . . I assume your interest is purely professional?"

McDougall's lips pulled up slightly at the ends. "Mostly."

Warren laughed, glad to see his friend making progress in that department. "I'll think about it. On one condition."

"What's that?"

"I want to meet this spy you have a mostly professional interest in."

# Chapter 16

*September 1916, Paris, France*

EVETTE TOOK A DEEP BREATH before joining Monsieur McDougall at the small table outside a café. Even after three months of training and one month of following whomever he suggested, her most recent assignment had left her on edge. Her assignments always did. And she felt self-conscious sitting in a café patronized by officers and bourgeoisie civilians. One of McDougall's associates had given her a wardrobe that helped her blend in, and today's black brimmed hat and ankle-length dress wouldn't reveal her peasant roots, but other things might. McDougall had assigned her a code name: Agent Sparrow. She found it fitting. Like a sparrow, she was common and tended to blend in. But what would the lieutenant's friend think of her when they were introduced? Ordinary sparrows didn't share cages with canaries or parakeets.

"You look lovely today," McDougall said.

"Thank you, monsieur."

His lips hinted at a smile. Did he find something amusing? "What did you learn of Monsieur Michel?" He kept his voice a whisper.

"He's a heavy drinker. Two of the three nights I watched him, he sat with the same people and paid for their supper. I followed the other men, who were both staying in the Hôtel de Crillon. One of the hotel workers said they're Swiss businessmen who often travel between Bern and Paris."

"And from Bern they could take messages to Berlin if they wished."

"Yes, sir."

"Anything else?"

"He arrives at his office a bit past ten most mornings. Takes a leisurely break four hours later. Usually he eats, but occasionally he visits . . . um . . . a house with ladies of low repute."

McDougall's hand clenched into a fist, as if in triumph. "That is where we shall catch him. When his guard is down with a woman. I'll recruit a few and have them ask all the difficult questions. Any particular woman he favors?"

"I'm not sure, sir." Evette hoped McDougall wouldn't ask her to find out. She preferred to keep her distance from places like that.

"Ah, here's the friend I mentioned."

Evette followed McDougall's gaze to a tall Royal Flying Corps officer with sparkling brown eyes and a kind face.

McDougall stood to shake his friend's hand. "Thanks for coming, Flynn."

"I insisted, remember?"

McDougall ignored the remark. "Lieutenant Flynn, may I introduce Mademoiselle Evette Touny?"

He inclined his head slightly. "Pleased to meet you."

As the two men sat, McDougall turned to Flynn and lowered his voice again. "As I was telling you at the aerodrome, having Mademoiselle Touny stay with the Donovans would be most convenient."

"And if you were followed in the course of your counterintelligence work?" The lieutenant scrutinized her with tense eyes. His French accent was off, but she could understand him when she concentrated.

"First I would try to lose my tail, go to a more crowded area, and try to slip away. If that failed, I would try to bore them. Stand in lines, slowly eat a multi-course meal."

The lieutenant leaned forward. "But what if the person following you is so good that you don't notice him?"

McDougall cleared his throat. "That is rather unlikely to happen."

Lieutenant Flynn turned to his friend. "But not impossible."

"Perhaps you could stop fretting over the worst that could happen and help do what ought to be done." McDougall's voice was terse. "We are discussing matters of serious national consequence."

"Matters which could affect Claire's safety."

Evette glanced at Lieutenant Flynn's face, finally understanding his hesitation. It was in his eyes, in the way he said her name. Whoever this Claire was, the lieutenant was deeply fond of her. "I don't want to be any trouble, and I certainly don't want to put anyone in danger."

"You won't be any trouble," McDougall said. "You are among my most competent agents in Paris. I have complete confidence in your ability to elude pursuit in the highly unlikely event that you are detected."

"And if not?" Flynn asked.

"If not, the Donovans have a telephone with which to call the police." McDougall tapped his fingers on the table. "Flynn, I am not asking you to force anything on the Donovans, but Miss Donovan is, after all, partially English. She may want to help."

"Yes, but that doesn't mean she should." Flynn sat back in his seat and crossed his arms.

McDougall glanced around to ensure no one was nearby and lowered his voice even further. "This is important. The Germans have organized a system, a league for gathering information and sabotaging French factories. There is work to be done, vital work. We won't win the war if we can't stop this group."

Lieutenant Flynn nodded. "I'll think about it."

Evette watched the airman, understanding his reluctance but hoping it wouldn't prevent him from making a decision soon.

# Chapter 17

WARREN RAN HIS FINGERS ALONG a row of books in the Donovan library, inhaling the scent of ink, paper, and dust. He randomly picked one and pulled it from the shelf. *Romeo and Juliet.* He turned the book so Claire could see the title. "You know, I never got around to reading this."

"You may borrow it if you like. It's one of my favorites."

Warren put the book away. "Romance isn't really my thing."

Claire laughed. "I've noticed. But maybe Shakespeare could change your mind."

"I've heard about it. Two young fools falling in love and acting rashly, both of them ending up dead. Doesn't sound very happy to me."

"It's not happy, but it's beautiful."

"Oh, how?"

Claire walked over to the piano and sorted through her music, but she didn't start playing. "To love someone like that, so suddenly and so completely that you can't live without them." She sighed. "It's powerful."

"Love at first sight is ridiculous."

Claire kept her face toward the piano and flicked her hair over her shoulder. "I disagree. I think it's romantic."

"Come now, Miss Donovan. Love is about more than getting swept off your feet. What about friendship and trust, common interests? Respect?"

"Why can't sweeping a girl off her feet go with friendship and respect? They aren't mutually exclusive."

"Friendship isn't developed in an instant. So falling in love at first sight rules out a relationship between friends."

"I think Romeo and Juliet had everything."

"No, they had infatuation, nothing more. Besides, look where it got them. Romantic love like that is the stuff of fairy tales. It doesn't exist in real life. And if it does, it's not healthy."

Claire scoffed. "It does exist, and it is the loveliest thing in the entire world. What could be better?"

Warren shook his head. "It doesn't work in the real world. Take the Tsar."

"What about the Tsar?" Claire turned around to face him.

"He's rumored to have an exceptionally happy marriage."

"Good for him."

"And he's losing his empire."

"Those two facts aren't connected." Claire frowned, scolding him.

Warren hated it when she did that. He hadn't meant to start an argument with her, especially not the first afternoon of his leave, but she needed to hear reason. If she had her head in the clouds, expecting something that didn't exist, she'd never be happy with a mere mortal and certainly wouldn't be happy with him. "There's a connection, all right. Nicholas has been so absorbed in his family that he's neglected his empire, and now he's paying the price."

"A better man could do both." Claire turned her back to him again.

"If you find such a man, please introduce me because I don't believe he exists."

Claire started playing Beethoven. He wondered if she'd picked a German composer on purpose. Warren walked back to the bookshelf, thinking perhaps he should have gone to London instead. What was it about his relationship with Claire? It could be completely smooth one minute, and then the next he was saying all the wrong things. He'd often thought of courting her more seriously, but every time he was ready to pursue a permanent relationship, something like this happened. He glanced at the titles on the shelves, but he didn't read them.

Partway through her sonata, Claire pushed the piano bench back and screamed.

Warren was behind her in two strides. "What is it?"

Claire stepped away from the piano, backing into Warren with a shaky finger pointed at the floor. "That's got to be the largest spider I've seen in all my born days."

Warren followed her finger and bent down to inspect the creature. It was larger than average but hardly worth fussing over. Since it was on an expensive-looking rug, he caught the spider in his handkerchief, went over to the window, and threw it outside. When he turned back, Claire was still pale. He'd been teasing her about her fear of spiders for almost two years but decided not to say anything today. Maybe holding his tongue would make up for their earlier disagreement. And maybe Claire would see something romantic in a man who could defeat a horrible spider since she didn't seem impressed by anything else about him.

* * *

That night it was easy to avoid discussion of romance. Mr. Donovan wanted to hear the latest news from the front, and Claire didn't complain as Warren answered each question about his squadron's activities. Even the butler lingered as if he too shared Mr. Donovan's interest in the war. The only person who didn't seem riveted was the person Warren most wanted to impress: Claire.

The next day, Mr. Donovan spent the morning in his office, then left for business that afternoon.

"Shall we stroll through the garden?" Claire asked.

Warren followed her outside. The air had a chill to it, so he wrapped his silk scarf around his neck.

"I've seen other pilots with scarves like that. Why do you all wear them?"

"Turn your head."

Her lips tightened in displeasure, but she obeyed, glancing to the left.

"No, really, turn you head like you're searching for a Hun scout plane."

Her next attempt was better. She wiggled her head up and down and whipped it from left to right.

Warren took the scarf from his neck and held it out to her. "Now undo your top button."

Claire stepped back abruptly, and her eyes squinted in disbelief. "Mr. Flynn, I don't know what you're suggesting, but—"

"Never mind. Just tuck this in under your collar. It would be easier if you unfastened your top button, but do it your way." He handed her the scarf, and she reluctantly took it, then turned her back to him while she placed it around her neck. "Now look around again."

She craned her neck from side to side, then turned back to him with a smile. "You know, it does go smoother with a scarf."

"And that's why all the pilots wear them. It also comes in handy if the engine spits oil on your goggles."

Claire pulled on the ends of the scarf, checking for oil stains. "And all this time I thought it was meant to make you more dashing."

"Does it make me more dashing?"

Claire's lips curved upward. "More dashing than what?"

"More dashing than your other suitors?"

"I don't have any suitors, silly. Unless you count as one."

Warren didn't know what to say to that. He liked Claire, except when she wallowed in her quests for unrealistic romance. And there was a war on. Almost weekly someone from his squadron didn't return to the aerodrome; some weeks the deaths were more frequent. It wasn't the best time to pursue a long-term relationship. "You can refer to me however you wish."

"Hmm." Claire strolled under an ivy arch and continued down the flagstone path. She fingered an overgrown rosebush as Warren caught up to her. "Maybe I ought to take up gardening. Our gardener was called up a month ago, and the grounds are showing signs of neglect."

"My grandmother's gardener was called up too. And her maid went to work in a factory. I wonder who she'll lose next. And who you'll lose. The cook? The housekeeper? The butler?"

Claire frowned. "We seem to go through a new cook every few months anyway. I think my father likes the variety. We lost a footman. A maid too, but we found another. No one else would hire our arthritic housekeeper, so she's stuck with us. And I'm not too worried about Franke. He's long past military age, and even if he weren't, he's German. Been in France for forty years, but my father still had to jump through all sorts of hoops to keep him in Paris."

"I wouldn't have guessed. He seems French."

"He is in all aspects other than birthplace. But that didn't stop the authorities from threatening to expel him. Everyone went crazy when the war started. Can you imagine it—our butler a security risk? He loves Paris."

"And you? Do you love Paris, or do you miss Charleston?"

They walked in silence for a few paces as Claire thought. "I like Paris, but it's been so dreadfully dreary lately. Massive battles and massive casualties. London was just as drab when I visited my grandmother last month. The only difference is they talk of the Somme instead of Verdun."

"Perhaps they should talk of something else?"

"They do. They complain of the poor food and the shortage of proper dress material." She turned toward him, her lips pulled downward. "You must think me horribly selfish to complain. Compared to the soldiers', my life is luxurious. I just didn't expect to be so lonely here." She fingered the wilted petals of a flower. "Papa is willing to put aside whatever he's working on if I want to talk to him, but he's gone so often. I think I've seen him more since you arrived than I did the entire month of August."

"That busy?" The demand for munitions was enormous, and there were more jobs than men to go around, but Warren was surprised someone as rich as Mr. Donovan couldn't hire more assistance.

"Yes. And I hate to say it, but his business has not only been busy but also quite profitable."

Warren wove a lose sprig of ivy back into its place on the wrought-iron fence. He thought of Miss Touny. She seemed pleasant, competent. He assumed McDougall's confidence in her abilities was justified. He was hesitant to suggest that the French girl stay with the Donovans just to make McDougall's projects easier, but maybe her presence would fill a genuine need for Claire too. "I have an idea that might help with the loneliness."

"I hope your idea has something to do with more frequent furloughs."

"No. But one of my old classmates was wondering if you might take in a houseguest."

"Who?"

"A French girl. She's willing to step in when your housekeeper can't work. I imagine she could help in the garden too, if needed, or talk to you when your father is busy."

"Where is she from?"

"Some village in Picardy."

Claire's head tilted to the side in surprise. "You want me to take in a French peasant as an extended houseguest?"

"It will give you someone your own age to talk to, someone to go on strolls with when I'm not here to take you myself, someone to practice your French with."

"Does she speak French or just patois?"

"Her French is better than mine." Evette Touny seemed reserved and quiet, but Warren had managed to get a few sentences out of her.

"That's not saying much."

"My French might not be as good as yours, but I didn't have tutors from the time I was five."

Claire smiled. "Yes, I sometimes disremember your origins. Not so different from that French girl, I suppose."

"Having her here will add some excitement to your life. And there's something else. She has a violent relative she needs to hide from. You'd be helping a woman in need."

She sighed. "My father always manages to come home for supper when you'll be dining with us, so I suppose, *for you*, I might could discuss it with him tonight."

She glanced up at him, her blue eyes teasing him from the ivy's shadows. She was beautiful. He was tempted to grab his scarf, still lying around her neck, and pull her close enough for a kiss, but he wasn't sure what that would do to their temporary truce.

# Chapter 18

LISTENING TO CLAIRE CONVINCE HER father to invite in a French houseguest was almost comical. She used all the same arguments Warren had—that they needed occasional help, that it would be nice to have someone her own age to talk with, that it would give her the opportunity to improve her French.

"It doesn't differ to me. Go ahead if you think it best," Mr. Donovan said.

"Thank you, Papa." When her father turned to the butler, Claire gave Warren a slight nod as if to emphasize the fact that she was making the request only as a favor to him. As Warren savored the roast beef prepared by the Donovans' current cook, he hoped the arrangement would benefit Claire as much as it benefited Miss Touny.

After their meal, the three of them went to the library. Claire played a few songs—classical, not ragtime—then finished the muffler she was knitting for the Red Cross and excused herself. Warren had to peel his eyes from the doorway she'd walked through when Mr. Donovan spoke.

"So, Lieutenant, what do you think the chances of victory are in, say, the next six months?"

Should Warren do what everyone else did and be optimistic? Or be honest? He decided on honesty. "Slim."

"Hmm. I hope that doesn't mean you think the Germans have a shot of winning."

"Not in the next six months. Their planes are better than ours, but they won't drive us from the sky. And I hate to admit it, but I don't think the air war will be decisive."

"What do you think will be decisive?"

Warren frowned. "Nothing."

"Nothing?"

"I don't think the war will be won with a decisive battlefield victory or with some new weapon. You've followed the news from Verdun?"

Mr. Donovan nodded.

"And the Somme?"

"Yes."

There was talk that a breakthrough was imminent, but Warren wasn't convinced. He had heard hushed rumors of sixty thousand British casualties from the initial day of the Somme alone. Nothing less than a dramatic turn in the war could have made such a sacrifice worthwhile, but so far nothing more than a slight shift in the front lines had been achieved. He didn't want to think about how many men had died for each yard of ground. "I fear this is turning into a war of attrition. The side that can endure the longest will be the side that wins."

"And will that be our side?" There was a slight hesitation before Mr. Donovan said *our*, as if he wasn't sure he could include himself in the coalition fighting the Central Powers. He turned to Mr. Franke as the butler came into the library to bring him his pipe.

"I don't know." Warren shifted in his seat. "American support would help us outlast the Hun."

Mr. Donovan struck a match and lit his pipe. "I will continue to provide shells, but I don't think the United States is ready to provide blood. Not yet."

*Not yet.* Warren chose to find hope in that phrase. Maybe at some point, preferably before the British Army was whittled down to nothing, help would come from America.

As the conversation died, Mr. Donovan picked up an American magazine. Warren browsed through a newspaper. Most of the articles were about Verdun and the Somme, but there was also a piece about the fighting in Romania and something about spy networks in Paris. "What the devil . . . ?"

"Hmm?"

"This article on the Lothair League. I've never heard of it before."

Mr. Donovan puffed briefly on his pipe. "Quite a write-up. Even if none of it's true, it makes a good story."

According to the paper, the Lothair League included a large network of spies and saboteurs, most of them from Alsace and Lorraine so they could blend in with the French population. Warren had witnessed plenty of spy scares before the war began, but this seemed more realistic. Specific acts of sabotage were credited to the League, questionable occurrences attributed to their spies. Frankly he was surprised the article had made it through the censors. "I wonder . . ."

"You wonder what?"

Warren wished he had kept his mouth shut, but he wanted to impress Claire's father, and Mr. Franke had left the room already. "I have an old schoolmate in British intelligence. He's trying to track some organization of spies and saboteurs. I wonder if it's connected to this League."

Mr. Donovan leaned forward. "Your friend. Has he had any luck?"

Giving out the scant details he'd heard about McDougall's projects would be frowned upon, so Warren downplayed his knowledge. "I hope so, but I don't really know." That was true enough. They weren't officially working together. McDougall only came to Warren when he needed help, and even then he gave him few specifics. All the same, Warren's curiosity was piqued.

* * *

The morning of Warren's departure, Mr. Donovan stayed home for a late breakfast. "Do come again. And keep me posted on the news from the front." The two men shook hands, and then Mr. Donovan left for business, leaving Claire and Warren with the household staff as chaperones.

Warren still had a few hours before he needed to head back. "Would you care to join me in the library?"

Claire followed him, and when he explained what he was searching for, she quickly offered her help.

"Lothair was Charlemagne's grandson," Claire said, still perusing an encyclopedia. "Had stormy relationships with his family—deposed his father once, got into a civil war with his brothers. He had a son by the same name. Lothair II's territory included Alsace and Lorraine."

"And did Lothair II turn his kingdom to the east or to the west?"

Claire skimmed more of the article. "Both, depending on which was most convenient. But overall toward areas that now make up Germany."

"So the Lothair League, like Lothair, wishes to turn Lorraine and the surrounding areas—roughly the Western Front—back to Germany."

"That's terrifying."

"If they're having any success, yes." Warren glanced at the clock. "I best be on my way. Thank you for your help."

"My pleasure."

When Warren brought his bag down to the entryway, Claire was waiting. "Do you still have my scarf?" he asked.

"Yes."

He expected her to go retrieve it, but she didn't move. "May I have it back?"

"I prefer to keep it."

"So I can have a sore neck and get shot down by the Hun?"

"No. I expect you can get another. But the newspapers are calling pilots the new knights of the air. Medieval knights often carried a handkerchief from a lady for good luck."

"So you want to reverse it and keep my scarf for good luck?"

Claire nodded.

"You do realize that tying my scarf back to medieval knights won't change who I am. I'll never be a romantic hero like the ones in your books."

She looked down. "I know . . . but I wanted something tangible to remember you by. If you want your scarf back, I'll fetch it."

Warren put a finger under her chin and tilted her head up. "If you want it, keep it. But remember it belongs to an ordinary man."

"The oil stains will remind me of that."

Warren chuckled. "Good. Maybe next time I visit I'll bring you something better."

"But, Mr. Flynn, that would be highly romantic, and you've made it quite clear that you're not romantic."

"That would be good manners. And my mother and grandmother taught me a few of those."

That brought a curve to her lips. "Do you remember the first time we met?"

"Of course. My grandmother dragged me along to your grandmother's house for tea. You were sixteen and just in from Charleston for a month-long visit. And you ended up being more amusing than I expected."

"Amusing. Is that the first thing you thought about me?"

"No. The first thing I thought was that your nose looked exactly like your grandmother's only significantly younger and with more freckles. And your hair was shiny when you stood in front of the window."

Claire groaned. "My freckles? Couldn't you at least say my nose was like porcelain and my hair was luminous in the sunlight?"

"I don't normally think in such poetic terms."

She crossed her arms. "I've noticed. Does it take effort to be so completely unsentimental, or do you do it naturally?"

"It's natural, I assure you." He didn't add that a few years later he'd decided she was the most beautiful girl he'd ever seen. Warren brought his peaked khaki hat up to place it on his head, and at the same time, Claire moved her hand, probably to pat his arm good-bye. Their hands collided, and Warren's hat fell to the floor.

"I'm sorry." Claire bent to retrieve it, but she paused before giving it to him, weighing it in her hand. She flipped it over and found the teacup handle he'd put inside the band. "What are you doing with a piece of broken china in your hat?"

"Don't you recognize it?"

She glanced at it, then at him. "It's not my grandmother's, is it?"

"You gave it to me."

She laughed. "Goodness, you kept it?" She turned it over in her hand. "Why on earth do you still have it—inside your hat, of all places?"

"I thought it might bring me luck. And it reminds me of good things. The time before the war started. And you."

Claire gazed up in astonishment. "You keep a piece of trash to remember me by? And I thought I was the sentimental one."

The conversation had turned awkward, but Warren nodded as he reached for the broken handle and his hat. Claire gave him his hat but kept the china.

"You can't keep it in your hat. What if you crash and shards of porcelain get mashed into your head?"

"I don't wear that hat when I fly, so I move it to my pocket."

"So the shards can end up in your hip instead?"

"I've crashed with it before and had no unpleasant side effects—none from that anyhow."

Claire shook her head and put the broken-off handle in her pocket. "I'll give you something else." She held up her wrist to display a delicate golden bracelet with a flower charm dangling from it.

"I can't take your bracelet. Give me back the teacup handle."

"You're letting me keep your scarf."

"My scarf with oil stains. Your bracelet looks new and is no doubt considerably more valuable than a piece of silk."

Claire ripped the bracelet from her wrist. "It's broken now. I can't use it. You may as well keep it."

"Claire!" He examined the newly broken clasp as she handed it to him. "You just ruined a perfectly good bracelet."

"It's not a bracelet anymore; it's a good-luck charm. One that's slightly romantic, if I do say so myself."

Warren shook his head. Claire was a handful. He wasn't sure if he had the right to, but he leaned in and kissed her on the cheek anyway. "Thank you, Claire. Take care of yourself."

She seemed surprised by his stolen kiss, wide-eyed and tongue-tied for a few long moments before the blood rushed to her cheeks and a smile crept across her lips. "You too, Warren. Be careful."

# Chapter 19

*December 1916, Essen, Germany*

Too much rain in August had ruined the majority of Germany's potato crop, so even though there were few smells more repugnant than rotting potatoes, Julian carefully saved what he could from each nauseating lump. Dorothea had bartered a set of bedroom furniture for a hundred kilograms of potatoes, but it wouldn't be enough to last until next year's harvest. The food situation was looking especially bleak after yesterday's discovery that most of the preserved fruits and vegetables from the garden had spoiled. Julian supposed it was a combination of Dorothea's inexperience and Mathilde's age, but somehow the jars hadn't been sealed properly. They couldn't waste any of the remaining food, not even questionable potatoes. Over the next hour, he managed to salvage two thirds of the small pile, just enough for the midday meal. He didn't peel them—good Germans didn't do that anymore for fear of wasting food—but he chopped the large pieces and put them all in a pot. Dorothea and her father wouldn't eat the peels, but Julian and the boys didn't mind them.

He stretched his neck in the chilly kitchen and held back a yawn. He'd spent a late evening listening to three slightly intoxicated factory workers complain about the long shifts and their fears that the new gas shells they helped produce would leave them permanently disabled. He'd compounded his exhaustion with a nocturnal visit to Herr Sauer's study. According to Herr Sauer's diary, Lohr was running four different intelligence rings in France. None of the spies were named, but Julian included the clues he'd gleaned in his report, along with mention of decreased civilian morale at what was being called the Turnip Winter.

Julian moved the pot to the stove and added pieces of a duck Willi had brought home the day before. Willi had probably poached it, but Julian hadn't asked. Duck was one of the few meals Gerta didn't complain about. Julian went into the dining room and found the little girl sitting in a dark corner, her legs pulled to her chest and her arms wrapped around her knees. "Gerta, what's wrong?"

She shrugged.

"I hope the floor is clean. Your mother might be unhappy if you get your dress dirty. She waited in line half a day for soap and can't get any more until next month."

"This dress is too short anyway." Gerta stood to show him.

"Yes, you're getting taller. But there might not be material to replace the entire dress. If I know your mother, she'll add a ruffle to the bottom. Perhaps one that will look like a flower if you twirl."

Gerta spent many an afternoon spinning in the sunlight, watching the way her skirt flowed around her, but Julian's suggestion didn't even bring a smile, so he tried a new tactic. "What if we were to decorate for Christmas a little early this year?" Christmas was still a few weeks away, but the snow outside provided the right atmosphere.

Gerta shook her head.

"Hey now, why so sad? It's the best time of the year. Maybe Mathilde will make a special treat."

"Mathilde doesn't cook anymore. You and Mama do. And soon Willi will go away and you too." Gerta burst into tears, and Julian couldn't think of anything to say that would comfort her. Willi would leave in the coming month with all the other boys who comprised the conscription class of 1918. The call-up was a year and a half earlier than expected. As for Julian, a new law meant to ensure enough labor for Germany's vital industries threatened to end his time with the Kallweit family. The scars on his forehead and side wouldn't be enough to ensure his continued exemption from the war effort. "Why does everyone have to go away?" Gerta sobbed. "I hardly remember Papa or Kurt."

Julian knelt next to Gerta and gave her a hug. He wondered which lot was harder—Gerta's, because she didn't remember her family members who were gone, or his, because he still thought of his parents and his dead brother daily. He didn't cry over them, but he missed them. Bittersweet memories of their times together permeated his thoughts and came to mind with most of his actions. But Gerta didn't even have memories to hold on to. "Come, Gerta. Let's go read that last letter your father sent."

* * *

Whenever he had an evening off, Julian went out. He would have rather stayed at the Sauer estate and caught up on his sleep, but spending time with the workers relaxing after their shift at the Krupp factory often proved worthwhile. Sometimes he wondered if he was crazy, socializing with people who would rip him apart if they knew his true origin. Ironically, he expected more mercy from front-line German soldiers. In parts of the front, it was wiser to live and let live, easier to feel sympathy for the men across no-man's land stuck in the same awful conditions than to feel a connection with the officers handing out orders or the civilians living in relative comfort back home.

This evening's stop, however, was not about gleaning information from factory workers. Julian walked around a city block, then doubled back to make sure no one had followed him. He crept into a building that stood amid a row of apartments and checked the third door from the main entrance. As expected, it was unlocked. Julian glanced over his shoulder to make sure no one was nearby, then went inside.

A broad, sixty-year-old Dutchman waited in the front room, his hand in his pocket, where Julian suspected he hid a pistol. Julian nodded his recognition and went into the back room, where Lieutenant McDougall waited.

"Glad you made it," Julian said. McDougall spoke extremely poor German. He depended on the Dutchman to see him safely in and out of Germany and a British sailor to see him in and out of Holland.

McDougall gestured to several discarded strips of cloth. "I wore a bandage around my head with a spot of blood on it and put my arm in a sling. No one expected me to converse with them."

Julian filed the technique away in case he needed it later.

"I have a list of letter boxes for you. A bookstore in Düsseldorf, a grocer in Bonn, a butcher in Recklinghausen. Only use them three times each. By then I will have others for you."

Julian took the addresses. He would mail his reports there, and the new contacts would see that they were sent on either through Holland or through Switzerland. "I'm a little nervous about the auxiliary service law that just passed."

"The what?"

"The Hindenburg program. All German males are now required to serve in a vital industry. Either the armed forces, government work, war industries, or agriculture. My name isn't listed on any national register, but locally they know who I am."

"See if Herr Sauer will help you apply at the Krupp works. I would very much enjoy inside information about their production. Offer to do small jobs for him in your free time so you can continue to live at his manor."

"Yes, sir." Julian hesitated before bringing up his next concern. "I worry that anyone healthy enough to work in the factory and do odd jobs at the

Sauer estate will be considered healthy enough to go back to war. I don't want to serve in the German Army."

"If it comes to that, you have my permission to leave. Frau Von Hayek can help you to her brother in Holland, and we can extract you from there."

"Thank you, sir."

"Is the ink still working?" McDougall pulled out a vial of liquid.

"Fine on my end. You're able to read my reports?"

"Yes. Well done thus far. We've found several of Lohr's men with your information. That vial is more ink, should you need it."

"Thank you." Julian slipped the ink into his pocket.

"Anything else before I leave?"

"I have another report, sir. And a real letter for my parents. Would you mail it for me?"

McDougall took the report eagerly and the letter with less enthusiasm. "A letter in French does not fit with my masquerade as a wounded German officer."

"I realize that, sir. So I wrote it in German. My mother is fluent, and I used a limited vocabulary so my father can read it too."

McDougall sighed and took the letter. "I suppose I sometimes forget that most people have a relationship with their parents worth preserving. A personal letter increases the risk to both of us. I will mail one for you this time but not the next."

Julian wondered if there would be a next time. He had been in Germany slightly over a year, and this was McDougall's second visit. Julian had only a modest hope that he would survive until the next meeting at least six months in the future. But in the meantime, he had other things to worry about, like how he was going to manage work at the factory, work at the Sauer estate, and biweekly midnight escapades into Herr Sauer's study, all on limited rations. It sounded exhausting.

# Chapter 20

*December 1916, Paris, France*

WHEN SHE HAD FIRST COME to stay with the Donovans, Evette had expected to dwell quietly alongside the family, assisting them when needed but otherwise keeping out of sight and out of mind. Claire had different expectations. She had pulled Evette into knitting projects, piano lessons, and shopping expeditions. Evette looked forward to their evenings in, knitting together by a warm stove or gathered around the piano in the library. Shopping, in contrast, was a shock. Despite the war and the dizzying inflation, restaurants, booksellers, and jewelers all seemed to be doing well, and other businesses were managing to muddle through. It felt strange shopping with Claire while Evette's brother was manning a frozen trench somewhere east of Paris.

Perhaps even more strange than the shopping were their tickets to the opera. The Paris Opera House had opened in November after two years of closure. Mr. Donovan was preoccupied with a work emergency and unable to use his ticket, so Claire was taking Evette instead and arranging her hair for the occasion. Between training and observation, Evette had learned how to blend in with the upper class, but she was still a little nervous.

Claire's look of concentration reflected back at Evette from the mirror. "Your hair is so different from mine." A lock of Evette's straight hair slipped from Claire's fingers, and Claire sighed with frustration.

"I don't mind doing it myself."

"I know, but it sounded fun to do it for you." Claire gave up on whatever she had been trying to do with Evette's hair and began a braid instead. "My best friend in Charleston had a younger sister, and she always did her hair, even though they had a nanny who could do it. I was jealous. It would have been fun to have a sister. I had to be content doing the doll's hair."

Evette laughed softly. "I'm sure yours was the best-dressed doll in all of Charleston."

"Maybe it was. You have sisters, don't you?"

"Two. And when I was young, they would arrange my hair for me."

"Ah. That's why you are so patient. You've had practice."

Someone knocked on Claire's door.

"Come in," Claire said.

Mr. Franke appeared on the other side of the door. "A note for Mademoiselle Touny."

Claire took it from the butler and handed it to Evette. Monsieur McDougall had told Evette he would send word when he had another assignment for her, and Evette recognized his handwriting. She opened the note, praying it wouldn't interfere with the opera. She didn't want to disappoint Claire by cancelling. The note read, *Tomorrow, eight am*, so Evette still had the night free.

"What is it?" Claire asked.

Evette glanced at Claire, but she didn't think her friend had read it over her shoulder. "A message from Monsieur McDougall."

"Do you suppose he's trying to court you?"

Evette stopped herself from shaking her head and ruining all of Claire's handiwork. It was better for Claire to assume Evette's connection with McDougall was about romance rather than espionage. But she didn't want to lie. "I'm far beneath his social class."

"Maybe he doesn't care. Do you want him to court you?"

"I'm not sure." Before moving in with the Donovans, Evette never would have considered the possibility of someone as educated as Monsieur McDougall courting her. Even after working at the factory, she was far too poor, far too simple.

"Well, either he's your ideal man or he isn't."

Evette met Claire's eyes in the mirror and couldn't hide her confusion.

Claire pinned back part of Evette's hair. "Surely you've considered what you want in a husband. If Monsieur McDougall meets the requirements, we will have to convince him that class differences aren't important."

"I just want someone who won't hit me."

Evette's hair slipped from Claire's fingers and began to unravel. Claire squeezed Evette's shoulder. "I'm sorry. I forgot. Papa's never raised a hand against me, so I can't imagine what you went through."

Evette reached up to take Claire's hand for a moment. "It's in the past now."

Claire nodded and started over on Evette's hair. "No man should hit a woman. Ever. But, Evette, you can't settle for any old chap who doesn't hit you. That's the majority of men, including many of the ugly ones. You deserve more than that. What about real love? Don't you have any dreams?"

"Dreams?" Evette felt Claire twist a lock of hair up on top of her head. "I suppose so. Being safe and not starving."

Claire shook her head. "No, not dreams like that. I want to fall madly in love with someone who's handsome and brave and will love me to distraction. Surely you have some aspiration beyond a man who will feed you but won't hurt you."

"If I keep my expectations simple, they are more likely to be met."

Claire laughed softly. "Evette, you're almost as unromantic as Warren. What do you have against love?" Claire was starting to sound like Evette's sister Rosemonde. Evette enjoyed their time together—sometimes it felt like they were almost sisters—but she didn't want Claire to repeat her sister's mistakes.

"*Love* is an excuse people use to justify a lack of self-discipline. It leads to unwanted babies and ruined reputations and lives of poverty and misery and dishonor." Five years ago, Evette had been sent to find Rosemonde. She had heard her sister's laughter, seen her discarded clothing, been shocked by a glimpse of the naked young man lying beside Rosemonde.

Claire fingers paused. "Does it?"

"It did for my sister. She said she was in love, but the young man disappeared. No one wanted a bastard baby, so my parents convinced her to marry a man twenty years her senior. He was awful." Evette had loved her sister even after Rosemonde had gotten herself into trouble. Evette had wanted to help, but she couldn't change her brother-in-law's cruel tongue, nor could she ease her sister's difficult labor. "They weren't married long. My sister died in childbirth. So did the baby." Evette stared at her hands. "The rumors lasted longer. I had few marriage prospects even before the war snatched away all the young men in the village. I can't afford to be choosy."

Claire pinned back more of Evette's hair, seeming deep in thought. "What you speak of is lust. It is different from love, but people often call it the wrong name. Real love obeys boundaries and stretches hearts, makes you feel like you can fly but always keeps the other person's happiness at the center of your thoughts and deeds. Real love doesn't take what it wants and leave the other person with the consequences. Real love is patient. Real love is kind."

Evette stared at her friend. What Claire had spoken was beautiful, as if she was describing a dream. Evette wanted to believe there was an alternative to the love Rosemonde had spoken of, something better than temporary bliss that melted into misery. "Have you found real love, Claire?"

Claire sighed. "No. I'm still waiting for someone who will sweep me off my feet and make every moment together magical."

"Oh. I thought perhaps Lieutenant Flynn . . . When you spoke of feeling as though you could fly . . . You didn't mean him?"

"Warren flies airplanes, not hearts." Claire frowned, then her face softened again. "Sometimes I wish I was in love with him. He's a good man. My grandmother loves him, and my father seems to approve. He is patient and considerate, and he treats me as an equal. He looks dashing in his uniform, and I love his eyes. But he's so unromantic. He must put effort into it—almost as if he's trying not to impress me. It would take so little on his part. A bouquet of flowers, a poem—he wouldn't even have to write the poem himself; he could just recite it to me. Instead, he carries garbage to remember me by."

"Garbage?"

"Right before he shipped off to war, he dropped one of my grandmother's teacups. He kept the broken handle as a memento."

"He keeps a token to remind him of you? Is that not romantic?"

Claire slipped hairpins into Evette's tresses. "I made him return it and gave him something else. Broken pieces of porcelain are not in the slightest bit romantic."

"Oh." If that was the case, Evette obviously knew nothing about romance.

"And then there are his letters. He always begins them with *Dear Miss Donovan* and ends them with *sincerely.* He could at least say he misses me or call me *Darling Claire* or sign off *yours.* When he comes to visit, I'm convinced he's fond of me, but every time I read one of his letters, it's as if he's talking to an old schoolmate, not someone he might be in love with."

"Perhaps he hesitates to share his feelings during war. Pilots have dangerous jobs."

Claire huffed. "A dangerous job is a good reason to say what you feel while you have the chance. If something did happen to him, I'd be forever uncertain about his feelings for me." Claire stepped back to examine Evette's hair from a distance. She'd somehow made Evette's hair look twice as thick as it was, with a loose, twisted arrangement. "I'm sorry. I'm talking far too much about myself. What about you? Have you ever met someone who made your heart skip a beat?"

"My heartbeat is quite normal."

Claire sat in a chair and leaned forward. "What about a handsome face that made you want to keep staring or a voice that made you want to listen for hours?"

Evette bit her lips, thinking. "Once."

"Well?"

Evette shook her head. "He was a soldier. Only a little taller than me, with hair the color of cinnamon and eyes the color of coffee. I don't even know his name, but he was kind. He helped me move my mother, and then he gave me money for my ticket to Paris. That was over a year ago. But him, or someone like him . . ."

"Then I suppose we shall wait and see what Lieutenant McDougall's intentions are. Or if your mystery soldier shows up again."

Evette smiled but mentally discarded Claire's final words. McDougall's note was about their work, and the kind poilu might be dead.

* * *

The next week Evette helped track down another of Lohr's spies. After his arrest, the arrogant traitor claimed there were dozens just like him, each with their own ring of sources feeding information to the League. McDougall's other agents caught two of the man's contacts, then they ran into dead ends.

Evette had a few days with no assignments. Then, one afternoon, Franke told her Monsieur McDougall awaited her in the parlor. She excused herself from the library and went to meet him.

He stood as she entered the room. They spent a few minutes on pleasantries before he gave her a new assignment. "Tomorrow morning I would like your assistance tracking a saboteur. We believe he has plans to damage shipping along the river." He handed her a slip of paper with an address. "Meet Agent Moreau there at seven tomorrow morning, and he'll point out the subject. Fournier will work with you to track him. I hope he will lead us to more members of the League. At the very least, I would like you to find his supply of explosives."

"Is he connected with the man we caught last week?"

"No. Not directly."

Evette nodded. "How did you learn of his plans?"

McDougall paused before answering. "I am obliged to keep all sources confidential."

Evette didn't reply. Knowing more about where the tip came from might aid her in her task, but she didn't think anything she said would change his mind. Perhaps Agent Moreau or Agent Fournier would have more information. She walked McDougall to the door, then went back to her room. She'd been inside only a minute when Claire knocked on the door.

"Come in," Evette called.

Claire's face was serious as she came in and shut the door behind her, leaning against it as if hesitant to come farther into the room.

"Is something wrong, Claire?"

"I, um . . ." Claire looked at the floor. "I'm sorry, Evette. I love the idea of a mystery soldier, but marrying up the social ladder would also be extremely romantic. I wanted to judge for myself how serious McDougall's intentions are toward you. And I overheard your conversation."

Evette swallowed and felt her palms grow clammy with panic. What would happen now? The Donovans weren't supposed to know about her work.

Claire looked up again. "Why does he want you to follow saboteurs, and what does he mean by the League? Not the Lothair League?"

"You've heard of the Lothair League?"

"Yes. Warren was trying to find out more about them."

"Then you know they have to be stopped before they win the war for the Germans. It's my job to help find them. McDougall isn't courting me. He's employing me."

Claire's eyes widened.

Evette turned to the wardrobe, wondering how quickly she could pack and where she could go. "I suppose you'll want me to leave now." No one wanted a spy for a houseguest.

"No! Stay!"

Evette turned around.

Claire grinned. "You can't leave now. Do you have any idea how exciting it is to have a houseguest with a secret occupation?"

# Chapter 21

*February 1917, Essen, Germany*

JULIAN TURNED OFF THE STREET and walked to the Sauer home at the same time as Franz, who was coming from the other direction. Franz grinned when he saw him. "Is the strike over, Herr Becker?"

"Not yet. Maybe tomorrow." Julian hadn't been involved in the recent rash of labor unrest stemming mostly from a flour shortage, but he wasn't sorry for the time off. "What have you been up to?"

"Collecting scraps." Franz turned to wave good-bye to a group of boys and girls his own age who were accompanied by a priest.

"Ah." Scrap drives were becoming more and more common. Julian hoped it was a sign that Germany's resources, and their ability to wage war, were wearing thin. "Any luck?"

"A bit. No one wants to part with their copper kettles though."

"I should think not."

"Yes, but the copper is valuable. It's hard to get from anywhere else." Franz opened the front door, and Julian followed him inside. "I'm supposed to ask Mama and Mathilde if they're willing to part with any."

"Hmm. It's dangerous business to ask a woman to give up her pots, especially when she's already had to give up butter, cream, sugar, and most flour."

"And meat. Yesterday I had a dream about pork roast and dumplings."

Julian laughed. "And woke up with a pillow wet from drool?"

Franz balked. "Of course not." Then he lowered his voice. "Maybe a little. I'm hungry all the time now."

Julian put a hand on the ten-year-old boy's shoulder. Julian's family was poor, but he'd never had to go to bed hungry. That had happened often enough in the trenches if the rationers couldn't find their squad or if shelling prevented their approach, but it was harder for a boy to go without enough nourishment.

Dorothea approached from the dining room. She'd lost more weight the past few months, taking smaller portions of the limited food so her children could have more. The shoulders of her dress sagged, and the cinched-in apron couldn't disguise the excess fabric gathered about the waist. "Herr Becker, I'm so glad you've come. One of the pipes is leaking—frozen, I'm sure. Would you see if you can fix it?"

"I'd be happy to look at it, Frau Kallweit. But I can't make any promises. I have little experience fixing pipes." And Julian had no idea where he could get a replacement if the pipe was broken.

After a meager supper of turnip soup, Julian went to examine the plumbing problem. Indoor plumbing had been added to the house after it was built, so the pipes were affixed to the walls. Julian walked along the hallway until he found the drip, then turned off the water source and removed the leaky pipe.

While Julian was working, Dorothea put Gerta and Franz to bed, then went to see her father in the study, where Julian could easily overhear them.

"Papa, we can't go on like this."

"Like what?"

"No food, no heat, and Gerta so weak she won't even go outside to play."

"It's February," Herr Sauer said. "Few children play outside in the winter."

"My children do. And Gerta has plenty of hand-me-down hats and socks from her brothers. I've patched them, and she still won't go outside. It's not because it's cold, Papa. It's because she has no energy."

"Wasn't she always sickly? Even as a baby?"

"That was Willi. Gerta has always been robust until now. But she's a finicky eater, and she detests war bread. Can't you do something? She's becoming malnourished."

Something clinked onto the desk. Julian suspected coins of some sort. "Offer to pay a little more for something she'll eat."

Dorothea's voice was low and beaten. "None of the local merchants know me, so they won't give me anything we don't have coupons for."

"They know me."

"No, they knew your former housekeeper, and they didn't like her."

"So trade away the china to the local farmers. Get food that way."

"I've already traded the china. It's gone now. So is most of my jewelry."

"Then take my pocket watch. Take the motorcar and the furniture."

"And what will we do when we run out of furniture?"

Herr Sauer huffed. "What do you want me to do? Write the Kaiser and tell him he ought to give in to Entente demands so the blockade will end? They want Alsace and Lorraine back and pieces of Austria for Italy. Those aren't light things to give up."

"My children cry at night because they are hungry." Dorothea's voice cracked. "What do I care about faraway provinces?"

"Honor is worth dying for."

"But land is not."

"Land is honor. Negotiation without victory may bring an easement of the blockade, but it would create problems far worse than what we have now. You think things will go back to the way they were before the war if we don't win? No. They'll want reparations and our African colonies. Nothing will be the same if we lose, and peace can't guarantee a good harvest."

"And if we continue? How many people will die, Papa? Not just soldiers— civilians too, including your granddaughter."

Julian could hear Herr Sauer's sigh from the hallway. "Even if I wanted to, I couldn't stop the war. Herr Meyer respects me, and he's close to the Kaiser, but General Hindenburg and General Ludendorff are the real leaders of Germany now. We'll have to fight to the end."

"And when will the end come?"

"The scientists and engineers working with Krupp are constantly coming up with better shells, new gases, more accurate mortars. They tell me they're nearing a breakthrough."

"I've heard that before."

The conversation ended. Julian pretended to be working on the leak when Dorothea walked past him, but he could see her tears, and as she turned the corner, he heard her sob.

\* \* \*

The strike ended the next day. Julian took the pipe to the factory and borrowed a welding torch to fix it. The end result was rough and unpolished, but he could turn the uglier side toward the wall.

Julian's normal work involved transporting parts for artillery pieces to the assembly line. He always said a few words to those he came in contact with, and his friendly greetings and ability to remember what other workers said during small talk proved useful in getting Herr Sauer's pipe fixed. He hoped it would be helpful in his next endeavor as well.

"Herr Gottschalk, have you heard much about the new gun? The big one?"

Gottschalk helped Julian lift a box and place it next to his machine. "The shells weigh 106 kilograms. Have a range of over 100 kilometers. Guess they'll be testing them elsewhere, eh? On Paris, maybe."

Julian covered his horror with a grin and moved his cart of boxes to the next station. Over the remainder of the day, he tried to steer other conversations to what was being called the Paris Gun. He heard conflicting information about its size and range, but by the end of his shift, it was clear he needed to search the offices near the testing grounds to see if he could dig up more data.

The Krupp works had four firing ranges, each as impressive as any built by the German government or its neighboring countries, but Julian didn't have time to visit the Essen range that night. There was the pipe to replace, and he was worried about Gerta. She usually went to bed before he returned from his shift, so he'd seen little of her since starting at the factory. That morning before work, he'd asked Mathilde for more details on the girl, and her report had been terrifying. The normally energetic child was languid, her smile absent, her voice barely audible. Long factory shifts weren't the only reason he was seeing less of Gerta.

"How is your sister?" Julian asked Franz when he returned to the Sauer estate. The boy was already dressed for bed, wearing two sets of pajamas to combat the cold.

"The doctor said she has pneumonia."

Julian walked to the bedroom where Gerta slept. Through the cracked door, he could see Dorothea bent over her daughter. He knocked gently and came inside when Dorothea glanced up. "How is she?"

Gerta looked as though she was just sleeping, but Dorothea's face told the full story. Her eyes were sunken and bloodshot, her lips cracked, probably from the way she bit the upper one when she was worried. It was the face of a mother who feared for her child's life. Dorothea took a deep breath before whispering, "She's so warm."

Julian felt the little girl's forehead. He'd never felt human skin that hot. "Will she eat anything?"

"She didn't eat breakfast, and she hasn't even opened her eyes since noon." A bowl of water and a pile of rags sat on a table near the bed.

"Have you eaten anything today, Frau Kallweit?"

"Not since breakfast."

"Would you like me to change out the cloths for a while?"

Dorothea didn't answer right away, caressing her daughter's face and putting a fresh wet rag on her forehead.

"You can't take care of her if you fall ill," he reminded her.

"But you have work."

"I can miss a shift for a family emergency. They need workers. They may dock my paycheck, but they won't send me away."

"Family emergency . . ." Dorothea nodded. "You have become like part of the family."

"Get some food, and then get some rest."

Dorothea kissed her daughter's forehead, mumbled her thanks to Julian, and left.

Gerta's breathing was uneven, the pauses between breaths sometimes so long that Julian worried she had breathed her last. He replaced the rags on her forehead every few minutes and rubbed them along her cheeks and neck. The little girl's blonde hair was damp with sweat despite the room's cool temperature. Julian spooned drops of water into her mouth, hoping the trickle would ease her cough.

Herr Sauer brought in a boiling tea kettle later that evening. "The doctor said the steam might help. It's about time to try again."

Julian lifted the little girl and held her over the mist until the water stopped steaming. "Perhaps some wet towels to keep the air moist?" Julian suggested.

Sauer nodded and brought the linens. Every few hours he heated a tea kettle and rewet the towels.

Julian wasn't sure what else to do. Herr Sauer said Dorothea and Mathilde had followed the doctor's suggestions day and night all week, but Gerta hadn't improved. Julian prayed for the little girl, for her family, pleaded that she would recover, but if the Lord saw fit to answer his prayer, the changes in Gerta's body were imperceptible.

As the sky outside eased from black to gray, Julian realized that Gerta was one more victim of the war. Her small body, too long deprived of sufficient nourishment, was no longer strong enough to fight her illness. Some might scruple that she wasn't hit by a shell or a bullet, so it wasn't the same, and it was different, but war was still the cause.

In the morning Dorothea came to check on her daughter. "Gerta?"

At her mother's voice, the girl woke and managed the slightest slip of a smile. Julian fed her vegetable broth, but she took only three spoonfuls before shaking her head slightly. Dorothea cajoled her into taking a few more bites, and then Gerta cried and patted her swollen throat.

At Dorothea's urging, Julian went to rest. He lay in bed but didn't sleep, and it wasn't the sound of Herr Sauer pacing in the study above his basement room that kept him awake. He had a sinking feeling in his chest that sweet five-year-old Gerta wouldn't last the week.

* * *

The doctor was on his way out when Julian gave up on sleep. "Is there anything you can do for her?"

The gray-haired man had to be nearing ninety years of age. Perhaps that was why he wasn't treating wounded soldiers. "She's in bad shape, and there's not much anyone can do other than wait. Keep giving her aspirin to keep the fever down. I left herbal tea with the cook. Try to get her to drink that. Keep her cool, and keep the air damp. I'm sorry I can't stay longer, but I have many patients this winter."

After seeing the doctor out, Julian found Franz in the dining room. The boy was faced away from Julian, his arms on the table, his head resting on his fists. "Dreaming of food, Franz?"

The boy straightened, and a hand flew to his eyes. Julian hadn't realized he was crying. "The doctor's come every day this week. Gerta's still not better." He took a deep breath. "Kurt hasn't written in a week. Willi hasn't written in two weeks."

"Mail can get held up, especially if their units are seeing a lot of action."

"But Gerta—she won't even respond to me."

Julian sat next to the boy and placed a hand on his arm. "Gerta is a special little girl, isn't she?"

Franz nodded and sniffed. "She always laughed when I said something funny, even when no one else did. She never tattled when I borrowed Willi's models without asking or took one of Grandpapa's books. A few months ago, I skinned my knee. She ran to the house and got a rag to clean the cut for me. And whenever one of Grandpapa's guests brought a piece of candy for her, she let me have half."

Julian and Franz spent the rest of the morning in the kitchen, boiling handkerchiefs and brewing tea. Julian was about to take the tea to Gerta when a heartrending sob tore the air. Julian motioned for Franz to stay where he was while Julian investigated. He was saddened but not surprised to learn the cry had been Dorothea's as Gerta had taken her last breath.

Mathilde and Franz came down with similar respiratory infections three days after Gerta passed away. Franz was so ill he was comatose for two days, but he recovered. Mathilde died after a short, bitter struggle.

In the weeks that followed, the Sauer house felt empty and lifeless. Franz's strength was slow to return. Julian would often come back from the factory to find the boy sitting next to the window, a blanket wrapped around his shoulders, a ball in his hand. He never tossed the ball, rarely even rolled it along the window seat. He just held it and stared out the window.

Herr Sauer threw himself into his work, spending hours in his study with the door shut. Julian followed up on the long sessions behind closed doors, but if Herr Sauer was busy, he left no written evidence of his accomplishments. He took frequent trips to Berlin, claiming there was an urgent need for his expertise, but Julian suspected he was trying to escape the house, with its bittersweet memories of the golden-haired girl who no longer left her dolls on his armchair, begged him for sweets, or searched his library for books with pictures.

Dorothea took it harder than the others, though Julian rarely saw her. She had been an early riser, but according to Franz, she now stayed in her room until noontime. Her face, already gaunt, looked twenty years older. With Mathilde dead and Julian working long hours, shopping and meal preparation fell to Dorothea. It was below her social station, and her lack of experience showed in the meals, already doomed to mediocrity because of rationing. She didn't complain about the long lines for rationed food, didn't talk about her daughter, didn't write to her husband or her sons. But from time to time, Julian would see her holding Franz, running her hands through his hair, and pulling him close as tears trickled down her cheeks.

Julian was fighting a war against their country, but their loss was his loss, their grief, his grief. He wanted Germany's armies vanquished, but defeat for individual families brought him no hope, no satisfaction that Germany, like France, was suffering. He felt only sorrow. Sorrow for the war, and sorrow for little Gerta.

# Chapter 22

*March 1917, Champaign Province, France*

WARREN WAS IN LOVE. HIS new airplane, a Sopwith Pup, had to be the finest machine ever built. There were other good planes, like the French Spad and the German Fokker. They might even be better in some ways, but he doubted any of them were as fun to fly, and none beat the Pup at high altitudes. In the ten days he'd had it, he'd shot down nine German planes, two of them on the same day.

He was a captain now, commanding his own flight. After his takeoff, he circled the aerodrome, waiting for two other pilots from C squadron to catch up to him.

The cool, crisp air blew through the open cockpit and kept him alert as he led his group toward the front lines in search of German opponents. The Sopwith had finally given his men the plane they needed to go head-to-head against German scouts like the Fokker and the Albatross. Peering into the distance, Warren thought he saw a group of small black specks.

*Speaking of German scouts . . .*

Ready for a fight, he turned toward them. They were at a similar altitude to his group, so it would be an even match. No . . . He could make out four planes, so his team was outnumbered. But Nelson and Grimsley, the men he flew with today, were experienced pilots, and they were high enough that most other planes would lose some of their aerobatic abilities, giving the Pups the advantage.

The two groups closed the distance quickly, meeting each other in a burst of machine gun fire. Warren twisted his plane around to chase the Germans, who couldn't match the Pup's tight turns. The Albatross D.IIs were good planes though, and the enemy pilots didn't make it easy to get around behind them.

Both formations broke up. Warren attacked one of the German planes from slightly above, riddling it with bullets but not downing it. He adjusted his plane and Vickers machine gun for another try, then noticed two of the Hun planes ganging up on Grimsley.

Warren turned to stop the planes diving on his comrade. He put a line of bullets through the fuselage of one, and the plane flew away with an engine fire. By the time Warren turned around to dive at the other Albatross, Grimsley had gotten away, as had the other attacker.

Warren pursued a new target, focusing on the Albatross he'd shot up before breaking off to aid Grimsley. The plane was limping home, but before Warren was in range, the dogfight to his left distracted him. The fourth Albatross had shot the wing off Nelson's plane. His friend's face filled with horror as the plane fell apart underneath him. It was impossible to glide a plane to a gentle landing with only one wing, and the Royal Flying Corps didn't issue parachutes to pilots.

The Albatross pilot who had shot Nelson ended his pass with a few bullets into Warren's plane. Warren grabbed the end of his silk scarf and wiped at his goggles to clear them of oil from his damaged engine. He made Nelson's killer his next opponent. It was tricky maneuvering into position behind such a skilled pilot, but eventually he was within range. He squeezed the trigger in a rage but missed. He fought the wind and wiped at his oil-splattered goggles again, but just before he had the plane lined up in his sights, it dove away.

The two other surviving Albatrosses joined him, heading for their own lines. Maybe they were low on fuel. Nelson's expression still fresh in his mind, Warren wanted to chase them. He'd crippled one of them, and Grimsley had gotten a few good shots in as well. But both Pups were damaged, and attacking a superior number of planes with an imperfect engine was unlikely to achieve successful revenge. Warren signaled to Grimsley, and they turned for home.

When he landed, he checked the damage to his engine.

A mechanic joined him. "That will take some work to fix, sir."

"Grimsley's plane will need repairs too," Warren said.

"And Nelson?"

"Shot down."

The mechanic bowed his head in a gesture of respect.

"Has A squadron made it back?" Warren had planned a trip to a nearby village with Captain Prior, who was seeing a local girl. Warren had intended to purchase birthday gifts for his grandmother and Claire, but with Nelson's death, a shopping trip no longer sounded enjoyable.

The mechanic nodded, but his frown sent goose bumps forming along Warren's arms. Not more bad news.

"And?"

"Not all of them made it back, sir."

"Captain Prior?"

"Haven't seen him yet."

Warren left his beloved plane to the mechanic and strode to the tent where Major Cook debriefed the men after each flight. He pushed aside the flap as the intelligence officer hung up the telephone. Warren waited.

The intelligence officer gave Warren a nod, then turned to Major Cook. "An artillery battery saw two of our planes attacked by three German fighters. Our boys had one victory, but they both went down."

"Did they see which planes?" Warren asked.

"Blue nose on one, red wheels on the other."

Warren swallowed hard. That meant Prior and Nesbeck had been shot down on the same day he'd lost Nelson. "Which side of the line?"

"Ours."

"Where?"

"North about twenty miles. The artillery that called it in is supporting the 51st Highland Division."

Warren left the tent, rushing to find a car. Maybe they'd survived their crashes. He drove as fast as he could along the muddy road often blocked with men and supplies moving to or from the trenches. He stopped some of the soldiers for directions and eventually found his way to the correct artillery battery.

"Those two planes, where did they crash?"

One of the men made a vague gesture to the west.

"Has anyone checked them?"

The man nodded.

"And?"

"Neither pilot made it, sir. I'm sorry."

Warren couldn't bring himself to reply. He drove slowly back to his aerodrome, a heavy sense of gloom surrounding him, eating at him. Prior, Nesbeck, and Nelson had been good pilots and good men. He was going to miss them.

* * *

A few weeks after Captain Prior's death, Warren's wing moved closer to Paris. It was close enough that he could visit the Donovans if he had a day off due to poor weather, but it was another month before he got around to it.

Mr. Franke, the butler, showed him to the library, where Claire waited in front of the piano. "When I looked out the window this morning and noted rain for the third day in a row, I said to myself, 'Perhaps Mr. Flynn will come visit as he cannot fly and will have already taken apart and adjusted everything on his airplane.' Ever since I received the letter about your new aerodrome, I've been hoping you'd accept one of my invitations. I had our cook plan an elaborate supper for if you came. Will you stay long enough to join me?"

He nodded.

"I missed you, Warren." She faced the piano as she said it, as if hesitant to be so blunt and look him in the face at the same time.

He knew he should say something about how much he'd missed her, but he kept silent as he took the seat next to the piano. "Any new music since I was here last fall?"

"Yes."

"Will you play for me?"

She complied, her lithe fingers playing first a classical piece, then a ragtime piece. As she finished, she rubbed her hands together. "It's still so cold all the time. I'm looking forward to summer."

"Coal shortage?"

"Yes. Papa usually manages to buy enough, but he didn't think it would be cold for so long."

"I have an idea." Watching Claire play was pleasant, but he wanted to be closer, wanted to hold her. He went to the gramophone and selected a disc. As the music started, he held out his hand. "We can dance to stay warm."

Her fingers slipped into his, and as she stood, he placed his other hand on the back of her narrow waist.

"You know, I think you've gotten prettier since my last visit."

One of her eyebrows rose. "And you seem to have grown more romantic."

"You know better than to assume something like that."

Her smile made her dimple show, but she didn't look convinced as he led her in a waltz. He was tempted to say something completely unromantic just to prove his point, but he found watching her more enjoyable.

"You seem to be staring at me, Captain Flynn."

"I'm counting your freckles."

She turned away with a grin and a blush.

"You moved; now I have to start over. I wonder if you have more freckles or if I have more kills. I'm up to thirty-four now." When Warren realized what he'd said, his feet stopped moving. He usually thought of his opponents as machines to eliminate, but there were people inside the planes too. How many of them had squadron mates mourning their loss, just as he mourned Captain Prior's and all the other men's who'd been shot down? The poor devils. "I'm sorry, Claire. That was a rather insensitive thing for me to say."

He rushed from the library to the garden. He needed fresh air despite the rain. Lately the war had him feeling as confused and out of place as a cavalry officer on a U-boat. He still exulted in each triumph over another pilot, but when he thought about how many people he'd killed, it made him sick. What type of man went up in a plane and shot down other men, then celebrated the event? And what was the alternative? Doing the same thing only with a rifle aimed across no-man's land? War turned the world upside down.

"I brought you your hat."

Warren glanced back at the doorway, where Claire stood with a shawl wrapped around her shoulders. She walked over to stand next to him and offered him his hat.

"I noticed you still have the good-luck charm I gave you. Lately your letters have been so infrequent." She looked away. "I wondered if perhaps there was another girl somewhere."

He took his hat. "No. No girl. I've just been busy turning into some type of despicable killing machine."

"You're doing your duty."

"Hmm."

Claire pulled her shawl more tightly over her shoulders. "My mother would have known exactly what to say to make you cheerful again. She had a way with words, could always read people. I wish I had that gift, especially now, because I don't know what to say." She put her hand on his arm. "I'm sorry that war is so awful and that you have to be part of it. But I'm here, and I want to help."

Warren took her hand and held it as he stared at the ivy. He didn't put as much pressure in his grip as he did on his stick when pulling his plane from a dive, but he grasped it with equal desperation. Having her nearby was helpful, even when she said nothing. The two of them would be as soggy as a duckboard in Flanders if they stayed outside much longer, but somehow the drops of water seemed cleansing.

"Do you ever miss your mother?" Claire asked.

It wasn't something Warren usually admitted, but he nodded.

"Still?"

Sixteen years had gone by, but he thought of her often. "Yes."

"I miss mine. Every day. I was hoping it wouldn't be so bad after a decade."

"It isn't as bad as it used to be. But it hasn't gone away. I doubt it ever will completely."

"Sometimes I wonder if she looks down on me and what she thinks."

Warren studied Claire. Her red curls were growing heavy with rainwater, and several drops hung on her eyelashes. "If she looks down on you, I'm sure she's pleased with the woman you've become." On the other hand, if his mother was watching, and if all she had taught him about right and wrong was true, Warren had a gnawing fear that she'd be horrified by the war and by his role in it.

# Chapter 23

*March 1917, Paris, France*

"I want to do something more," Claire said.

Evette looked up from the pot of soup she stirred. The Donovans were between cooks again, so she was filling in. "Like what?"

"When Captain Flynn came to visit, we spoke a little of our mothers. We both lost them when we were about the same age. And it got me wondering what she would think of me."

"You're well educated, you've become an accomplished pianist, and you manage to maintain a social grace without hiding your opinion. She'd be pleased, I'm sure."

"Those are things I can do, but what about who I am? I'm spoiled. I can have new clothes whenever I like, I live in a home far bigger than I need, and Papa always manages to find enough coal to heat the home, even if I have to wear an extra layer. Millions of soldiers are eating cold, pitiful meals and sleeping outside all winter, and I complain about the inferior bread and the need to put on a sweater. I want to do something worthwhile, something that will make a difference."

"You think you'd be a better person if you suffered like the soldiers?" Claire had been given more than most people, but that didn't mean she was a bad person. If she was spoiled, it was her father's fault.

"Not necessarily." Claire delicately sat on a high stool. "But I want to do more than knit socks. Can I help you?"

Evette added herbs to the soup and stirred them in, trying to hide her surprise. "Maybe."

Claire leaned on the countertop. "That sounded very much like a no."

"I'm grateful for your offer . . . I'm just not sure it would work. Monsieur McDougall hired me in part because I blend in. I'm ordinary, whereas you're elegant and obviously of good social standing. If I can think of a situation where something like that wouldn't be a liability, I'll gladly accept your help."

Claire seemed mollified, if not exactly happy. "Did Monsieur McDougall say you were ordinary?"

"Yes."

"Hmm." Claire's eyebrows scrunched together. "I've seen him with you a few times since I learned he was your employer. I've noticed how he looks at you. I don't think he considers you ordinary, not in the least." Claire forsook the kitchen for the library and its piano, leaving Evette to ponder two strange ideas. Was there a way to let Claire help with counterintelligence work? And if Claire was right and McDougall was fond of her, how did Evette feel about him?

* * *

Evette peered around the corner of a dark alley at the suspected member of the Lothair League. He was alone but seemed to be waiting for something. His stride was lopsided, indirect, as if he wanted to linger without appearing to loiter. When she was alone like this at night, following someone significantly larger than she, Evette was tempted to ask McDougall for a weapon.

Claire's words about McDougall one week ago in the kitchen had left Evette perplexed. She rarely saw him interact with women other than his middle-aged housekeeper, so she had nothing to compare her treatment to. Two years ago, knowledge that a gentle, well-educated man was interested in her would have brought contentment. But Claire's ideas from Christmastime on love and romance lingered, as did Evette's memories of the poilu who had given her money for a train ticket. When it came to men and romance, uncertainty reigned.

Evette shook her head to clear it. Claire might be mistaken about McDougall's feelings, and the poilu could be married, could be dead. In any case, she was unlikely to ever see him again, and she needed to concentrate on the man walking toward her. She was concealed behind a large barrel but could follow his movements by looking through the space between the barrel and the wall. Midway down the alley, he stopped and bent to the ground. His hand momentarily rested on a stone, then he straightened, and his stride became purposeful as he stalked past the barrel and turned left onto the main street.

Evette bit her lip in indecision. She didn't want to lose the man, but he would notice if she followed him too closely in the nearly deserted streets. And there was something odd about his gesture with the stone. She waited until the man was out of earshot, then rushed down the alley to where he'd bent over. When she moved the stone, she uncovered a folded envelope. She slipped it into her coat pocket and hurried to catch up to her quarry.

She arrived on the main road in time to see him turn into a side street a block away. She sighed with relief. She hadn't lost him. During her pursuit, she stayed a half block behind. When he went into a narrow row house, she found a convenient recessed doorway to slink into and watched. An hour later, she concluded the row home was his residence.

She went back to the street corner where she had left her bike and pedaled to McDougall's residence rather than his office. The woman who managed the boardinghouse, Madame Morel, answered Evette's knock. She wore a dressing gown, and her hair was in a long braid. Normally she wore her hair up, so Evette had probably roused her from bed.

"May I see Monsieur McDougall, please?"

Madame Morel's gray eyebrows drew together in disapproval, undoubtedly because of the late hour, but she nodded and climbed the stairs. That meant McDougall wasn't in his ground-floor study. Perhaps he had also gone to bed, but that couldn't be helped. As Evette waited, she pulled the envelope from her pocket and broke the seal. Taking advantage of the indoor light, she read the message. The words inside made all traces of reluctance for disturbing both Madame Morel's and Monsieur McDougall's sleep vanish.

"Mademoiselle Touny, what a pleasant surprise. Shall I have Madame Morel make some tea?"

Evette glanced up to see McDougall descend the last few stairs. Madame Morel was behind him and didn't look at all as if she wished to make tea. "No, thank you. That won't be necessary."

McDougall motioned toward the study and followed Evette inside. "That will be all, Madame Morel," he said as he shut the door securely. "Well, did you find out where he lives?"

"Yes." Evette handed over the paper. "He left this under a rock in an alley."

McDougall read the sheet of paper to himself. Evette remembered it word for word: *Munitions train will stop at Gare Montparnasse, 11pm Thursday. Guards bribed to leave cars for ten minutes. Plant device by 11:10.*

McDougall reached for his phone and was soon speaking with someone but in English, so Evette understood only snippets. When he hung up, he put the message in a fresh envelope and sealed it. "That was my superior. He will contact his French counterpart and send a pair of gendarmes here to escort us back to the alley. You will replace this note. They will stay and arrest anyone who tries to collect it. Then you can show me where this man lives, and I shall have him apprehended too. Tomorrow someone will arrest the bribed guards. Well done, mademoiselle."

"Thank you, sir."

As they waited for the French police, McDougall paced. Evette concluded Claire must be making things up. McDougall's focus was completely on his work. He wasn't the type to let a woman distract him.

# Chapter 24

EARLY THE NEXT MORNING, A knock roused Evette from her sleep. She slipped into one of Claire's old wraps and went to answer her bedroom door.

Mr. Franke stood in the hallway. "Monsieur McDougall is here to see you. He's waiting in the parlor."

"Thank you. I'll be right there."

Evette dressed, then brushed and pinned up her hair. She supposed it was fair that McDougall had disturbed her sleep; she'd done the same to him the night before.

The Donovans' new cook had already brought coffee and rolls into the parlor when Evette arrived. McDougall brushed a few crumbs from his hands and stood to greet her.

"I apologize for waking you, but I have something urgent."

"What is it?"

"No one came to retrieve the note."

"They probably checked while I was watching his home or reporting to you."

McDougall nodded. "Aye. And we questioned the man we nabbed last night, but we do not believe he is the mastermind."

"He's in the middle? Taking orders from someone else and passing them on to the saboteurs?"

"Yes. He bribed the guards, hired the saboteur, and learned the train schedule. He admitted to working for the League."

Evette took a seat. "Did he say who his contact with the League is?"

"No. Said the man always contacts him, not the other way around. We will continue to question him, but I have a feeling that even if we find the saboteur and the guards, we won't get the League man."

"So it's a dead end."

"Perhaps. I have one idea, but it is rather a long shot. The man we arrested had a dog. I want you to take it for a walk. See if it recognizes anyone coming to visit his master. I shall arrange to have backup nearby to assist if the dog finds our man for us."

"All right."

"I need to coordinate a few things, but I will meet you in an hour. Anything earlier would be uncivilized." McDougall glanced at his watch. "Which means I disturbed your sleep at a rather uncivilized hour, but I shall make it up to you, I promise."

McDougall took another roll and let himself out. Evette looked at breakfast, but she had no appetite.

She remembered Claire's desire to help and stood, leaving breakfast untouched. On her way to her friend's room, Evette almost bumped into Mr. Donovan when she came around a corner too quickly. "I'm sorry, sir."

"Don't mention it. I have an early meeting, but will you tell Claire I'll try to join her for supper?"

"Yes, sir."

"Thank you." He smiled his gratitude.

When Evette knocked on Claire's door, she heard a sleepy voice telling her to come in.

Claire was still fastening the tie on her robe when Evette entered. "I hope you were involved in something exciting yesterday. You missed the best dessert I've had in ages."

"I was catching a saboteur."

Claire's jaw dropped.

"But there are a few of his friends to catch still, if you'd like to help. I need to walk a dog."

\* \* \*

McDougall was waiting with a leashed terrier when the women arrived. His lips turned down when he recognized Claire.

Evette spoke first. "She offered to help, sir. I thought if we switched off it would look less suspicious."

"Perhaps, but don't let Captain Flynn know I've dragged you into espionage. If he finds out, he may never speak to me again."

Claire's eyes widened in mock innocence. "Why should Warren care if I get involved in a little spying? One of the reasons Evette came to live with me was to help relieve boredom. Besides, the United States is bound to declare war soon. I want to help my country."

McDougall hesitated before answering. "I supposed this assignment is safe enough. Two gendarmes are waiting in the man's rooms, watching through the window to see if the dog recognizes anyone. I would appreciate your report when all is finished, Mademoiselle Touny."

"Yes, sir."

When McDougall was out of earshot, Claire put her hand on one hip. "The last time I saw him, I was certain he fancied you, but today he seems cold."

"I doubt he slept much last night. He oversaw the arrest, then he helped question the man they caught."

Claire bent down to scratch behind the dog's ears. The terrier yipped cheerfully. "I wonder what sort of questioning they do."

"Nothing we want to know about."

Claire frowned. "We shan't think of it, then. And a great deal of romance novels have heroes who appear cranky at first. No doubt McDougall is simply hiding his feelings."

Evette chuckled. She'd long ago learned not to argue with Claire about romance.

They spent the morning walking the dog back and forth along the street in front of the saboteur's home. At first they went together, then they took turns while one of them took a break on a nearby bench. By noon, the dog needed a rest.

"Come on, boy," Claire said. "Don't you want to walk a little longer?"

The dog lay on the new spring grass and put its head on its front paws.

Clair sighed and sat beside Evette. "Fiddlesticks. I suppose you'll have to tell McDougall the dog stopped cooperating."

"Maybe he needs a nap."

"Maybe."

They sat there for perhaps a half hour, watching people pass by. The puppy ignored them all. Finally, a hatless man in a well-worn suit coat walked past them. The puppy wagged his tail and stood, then trotted to the man, who looked from the dog to the women and then back again.

"Do you know this puppy, sir?" Evette asked. "We found him wandering about, and we're trying to find his owner."

The man bent and picked up the dog. "Yes, I know where this one belongs. I'll take him if you like."

Evette handed over the leash, wondering if she was handing it to the saboteur or to the League man. It felt dishonest, trapping him this way, but soldiers like her brother were desperate. If this man really planned to destroy a train full of munitions, he was a traitor and had to be stopped. She forced a smile. "Thank you, sir."

"You're welcome."

Evette and Claire watched the man walk into the row home. Ten minutes later, he came out under arrest.

"I almost feel sorry for him," Claire said. The dog came out after the gendarmes and their prisoner, but the men ignored the animal. "And I do feel sorry for the dog. It's not his fault his previous master was a traitor. Do you think McDougall would mind if I took him home with me?"

"I'll ask."

Claire scooped up the puppy. "I'll bring him with me for now. I doubt he's been fed, and we wore the poor little thing out."

The two of them walked back to the Donovan manor. From there, Evette took her bicycle to McDougall's office to make her report.

"We found a man, sir. I have no proof that he's involved, but he knew the puppy. I suppose the gendarmes will report to you soon."

McDougall closed a file of papers and locked it in a desk drawer. "Well done, Evette. Thank you."

Evette's eyes had wandered to the window, but she turned back to him sharply. McDougall had never called her by her first name before.

"I didn't mean to be forward. But I thought perhaps we were on friendly enough terms to call each other by our given names. If you prefer Mademoiselle Touny, I shall continue to call you that. But in either case, please call me Howard."

"Evette would be fine, sir. I mean, Howard."

He smiled and rubbed the back of his neck. "I still need to monitor the arrest at the train station, but hopefully after that, things will calm down. I will fill you in tomorrow. You can take the rest of the day off."

"Claire was hoping to keep the puppy. Did you have other plans for it?"

"She can have it. If I need it again, I shall know where to find it, eh?"

When Evette returned to the Donovan manor, the little terrier was a firmly established resident. Evette heard Claire's giggles from the front parlor the instant she stepped inside.

"You're back." Claire grinned when she saw Evette. "I think our little puppy will be a perfect fit here. He took an instant liking to Papa."

"Just remember the dog is your responsibility," Mr. Donovan said with an indulgent smile.

"You already told me that, Papa."

"Yes, but last time you had a puppy, I ended up doing most of the work."

"That was thirteen years ago!"

Mr. Donovan laughed. "Yes, I suppose you deserve another chance."

# Chapter 25

Evette rushed to the train station, hoping she wasn't late. A week had passed since McDougall had arrested the guards willing to accept bribes at this same station. They had nabbed the middleman, the saboteur, and the corrupt soldiers, but the League's mastermind was still at large, and that made her nervous.

She banished work from her mind as the crowds disembarked from the train. "Emile!" She recognized her brother and waved to him.

He made his way through the crowd and wrapped his arms around her. They hadn't seen each other since he'd been mobilized in August 1914, two and a half years ago. He had been given two previous furloughs but had always gone back to the village to see their mother and surviving sister. For this furlough, he had left the village a day early to meet Evette for an afternoon.

"Look at you," he said, holding her at arm's length. "You've grown up. And you don't look like a peasant girl anymore." He glanced at her clothing.

"The Donovans have been generous." She wished she could tell him about her real job, but she wasn't supposed to discuss it.

"Hmm. Let me get my things."

Her brother disappeared, then returned not long after with a pack.

"Ready?" she asked.

"Yes." He seemed deeply weary, as if he was at the beginning of leave instead of at the end. The result of traveling or of something else?

"I can't wait to show you Paris," she said, hoping her enthusiasm would spark some interest. "First I'll get you something to eat. There's a wonderful restaurant not far from here. Claire—Mr. Donovan's daughter—took me there about a month ago."

It was only eleven in the morning, so the restaurant was nearly empty when they went in. Evette paid for the steaks as soon as they arrived, a habit she had picked up while working for McDougall. If her meal was already paid for, she could leave whenever she wanted without creating an incident.

"You know what we eat in the trenches?" Emile asked partway through the meal.

"No."

"Sometimes nothing. It's easy for the rationers to get lost, especially in the dark when we're in a new area. The trenches can be like a maze. Or our relief is late, so we're stuck up front longer than planned, and none of the officers bothers to adjust the supplies." He took a sip of his drink. "In the winter, our substitute coffee is usually frozen by the time it gets to us. When we do get food, it's cold ratatouille, hard biscuits, muddy bread, soup made from animal scraps." Emile speared a piece of steak with his fork. "I haven't eaten anything like this in years."

Evette set her fork down as guilt swept over her. She didn't eat steak often, but even the occasional indulgence now felt sinful. "Does everyone eat that poorly?"

"Heavens no. Not the officers. They have their own cooks. And they don't sleep in the mud like the rest of us. They have nice little dugouts along the communications trenches." Emile ate another bite, but the expression of pleasure from the food quickly dissolved into bitterness. "The difference is even more dramatic when we're pulled into reserve. The officers find nice chateaus for themselves and leave forty of us to sleep in a roofless barn with moldy hay. When we ask the farmers for straw to sleep on, they refuse, and the officers side with them." He set his jaw and shook his head in frustration. "The officers are all fools. Once we were marching in the rain and were told we could only wear horizon-blue uniforms, and that was after we'd been outfitted with surplus British raincoats. The idiots made us take our coats off because they were khaki, and when a few of the men got sick, the medical officers refused to see them. It's like we're animals rather than men. The generals will sacrifice thousands of us for a few meters of ground as long as they can have an advance to report in their dispatches. At the rate we're going, we'll all be dead or maimed in another year or two."

"But the newspapers say you're being well fed and that they've set up rest camps and—"

Emile leaned forward and lowered his voice. "The last rest camp I was in, I slept in a tent. It was snowing, so they gave us two blankets instead of one. My feet weren't dry the entire four days we were there. That was our rest. The papers only report eyewash."

He finished his food, and Evette pushed hers toward him. She was no longer hungry, but her brother seemed physically, as well as emotionally, at the end of his strength. "Why didn't you tell me things were so awful?"

One side of Emile's lips lifted up slightly. "I tried once. The censors read the letter, and as punishment, I had to stay up the line when my unit rotated back for rest duty. If they would send me to prison instead, I'd write inflammatory letters every day. Prison would be like a holiday compared to the army."

"So that's why your letters are so . . . so vague?"

Emile nodded. "Thank you for the food."

"Thank you for helping me get to Paris." She contemplated telling him about the soldier who had given her the rest of the money, but she wasn't sure Emile would approve. As they left the restaurant, she wondered if he would approve of anything she'd done lately.

They walked past a jewelry store, and a middle-aged couple emerged, chatting about their purchase. Emile watched them with narrowed eyes until they climbed into a cab and were driven away. "There are two Frances, Evette. Those who didn't start the war and now can't escape it, and those who are profiting from it." He glanced at her dress. Evette had worn her favorite outfit to meet him, but as she looked over the unfaded richness of her skirt, she wished she had chosen something else.

Did Emile think she was part of the France that was profiting? She was better off than she'd been in the village, with more money than she'd dreamed of earning three short years ago, and she no longer wore typical peasant garb. She had enough blankets to keep her warm and had sufficient food. "I'm trying to help."

"Yes, someone has to keep that rich American happy so he'll continue supplying us with shells." His tone was caustic, like some of the chemicals she'd used at the munitions factory.

Evette bit her lower lip, wishing she could tell him about the sabotage she'd thwarted, about the spies she'd helped track down. "What do you want me to do?"

Emile didn't answer for a while, staring at the ground. Finally he looked up. "I don't know." He meandered along the street, and she followed. "You're my sister. I want you to be happy. I'm glad you're away from Gaspard and that you have nice clothes. I just . . . I don't know. The war is taking a lot from some people and very little from others."

Originally she had planned to show him the Eiffel Tower, the Arc de Triomphe. They seemed like such petty destinations now. "How can I help you? Can I send you more food? Knit socks for you?"

He shrugged. "Before I left for furlough, there were rumors that General Nivelle's planning a big offensive, one that will decisively win the war. I think it will happen soon, so I was lucky to get leave. I don't believe anything an officer tells me anymore, so I doubt it will lead to victory. But if it's as big as they're saying, it might be the end of my agony."

"Emile, I . . ." Evette felt her throat tighten. He spoke so casually about the possibility of death. Was this really the same boy who had laughed with her during harvest and changed the lyrics of children's songs so they were always about her? "Isn't there something I can do?"

Emile shook his head. "No. You and I, we're just little people stuck in the designs of our leaders. Life is cruel and blessedly short. The only thing we can hope is that the next life will be better."

As Evette watched the train pull away a few hours later, an intense melancholy gripped her heart. The years of war had killed everything joyful in her brother, leaving him bitter and changed. She didn't blame him, but she mourned the difference. Would he ever smile again? Could he ever forgive his country for putting him through such horror and for treating him so abominably? Before the war, he'd been a gifted student and shown promise as a writer. He'd planned a future as a journalist. But now he hated the newspapers, and it seemed he wasn't planning any future at all.

Evette was doing her best to combat the spies and saboteurs McDougall asked her to tail, but unlike her brother and the millions of other soldiers, she wasn't suffering. It wasn't fair, and she didn't know how to fix it.

# Chapter 26

*May 1917, Artois Province, France*

APRIL 1917 HAD BEEN A singularly poor month for the Royal Flying Corps. *No*, Warren corrected himself, *a singularly poor month for the Allied armies.* The Nivelle Offensive, a joint British and French attempt to burst through the German lines, had turned into an unmitigated disaster. Bloody April, as the air war was called, had turned into May, and several new pilots would soon join Warren's flight. The new pilots kept coming, but they needed more training. They were eager to fly and could control a plane during normal conditions, but they were no match for experienced German pilots, especially when the enemy attacked in packs. Some of the German pilots were becoming legends, like Manfred von Richthofen, leader of Jasta 11 and pilot of an all-red Albatross D.III. But whether they were shot down by the Red Baron or a less famous opponent, the new men were just as dead.

Warren was desperate for replacement pilots, but he wished the RFC would keep them in training a little longer. After April, he was hesitant to even learn their names, let alone befriend them. And he dreaded the inevitable letter he would have to write to their next of kin. He had written so many of them now that he could finish a letter in five minutes. *I regret to inform you that your son has been killed in action. His courageous service was an asset to his country, and he will be sorely missed.* He always said the fallen had died in action doing something brave, even if they'd really done something as foolish as flying into a tree during takeoff.

Sitting at the desk in his tent, Warren finished his latest letter of regret for a pilot who'd been shot down on his second combat mission. The poor chap's wings had been shot off, and he'd had a long tumble to the ground. Why did the RFC still have a no-parachute policy? Supposedly there was fear that pilots would abandon damaged planes too quickly if they could bail out, but good pilots were just as hard to replace as quality airplanes. Not that the new men survived long enough to become good pilots.

After the letter, Warren sorted through his mail. The handwriting on most of the envelopes was unfamiliar, probably written by people he didn't know, replying to one of his condolence letters. He hated it when they wrote back to ask for more details about their son's or brother's deaths. The last thing he wanted was to write to the dead men's families and tell them the pilot had burned to death when his engine had caught fire or been cut in pieces by the Red Baron's twin Spandau guns. He would write back eventually, but first he found one of Claire's letters and savored each word. More about the new puppy and the latest collection of sheet music. It was all so different from the slaughter over Arras. He needed that—a reminder that somewhere life was continuing as usual.

"Sir?"

Warren looked around to the open tent flap. "Yes?"

"The new men are here."

Warren stowed away the letters and went to meet the recently arrived pilots. Dare he hope they would last long enough to become experienced? As he walked toward the waiting pair of men, one of them seemed familiar. "Boyle?"

Warren's old observer and mechanic smiled. "Yes, sir."

"Congrats on getting your wings, Flight Sergeant Boyle."

"Thank you, sir."

Warren relaxed a little. At least one of the men was an old sweat, even if his experience was with observing rather than flying, and mechanical skills like Boyle's often came in handy in the air. Maybe the tide was about to turn.

* * *

After a few days of training his new men, Boyle and Reeves, Warren led them up for a midday patrol. The Huns preferred to do their reconnaissance then, when the sun was bright and shadows were small. Reconnaissance planes made good targets for men on their first mission. Warren led them up to altitude and waited, but the Hun was late this morning.

It was nearly time to turn back when Warren spotted something to the north. The speck grew larger and larger until he recognized it as a two-seater plane. Even better, it was heading for the British side of the front. Warren held back for a few minutes, letting the reconnaissance plane fly deeper into enemy territory, where, if it was shot down, the crew would be captured rather than rescued by their compatriots.

When the time was right, Warren led his squadron in the attack. The German plane soon noticed them and circled north to postpone their meeting. But Warren had let the plane come too far west to escape completely. The Sopwith

Pup's superior speed easily closed the distance. It was a pity there weren't more targets to go around. As previously agreed, Warren would keep the lead and the new men would follow, gaining experience so that eventually they could claim victories of their own.

The Hun observer aimed well, but Warren came from below, presenting his enemy with the smallest possible silhouette. He dodged the German bullets and saw his own projectiles hit home. It wasn't a perfect run, but it was sufficient to send the enemy plane to the ground.

Warren decided to follow it as it crash landed. New men were usually in search of souvenirs, and the damaged German plane was heading for a decent field. If Warren led the men back to the aerodrome, the enemy plane would be picked over by infantrymen before they could reach it. By following it in, his men would have first dibs, and seeing an enemy plane up close, even a wrecked one, would give them additional knowledge for the next engagement.

He gave the AEG C.IV a wide berth when he landed. Most German airmen wouldn't shoot at a plane while it came in, even if it was the plane that had shot them down, but there were always exceptions. After Boyle and Reeves landed, Warren led them to the wrecked German craft. An artillery crew had beaten them there and were taking custody of the pilot and his gunner.

A pair of British artillerymen lifted the wounded pilot out. The gunner, who had left the plane under his own power, immediately rushed to the pilot's side, his words foreign but urgent as he motioned for the pilot's wounds to be treated. He removed a scarf from his neck to staunch the blood flow, and the British men did their best to help but to no avail. It was a sucking wound, most likely a bullet through the lungs, and each gasp from the mouth caused a corresponding gurgle from the chest. The pilot reached a hand out to his gunner and gave his arm a weak squeeze. Then his hand fell away, and the man died beside his plane. The captors seemed subdued, the gunner devastated.

As the artillerymen led their surviving prisoner away, Warren sighted tears on the gunner's cheeks. More noticeable was the expression on his face. His chin was clenched, his lips trembling. His eyes were numb at first, until they met Warren's. The power of his accusation went directly into Warren's soul.

* * *

Two weeks passed, and Warren still couldn't forget the way the downed German gunner had looked at him. For some reason, it made him miss Claire. Even when she couldn't put it into words, he felt her comfort, her lack of condemnation with each touch of her hand.

Warren's own hands might be covered in German blood, but he was doing his best to minimize British deaths. He had given Boyle and Reeves regular, consistent missions, and Boyle was now one of the best pilots in the squadron, rivaling men who had been with Warren since his promotion to captain.

After receiving their next assignment, a patrol deep into Hunland rather than on the line, Warren walked with Boyle to his plane. "You're doing well, Flight Sergeant."

"Thank you, sir." Boyle grinned. "I'm trying."

"You're succeeding. Good luck up there today."

"Same to you, sir."

Warren glanced at Boyle's flash of teeth and went to his own scout plane with a smile, remembering Boyle's hesitant admission earlier in the war that he wanted to fly. The war had destroyed a multitude of dreams and crushed a mass of hopes. Maybe that was what made Boyle's advancement so satisfying. It was one small bright spot in a world gone dark.

When they reached altitude, Warren led the four other planes east in search of German targets. He hoped they would be fighters. Reconnaissance planes observing the British troops or spotting for Hun artillery made easier targets, but the same was true in reverse. German fighters had an easy time shooting down British spotters, but if the squadron could knock out a few of the aggressive Hun machines, the air would be safer for other British pilots. Warren was up for the challenge, and so were his men.

Twenty minutes later, he spotted a pair of German two-seater aircraft. They weren't fighters, but he turned toward them anyway, slowly gaining altitude as he closed the distance. When the Huns noticed, they split up. Warren motioned for three of his pilots to follow one while he and Reeves followed the other.

Warren caught the plane, dove, and sheared off a wing before the Hun could return fire. He watched the plane fall, then noticed Reeves signaling east. Two Hun fighters were flying toward them. Warren made a smooth turn so he would meet the Albatrosses head-on. Reeves stayed on his left wing. One of the Hun planes had a trio of red stripes on each of its four wings, but neither of them was painted solid red. That was a relief. Warren was in a good position for the attack, but he didn't want to face off against the Red Baron.

Bullets flew as the two flights neared each other. Several ripped through Warren's right wing, but he saw his bullets do the same to his opponent's engine. Black smoke bellowed from the enemy fuselage. Warren glanced behind him. Smoke streamed from Reeves's plane too.

As the two injured planes turned for home, Warren looped his plane into a tight turn and went back for a pass at the other Albatross. The second German fighter appeared undamaged and turned to meet him. As Warren passed it, he felt a whir of bullets whizzing past his head, but he managed to shoot his opponent's engine. The German plane spiraled out of control. Warren didn't envy the man. Nor did he envy the other German pilot when he saw the first plane's engine burst into flames.

That made three victories for the day. Three fewer planes to fight the Allies, three fewer trained pilots, and one less gunner. But Warren didn't feel like celebrating.

He picked out Reeves, now in the distance. Even if he didn't make it back to the aerodrome, it looked as though his plane was functioning well enough to land within Allied lines. Warren searched for the other half of his squadron, but he hadn't seen them since they'd chased the other observation plane. It was probably time to head back anyway, before he ran out of fuel.

After landing his plane and examining the minor damage to the canvas, Warren walked to Major Cook's tent. One of his pilots, Flight Sergeant Grimsley, was already inside.

"Grimsley, how did it go?"

"We got him, sir. But then we got jumped by three Hun fighters. I barely made it back. Potter looked like he was going to crash land on our side of the line."

"And Boyle?"

"He shot down one of the Hun scouts, sir, but he'll not be coming back."

"What happened?" Warren's muscles tensed, but maybe Boyle had landed behind German lines. Being a POW was better than being dead, and sometimes prisoners escaped.

"Gone west, sir. His plane caught fire. Turned into a flamer."

Warren left the tent. He'd seen and heard of so many deaths—what was one more? Yet when he thought of Boyle's grin, of his enthusiasm for flying, of the way he had bucked social norms and gotten into pilot training, this one hurt more than the others. And going down in flames—what an awful way to die.

With his eyes to the sky, Warren whispered the Royal Flying Corps motto. "*Per ardua ad astra*, my friend." Through adversity to the stars.

# Chapter 27

*June 1917, Essen, Germany*

JULIAN SLOWLY EXTENDED HIS WEIGHT farther onto an oak branch. While growing up, he had never suspected his propensity for tree climbing would one day lead to some of his most successful moments of spy craft, but the tree on whose branches he was currently perched grew perfectly over the one-story building he was trying to sneak into. Krupp's Essen testing range spread out before him, silver in the moonlight. Written results of the tests performed there were stored in the building below.

He lowered himself to the roof and crawled toward the vent. He waited until the guards below finished their patrol before he removed the vent cover and lowered his rope. Then he dropped into the room, a long, closed-off chamber with no direct outside access. He lit a candle. Little had changed since his first visit two weeks before: crates were stacked along the walls, and shells were lined up in neat rows. But for years Krupp had tested shells at a rate not unlike that of a battery on the Western Front, so there were different boxes on this visit. A scattering of shells and shell parts lay along a central countertop. He noted the types but expected the real information harvest to come from the reports the scientists wrote.

He blew out the candle and left the storeroom. The scientists and engineers who worked there all had offices with windows. One by one, Julian searched them, hoping to find out which new munitions were successful and whether the Paris Gun was truly capable of firing a one-hundred-kilogram shell more than one hundred thirty kilometers. On his last visit, he'd come when the moon had been only a sliver, expecting the darkness to mask his entry. It had, but the curtains were too thin to hide candlelight from the guards, so the lack of moonlight had meant he was unable to read anything in the offices. Tonight, he carefully pulled the curtains back so the moon could illuminate the copious collection of documents.

He found reports of failed modifications, unreliable powder, and faulty barrels. But he also found reports that indicated the Paris Gun was moving ahead. He wrote down its range and accuracy. His scraps of paper would be proof of espionage should he be caught, but he couldn't remember everything without them. As he left each room, he placed the curtains exactly as he'd found them and left the reports and notes stacked in their same order and position.

When he had examined every office, he returned to the storeroom and climbed up through the vent. Then he listened. The noises of the night—crickets and an occasional nocturnal bird—greeted him. Julian was ravenous. He had eaten with the Kallweit family before leaving with the excuse that he had friends to meet, but the meal had been small and served hours ago. It had also been one of Franz's wartime favorites, so Julian had given the boy part of his own portion.

Julian crept to the edge of the building above the front door. He could smell one of the guard's cigarettes.

"It's your turn to check the perimeter," a voice from below said. Julian tensed at the sudden words. Though spoken quietly, the sound of another human after hours inside the empty building seemed loud.

"All right. As soon as I finish this."

Julian waited until the guard finished both his cigarette and his patrol. Then he reached for the tree branch and climbed down the oak. When he passed the gate, he allowed himself a sigh of relief.

The eastern horizon was turning gray as he reached the Sauer estate. He still had his report to write and his notes to destroy, so he would get no sleep that night. No sleep until another long shift at the factory had ended. Julian stifled a yawn as he crept in through the back door, taking care not to make any noise. He didn't want Sauer or Dorothea to suspect he'd been out all night.

When the cover letter and report were written and the notes were burning, Julian ruffled the blankets on his bed so it would look like he'd slept. He didn't think anyone came into his room, but he couldn't risk letting his guard down. He ran a hand along the feather pillow but resisted the urge to sleep. It was time to head to the factory.

* * *

Julian was exhausted by the time he finished his shift, posted his report to the letter box in Düsseldorf, and returned to the Sauer home. He was hungry too, but that was normal. Sleep was his top priority, but he stopped as he walked past Sauer's study.

"Out all night, no doubt up to no good. I'm not sure I want that type of influence around Franz," Dorothea said.

"You enjoy the extra rations he brings in and the work he does around the house."

"Yes, but what if it becomes a habit?"

Sauer's deep chuckle crept into the hall. "Once is hardly a habit. And he's a young man, Dorothea. Perfectly ordinary if he occasionally gets so drunk that he doesn't make it home or decides to spend the evening with a woman."

"That's not the type of behavior I want Franz emulating."

"And what do you think Kurt and Willi are doing during their breaks from fighting?"

"I raised my boys to avoid such unseemly behavior!" Dorothea's voice was so loud Julian worried Franz would come investigate and find the Frenchman lingering in the hallway.

"If you aren't worried about Kurt and Willi, I don't think you should be worried about Franz. I'm heading to Berlin tomorrow. I'll be gone a week. If you're still concerned when I get back, we can discuss this further. But perhaps you're assuming the worst. Just because you saw him coming in at dawn doesn't mean he was up to mischief."

Julian left before he was discovered. Perhaps he could think of some excuse for being out all night, something that didn't involve espionage or drinking or carousing with loose women, but just then he was too tired to come up with anything. It was strange to feel shame for something he hadn't done, but he could live with a tarnished reputation as long as no one knew where he had really been the night before.

# Chapter 28

*June 1917, Paris, France*

Lieutenant McDougall looked exhausted when Evette met him in his office.

"Are you all right, monsieur?" she asked as she sat across from him.

He rubbed his eyes with his fists and fought back a yawn. "The Germans seemed aware of our plans this spring. My superiors think I should have done more to prevent the information getting out." The spring offensives had resulted in a high death toll with few gains, giving the two of them long hours but little to show for it.

Evette glanced at the men sitting behind their desks in the large open office or pacing away in smaller private rooms. She wondered which of them had chastised McDougall. "You did everything you could. We've followed up on every lead, and you caught nearly everyone."

"I didn't catch Lohr."

Evette folded her arms. "No."

McDougall stared out the window. "Somehow they knew. I wonder if he was their source."

Lohr seemed behind everything Evette had been fighting, but she didn't think it fair for the other officers to blame McDougall. He'd done his best, and she doubted Lohr was the only one who had known about the Chemin des Dames offensive. "It was an open secret. People talked about it in cafés and wrote letters about it. Anyone could have found out and passed the information on."

He turned back toward her and leaned forward. "I have another problem just as big."

"Another secret to keep?"

"Yes. One I am not sure can be kept. The French Army is in a poor state."

"Near the end of their strength, I imagine." The casualties that spring had been horrendous, and if Emile was a typical example, the army had been exhausted long before April.

"More serious than that. Mutiny."

Evette gasped. "Mutiny?"

"Yes. And if the Germans find out . . ."

"They could break through the lines and end the war."

McDougall nodded. "We are in a bit of a spot. No one is sure how far the unrest will spread. Censors are blocking news of it for now, and the French have the most mutinous units contained. But it only takes one spy to inform the Germans that large numbers of French troops are no longer willing to fight, and then disaster. We've got to round up the German spy networks once and for all."

"But how?" They'd already investigated or arrested everyone suspicious other than Lohr.

"I have permission to try something risky. We will release one of the spies we have already caught. Tell him the evidence against him was insufficient so he thinks he is really free. Follow him and see who he meets. We shall have to watch him around the clock, watch everyone he comes in contact with. Hope we are led to the right network. I plan to release someone who knows nothing about the mutiny, of course, but that doesn't mean he can't learn of it and tell the wrong people."

"Like playing with a live grenade . . . but if we don't try, we may not have any leads."

"Exactly." McDougall smiled slightly. It made him seem younger, more at ease. "Can I enlist your help?"

"Of course. Who are you releasing?"

"The man you found a few months ago who was planning to blow up train cars full of munitions. He had contact with the saboteur and the guards, and he must have contact with someone higher up."

"The one who owned the dog?" Evette remembered him, but she didn't think he would remember her face, which made her job easier.

McDougall paused as if searching his memory. "Yes. His name is Raoul Simon."

"When will you release him?"

"Tomorrow. Midafternoon."

Evette straightened in the chair. "I'll be ready."

"I shall see you have assistance. I want at least one set of eyes on Simon around the clock. Can you be here tomorrow at three in the afternoon?"

"Yes."

"I knew I could count on you." His gaze locked on her face, as it often did. "You know, Evette, you have beautiful eyes. Like a meadow after the rain."

Evette was silent for an awkward second, unsure what to say. No one other than her mother and Claire had complimented her before. "Thank you, sir."

"You can call me Howard, remember?"

"Thank you, Howard."

* * *

Evette spent the next six evenings tailing the released prisoner. Perhaps exulting in his new freedom, Simon ate well for supper, then took long strolls along the boulevards, making it difficult for her to follow him without being seen. She was forced to monitor him from a distance, left to hope the newspapers he purchased were simply for reading and didn't contain any secret messages. After he bought a paper from the same newspaperwoman the third day in a row, she suggested McDougall investigate the lady, but nothing came of it.

The following week, Evette loitered at cafés while he shopped at bookstores, sat on park benches while he spent his mornings at home, and wondered if something was finally happening when he left his apartment late one night. The sun had set, so it was easy to follow him as he walked five blocks to the east, then circled around the neighborhood. She worried he had seen her, but he doubled back without really looking around, as if following a set procedure rather than instinctively checking his back.

He eventually went into a home set back from the street with a yard full of overgrown bushes. Perhaps the inhabitants had lost their gardener to mobilization just as the Donovans had. Whatever the reason behind the neglect, the unruly vines made it easy for Evette to sneak through the iron gate and move toward the home without being seen.

Approaching the house benefited her little because the windows were darkened with blackout curtains. Something in her gut told her this wasn't an ordinary social call. She hesitated in the overgrowth. How long should she wait? Simon had already dined, but there were plenty of other possibilities.

Then a second man strode from the street to the home—Lohr.

Simon had become so monotonous that she was the only one watching him that night. Should she wait and tail Lohr instead? Or follow her instructions and stick to the original target? *Lohr.* That was the best option. But she also wanted to know what the two men would say to each other.

She crept around the house until she found a back door. It was locked. A nearby window, however, opened with only the faintest of squeaks, and she assumed the wind would disguise the slight sound. She had grown proficient using windows for entry and exit while trying to avoid her half brother.

Living with Gaspard had also taught her to walk silently, so she stepped first with the outside of her foot before putting her full weight on the floor as she crossed a kitchen illuminated by the embers of a dying fire. The kitchen exited into a dining hall. When she was halfway across the massive room, the sound of male voices suddenly sounded, coming closer. In panic, she looked around. Candles lit the room, but they revealed no hiding spots, and she didn't have time to search out the broom closet. A clean cloth covered the long table in the room's center, the edges reaching to the seat of each chair. She ducked under the table and stretched herself across four of the chairs. She was invisible there as long as no one pulled a chair out.

"I sent the cook and housekeeper to their quarters. Checked all the windows before you arrived."

"Hmm. But how did you get out of prison to meet me in the first place?"

"They let me out. Said they didn't have sufficient evidence to keep me."

"Lack of evidence usually doesn't stop them from holding someone who might be a danger to them."

"I have a few connections. Perhaps they assisted me anonymously."

The other man chuckled, a low, menacing sound. "Few people assist anonymously. They'd rather have credit, a reason to call in favors later."

"I told you I wasn't followed. I completed all the precautions you gave me."

"A source told me the British released a prisoner so they could follow him. I assume my source meant you."

Under the table, Evette nearly gasped. Lohr had a source who knew McDougall's plans?

Lohr continued. "Perhaps you succeeded in boring your tails."

"There weren't any tails."

"Or the tails are more skilled than you. Do you have any information for me?"

"No. I didn't dare look up my old contacts until I saw you. Besides, I don't have direction on how to proceed, nor the necessary funds. And if you think I'm being followed, perhaps I should delay further."

There was a pause and the sound of pacing. "I need you to get back to work. We need action. Just make sure you aren't followed. Hire all the saboteurs you can, use your previous contacts to determine the best targets. But be careful."

"I'll need money to hire saboteurs."

"I used what I had to bribe my source in British intelligence. He's expensive. Told me they have sources in Essen and in Munich but couldn't tell me anything about them. Said he needs more time to get his information and more money if he's to disclose it. I'm going back to Germany tomorrow. I'll bring what you need when I return in a few months." She heard the scratch of pen on paper above her on the table. "Another contact. One I knew before the war. He's not an idealist, so don't talk politics. But he can arrange funding if you say you're with the League."

Evette wished she could see what was written on the paper, wished they would name the source who had told Lohr about McDougall's plans.

Footsteps sounded, and the men moved farther away.

"I haven't learned much on this trip," Lohr said. "Almost nothing to speak of as far as useful intelligence, so I need results from you soon."

After that the voices were too muted for Evette to make out. She took a few deep breaths. She hadn't been discovered. Lohr didn't know about the mutinies. But Lohr did have multiple sources, and unless rearrested, Simon would soon been conducting sabotage projects all across Paris.

Evette slid from her hiding place and rushed to the window. She lifted the pane as she heard the front door close and voices, probably the servants, chattering a few rooms away. She waited until the men were out of the garden before following them, knowing she was leaving two windows open, something that would surely arouse suspicion. Regardless of the risk, she wanted to follow Lohr. Perhaps they could catch him before his return to Germany.

But when she reached the road, both men had disappeared. The only sign of life was a horse-drawn carriage turning the corner at the end of the street. She checked again that neither Lohr nor Simon was visible, then ran after the carriage. When she followed it around the corner, it was gone.

# Chapter 29

Unable to find Lohr or Simon, Evette went to McDougall's home to confess her failure. Madame Morel gave her the usual look of disapproval but went to rouse McDougall from his bed. She wished McDougall would tell Madame Morel what his work involved so she would stop assuming the worst.

"Evette?" McDougall turned back briefly. "Thank you, Madam Morel."

As soon as the housekeeper left, Evette spoke. "I lost him."

"Well, we know where he lives. I expect he shall return there before long. Hopefully he won't arrange anything untoward in the meantime."

"It's worse than that. He met with Lohr. I crawled through a window and listened to part of their conversation, but I lost them when they left." Evette looked at the floor, not wanting to see the disappointment in McDougall's eyes.

"Come into my office." He placed a gentle hand on her elbow.

When they were seated, Evette forced herself to look up.

McDougall watched her but didn't seem to condemn her. "So he met with Lohr?"

"Yes. Lohr told him he wants sabotage, lots of it, quickly. And he has at least two sources here in Paris. They didn't say either name, but one arranges money for the League, and the other is selling them information." Evette was about to tell McDougall that the second source was with British Intelligence, probably someone McDougall worked with, but would he believe her? What if he included the information in a report and Lohr's source found it? Or worse, what if McDougall was somehow involved? Evette pushed the thought from her head. She'd worked with McDougall for almost two years. He couldn't be a double agent. Still, she held that piece of information for later, focusing on the more urgent facts. "Lohr said he was leaving for Germany tomorrow, but he also said he hadn't learned much of significance. I assume that means he doesn't know about the mutinies."

"I can issue an alert with his description and try to stop him at the borders. I don't know how he's getting in and out, but I shall see that the appropriate people are watching for him." McDougall opened a drawer and held out a set of three keys to her. "Skeleton keys, in case you have to follow him inside again. Perhaps he has made it home."

It was a long, dark walk back to Simon's flat. A light shone through a crack in the curtains, so she assumed he was inside. Agent Fournier was due to relieve her at midnight, but he never came. She hid from yet another police patrol out looking for anything suspicious and cursed Fournier. Simon had been boring recently, but that wasn't an excuse to neglect one's duty.

Dawn found her bleary-eyed and hungry, but a scream and several loud, excited voices drove the sleepiness away. The noise came from farther down the block. As Evette approached, she saw a small crowd forming. In the center of the commotion, she recognized Agent Fournier sprawled on the grass next to the sidewalk, a knife protruding from his back. Evette gasped and took several steps backward on shaky legs. A middle-aged woman sobbed and gestured as she recounted how she'd discovered the body.

Evette's relief had come; he just hadn't made it to her. Fournier's murder escalated her assignment from dangerous to deadly.

She couldn't neglect Simon, especially not while Lohr was in France, so she returned to her post. She was terrified that he might be the murderer, but she followed him anyway when she caught sight of him leaving his house. Where was he going so early after such a late night?

Six blocks later, he stopped and sat at a table outside a café. Evette held back until a French officer joined him and Simon slid an envelope to him. She suspected it was a bribe of some sort, which meant Simon had gotten money while she hadn't been watching. She sat a few tables away with her back to Simon, but she faced the reflective glass window of the café so he couldn't sneak away without her knowledge. She ordered and paid for coffee and a roll while the men did the same.

"Things are bad," a voice said in a whisper.

"How so?" Simon asked.

"The poilus are sick of fighting. All along the front, the men are saying they'll hold the line but they won't attack. Soldiers singing the 'Internationale,' issuing manifestos, refusing to obey orders. It's mutiny on a scale so large it's frightening."

"Is the Communist revolution spreading to France?"

There was a pause. "I wish that were the case. Some involved are Communists. Most have just lost all trust in their leaders. They've been at war a long time, seen a lot of men killed. They aren't willing to die for some general's glory anymore. They'd rather live."

"Imagine that—wanting to live."

The officer muttered something unintelligible.

"I have a friend who might find this information useful. You're sure it's as bad as all that?"

"Yes."

"Enjoy your breakfast. I need to catch him before he heads out of town."

In the window, Evette saw Simon leave his table and rush away. If Simon told Lohr about the mutinies, it would be a disaster. She slowly counted to twenty, then calmly stood and followed, hoping the officer wasn't paying attention.

Simon's rapid stride drew curious glances from other passersby, and since she had to match her pace to his, so did Evette's. Dozens of other pedestrians hid her from Simon, but she wished another of McDougall's agents were there to help her. Outside a hotel, Simon questioned a heavy-set woman wearing a porter's uniform. Evette was too far away to hear what was said, but the woman gestured to the lobby, and Simon darted inside.

Evette followed.

"May I help you?" The porter scrutinized her through narrowed eyes, making Evette suspect that her all-night vigil was evident in the state of her hair and clothing. "The hotel lobby is for paying guests and their friends only."

"The man who just went inside is my husband. I want to make sure he's not meeting another woman." Evette's simple lie made the porter hesitate long enough for Evette to brush past her.

Inside, Simon paced across the lobby. He saw her when she arrived, but his attention quickly turned to Lohr, who descended the staircase with his luggage.

Evette scanned the lobby. An elderly man was stationed at the desk, and a few prosperous-looking couples sat in plush armchairs, reading papers and chatting. Ideally, both Simon and Lohr would be arrested. She walked to the clerk and whispered, "Please call the gendarmes at once."

He raised an eyebrow.

"It's urgent. Please. A matter of national security. Those two men are spies."

His scowl told her he didn't believe her. With all the spy scares over the past few years, it wasn't surprising, but it was disappointing.

Lohr noticed Simon and strode toward him. The clerk and the porter wouldn't help her, and Evette wasn't sure any of the hotel patrons would either. Desperate to prevent the two from talking to each other, she took a chance. "Stop those men!" she shouted. "They're spies!"

All noise ceased. The middle-aged women stared, and their husbands rose to their feet but didn't move forward.

Lohr and Simon proved their guilt by bolting for the door. Evette flew after them, but they turned opposite directions when they reached the street.

"Stop!" she yelled again. "He's a spy!" She turned after Lohr, chasing him until he shoved a coachman from his parked carriage and shook the reins, urging the horse into a trot.

Her lungs ached as he drove off. She searched for a horse or a car, but there were no other horses nearby, and all the automobiles were empty, so she couldn't ask for a ride, and she didn't know how to drive. She ran after the carriage for a block but fell farther and farther behind. A gendarme stopped and questioned her. He was skeptical while she explained the situation, and in the meantime, Lohr vanished.

When it was over, she walked slowly to McDougall's office, fighting back tears of frustration and exhaustion.

He listened in silence while she told him about his dead agent and the successful escapes of both Simon and Lohr. "I'm sorry," she finished. "I tried, but I didn't know what else to do."

"We shall catch them yet. The important thing is you prevented Lohr from hearing about the mutinies. That act alone may have saved the Allied cause."

# Chapter 30

DESPITE MCDOUGALL'S REASSURANCE, EVETTE FELT her failure for days. Perhaps she should have followed the men instead of interrupting them. Maybe a gendarme or an army officer would have arrived in time to arrest them. Or maybe McDougall was right, and waiting would have allowed vital intelligence to make it to Germany.

Now that Simon knew Evette's face, she no longer watched his flat. According to McDougall, he hadn't gone back. He had disappeared, just as Lohr had. After the all-consuming assignment, she needed the break, but it only gave her more time to wish she could have done things differently.

Claire tried to cheer her up with piano lessons, and Evette cleaned the entire Donovan mansion, learned how to cook dozens of new dishes, and wrote frequent letters to her brother. She hadn't heard from him in weeks, and she was starting to worry.

Two weeks after the incident at the hotel, she went out for a bit of fresh evening air. As she neared the end of her stroll and the Donovan home came into view, a man emerged from the gate. Evette caught only a glimpse of his face, but it was enough for her to recognize him. Simon. He had found out where she lived.

He hadn't seemed to notice her, so she pulled the brim of her hat down and crossed to the other side of the street as he came her direction. He might have been responsible for the murder of the other agent, and she didn't want to give him the opportunity to repeat the crime. She watched him in her peripheral vision and only breathed without constriction after he passed her. She turned and tried to work up the courage to follow him as he strode away.

She hesitated. Would Simon come back and attack her in her bedroom? Had he left a package for her, one full of phosgene gas? Had he done something to Claire?

Concern for her friend drove her across the road. She had promised she would never endanger the Donovans, but Simon had thwarted her efforts to keep them safe. She remembered Captain Flynn's worry, his concern that having a spy live with Claire was a bad idea. He'd been right.

"Claire?" Evette called as she rushed inside. "Claire?"

Mr. Donovan stepped from his office. "Claire went to play the piano at the hospital."

Evette nodded, remembering now. Claire had left to do her new volunteer work shortly before Evette had gone on a walk. "Did anyone stop by while I was gone?"

"No."

"Was there anything in the mail for me?"

Mr. Donovan shook his head. "Mademoiselle Touny, is something wrong?" When she didn't immediately answer, he motioned her into the parlor and continued. "Have a seat. I know you have done your best to keep your employment secret, but I'm not so witless that I haven't guessed, and discretion isn't one of Claire's strengths. She's let enough slip to confirm my suspicions. Are you in some kind of trouble?"

Evette stared at Claire's father. "You know what I do?"

"Tracking spies and ferreting out saboteurs? If you've had any success, France owes you her thanks. The United States too, now that we are officially allies."

Evette absorbed her shock and took a calming breath. "One of the saboteurs escaped. I just saw him outside your garden. I must have somehow led him here. I didn't mean to, but I fear I've put both you and Claire in danger."

Mr. Donovan studied her carefully for a moment, then called, "Franke?"

The butler came a moment later. "Yes, sir?"

"Have the coachman get the carriage ready, please." As soon as Mr. Franke went to complete his errand, Mr. Donovan turned back to Evette. "I don't want Claire coming back unescorted. I'll pick her up. I guess you better come with me. But first we'll call the gendarmes. You can provide a description of this man?"

"Yes."

"Good. We'll go make the call."

She followed Mr. Donovan into his office, grateful for his all-business and no-blame manner. She had put him and his daughter at risk, but rather than making her feel guilty, he was doing his best to fix the problem.

* * *

It took them two weeks, but eventually the gendarmes arrested Simon. Unfortunately, he held his tongue regarding his upcoming projects, his methods of contacting Lohr, and how he had tracked down Evette. Two days after his arrest, a boxcar full of 75mm shells exploded at the train yard, and Simon took credit for it. Then a munitions factory caught on fire, and a ship sank in the English Channel. Simon took credit for those too and said the League was behind seven other disasters that followed Lohr's most recent trip to Paris.

Another week passed, and Evette was finally starting to feel safe again when Mr. Franke told her a French soldier awaited her in the parlor. She wasn't expecting anyone. McDougall was on leave in Scotland, and even if he wasn't, he wore a British uniform, not a French one. Emile was the only French soldier who knew her address, but he would have written first. When she came into the parlor, the man who stood before her was a stranger. He was of average height, with dark hair and a well-worn but clean uniform.

"Are you Evette Touny?"

"Yes."

"I was a friend of your brother's."

A chill crept through Evette's veins. "Was?"

"I'm sorry to be the one to tell you. He died about a month ago. He asked me to deliver a letter because he knew it wouldn't make it through the censors. I had to wait until I was on furlough before I could come."

She took a deep breath, struggling against the tightness gripping her throat. "How did he die?"

The man held the letter out. "I think the letter explains. Most of his effects were shipped to your mother, along with official word of what happened. But Emile's version is here." Evette took the letter with trembling hands. His delivery made, the soldier excused himself and left as quickly as he could.

Evette collapsed into a nearby armchair and forced herself to breathe. She had known Emile's life was at risk from the moment he was called up, had worried something was wrong when she'd stopped receiving his letters. But if he had died on the battlefield, how could he have written to her? Had he been wounded? Was the letter written in a hospital while he slowly succumbed to mortal wounds?

It took her a few minutes to work up sufficient courage to open the last letter she would ever receive from her brother. Tears blurred her vision, but curiosity forced her to blink them away long enough to read his words.

*Dear Evette,*

*I assume you have now heard that I am dead, either from the bearer of this letter or perhaps through Mama. I'm not sure what they'll tell Mama when they inform her of my death. Maybe nothing. Maybe the truth. Maybe they'll weave one more lie and tell her I died in action. They're good at lies.*

*Today I was court-martialed for mutiny. I don't suppose word has leaked to civilians yet, but our army is spent. Not only in my sector but everywhere, if the rumors are true. It's unwise to trust rumor, but the poilus are less likely to create fiction than the newspapers are. All their propaganda—saying the Boches are inept when they're well-trained and determined, talking of glory and honor where none exists. It's all eyewash. I take some solace in knowing I will no longer be subject to their twisted version of the war.*

*My squad was ordered to advance across ground covered by Boche machine guns. The orders specified we were to move at once, during daylight, rather than wait until dark. Taking the trenches on the other side of no-man's land wouldn't have gained anything for France, and it would have resulted in most of our deaths. But a colonel wanted to have something to report in dispatches, some gain, no matter how useless, even if it cost us our lives. We stayed in our trench. They can't execute everyone who refuses orders. To do so would cull the French Army more than Verdun did. I was the spokesman, so the punishment has fallen on me.*

*I am to be executed in the morning.*

*You'll probably think me a coward. I've been told that such I have become, as well as a traitor. But you can't understand how hard it is to know your life is of less value than a box of ammunition. Our leaders don't care how many of us perish as long as the enemy loses more men before we're exhausted. I can't go on in a war I didn't ask for and that I can't win. I've given everything I can for three long years and am valued less than a broken artillery piece. At least the artillery can be used for scrap metal. The poilus, even the living ones, are only good for absorbing Boche bullets and Boche shells. I've been told I'm a defeatist. I feel not like a defeatist but like a man who has been awaiting execution for years. It will happen in a few hours by my own countrymen instead of my hereditary enemy. The means are surprising, but the end is not.*

*I am sorry for the dishonor I will bring to your name. If I go to heaven, I shall look down upon you often. If I go to hell, Verdun has prepared me. I can't imagine damnation being any worse than what I've already seen.*

*I regret the way our last meeting ended. The war isn't your fault, and it isn't your fault that your role in it has been less difficult than mine. I wouldn't want you to suffer. I really wouldn't. It may take time, but I hope eventually you can think of me without repugnance. Remember me as I was before the war, before the army crushed my soul and robbed me of my life.*

*Your brother,*
*Emile*

Evette sat in silence for a long time after she finished the letter, ignoring the little terrier at her feet, trying to understand all her brother had said. She didn't feel repugnance at his actions, just sorrow at what the war had done to him and to countless others like him. It wasn't fair. It wasn't right. Pain clutched her heart, holding it so tightly she doubted she would ever be the same again.

* * *

"I have seen you nearly every day since I returned from leave, and you have been wearing black each time," McDougall said to Evette. "And during that same period, I haven't seen you smile, not even once. Is something wrong?"

Evette sat across from him in his Paris office, reviewing leads and discussing which of their tips and suspicions were worth pursuing. "I'm in mourning. My brother is dead."

"I'm sorry." Then he hesitated. "The abusive brother?"

"No. The kind one. My full brother."

"You were close to him?"

"As close as one can be with a man controlled by the army and its censors."

The features of McDougall's face softened as he studied her. "I had a brother. He died at the beginning of the war. I wish I could say we were close. He was a year and a half older than me, but he seemed to do everything right. I seemed to do everything wrong."

"Were you a troublemaker?"

"No. But I was never as smart or as handsome or as brave as Henry was, not according to my father. Not that it matters now." McDougall shook his head. "Would you like some time off? I know death is common, but that does not mean it is easy."

She thought of sitting around the Donovan mansion with nothing to do, searching for ways to amuse or distract herself. What would Emile think of that? "I think a break would make it worse."

"May I ask how he died?"

Evette had feared that question. She wasn't ashamed of her brother, but she knew how it would sound to everyone else, to all the people who hadn't seen what the war had done to him. Still, she told the truth. McDougall had probably been trained to detect lies. "He was executed for mutiny."

She wondered if the news would make him think less of her, but he reached across the desk. "You are better than both your brothers, Evette. You are neither a bully nor a coward." He grasped her hand, and she knew he didn't condemn her. But what she really needed was someone to believe her when she said her brother, despite his execution for mutiny, was no coward. He was just a different type of casualty.

The next day Evette received a box from McDougall. Inside was a bracelet with semiprecious stones in a rainbow of colors fitted in gold. A note accompanied it. *Losing a brother is hard no matter how he dies.*

"It's beautiful," Claire said when Evette showed it to her. "That's a generous gift from someone on a lieutenant's salary. I knew he fancied you."

Claire's simple statement caused something to click in Evette's head. Lohr had bribed someone in British Intelligence who knew about Simon's release and the plans to tail him. She hadn't thought McDougall would sabotage his own project, but she hadn't thought her brother capable of mutiny either. Was McDougall's expensive gift purchased with Lohr's money?

# Chapter 31

*September 1917, Essen, Germany*

JULIAN WAITED IN THE HALLWAY outside the study after serving Herr Lohr and Herr Sauer their ersatz coffee.

"I arranged for a group of agents to watch the port in Marseilles," Lohr said. "They'll send in information about departing ships so U-boats can sink them. Then I went to Paris. I've a new source there. Someone in British Intelligence."

Sauer's intake of breath was audible. "I'm impressed. How?"

"Bribery. But he's expensive."

"If you keep getting the results you're getting, I'll see to it that Herr Meyer continues your funding. Increases it if necessary."

"He said they have men in Germany," Lohr said. "Couldn't give me details like an address or an alias, but one is in Essen."

"Here?"

"Yes. If I pay him enough, he'll find more information for me. If not a name, then a list of information they've gotten from him. If we can look at what he's telling them, we might find our man."

"Spies. I hate the lot of them, present company excepted. The sooner we string the British informer up, the better. When will you go back?"

"I'm not sure. It's getting more difficult to cross the border, and I'm tired. I thought the week I spent resting in that Bavarian inn would help, but the weariness goes deeper than that. I didn't know the war would last so long."

"It was supposed to be over before the leaves fell," Sauer said, his voice worn. "It wasn't supposed to last long enough to kill my granddaughter or call my second grandson to the front."

"I'm sorry for your loss."

"If we don't win the war, more disasters will follow. I hope your health improves quickly, because I need you in France."

"There is another reason I'm reluctant to return. I ran into a problem in Paris. One of my contacts was arrested in February, released in June. I was hesitant to meet with him when I was last there, but he insisted. I hid after our meeting and saw a shadow chase the carriage I put him on. Someone was following him. He got away that night, but a woman interrupted a meeting the next day, nearly got us both arrested. If he can stay clean for a few months, I'll assume the threat is past. But I fear they'll find him again. I just hope he won't lead them to any of my other sources."

"Does he know many of them?" Sauer asked.

"A few saboteurs. And one other."

The men were quiet for a time, so Julian sneaked away. He wished Herr Sauer would discuss Gerta's death and Willi's enlistment with Dorothea the way he had with Lohr. She needed her father's comfort, needed to know that he too was hurting despite his calm appearance. But Julian's concern for Dorothea's feelings were minor compared to the fear he felt for his life. He didn't doubt that he was the agent Lohr sought and Sauer planned to hang. Did anyone other than McDougall know his alias, his location? They could catch him with less. Sauer was brilliant; if he knew the spy reported on Sauer's work and about the Krupp factory, he would soon suspect his Alsatian groundskeeper.

During supper, Julian watched Lohr, thinking of the unshakable weariness he'd spoken of. Deep lines surrounded his mouth, dark skin shadowed his eyelids, and gray stubble aged his jawline. Julian recognized the signs of exhaustion because he saw the same things in himself whenever he looked in the mirror.

* * *

Julian rubbed the sleep from his eyes, lit a match, and checked his watch. It was still a few hours before dawn. He normally wrote his reports before he went to sleep, but he'd been so tired the previous night after staying up to eavesdrop on Lohr and Sauer that he'd postponed it. He lit a candle and frowned when he retrieved his invisible ink. The liquid was almost gone. This was probably his last report to write before he met with McDougall again in a few days, but it was a long one. He scrutinized the amount left and decided to add a little water so it wouldn't run out.

Taking the vial with him, he went upstairs to the kitchen and added about a teaspoon of liquid. Dorothea would be up soon, so he piled kindling in the stove and started a fire with the wood he and Franz had been stockpiling all summer. In the coming winter, the Kallweit family would have enough firewood to keep them warm. The food situation brought Julian less confidence. He had helped Dorothea preserve some of the garden's produce, but what would another harsh winter do to Franz's health? Would it leave the boy susceptible to otherwise mild disease just as the previous winter had left

Gerta weak? With Lohr on his trail, Julian was unlikely to stay the winter in the Sauer household, but he wanted the best for Franz, for Dorothea, maybe even for Herr Sauer. The crusty old man would eagerly execute Julian if he knew the truth, but his intelligence and hard-nosed mannerisms had won him Julian's reluctant admiration.

Back in his room, Julian pulled out rough-surfaced paper for a letter. He almost addressed it to his parents, but what if his mother hadn't survived the past winter? The letter wouldn't make it to Calais anyway, but the image of his father reading the letter all alone convinced him to switch recipients. Lately he'd been addressing letters to people he'd only met once, so he kept with that pattern and addressed it to Maximo's widow.

When the cover letter was sufficiently long to mask his report, he switched from black ink to colorless ink. Halfway through, a knock at his door startled him.

"Come in."

Dorothea opened the door wide enough to stick her head inside. "I made some ersatz coffee. It's hot now if you'd like some before you go to the factory. It tastes almost like the real thing."

"Yes, please. I'll be up in a few minutes."

Dorothea nodded, but her expression, downturned lips and pinched eyes, didn't change. She never smiled anymore. As she pulled back into the hallway, she stopped abruptly and stared at the little desk in Julian's room. Her eyebrows scrunched together, and she glanced from Julian to the desk before leaving. When the door closed, Julian realized what the problem was. He'd left his pen in the clear bottle of invisible ink.

* * *

Julian did his best to pretend nothing was wrong when he went to breakfast that morning. He caught Dorothea watching him several times, but she quickly looked away whenever he noticed. Before he escaped to the factory, he hid his report under his mattress and his ink outside in a tree, high enough that he didn't think Franz would find it, even if the boy decided to play outdoors.

His shift was normal, but a growing concern gnawed at him. Was it safe to go back to the Sauer estate? Dorothea normally gave Herr Lohr a wide berth when he visited her father. Lohr would leave that afternoon. Would she talk to Herr Sauer then? Or would concern for what she'd seen prompt her to talk to him sooner?

If Julian could make it another twenty-four hours, McDougall would be in town for their meeting, and McDougall could get him out of Germany. He had been hoping to last a little longer. The range tested new types of shells weekly, and the factory workers he went to the pubs with after their shifts ended were steadily growing more free with their information.

Could he last another month? More pressing, could he last another day? He approached the Sauer estate slowly after his shift, entering through the kitchen door, where he hoped no one would hear him. Maybe he could detect trouble, if it existed, while he still had a chance to escape.

Franz grinned when Julian walked in. "Hello, Herr Becker."

"Hello, Franz. I hope your smile means there is good news."

"Grandpapa went to Berlin this afternoon with Herr Lohr. He said he would bring me back a sausage."

"Food is the best kind of good news." Julian looked at what was spread out for supper. At least there were fresh green beans from the garden to go along with the cheap bread and turnip jam. "Have you and your mother eaten?"

"Yes."

Hungry and knowing he should eat now in case he had to run later, Julian got to work on his meal. "Anything exciting happen today?" He waited, wondering if Franz would mention visits from the police or worried conversations between the adults.

"A letter from Kurt arrived. I pulled dead plants from the garden after school. Then Mama had me work on my reading."

"You've done an excellent job with the garden."

"I have?"

Julian nodded. "Did you pick these green beans?"

"Yes."

"They are delicious."

Franz beamed and kept Julian company while he ate. The poor boy needed a father who could communicate in person, not merely through letters. Herr Sauer loved his grandchildren, but he didn't show it in ways a boy of eleven could easily detect. Julian supposed he was a type of father figure to the boy, but he felt inadequate, inexperienced. And in the back of his head was a worry that any good influence he had on the boy would backfire if Julian's real identity was revealed.

At twenty-six years old, Julian was old enough to be a father. Not to an eleven-year-old, of course, but if it hadn't been for the war, might he have found a nice girl to marry, someone like the one in Maximo's village, and had a few children by now? The thought of having a family was pleasant, but with Lohr and Sauer on his trail and Dorothea wary, his chances of becoming a husband and a father were so slight that they scarcely existed. It was time to get out of Germany before his future disappeared completely.

# Chapter 32

JULIAN DIDN'T SEE DOROTHEA THAT night. Franz said his mother felt ill and had gone to bed early. It was unlike her to retire without seeing Franz safely to bed, especially with her father in Berlin. Was she really unwell? Or did she suspect Julian? But if she suspected Julian, would she let him near her son?

The next day when he returned from the factory, it was almost an exact repeat of the night before. Dorothea was in her room, and Franz waited in the kitchen. Apprehension had whittled Julian's appetite down to almost nothing, so he gave most of his food to the boy.

After Franz went to bed, Julian took the report from under his mattress and walked farther into Essen. He loitered in the streets, watching for anyone who was doing the same. When he was confident no one was tracking him, he made a few turns, doubled back, and crept into an apartment building. The third door from the entrance was unlocked, and inside, the Dutchman waited. The two nodded to each other, and Julian strode into the back room, where McDougall sat.

Julian handed over his last report. To his dismay, his hands shook.

"Is everything all right?" McDougall asked.

"I think I've blown my cover. Frau Kallweit interrupted me while I was writing this. She saw the ink and saw that I was writing on a page already full of words."

McDougall's mouth turned down in alarm. "Has she said anything?"

"Not to me, but she's suspicious. Herr Sauer went to Berlin for a few days. He'll be back soon, and the two of them will figure it out."

"I was under the impression you were the one doing things like ironing and heating up ovens, so she can't use heat to reveal what you've written. Besides, I have your report now. It's completely safe."

"She's done more housework since I started at the factory." He imagined it had been a big adjustment for someone who had grown up with a maid and a cook. "They don't have to actually see the report to know what's going on." A mere suspicion would be sufficient for them to make inquiries into Alsace, where he claimed to have been born. Or they might lock him up without an investigation. War made people desperate, and Germany was in a life-or-death struggle.

McDougall pulled a small tube from his pocket. "New type of ink. Give me your handkerchief." Julian complied, and McDougall spread the paste on the white cloth. "Next time you need ink, dip your handkerchief in water, and you'll have an acceptable solution. This one has to have the proper reagent, not just heat, or it stays invisible. Neither Frau Kallweit nor Herr Sauer will have the correct chemicals."

"They have friends who might. What reagent does it use?"

McDougall was silent.

"Well?"

"I have been asked not to disclose that information."

Julian swallowed back a mouthful of worry. "Right. In case I'm captured. Because everyone knows my luck is running out."

"Nonsense."

"No, common sense. I can't last much longer, not with my cover hanging by a thread. And there's more. Lohr has a source in Paris, someone working with British Intelligence. They know there's a mole in Essen. They don't have all the information they need yet, but next time Lohr goes to France, he'll have plenty of bribery money. Even if he doesn't learn my alias, he'll learn what information I've passed on. It won't take them long to figure out I'm the man they want."

McDougall's lips hardened. "A source in British Intelligence? Impossible."

"I heard it from Lohr. There's no reason for him to lie about something like that."

"He could lie to get more money for himself. I will look into it, but don't assume Lohr isn't playing Sauer the same way he's playing his contacts in Paris."

"I want to leave, Lieutenant. You can get me out before Lohr pieces everything together. If we wait until your next visit, it will be too late."

McDougall's eyes narrowed. "You want to leave? Because one middle-aged woman saw you writing a letter and one man who lies for a living claims to have a source in British Intelligence? We need you here gathering information about that Paris Gun and collecting all your bits of information from those factory workers. You can't quit now." He rapped his fingers along the table and examined Julian the way a poilu looked at a louse before plucking it from his uniform. "Frankly I am shocked that you would ask to abandon your assignment when no one has yet confronted you."

"Once they confront me, it will be too late. Do you expect me to stick around until they arrest me?"

"I expect you to keep to your post until the war ends, or, yes, until you are arrested and executed. What I don't expect is for you to turn into a coward."

"A coward?" Julian had thought McDougall was different from the officers in the field, the ones who drove their men past the breaking point. He'd been wrong. "You try living a lie for two years and see how you manage!"

McDougall huffed. "So that's the problem? You're tired?"

"Yes, I'm tired of deception. You don't understand how difficult it is. The Kallweits are good people, and I'm lying to them. Every day I'm lying to them! And sending you information that's likely to get their sons killed. They've been kind to me, and I'm stabbing them in the back."

"So you want to leave and betray all the French soldiers who depend on your information instead?"

"None of them would see it as betrayal."

McDougall crossed his arms and slumped back in his chair. "No, the average poilu probably wouldn't. The French Army is practically in a state of mutiny."

"What?"

McDougall glanced over at him. "Same as you. They've had enough of war. Seen too many people die, too many men wasted in fruitless charges across no-man's land. They called General Petain in, and he quelled the problem, but it was dicey for a while. One wrong word and the Germans could have waltzed through the French lines."

"But they didn't find out?"

"A little sparrow helped me track a spy who was carrying the information to Lohr, who would have carried it to the Germans. Bit of a close call, it was."

Julian sat in the chair next to McDougall. "A sparrow?"

"Code name for another agent. One who hasn't given up on her duty."

"Her?"

"Aye. A lass helped prevent a disaster of enormous proportions by keeping the wrong information out of German hands. And I still need you here because if that factory down the road comes up with something that can break through our lines, we need as much warning as we can get, and you are in a position to give us that information long before it trickles down to a captured German prisoner."

Julian was quiet.

McDougall picked up the letter, skimming through the cover script. "I see this one is addressed to a friend's widow. Stay at your post, and keep a few more women from becoming war widows. Or turn coward, forget your duty, and let the Germans win the war. Your choice, Julian. Your choice."

\* \* \*

Julian stayed. He returned to Herr Sauer's home and continued his work, knowing it might soon lead to his arrest.

Dorothea's health recovered, but Julian saw little of her. She spent most of her time in the library tutoring Franz or outside strolling around the garden.

When Sauer returned, Julian was the first to greet him. "Welcome home, Herr Sauer." Julian took the man's coat. "I hope you had a good journey."

"Politically it was a nightmare. But the shopping was worthwhile." Sauer held up a potato sack and dropped it into Julian's outstretched arms.

Julian assumed Lohr hadn't managed a trip to France and back during the week Sauer had been gone, so Sauer was unlikely to suspect his employee for the time being. Julian hung Sauer's coat in the closet, then opened the sack. It contained a smaller pouch of sugar, several loaves of bread, and sausages. He smiled as he remembered Maximo and some of his other comrades calling the Germans stupid sausage eaters. Then his smile grew sad as he thought of little Gerta and what this nourishment might have meant for her last winter. It didn't matter that their countries were at war. The little waif still held a few pieces of his heart.

He took the food to the kitchen, debating whether he ought to cook a feast or ration the food to make it last longer.

Franz came bounding into the kitchen as Julian filled a kettle with water. "Grandpapa said he brought food."

Julian handed a loaf of rye bread to the boy, whose eyes widened as he saw it wasn't the normal war bread. When Julian was Franz's age, he would have ripped off a chunk and eaten it immediately, but Franz placed it on a cutting board, caressing it with care.

"May I cut a small piece now?"

Julian nodded his permission. "How are your mother's lessons?"

"They would be going better if Mama did not insist on having me memorize passages of Goethe."

"Goethe is perhaps a bit rough for an eleven-year-old. We need to find you some good adventure stories."

"Like what?"

Just like that, another hole in Julian's cover story appeared. Though his mother's first language was German, the only book she had in that language was the Bible. Borrowing books from his neighbors had turned up only French titles. Julian had no idea which authors were popular for young boys in Germany. "My mother wasn't as intent on encouraging me to read as your mother is,"

Julian lied. "So I didn't read as much as I should have when younger, but I hope you'll do better than I did. Perhaps your grandpapa can recommend something interesting. Or your brothers. Do Kurt and Willi have anything worthwhile on the bookshelves in their rooms?"

"They wouldn't let me borrow their books."

"You're older now, much more careful than you were when you were nine. Write to them and ask." Julian almost suggested other questions Franz should include to his brothers, thinking to learn information from them, but his cover was so fragile that he doubted either brother would have a chance to receive Franz's message, let alone return it, before Julian was executed. In that instant, Julian decided supper would be a celebration. It might be his last time dining with the Kallweit family, and he wanted Franz to have a good memory of it.

# Chapter 33

THE DAY AFTER HERR SAUER returned, the family received a telegram that said Willi was coming home. The telegram included no details other than the date, but in Dorothea's eagerness to see her second son again, she seemed too preoccupied to discuss the strange letter written by their caretaker with her father. Even the normally phlegmatic Herr Sauer was more cheerful than usual, anticipation coming out in an occasional whistle and more patience with Franz when the boy hid in Sauer's study to avoid his chores.

Three days after the telegram arrived, the promised date of Willi's homecoming, Julian returned from his shift expecting the house to be in commotion. He was surprised to find Franz sitting in the kitchen like normal.

"Has Willi come home yet?"

Franz nodded.

"Well, where is he?" Even though the young man had probably been shooting his countrymen, Julian was eager to see him.

"He's resting."

The telegram had said nothing of an injury, nothing about a medical convalescence. Everyone had assumed Willi was coming home for leave, but Franz was far too subdued. "Is something wrong, Franz?"

"His left arm is gone."

Julian took a seat by the boy.

"He said he couldn't hold paper and write at the same time, so he couldn't send us letters from the hospital."

Unless things were vastly different in German hospitals, Julian assumed Willi could have found a nurse or a Red Cross lady to help with a letter. But he'd seen other soldiers use flimsier excuses to postpone telling their families of an injury. "Did he say what happened?"

"A French shell shattered his arm. The doctor couldn't save it, so he cut if off." Franz bit at his lower lip. "But it's not just his arm. He looks like a ghost, and he seems so much older than the last time I saw him."

Julian put his hand on the boy's shoulder. "Amputations take time to adjust to. And he'll be extra tired from the journey. There were probably people staring at him, people asking him about the war."

"Will he ever be the same?"

Julian hesitated before answering. No, a man wasn't the same after combat or after losing a limb. Was Franz old enough to understand? "Well, his arm won't grow back."

"I know that." Franz wiped at a tear but tried to hide the motion. "But will he ever play with me again? Will he smile and tell jokes like he used to?"

"Give him some time. He'll laugh again, but probably not for a while."

Franz nodded and asked about the carrots in the garden. Julian was glad for the change in subject. When the boy seemed happier, Julian excused himself. Walking past Sauer's study, he overheard Dorothea speaking with her father.

"What will he do without an arm?"

"You can do lots of things with only one arm."

"Like what?"

"He could be a teacher," Sauer said. "A scientist. A politician."

"No, he won't be a politician!"

"Fine. But there are options. I'll see that he gets the best prosthetic money can buy. Any education he wants. He's still recovering, Dorothea, but he's a strong young man. He'll adapt."

Julian went on, stopping outside Willi's room. The door was open a crack, so Julian peeked in, but Willi was asleep. Franz was right; Willi looked older, like someone who had suffered a long illness. His complexion was gray, even in the sunlight, and his skin hung from his bones much like his mother's had since wartime rationing had so drastically reduced her weight. The sound of Willi's breathing reminded him of the other men Julian had been with in the hospital. Slightly strained, weary beyond anything a civilian could experience. But the permeating hospital scent of chemicals and infected flesh was replaced with the smell of pine coming from Willi's open window.

It was several days before Julian saw Willi awake. The boy sat outside one evening on a chair, a blanket on his legs, his shirt hanging strangely on him. Julian assumed Dorothea would soon tailor the lad's shirts to better fit him, part of the long road to adjustment.

"It's good to see you again, Willi."

Willi gave a half smile in momentary greeting. Julian sat next to him on the porch, and together they watched Franz pull weeds and dying plants from the garden.

"Does it hurt still?" Julian eventually asked.

Willi turned toward him, surprise on his face. "Yes. Even the part that's gone, but most people look at me like I must be lying when I say that."

"I was in a military hospital, and I've known other amputees. The nerves remember."

Willi nodded. "I'm glad to be away from there. The hospital was a foul place."

Julian had never been in a German military hospital, but he assumed it wasn't too different from a French military hospital. "Smelly, crowded . . ."

"Hopeless."

"Yes."

"No one seemed to care. The doctors and orderlies were always in a hurry, always needing to see someone else. It would have been so easy to let myself die, especially when they took my arm. The next hospital was a little better. There were nurses there, and some of them were kind." A wan smile pulled at his lips. "And some of them were beautiful. It was strange to see women again."

"I imagine it's also strange to be home."

"Yes. I miss Gerta. She could have made me glad to be home again. I didn't think I was ready to come back, but they needed the bed for someone else."

"Your mother is glad to have you. She would rather take care of you here than let a stranger help you."

"I suppose so."

"And Franz is glad to have you back, but he's also worried about you."

Willi stared at his brother more intently. "He's a good worker."

"You should see all the brushwood he gathered. And your grandfather bartered for mature trees." Julian had spent hours chopping them into logs small enough to fit into stoves made for burning coal. "You'll be warm this winter, even if you can't get any coal."

"Do you . . . do you suppose a man can learn to chop wood with one arm?"

Julian considered the question carefully before answering. "I'm not sure. Life will be different for you. But it can still be good."

Willi turned his gaze to Julian, a slight frown marring his face. "I didn't expect war to be like it was."

"No one ever does."

"Kurt ought to have warned me."

"Would you have believed him?"

Willi shrugged. "Maybe not. And I don't know if he could have put it into words anyway. How do you describe what it's like to see men all around you getting ripped apart by artillery? Or explain the horror of a tank coming toward you through a shroud of smoke? It's not at all how Grandpapa described it."

"This war is different from the one your grandfather fought."

"The more experienced men tried to explain. Taught us how to use holes and depressions in the ground to our advantage, warned us not to huddle together during a shelling. But when the first bombardment came, I couldn't think. I was too terrified to do anything but cower on the ground."

"That's normal."

"Maybe so. But it felt pathetic."

"The shellings were always the worst." Julian's eyes strayed west toward the front lines. "They were bad when I was there, and I hear they've only gotten worse."

"I thought I would hate them more."

"The artillery?"

"No, the British. And the French. But instead I felt sorry for them. They were stuck in the trenches just like me, hoping their officers wouldn't ask them to do anything stupid, praying the next round of artillery would fall somewhere other than on top of them. It's strange, but I felt a bit of a kinship with them. We had more in common than I thought we would."

Julian stared at his hands, thinking of all the times he too had felt sorry for the men on the other side of no-man's land. "Willi, you're a compassionate person. I'm glad the war didn't take that from you."

"No, it took my arm instead."

"Better your arm than your soul."

Willi's eyes watered. "I suppose I know that, but I don't feel it." He glanced at his empty sleeve. "I wish things had turned out differently."

"We all do, Willi. I think we all do."

# Chapter 34

WARREN SPENT HIS NEXT LEAVE in London with his grandmother. He'd had enough notice to write Claire and suggest she visit her grandmother at the same time, and she was waiting when he arrived.

On the second day of leave, he did something he'd been wanting to do for a very long time. He arranged to borrow a two-seater training plane and asked Claire if she'd like a ride.

"You want to take me up in a plane?" Her voice was quiet, and her eyes darted around her grandmother's parlor as if to make sure no one had overheard.

"Yes. If you think you'd enjoy it."

A slight smile crept across Claire's face. "Maybe I'll finally understand why you love it so much. Just don't let my father know; I don't think he'd approve."

"It will be our little secret." Warren ran his finger across her cheek, pausing at her dimple. Her cheeks flushed at his touch. "I should warn you, oil tends to leak everywhere, so wear an old dress."

They told their grandmothers they were going for a drive, which was true. They had to drive to the airfield. Then Claire watched as Warren inspected the Avro 504 and went through the preflight checklist.

"What does that do?" Claire pointed to the foot bar.

"It controls the rudder."

She went on to question most of the controls, and Warren eagerly shared his expertise, happy to combine two of his favorite things: flying and Claire. He finished his examination of the plane and turned back to her. "I'm going to take her up for a spin first. I've flown this type but not this plane. I want to make sure there aren't any problems before I take you."

Claire nodded, and one of the student pilots stood next to her to watch the test flight. Or was the student standing next to her for other reasons? Her dress, faded as it was, still accentuated her figure. Warren decided to make it a quick test flight. He wouldn't be doing anything rigorous with Claire in the training seat, so he fought the urge to show off with loop-the-loops or tight spirals.

He landed again, checked the aircraft, and then reached for Claire's hand. "Ready?"

"I suppose."

Warren slipped a cap over her head. "This will help with the noise and keep your hair out of your face." He helped her into her seat and fastened her belt. "Put these on," he said, handing her a pair of goggles.

She made a face as she obeyed. "No silk scarf?"

"Someone pinched my extra scarf." He tapped her lightly on the nose. "I don't think you'll need one for a flight this short." His eyes fell to her lips. He loved the way they curved, loved their color. He wondered if their texture was as soft as it looked.

He gave her a smile and pulled himself away, then climbed into his own seat and motioned to the mechanic, who spun the propeller, bringing the engine to life.

"Ready?" he shouted to Claire.

She turned around from the front seat and nodded with enthusiasm.

He started the plane forward. Not long after, it lifted easily, and he wondered if she experienced the same thrill he did at leaving the ground. He climbed to a few hundred feet but avoided the higher altitudes that might chill Claire. Besides, he only had permission for a short flight and didn't want to ruin his chances of borrowing a plane again should Claire want another ride. He kept his turns gentle and smooth in case she was sensitive to motion.

When she wasn't looking over the side of the aircraft at the landscape rolling past below, she grinned back at him. He decided to turn the plane into a sharp spiral to see what she would think, then he buzzed a nearby farm to give her a sense of their speed.

Reluctantly he headed back to the aerodrome and managed a flawless three-pointer landing, with all the wheels touching the ground at the same time. When the propeller had slowed to a near stop, he jumped from the plane and went to help Claire.

"What happened with the engine?" she asked as he undid her strap.

"Nothing. The engine was normal."

"It kept cutting out when you were getting ready to land."

Warren almost laughed. "That's the only way to control the speed in one of these planes. If you want to slow down enough to land, you have to turn the engine off, then turn it back on when you need the power."

"There is so much about flying that I don't know."

"Stay close, and I'll teach you."

He helped her to the ground, and she took his suggestion literally, staying within a few feet of him as he looked over the plane. When finished, Warren thanked the instructor for loaning him the plane, then offered Claire his arm and led her back to his grandmother's car. He'd parked on the other side of a hangar, out of view from most of the aerodrome. "What did you think?"

Her giddy expression was sufficient answer, but she used words too. "It was marvelous! I felt like a bird, only I watched us pass birds—we were going much faster. And we were so high."

"I kept us fairly low, actually. It's cold if you go much higher."

"Maybe next time you'll have to lend me your flight jacket."

"If I lend you my jacket, I might never get it back." Warren opened her door but kept one of his hands on the car, barring her entrance with his arm. "Next time? You liked it enough to do it again?"

"Yes. I loved it."

"Claire, you are a woman after my own heart."

"Careful, Mr. Flynn, that borders on something romantic." She glanced behind them, her hair bouncing as she turned back.

Warren brought one hand up to touch the red curls and put his other hand on the small of her back as he studied her face. He recognized excitement there and something else he couldn't quite pinpoint.

"What are you thinking, Warren?" she whispered.

"That I want to kiss every single one of your freckles."

Claire blushed and looked at her feet. "I have many, many freckles. So many kisses would surely be improper."

Warren pulled her toward him. "What about one kiss?" he asked softly.

Claire nodded, watching his lips as they drew near, then closing her eyes. He hesitated for an instant, feeling the warmth of her breath on his face. Then his mouth gently brushed hers once, twice. The third time, it was no longer a soft motion but something more intense. Her lips were every bit as supple as he'd imagined. She brought her arms around his neck and kissed him back, holding him tighter, her mouth exploring his. An aching spread in his chest, not an ache of pain but an ache of longing.

He pulled back reluctantly. "The scoundrel in me is tempted to kiss you until you melt in my arms completely, but the gentleman in me knows I should stop now."

* * *

The drive back to his grandmother's home was short, but it gave Warren time to put into words the feelings he'd been having and shape them into phrases Claire might find romantic. He kept glancing at her, wanting to kiss her again. In his grandmother's garage, he did kiss her again, more thoroughly than before.

"Claire, let's get married."

Her face seemed to glow as she beamed up at him. "You want to marry me?"

"Yes. I'm tired of saying good-bye all the time. I want your face to be the first thing I see when I wake up and the last thing I see before I fall asleep. I want to be able to kiss you as much as I want and spend every second of every leave by your side and find out if you have freckles anywhere other than on your face." She blushed and adjusted her mouth so her dimple grew more pronounced. "I need you, Claire. I need you to cheer me up and convince me that there's still something good and beautiful on this earth, no matter what I see on the front lines. I . . . " He leaned his forehead on hers, inhaling her soft perfume and feeling her silky skin. His arms reached around her waist to hold her. "I love you, Claire."

She stood on her toes and pressed her lips to his. The kiss was full of affection and touched with something more, some type of hunger that told him she was also tired of saying good-bye every night. She stayed in his arms long after the kiss ended. "When do you want to get married?"

"Soon."

"Good. The more I think of it, the more I want it to happen." She rested her cheek on the part of his neck that curved into his shoulder. "Have you talked to my father yet?"

"No." That was the proper thing to do, but it was more Claire's choice than her father's, and Warren was confident Mr. Donovan would have no objections. Why persist in inviting a pilot to spend leave at your mansion if you objected to him becoming your son-in-law? Warren might have downplayed his interest in Claire from time to time, but he'd never hidden it completely. He doubted her father would be surprised. "Shall we go see him tomorrow?" Getting Mr. Donovan's official blessing would make the engagement complete.

Claire stayed as she was for a few long seconds. He could feel each breath, each beat of her heart. "I don't want this moment to end."

He kissed her again, moving his hands up her back and into her hair. They were both breathless when they pulled apart some time later.

* * *

"Grannie, I think I should return to Paris tomorrow."

Claire's grandmother Huntley gently set her teacup in its saucer and set both on the low table in front of her. Warren stared at the food on his plate. Compared to the prewar years, the toast and jam were bland, but he knew Claire's grandmother was serving the best she had access to. "But your father isn't coming to escort you back for another week."

"Warren is going back tomorrow. I could go with him."

Mrs. Huntley raised one gray eyebrow. "I'm not sure that's the best idea, Claire."

"Traveling with Warren is safer. If U-boats are active, he's much more capable of plucking me from the ocean than Papa."

"Indeed, ma'am. I'll die before I let her drown."

Another raised eyebrow and a slow sip of tea passed. Finally Mrs. Huntley spoke again. "I am concerned with your safety, but I am more concerned with your reputation. I have seen many young couples buy the philosophy that normal standards are irrelevant when the young man in question might be killed within a fortnight, but I assure you the laws of propriety still apply now, and they will still apply after the war. To travel all the way from London to Paris in the company of a single man with no chaperone is simply not proper."

Claire frowned, sticking her lower lip out slightly like she did when she was trying to convince her father of something. She'd done it to Warren too, with generally good results. "We aren't trying to be improper, Grannie. But Warren's leave ends in three days, and we want to talk to my father about something before then. If I wait for Papa to come, we'll miss our opportunity until Warren's next furlough, and who knows when that will be. We could leave in the morning and arrive before nightfall. Surely it's not so improper if we travel during daylight?"

Mrs. Huntley took another slow sip of her drink, studying both of them over the rim of her teacup. She put the cup down with a sly smile. "You wish to talk to your father about something, do you? Something important, no doubt." The sparkle in her eyes told Warren she'd guessed exactly what they were thinking.

"Yes, Grannie. Life changing."

"Well, I suppose if it is that important, I could come as chaperone." She took a dainty bite of her toast and swallowed. Then she glanced at Warren. "Someone will have to go to ensure your Grandma Beatrice receives a detailed report."

Warren settled back in his armchair and relaxed. Everything thus far was going exactly as Claire had predicted.

\* \* \*

"Papa?" Claire peeked around the door to her father's office as soon as they arrived in Paris, displaying her most impish smile, the one she reserved for her father. Her right hand gripped Warren's.

Mr. Donovan quickly stacked his papers together and slid them into a drawer. "Come in, Claire, Captain Flynn." He pushed himself from his seat and strode to the front of his desk.

Warren looked at Claire, wondering if he should speak or if she should. She nodded to him, and he cleared his throat. "Mr. Donovan, I would like permission to marry your daughter."

Warren expected a hearty laugh and a quick approval. Instead, the muscles around Mr. Donovan's mouth tightened. There was no smile and certainly no laugh. "And when would such a union take place?"

*Tomorrow* no longer seemed an acceptable request, though that was what Warren really wanted. "Perhaps my next leave, sir."

"No, I don't think that's a good idea."

"But, Papa—"

"Absolutely not." Mr. Donovan folded his arms across his chest and eyed their intertwined hands. "Do you want to end up a widow, Claire? Flynn may be more skilled than the average pilot, but he won't last out the war. Sooner or later his luck will run out or his engine will fail, just like it did for Guynemer and Immelmann and Voss."

"Sir, just because I'm involved in a dangerous occupation doesn't mean I won't survive the war. And it doesn't mean I won't be a good husband to your daughter."

Mr. Donovan scowled. "The two of you are thinking about next week and next month. What about next year? What about fifteen years from now? I intend for Claire to make a good match when she marries, and having a dead husband of questionable social standing in her past will jeopardize her future options, not to mention break her heart in the short-term."

"We can't put our lives on hold just because something bad *might* happen." With effort, Warren held his temper in check, seeking a compromise. He couldn't change his social standing, but he had options when it came to his vocation. "I could request assignment back in England, training new pilots."

"Oh, yes, so you can die in a training accident instead of a dogfight."

Training accidents were as common as gas attacks, but Warren had hoped Mr. Donovan didn't know that. "Surely you've suspected my feelings for your daughter before now. If you disapprove of me, why didn't you make it clear sooner, before we fell in love?"

Mr. Donovan walked around his desk as if he needed a physical barrier between himself and the couple. "I've enjoyed hearing your war stories, Captain, and I admire your bravery. You've helped break up the monotony for Claire and for me with your visits, but I will not allow you to marry her, not while the war continues. It will be hard enough on her when you die without a marriage to make things even worse."

Warren placed his hands on the desk and leaned forward. "And what of your daughter's wishes? She seems willing to risk the chance of heartbreak in exchange for a happy union, even if its duration is relatively short."

Mr. Donovan met Warren's stance. "My answer is no, and it will remain such until the war ends."

"I can support Claire without your help." Warren's wages were adequate, and his grandmother would take them in if they needed a place to live.

"Oh, so now you're threatening to run away with her?"

"Only if you threaten to cut her off. Tell him, Claire. Tell him what we decided and how determined we are." Warren turned to Claire when she didn't answer right away. Tears streaked her cheeks, and her skin was pale.

She opened and closed her mouth a few times, but no words came out.

"Claire?"

"Warren," she whispered. "Maybe we are rushing things. We might should give it a little more thought."

He couldn't believe what he was hearing. Was she backing out? "But, Claire, I thought you wanted this as much as I did."

She sobbed and left the office. He followed her out and put a hand on her arm. "Claire?"

"I'm sorry, Warren. My father wants what's best for me. Maybe I should listen, at least think about what he's said. He's right—if you die, it will break my heart, but I think it would be even harder if we were married."

Warren stood absolutely still for a few long seconds. "Yes, maybe your father is right. If you can't think for yourself, then I guess you aren't ready to get married, especially not to me." He strode away from Claire, plucked his hat from the stand in the entryway, and slammed the front door on his way out.

# Chapter 35

*November 1917, Paris, France*

EVETTE HAD SPENT MONTHS HESITATING, not completely trusting McDougall but not convinced he was Lohr's contact either. She wished Lohr and Simon had given her more clues. Lohr had at least two sources in Paris. One had access to money, and the other had access to McDougall's plans. But McDougall's knowledge of his own plans didn't confirm his guilt. Nor did one expensive present.

Evette sighed. The doubt was driving her mad. But investigating her boss felt wrong, a show of disloyalty and ingratitude. McDougall had always been kind to her. He had given her a job and hidden her from Gaspard. Yet she couldn't ignore the feeling of unease she experienced every time she thought of Lohr's conversation. Her assignments had kept her busy all summer and fall, but soon she would have to do something about her nagging doubts.

Long hours tailing a suspected saboteur had kept Evette away while Claire's grandmother was visiting. But the day Lady Huntley left, Evette found Claire in the library, sitting in front of the piano but not playing. Her head was tilted to the side, her face turned toward the window.

"Claire?"

Slowly Claire turned around. Her eyelids were puffy, and the whites of her eyes were pink.

"Claire, what's wrong?"

Claire looked at her hands for a few moments before speaking. "Sometimes I'm rash. I jump into things without thinking them through. And other times I hesitate and let an opportunity pass, and then I regret it. How am I to know which is right?" The skin between her eyebrows scrunched together, and her lips pulled down in dismay. "Warren asked me to marry him."

Evette almost offered her congratulations, but if Claire had been crying, something obviously wasn't right.

"Warren asked me to marry him, and Papa said no—he was quite insistent on the matter. I really did want to be Warren's wife. But I don't want to be his widow. And I don't want to lose Papa."

Evette sat on a sofa, and Claire came to join her.

"Warren was upset." Claire sniffled. "Of course he was upset. I told him I wanted to marry him, and I backed out. But I was scared. That Warren would die, that Papa would disown me." Claire took a deep, shuddering breath. "Now, even if I did work up the courage to defy my father and elope with Warren, I don't know if he'd take me."

Evette put her arm around Claire's shoulder, wondering herself where the line was between being rash and letting opportunities slip past, never to return.

* * *

Evette didn't know whether Claire had made the right choice, but she did her best to comfort her friend over the next few days, even when she wasn't sure what to say. Maybe when the war was over, Claire wouldn't have to choose between her father and her ex-fiancé—but how long would the war last? Evette doubted Captain Flynn would ignore Claire forever, but she'd never been jilted like that, and there was no guarantee he'd survive the war.

Claire's problems were unresolved, but Evette finally worked up the courage to resolve her own. She was disgusted by her long indecision. The time for action had come. She had to find out whether she could trust McDougall, and she finally knew how. She would break into his office. McDougall knew of the plan to release Simon and have him tailed—he'd thought it up. If he also knew about the sources in Essen and Munich, it wouldn't prove he was Lohr's contact, but it would make it more likely. If she found no information about the spies, then Lohr had a different source, and she could trust McDougall.

Security in McDougall's office was strict, and the locks on the outside doors were secure. But those who worked there were used to seeing Evette. She arrived when most of the men were finishing their day's work. McDougall had already gone home, which suited her purposes. She went to the water closet and waited three hours until the lights had all gone out, the sound of footsteps had disappeared, and she was sure the building was empty. She lit a candle and crept out, making her way upstairs to the fourth desk on the left.

She ignored her guilt and used the skeleton keys McDougall had given her on the top drawer of his desk. Among the pens and pencils, she found a photograph of McDougall's brother, the one who had set a standard Howard felt he could never meet. Did he keep a picture of Henry out of affection or as a motivation to push himself?

Methodically she unlocked and examined the contents of the larger drawers, two on either side of the desk. She found money but only enough for a few meals at a café. It certainly wasn't bribe money, though she doubted McDougall would store money from Lohr here if he was accepting it. A copy of *The Iliad*, more loose paper, and a stack of unused envelopes completed the first drawer. The second drawer was full of memos from other staff members. She skimmed them as best as her primary-school English allowed but saw nothing about Essen or Munich.

The third drawer was more eye-opening. Buried under a week's worth of newspapers was a folder labeled *Spider*. She flipped through the sheets. She recognized them as German but couldn't read them. An address in Essen was written on the inside back cover of the file. A sheet labeled *letter boxes* included addresses in Düsseldorf, Bonn, and Recklinghausen, and half a dozen addresses in Holland. She'd heard the term before—letter boxes were safe locations for an agent to mail or leave a report, which would then be forwarded on. There were also maps of Essen and a letter from a Frau Von Hayek.

McDougall was aware of the Essen spy.

She looked more carefully at the other pages. Spider's reports? On closer inspection, she noticed words, very faint, written between the darker German lines. The letters weren't ones she recognized, and yet something about them was familiar. She stared at them until the candle's flame wavered, reminding her that time was limited. The words were almost like looking over someone's shoulder and seeing the reflection of a handwritten list in a store window.

She put the folder aside. She needed time and the use of a mirror to study it. If she found evidence of a spy in Munich as well, she would want the reports as evidence when she went to McDougall's superior. And if it turned out that McDougall was innocent . . . she would have to find a way to sneak the folder back to him.

The last drawer contained McDougall's counterintelligence papers, full of folders on all the men she had tailed, all the suspects they had observed or heard about. She flipped through them quickly, taking a little longer on the stacks dedicated to Simon and Lohr. The majority of the papers were in English, but enough was in French that she concluded none of them dealt with an Allied spy in Munich. Unless information from Munich was included in Spider's reports, Evette had searched an innocent man's desk.

She relocked all the desk drawers. Gripping the folder with Spider's reports to her chest, she returned to the first floor and let herself out through a back window. She scolded herself for not planning better—she couldn't lock the window from the outside, and eventually someone would notice it wasn't properly secured.

The night was dark, and it was late, but as Evette hurried to the Donovan home on the bicycle she'd left two blocks from the office, she had no plans for sleep, only a hope that the papers she carried would finally put her suspicions to rest.

* * *

Evette tiptoed down the hallway when she arrived and saw light showing at the crack under Claire's door. It was late, but Claire hadn't slept well lately. Evette went to her own room and read through the French part of Spider's reports, using a mirror to help her. The agent funneled out information about German munitions production, internal politics, and Lohr. If Spider knew Lohr in Germany, and Lohr knew there was an Allied spy somewhere in Essen, would Lohr figure out the agent's identity? She should have told McDougall months ago that word of spies in Essen and Munich had leaked to Lohr, but she hadn't completely trusted him then. She finished reading the final report. There was only one step left before she confirmed McDougall wasn't Lohr's source.

Claire's light was still on, so Evette knocked gently on the door. "Claire?"

"Yes?" Claire looked up from a novel when Evette came inside and shut the door behind her.

"How good is your German?"

"My tutor was as strict as General Falkenhayn. Why?"

Evette showed her the letters she'd stolen. "These are reports from an agent code named Spider. He's written his report in French, backward. The ink must have been invisible originally, but it's been made to show here." Evette pointed to the faint brown lines written between the black ones. "I've read his reports, but I want to know what else he's saying. The black ink is in German. It was probably written as a cover for the report, but I have to be sure."

Claire took the first letter and read it, her mouth tight in concentration. "It's a personal letter." She proceeded to read it, with frequent pauses as she translated the words in her head.

*To the widow of my best friend,*

*I often think of how wrong it is that your husband is dead and I am alive. It wasn't supposed to be that way. He volunteered to take my place when I was asked to deliver a message through a battlefield. I turned him down. I thought he would be safer where he was, led by a good leader and surrounded by our comrades. If anyone was to die, I thought it would be me—alone, running across open ground, an easy target for our enemy.*

*He loved you. I could tell by the way he reread your letters until the ink smeared and the folds were so worn that the paper fell into thirds. I knew you at once when I saw you, not just because of the picture he always carried but also because he had described you so completely. He was devoted to you. He may have looked at the war as an opportunity for adventure, but that was when we thought it would be over quickly. Very soon he came to wish for peace so he could go back to his life with you. He told me that when the war was over and he had saved enough money, he would to take you to the ocean. He wanted to watch your reaction to the sand between your bare toes. He loved everything about you, from your hair down to your feet.*

Claire set the letter down. "How frightfully sad."

"He can't have expected his report to be sent to a friend's widow, but do you suppose he really meant those words?"

"I hope so. It's tragic but beautiful."

Evette glanced at the clock. "Maybe we should see what the next one says."

Claire began reading.

*To my papa,*

*I often think of your selflessness. When I last visited, Mama needed so much extra care, and you always gave it willingly. I can think of no greater demonstration of love than that which comes in times of illness. Your devotion to her has made me think much of what love really is, what it requires, what it can give, and what it can become. Who will take care of you when you are old and in need of help? I want to be there, but I don't know if I will be.*

*I miss the dairy. I know I've done my share of complaining about the work it takes to care for the cows, tend the garden, and make cheese. So much work, and yet it produces something tangible. Food for nourishment, healthy animals to begin the process over again. So different from war, which produces only death, destruction, and grief.*

*I sometimes dream about going back to the dairy. You probably think I'm dead. And I may never have the opportunity to disabuse you of that belief because before long, it may be true. I pray sadness over my absence hasn't weighed down your already burdened spirit. And even though I know better, I pray I shall see you again. If I could return home, even for a few days, it would show a generosity from God not yet seen in my lifetime.*

*I wish you well,*

*Your son*

"He didn't write his name," Claire noted. "But whoever he is, he has a poet's soul."

"I wish I could meet him. His dairy sounds like a bit of paradise."

Claire looked up from the next letter. "If he's spying in Germany, I think it unlikely that you'll be introduced."

Evette leaned against Claire's headboard. "What an awful war this is, to take people like that, or like my brother, and send them to their deaths when their lives are just beginning."

Claire had already begun reading through the next letter. "Oh," she sighed. "He has a romantic streak too. This one is addressed to *the woman whose name I do not know but whose face I cannot forget*. What I wouldn't give for Warren to write a letter like this to me." She frowned. "I wonder if he'll ever write to me again at all. I hurt him badly. I didn't mean to, but . . ."

"Write to him."

"What would I say? I'm not ready to run away with him, and that's what he wants."

Evette tried to think of something useful to tell Claire, but nothing came to mind. In the silence, Claire began reading again:

*To the woman whose name I do not know but whose face I cannot forget;*

*I still think of you often, even though so much time has passed since our brief meeting. Did you make it to the city? Did you find work and somewhere to live? Have I crossed your mind even briefly since that day?*

*I sometimes wonder what would have happened if I hadn't been called away, if I had at least learned your name so I could write you a real letter. Do you still live in fear like you did that day I met you? I could see it in your eyes and in your shoulders: you were scared of something. At first I worried it was me, but then I realized it was someone else, probably your half brother. I wish I could have done more than give you money for a train ticket. No one should have to live in terror. I've been a soldier, so I know what it's like to fear for one's safety and to feel completely helpless. I hope you've escaped. I pray that you have.*

*I remember those green eyes of yours, like a meadow after the rain. That may not sound like a compliment, but I mean it as one. Open spaces are like home to me, and looking into your eyes gave me that feeling—like I was safe and home and that I could spend years there without ever wanting to leave. It's strange that I would feel that way about someone I've spoken so little with. Some days I wonder if I've gone mad. I don't believe in love at first sight. But when I think of you, love is the only term that explains what I feel.*

Claire set the letter down with the others. "I wonder who she is."

Evette sat very still, trying to wrap her head around what she'd just heard. It was impossible—and yet there were the words, and they proved it.

# Chapter 36

"Will you read the letter again?" Evette asked.

Claire complied, and Evette analyzed every word. She wasn't the only woman in France who'd been in an abusive situation a few years ago and not the only girl to be beaten by her half brother. But how many soldiers had bought train tickets for someone like her and failed to learn the recipient's name? A recipient with green eyes, no less.

"You're crying, Evette. I realize it's a beautiful letter, but it might only be cover for the coded report. He may have never even met her."

"No, she's real. They really met once."

Claire laughed. "I'm turning you into a hopeless romantic. Soon you'll be as bad as I am."

"Do you remember when I told you about that soldier I met, the one who gave me money for a train ticket?"

Claire glanced back at the letter. "That's right. You met the same way Spider and his secret love met." Then Claire's eyes riveted on Evette. "The violent relative you're hiding from. Your half brother?"

Evette nodded.

Claire reread the letter. "It's you. It has to be. You even have green eyes. Like a meadow after the rain. Oh, Evette, how romantic."

"I think he's in danger."

"He's a spy; of course he's in danger." She focused on the sheet. "And it seems he's in danger of losing his heart. How delicious."

"No, he's really in danger. Someone's been leaking information. I thought maybe it was McDougall, but—"

"McDougall? How could you suspect Lieutenant McDougall? He's one of Warren's friends, and he's your employer."

"He knew some information that got out."

Claire's lips puckered in concentration. "Is he the only one who knew it?"

"I don't think so. And I don't think McDougall knows everything that's gotten out, so at least part of the information had to come from someone else.

But I had to prove it wasn't him before I could trust him. That's why I broke into his office and took these reports."

Claire's jaw dropped. "You took these without asking?"

"I had to. He would never trust me with them. He thinks I'm capable if he needs someone to tail a suspect because I'm good at blending in, but he never asks for my opinion about anything important. I'm just a woman, just a pretty face." Evette stopped, stunned. "This summer he told me I had beautiful eyes. Like a meadow after the rain."

"Well, you do have lovely eyes—"

"Why would he use the same description?"

Claire looked at the papers. "I suppose because he read this letter, along with the report, and recognized it was the type of thing that might sweep a girl off her feet. I suppose it's not so original if he copied it from one of his agents, but at least he was trying."

"Or he didn't mean it."

"I think he cares for you, Evette."

"Like a man cares for a beloved horse or a loyal hound."

"No—he may not have a romantic bone in his body, but he fancies you." Claire smoothed out the creases in the report. "And so does Spider." Claire was suddenly quiet, a slight frown marring her face.

"Are you thinking of Captain Flynn?"

"Yes. He's like McDougall, I suppose. Not really romantic." She brought her hand to her lips. "But when he kisses me, oh, Evette, it's the most wonderful feeling in the world. Who cares for poetry with kisses like that? And now I wonder if I'll ever see him again, let alone be in his arms."

"Write to him. You told me love is patient. He's been hurt, but maybe he'll wait."

Claire ran her fingers along the bedspread. "He would have to be very patient, indeed, to forgive me."

"Ask."

Claire finally nodded. "I will write to him." She fingered the stack of reports still in need of translation and checked the clock. "But not tonight."

Dawn was only a few hours away. Evette groaned. She doubted the other letters would include information about Munich, so it seemed McDougall wasn't a traitor after all. What would she say to him when she returned his folder?

\* \* \*

Evette didn't make it to bed that night. After washing her face and changing her clothes, she went to see McDougall. The real traitor might work in the next desk over, so she went to his residence, not his office. When she arrived, she lifted her hand to knock, then hesitated. After a few seconds, her hand fell limply at her side. She fingered Spider's reports and thought of his smile that day they'd met. He had been in some type of pain, a sort of emotional anguish, yet he had helped her escape a situation that could have ended in her death. Now he was in danger; she was sure of it—more danger now due to her months of indecision. The least she could do was square her shoulders and confess her theft.

She knocked as firmly as she dared, and McDougall answered soon after. He wore only his shirtsleeves, trousers, and slippers. "Evette? Please come in. Madame Morel is finishing breakfast. I shall ask her to prepare another place."

Evette clung tightly to the reports, hoping she could draw courage from them. "Please, Monsieur McDougall, there's no need to trouble Madame Morel. I shall stay only a few minutes."

He led her into his study. "I assume this is not a social call?"

"No, monsieur."

"What's wrong, Evette? I thought we were familiar enough to use our Christian names."

"We were, but I've done something that will make you angry."

He sat back in his seat, waiting.

The clock ticked five times in the quiet house before Evette worked up the strength to speak. "Someone has been leaking information. When Simon met Lohr, I overheard more of their conversation than I originally told you. Lohr knew from someone, a source in British Intelligence, that a prisoner was going to be released so he could be tailed."

"Why didn't you tell me at once? That was back in June. Have you any idea how significant that information is?"

"Yes, but how was I to know that Lohr's source wasn't, in fact, you?"

"You doubted me?" He kept a normal volume, but he spat the words more than spoke them.

Evette swallowed. "Last night I broke into your office to be sure I could trust you." Slowly she handed him the reports from Spider. He looked at each one of them, then at her. "I know it wasn't you because Lohr said his source told him about two spies. One in Essen. One in Munich. You only have information about the one in Essen."

McDougall was quiet for a long time. "This means that someone with access to my project, as well as access to a project in Munich, is talking to Lohr. Someone that high up could cause a great deal of damage."

"Lohr said he was bribing the source. That the man was expensive. When Lohr came back, he was going to offer more money for more information."

"I need to figure out who has access to that information and what else they know."

"Sir, I was wrong not to tell you this summer. I'm sorry. And I'm worried. I haven't heard from or seen Lohr since Simon's arrest, but what if he's come back to Paris and gotten his information?"

"If he has come back, then Spider is in danger. So is the Munich spy, whoever he is." McDougall swore under his breath. "The only reason Spider is still in Germany is because I made him stay there. He admitted his cover was shaky, even asked to leave. I said some hard things to him, things I regret. If what you say is true, I need to get him out, now." He opened a drawer and took out a train schedule.

"Can I help?" Evette wanted make up for her mistakes. And if Spider was in danger, she wanted to help him.

McDougall didn't answer immediately. He stood, and she followed him. "Do you trust me now, Evette?"

"Yes. I'm sorry I doubted you. And now I've given you reason to doubt me." Her gaze slid to the floor, then back to his face. "Do you think you can forgive me?"

He studied her for a few seconds, then put his hands on her arms with a chuckle. "You are impossible to stay cross with. All is forgiven." He leaned closer and kissed her gently on the cheek. "I will see you when I get back."

"Where are you going?"

"A train ride to the Channel. After that, to the Ruhr to fetch my spider."

"And what about the traitor?"

McDougall tapped his fingers on a bookshelf as he thought. "I don't trust anyone I work with to head the search, but Captain Flynn's aerodrome isn't far from here. Write to him; ask him to help you. He'll get further than you will in an investigation like this. It's probably someone who supervises both me and whoever is running the Munich spy. Look for someone with expensive taste."

# Chapter 37

*December 1917, Paris, France*

WARREN HAD BEEN RELUCTANT TO go to Paris. When he'd received Evette's letter, he'd put the journey off for a few days. Only when a thick squall rolled in and prevented flying did he finally answer her summons. Her letter had said she would wait in a park at eleven in the morning each day, and she was there, on a bench, huddled under an umbrella when he finally arrived. He almost felt guilty for not coming until a rainy day, but he had his squadron to lead.

They exchanged greetings and started walking together. Even though he had committed not to talk about her, Warren found himself asking, "How is Claire?"

"She spends a lot of time playing the piano."

"What is she playing?"

Evette didn't answer right away. "Sad songs mostly." They walked a few more paces. "She still loves you, Captain Flynn, and she's miserable without you, but she's not ready to lose her father. She already lost her mother. I think she's hoping she won't have to choose between the two most important men in her life."

"And if she does have to choose between us, who do you think she'll pick?"

Evette looked away.

"Exactly. She already picked her father." Warren stomped away before remembering he was taking his anger out on the wrong person. "I'm sorry, Miss Touny. I just . . ."

"You just hurt inside. So does Claire. Maybe more than you, because she feels guilty too. She wants to be stronger, but it takes time to build the kind of tenacity that can walk away from her current life into something that might only last a few months."

"So you and Claire both think I'm unlikely to survive the war, do you?"

Evette was quiet for a while. "It's only that so many are gone already. But if you can just keep from dying, something tells me Claire will change her mind."

"Just keep from dying. Sounds so simple." Memories of Captain Prior and Flight Sergeant Boyle and dozens of other men came to his mind.

"You still want to marry her, don't you?"

Warren still loved Claire, but her decision to side with her father had hurt deeply, like a piece of broken propeller wedged into his heart. Part of him needed some change from her, some assurance that if they were married, her first loyalty would be to her husband, not to her father. Another part of him knew all she had to say was one word, and he'd instantly forgive her. "Yes."

"Then be patient. She loves you."

"But if her father never comes around, will she ever love me enough to leave him?"

Evette's brow crinkled. "I want to say yes. But I don't know."

At least she was being honest. Warren was grateful for that. "Does McDougall ever talk to you about the future?"

"Only the future of my next assignment."

"Hmm. Maybe I should talk some sense into him."

"I'm sure that's not necessary, Captain. We've time enough to sort personal matters out later."

"So where is McDougall? If he needs help, he usually asks me directly."

Evette glanced around the sidewalk, making sure they were alone. "He went to rescue a spider."

"Spider's in trouble?"

"You know him?"

"I flew him to his current assignment. Haven't heard much since. What type of trouble?"

Evette seemed suddenly reticent, as if she wasn't sure she could discuss espionage with Warren.

"Please, Miss Touny. We're on the same side. And I like the Frenchman. I don't want something to happen to him if I can do anything to help."

"We think someone knows who he is."

"Give me details."

"It starts with a man named Lohr. I don't suppose you know who he is, but—"

"McDougall mentioned him," Warren said. "Saboteur and spymaster, working for the Germans. Somehow manages to sneak back and forth between Paris and Essen."

"Yes. And Lohr has a source in British Intelligence, someone who knows about Spider and another man in Munich. The source sells the information.

When Lohr came this summer, he only discovered the location of the spies. But if he's come back and the man is still willing to sell secrets, he might provide names or summaries of what our spies have learned."

"So the next time Lohr goes to Essen, Spider will be arrested and executed."

Evette nodded, worry lines appearing around her lips as she frowned. "McDougall went to get Spider out before it's too late. He wanted you to help me figure out who's behind the leaks. It will be someone who outranks McDougall, someone with access to his project as well as whoever is running the spy in Munich."

"How did McDougall plan to sneak in?"

"He didn't say, but the last three times he's had a friend with a small ship sail him to Holland. Then he sneaks across the border with a Dutch contact, and they pretend to be in Germany on business. Or he pretends he's an injured soldier on convalescence leave."

"He's doing that for a fourth time?"

"I think so."

Warren shook his head. "Four times is pushing it. He should have called me. I can fly in and out in a night." Warren looked at the sky. The wind blew from the east, and on the eastern horizon, he could pick out clear sky. The weather just might cooperate with him. "You don't know how Lohr sneaks in and out of France?"

"No."

"Then he may very well beat McDougall there and set a trap to catch them both. I'm flying to Essen. Tonight, if the weather allows. Finding the traitor can wait a few days."

* * *

Warren went back to his aerodrome and spent the afternoon studying maps and questioning a pilot who had been shot down on the German side of the front and then escaped through the electrified fence separating occupied Belgium from the Netherlands. He had avoided a fatal shock by shoving a wooden cask between the wires and crawling through. Warren planned to fly out, but now he had a second option.

That night Evette helped Warren break into McDougall's office through a back window so Warren could see Spider's file. He had a feeling she'd done it before because it went far more smoothly than he would have expected. He read Olivier's reports and looked over another map of Essen. Spider's temporary home was within a mile of the Krupp factories in the Altendorf district, and he shared the dwelling with the Sauer and Kallweit families.

"Here." Evette handed him a paper. "It's a letter from Frau Von Hayek, one of McDougall's Dutch contacts, married to a German man. She sent this a year ago while visiting family in Holland. She recommended Spider to his current position. If he's in danger, so is she."

Warren skimmed the letter and copied the address he needed. "I'll try to warn her too. Maybe she can leave via Holland and catch McDougall before he gets to Essen." He studied the map again. A wide field lay only a few miles from the Sauer home. He had noticed it on an old map at the aerodrome and felt that field was his best option. He checked four other possible fields on the more recent map and eliminated two, leaving him with three choices. Warren glanced at his watch. "I want to make it in tonight, so I better get back to the airfield."

They snuck out the same unlocked back window. Before they parted, Warren turned to Evette. "If something happens to me, will you tell Claire I still loved her?"

"Yes. But come back to her. She needs you."

"Not as much as she needs her father."

"Give her some time, Captain."

Warren nodded, not in agreement but because he needed to get to his plane. His relationship with Claire was too complicated to sort out just then. Other things were higher priority, like saving Olivier and McDougall from Lohr.

The moon was bright, and the sky had cleared when Warren reached his aerodrome, driving the car he'd borrowed from the intelligence officer. He sought out Major Cook to explain his plan.

"That Sopwith isn't your personal property, Captain."

"Yes, but this is official war business. And I'd actually like to borrow a spotter plane instead of my scout. I hope I'll need the extra seat."

Cook hesitated only an instant before agreeing. "Make sure you bring it back in one piece."

"Yes, sir."

"And, Canada?"

"Yes, sir?"

"See that you come back in one piece too."

* * *

Warren vaguely remembered the countryside surrounding Essen from his flight two years before. Astounding, really, that Spider had lasted so long. His preferred landing strip bordered what looked like forest and a long stream. He hoped the map was accurate and that the field hadn't been turned into a practice artillery range or a training field for new conscripts. His other options would involve longer walks.

He flew over Essen to confirm his position. The people below would be able to hear him, and some would even recognize the sound as an airplane engine, but most Germans who could identify the type by its engine noise would be near the front line.

He banked back to the west, picked out the unmistakable outline of the Krupp factories, and switched his engine off to lower his airspeed. A few minutes later, he saw the stream glowing in the moonlight and dipped toward the enemy earth. The field was rough when he touched down, but the sturdy reconnaissance plane held. While the engine was still running, he drove the plane into the forest where it would be better hidden. He finally turned the engine off, then spent the next hour sawing off tree branches and using them to camouflage the spotter.

He went through his knapsack, keeping part of the food, leaving the saw and the spare airplane parts. He had extra petrol in the observer's seat. He'd refuel when he got back, then leave the petrol can behind.

Before leaving France, he had changed into civilian clothing. To German eyes, he was now a spy. He took the two-mile walk to the Sauer estate cautiously, pausing often to make sure no one could see him. He could speak a few phrases in German, but they wouldn't sound like they'd come from a native.

When the manor came into view, Warren waited, trying to figure out how best to approach it and find Olivier without disturbing the other residents. He hadn't expected the home to have so many rooms. If he wanted to return tonight, he should grab Olivier now and head back to the plane. But there was also the woman who had arranged Spider's position. If they waited one day, they could warn her too, and Warren could wait until Olivier appeared instead of trying to break into the home to search for him. The plane was reasonably well hidden in a quiet area. Once he made contact with Olivier, he could return to make sure it stayed safe.

It was a cold night, but he'd endured the cold before, and he had food. At least it was dry, and he was wearing appropriate clothing. Warren positioned himself where he could see anyone leaving the side or front doors and sat down to wait.

# Chapter 38

*December 1917, Essen, Germany*

WHEN JULIAN LEFT FOR THE factory that morning, the last thing he expected was to hear his Christian name. He'd been swallowed up in the persona of Hans Becker for so long that Julian Olivier had become someone from a different life. But a voice called from the woods to the side of the house as he walked toward the lane. "Julian."

He paused, startled, then bent down and fiddled with his already fastened shoelace in case someone was watching from the house. Slowly he turned his head to study the trees and let whomever had called know he had heard. He didn't go directly to the woods. He followed his previous course, only turning into the grove of trees when he knew anyone looking through the windows of the Sauer estate would be unable to see him.

Within a few minutes, he was back where the sound had originated, face-to-face with the Canadian pilot. "Lieutenant Flynn?"

"Captain, actually. I've come to take you back to France. Lohr has a source, and agent Sparrow thinks your cover is blown."

"That doesn't surprise me." He didn't know who she was, but McDougall had mentioned an agent Sparrow during his last visit. Julian examined Flynn's clothing. Civilian, at least, if not German.

"McDougall left France to warn you, but I didn't think he could sneak through Holland quickly enough to beat Lohr."

"When do we leave?" Julian hesitated to leave without McDougall, but it might be weeks before the Scotsman made it to Essen.

"Tonight. I brought in a little two-seater plane. If the German Jastas on the front lines can see us, they'll shoot us down, so we want to cross the trenches in the dark. I plan to go back to my plane for the day. It's through the trees, near the field by the stream. Do you know the area?"

"Yes. I've gathered mushrooms there with the Kallweit boys. It's a good location. Not many people go there this time of year. But don't light a fire; someone would notice the smoke. Will you be warm enough?"

"I'll manage."

"And food?"

"Cold bully beef."

Julian supposed the tinned meat was better than what most of Essen's population would eat that day.

"Before we leave, can you warn your contact, the lady who set you up here?"

"Yes." If Julian was going to leave that night, he could skip his shift at the factory and visit Frau Von Hayek instead. And as strange as it sounded, he wanted to say good-bye, in his own way, to the Kallweit family. "What time do we fly out?"

"Early morning. The sun doesn't rise until eight, so we should leave between five and six. Then it will be dark when we cross the lines, but we'll have a bit of light to land by."

Julian thought of the information he'd gathered in Essen. And of the information he still hadn't gathered. He wanted to spend the day hiding beside the plane, but McDougall's chastisement from their last meeting continued to sear his conscience. There were still things to learn, things that might help the poilus in the trenches. "I've been monitoring results at the Krupp testing range. They're on to something major—a huge gun with an unheard-of range—and new shells that are supposed to be even more deadly. I can only break in when the moon is right. I should go tonight. It will take a few hours, but I'll be finished before we need to leave."

"Right. Do you need help?"

No one in Germany had helped Julian with his espionage work since Frau Von Hayek found him his cover job, but he quickly saw the benefit of having a lookout. "Yes. I'll meet you by the plane this evening. We'll hit the range at about nine. Most of the men don't work past then no matter how important their projects."

\* \* \*

Julian saw Frau Von Hayek that morning, and she assured him she would leave at once for Holland. On Captain Flynn's suggestion, he also asked her to contact McDougall to tell him not to come to Germany. In case he had already crossed the border, Julian placed an ad in one of the local papers: *Spider is going home.* He hoped McDougall would remember to check it.

Willi and Franz were playing chess when Julian returned to the Sauer home and walked into the dining room.

"Grandpapa said someone is coming to see him tomorrow," Franz said.

"Do you know who?" Julian asked.

"No."

Julian mulled over Franz's information. Part of him wondered if he should stay an extra day and listen to one last source. But if the expected guest was Lohr, Julian was leaving just in time. "I'll make sure the spare room is ready. Good thing the factory let me off early."

Franz's grin was so large that Julian guessed it would have been his job to prepare the room if Julian hadn't volunteered. "Grandpapa seems to know everyone."

"That's not always a good thing," Willi said.

Franz looked up quickly. "Sure it is."

Willi sat back in his chair, his eyes still on the board. "Have you heard of Dr. Faber?"

Julian and Franz shook their heads.

"Grandpapa knows him. More than anyone in Germany, he's responsible for gas warfare. He's a brilliant scientist, and I suppose I should admire him, but instead I feel distaste for him."

Julian felt the same thing but swallowed it back.

"His wife was a chemist too. A brilliant woman. She committed suicide shortly after we used chlorine gas at Ypres." Willi moved one of his pieces and waited for Franz to decide on his next move. "Grandpapa said it was necessary. With the British blockade, we have to use all available sources to fight our enemies. But Mrs. Faber must have disagreed."

Franz looked back and forth between the two men, obviously worried by the turn and tone of conversation.

Willi fingered one of the pawns he'd captured from Franz. "I was in the hospital with men who'd been gassed."

"So was I," Julian said before he had time to think it through. The British hadn't used gas until after Julian was released from the hospital. He quickly amended his statement. "The wind changed during the attack, and it was our own gas that got them."

"I sometimes think of Mrs. Faber. Did she know her husband was capable of evil? Or was it a surprise? Some men have their weaknesses on display for all to see. No woman will marry me and only then notice I'm missing an arm. Others might disagree, but I think an open weakness is better than a hidden evil."

Franz turned to Julian. "Mama's friend came to visit today. She brought her daughter."

Julian pulled out a chair and sat. "How old was this daughter?"

"About my age." Willi moved one of his pieces forward.

"Was she pretty?"

"Beautiful."

Julian had never heard the word uttered with such frustration. "But?"

"But her eyes were full of pity. I suppose that's marginally better than disgust." Willi flicked one of the chess pieces across the table. It clattered to the floor, and Franz went to retrieve it.

"There are other women," Julian said.

"Will they be any different?"

Julian wondered what he could do here on his last day to encourage Willi. He was a bright young man, a hard worker, and he had the self-discipline to do nearly anything as long as he could kick his depression. "Unfortunately I'm not very experienced with women."

"Nor am I," Willi said.

"Find someone who sees your good qualities and loves those. If she also pities your lost arm, so be it, as long as she admires what is left to admire. And, Willi, there is much left in you to admire."

Willi seemed to be fighting emotion, so Julian excused himself to go prepare the guest room. It was strange. He was eager to return to France, yet something inside him was sad to leave Germany. He wasn't sure Franz and Dorothea could give Willi the support he needed—not from lack of effort, but they hadn't seen war, so they didn't understand. Julian wished that before he left he could be sure Willi was on the road to full emotional recovery.

\* \* \*

The Krupp guards were easy to get around when it came time to visit the testing range. Julian had watched them before. They were alert but predictable. Captain Flynn waited nearby in the trees. He promised to throw a rock at a window if the guards did anything unusual.

Julian crept inside by climbing the tree, then sneaked into each room and took notes on the latest developments. The Paris Gun was progressing and would soon menace France. The new high-explosive shells had proved slightly more effective than the previous type, but they used twice as many nitrates, so Julian doubted they would be adopted.

He was nearing the end of his tedious circuit when he heard a crash toward the back of the building. Flynn? Julian froze, his ears straining to hear more. He was almost finished, but he didn't want to push the miraculous luck that had sustained him since 1915. He tiptoed back to the storeroom, planning to crawl through the vent and end his night's work. There might not be anything useful in the last office anyway—it was Julian's habit to start each search in the offices of the most senior men and work his way down from there.

Inside the dark storeroom, Julian's hands gripped the rope hanging through the vent. Then the light switched on, and he blinked at the sudden brightness. Lohr stood in the doorway, his pistol aimed at Julian.

"I thought I might find you here." Lohr walked toward him. There was only one door into the room and no windows. Julian stepped slowly around the counter in the room's center, keeping it between him and the man from Lorraine. "Stay where you are, or I'll shoot. I want to see your hands."

Julian lifted and held them in front of his shoulders. "I didn't know you were in Essen."

"I just arrived. I came earlier than scheduled because as soon as I heard someone was feeding the British results of the artillery testing here in Essen, I suspected you. Then Frau von Hayek's name was mentioned, and that made it certain." Lohr strolled even closer, his tone conversational. "But how were you getting your information? At first I assumed Herr Sauer was bringing results home and you'd gleaned your reports from him. But artillery isn't his specialty. Then I thought perhaps you were friendly with the men who work here. That was a good possibility, but then, so was the chance that you were simply breaking in, especially when Sauer remembered his daughter had seen you come in early one morning like a thief sneaking back to his roost."

Julian stared at Lohr's pistol and wished he had borrowed Flynn's revolver. Or maybe he should have stayed in the woods and ignored the Paris Gun and McDougall's insinuation that leaving was cowardly.

The counter in front of him was covered with pieces of partially disassembled artillery shells. Some of the items were small enough to throw, but Lohr caught Julian looking at them and motioned him back. Julian stepped toward a box of shells, but they were all too big to use as bludgeons. Even if he could arm and detonate one, which was doubtful considering Lohr's steady gaze and deadly weapon, the explosion would kill him along with Lohr.

"Two years." Lohr raised an eyebrow. "That's an impressive run. I have few agents who last more than two months."

Julian took a slow step toward the counter. It might not stop a bullet, but it would at least block Lohr's view if he ducked behind it.

"I said don't move."

"Are we to stand here all night?"

Lohr's mouth turned up in a grin. Was it Julian's imagination, or was there a sadistic quality to Lohr's smile? "No. Move your hands to your head and turn around."

Julian obeyed.

"Were I kind, I would shoot you now. But I imagine the engineers who work here would be most disconcerted to find your blood on their floor in the morning."

Lohr's footsteps echoed around the room as he came up behind Julian and pushed the handgun into his back. "Outside."

As Julian walked forward, his mind reviewed his training in hand-to-hand combat. When they neared the door, he arched his back and smashed his head into Lohr's nose.

Lohr grunted, and Julian turned in one quick motion, gripping the pistol and turning it to the side before Lohr could squeeze the trigger. Lohr recovered and tried to jerk the handgun away, but Julian held it and smashed his foot into Lohr's insole. The result was a slackened grip but not a full release. With one more twist, the pistol clambered to the floor and slid toward a pile of high-explosive shells stacked along the north wall. Julian dove for it, but Lohr wrapped a muscular arm around his neck and yanked.

Gasping for breath, Julian gripped Lohr's arm to ease the pressure. They remained locked in their deadly embrace, the seconds stretching out the same way an artillery barrage in the trenches did. But Lohr was the stronger man. With a sudden burst, Julian felt himself lifted from his feet and smashed onto the countertop. He slid halfway along its length, knocking munition pieces to the floor. Several of the sharper edges bit into his skin.

A hissing sounded. One of the shells that had fallen between Julian and Lohr released a thick greenish gas. Without stopping to retrieve his weapon, Lohr ran for the door.

Gasses formed all around Julian from the other disrupted shells. Still stunned from Lohr's powerful slam, he held his breath and stumbled toward the door. Already a headache was building, and his eyes stung. As he took in gulps of foul air from the hallway, his throat first itched, then burned. His movements were becoming less coordinated. He took long, agonizing steps, stumbling like a drunk into one of the offices.

If he could just make it to the window.

Surely the fresh air would help.

Why was the lock so difficult for his trembling hands?

If he could just make it outside . . .

# Chapter 39

WARREN USED HIS WEBLEY REVOLVER to take another shot at the guard rushing into the building. The other guard had run off, probably for reinforcements. The same civilian whose appearance had prompted Warren to throw a rock at one of the back windows came stumbling out and grabbed the guard by the shoulder. He yelled something in German. Warren couldn't understand the words, but he grasped the meaning. Something inside was no longer safe.

No matter how good Olivier was, a single, unarmed man was unlikely to scare a guard with a rifle, so Warren assumed the danger was something else. He went back to the building's rear, wondering if he should follow Olivier in through the vent on the roof. As he jogged to the tree, Warren heard the squeak of a window and a cough worse than the time he'd listened to the German pilot drown in his own blood.

If he hadn't recognized the man at the window, he would have fled. "Spider?"

The Frenchman didn't answer, struggling for breath as he tried to push the window up. It seemed jammed somehow, so Warren moved to help, but it slid open easily for him. He grabbed Olivier underneath the arms and pulled him outside.

Olivier immediately slumped to the ground, barely awake.

"Come on, Spider." Warren patted the man's cheeks, hoping to revive him, but he only winced. Noise from the front of the building told him the reinforcements had arrived. "Thank you, McDougall, for picking a small spy." Warren tugged Olivier from the ground and balanced him on his shoulder. He was heavy, but Warren could manage for a while. He ran, eager to put some distance between the two of them and the guards.

He rushed past a road and paused, listening for anyone who might be chasing them. He was met with silence. Maybe they were going to get away after all. He began moving again, afraid if he stopped for too long he wouldn't have the energy to start again. It was a long way back to the plane. Could he carry Olivier that far?

Olivier gagged and vomited all over Warren's back. Warren shuddered at the thick wetness, but the wind and the chill kept most of the smell away. Someone yelled, and Warren ran faster. Then a shot rang out, and Warren felt a painful blow in his thigh. He tumbled to the ground, dropping Olivier in the process.

* * *

Warren sat in the cold German jail cell with his knees pulled to his chest. The floor was hard and frozen, but there was only one narrow bench in the cell, and he'd laid Olivier on that. He'd also given the Frenchman the cell's single blanket. Blisters surrounded the edges of Olivier's nose and mouth, and each breath sounded like a gasp. He'd vomited again when they'd arrived. Warren had done his best to wipe away the mess, most of it blood.

Olivier was unresponsive. Warren didn't know what he'd been exposed to, so he wasn't sure how to help. The truth was, most forms of gas poisoning couldn't be treated in jail anyway. They'd probably both be executed in the morning, so at least it would be over soon. Listening to Olivier's struggle for breath, Warren thought it would be over for Spider well before dawn.

A German doctor had removed the bullet from Warren's left thigh and stitched it up. The man had even spoken English, told him it was only a flesh wound, that if he kept it clean and if he lived long enough, it would heal. It ached now, the pain flaring whenever he moved. The doctor had disinfected the wound but had spared no morphine for a prisoner.

At the beginning of his assignment in Essen, Olivier had told Warren that being executed wasn't any worse than dying in the trenches. It couldn't be much worse than burning to death or falling ten thousand feet from a broken air-plane either, but the apprehension gnawed at Warren's stomach. Apprehension and regret. He would have rather died in the air.

He shivered in the chill that penetrated all the way to his bones. Either the Germans didn't waste coal on prisoners, or they were as desperate for fuel as the French were. Would they freeze to death? He'd heard dying of cold was relatively easy after one turned numb. A draft sailed through the bars at the front of the cell. A narrow window on the back wall, also crossed with bars, let in an even bigger draft. Concrete blocks formed the rest of the cell.

Despite his injured leg, Warren was driven to his feet by the cold. The bars on the window were solid, and the opening was too small and too high to climb through anyway. The lock at the front of the cell looked solid, and a few moments of fiddling with it earned a shout from the guard.

Eventually Warren went back to his spot on the floor, listening to what he was sure were Olivier's death throes. Depression settled on him like a well-aimed artillery shell. His mother had told him stories about dark times and dark places. She'd told him he was never alone, that he could always pray. She had been so sure, but if she was right, why hadn't all the prayers on her behalf done her any good when she'd lain dying of cholera? Prayer was just something people did to make themselves feel better; it couldn't change anything. It wouldn't release them from prison or make the blisters in Olivier's lungs go away. Warren rubbed the ground with the heel of his healthy foot, thinking, remembering, but not praying.

He dozed off and woke with a crick in his neck. As he tried to rub it out, his mother's words about people with stiff necks and hard hearts came to mind. He felt a small smile pull at his lips. Then it faded. His mother, half the men in his flight squadron, and thousands of men in the trenches. All full of faith that hadn't saved them. Not physically. But he also knew physical salvation had never been as important to his mother as other types of salvation.

He hadn't prayed much since his mother had died. He'd said a few family prayers when his father had requested it but none with faith since the cholera and none at all since leaving Cardston. If he were to pray now, no one would know. Unless God was real, and then He would know. But if He was real, praying wouldn't be a sign of weakness or evidence of gullibility. It would be the right thing to do.

Olivier's breathing grew more strained, the gasps coming with a rattle. Praying might not help the injured Frenchman, but it couldn't hurt him either. After a few moments of thought, Warren bowed his head and started talking to God.

\* \* \*

Warren fell asleep sometime during the early hours of the morning. When he woke, a pale gray light shone through the barred window, and the cell was silent. His limbs were numb with the cold, and each breath he released hung in the air as a small white cloud. It took him a few seconds to remember where he was and what had happened. Then he panicked. If he couldn't hear Olivier, it probably meant the Frenchman was no longer breathing.

When he approached the bench, he saw Olivier's chest rising and falling in a steady rhythm. Perhaps Spider had an abnormally robust constitution. Or perhaps the Germans had come up with a new type of gas that had only temporary effects. Or maybe, *maybe*, it was a miracle.

Relief was short-lived because Warren fully expected the two of them to be sentenced and executed during the coming day. Had Olivier been healed just so he could stand before the firing squad or the hangman?

"Julian?" Warren whispered.

Olivier's eyelids closed more tightly, and a muffled grunt came from his throat.

Warren waited, wondering if he should wake him further, but being awake wouldn't do Olivier any good. Warren paced the cell a few times, partially as a distraction, partially to keep from freezing. As the blood worked its way through his body, the ache in his thigh flared.

"Flynn?" Olivier's voice was barely audible, a muffled utterance from someone on his deathbed.

"How do you feel?" Warren asked, sitting on the edge of the bench.

Olivier lifted a hand a few inches and turned his neck to the side. "I can move a little. That's something. And I can breathe. But everything hurts—especially my throat and my nose." He paused. Warren picked out a slight rattle in his breathing. "I didn't expect to be alive this morning."

"We might be shot before the morning's over."

Olivier frowned. "Tell them you crashed a few months ago on the German side of the line and you escaped from a prison camp. You're a POW, not a spy. Maybe they'll just send you to prison."

Warren almost laughed. "Lie while your body is being riddled with bullets from the firing squad?"

"It's not lying; it's self-preservation. And it would be foolish for you to die when there's a chance you can live. You've only been a spy for a few hours. Stick to being a pilot."

Chances were someone would find Warren's plane, and that would prove the lie false. Warren was glad he had borrowed an older model for the flight. The Germans wouldn't gain any new technology from taking the R.E.8 apart.

Their jailer came toward them, preventing any further discussion. He said a few sentences in German and held out two pieces of a substance that vaguely resembled bread. Warren hobbled to the front of the cell to receive it. When the old jailer walked away, Warren turned to Olivier for a translation.

"He said his lieutenant is on leave until after Christmas. While he's away, our guard is in charge. He said he's seen enough death to last him a lifetime, so he'll wait until the lieutenant returns and he's ordered to execute us. We have a few more weeks of life, I suppose."

Warren limped back to the bench. Another miracle? Or a mere postponement? Knowing Olivier couldn't feed himself, Warren broke off a small piece of bread and put it into his friend's mouth. Feeding the bread to Olivier was a slow process, but they had nothing else to do, and anything that could make their meager ration last a little longer felt worthwhile. The small pieces reminded him of Canada and his father, of breaking bread for their worship service, of all the symbolism that went with the sacrament. Those were his parents' beliefs, not his, and yet there was comfort in their faith and devotion. And maybe comfort wasn't an illusion after all, but something to seek after, worthwhile for its own sake, and evidence of a benevolent God.

# Chapter 40

*December 1917, Paris, France*

When McDougall and Flynn both disappeared, Evette took it upon herself to find the traitor in British intelligence, but she had no authority and few clues. She began by tailing everyone who worked in McDougall's office with the rank of captain or higher. It was a tedious process. She had hoped she might catch them meeting Lohr, but nothing so dramatic occurred. The men went to the office as expected and ate sometimes at a restaurant and sometimes at their various residences. She learned which post offices they used, where they banked, how often they shined their shoes and cut their hair. If one of them was a traitor, he did a good job hiding it.

Weeks went by, and 1917 drew to an end. Christmas Eve that year lacked the spirit Evette usually found in remembering the birth of the Christ child. With Emile gone, she felt more alone than ever. And she felt guilt. Had she allowed a silly infatuation with a soldier she'd met once to color her judgment and send first McDougall and then Captain Flynn off to rescue someone who was already lost? And were all three now dead?

Claire suggested they go to midnight mass, and Evette agreed, hoping it would cheer her. Many of the parishes weren't holding a service, so they pedaled through the cold, dark streets to several churches before finding an open one. The inside of the church was scarcely warmer than the street, but at least it was sheltered from the biting wind.

The war hadn't made her lose her faith, but it had made her question it. Evette tried to focus on the familiar carols, the candles, and the promise of the infant Savior. This year the ceremony was simpler, less elaborate. She found that appropriate. The birth of the baby in Bethlehem had, after all, been a simple affair. As the service ended, she felt a sliver of hope. Perhaps like the Wise Men seeking earnestly for the King of kings, she would have a long journey, but maybe something good waited at her final destination.

\* \* \*

Evette dined with the Donovans on Christmas afternoon. The meal would have been considered a feast in her village, especially since the war began, but it was a relatively humble supper for the wealthy Americans. After the meal, Claire played Christmas carols on the piano while Mr. Donovan, Evette, Mr. Franke, and the cook sang. The rest of the staff had the day off. As the sky grew dark, the others excused themselves, leaving Claire and Evette alone in the library.

"If you could have anything for Christmas, what would it be?" Evette asked.

Claire smiled wistfully. "I should say peace, and I would like the war to end. But I'd settle for a letter from Warren. I wrote him three weeks ago, and I haven't heard back."

Evette's cheeks burned. "Claire, I have something to tell you."

"Yes?"

"Monsieur McDougall told me to ask Captain Flynn for help with one of our projects, so I wrote to him. But when I explained what had happened with Spider, he flew to Germany to try to rescue him. He was only supposed to be gone a day or two. But . . . but something must have gone wrong. I haven't heard from any of them. I'm so sorry, Claire. If I'd known what would happen, I wouldn't have written to him."

Claire didn't respond. She stared at her fingers, still on the piano keys.

"He told me if he didn't make it back to tell you he still loved you."

That brought a sob and a sniffle.

"He may be fine," Evette added. "I've read accounts of pilots crashing on the wrong side of the lines and sneaking back through Belgium or Holland. It just takes time."

Mr. Donovan returned to the library, the terrier at his heels. "Who's ready for a Christmas toast?"

Claire ran from the room, tears streaking down her cheeks.

Mr. Donovan watched her go, then turned to Evette, a bewildered look on his face. "Whatever is wrong?"

"Captain Flynn is missing."

"Oh." Mr. Donovan sat in his favorite armchair, and the dog curled up near his feet. He could have said he'd been right all along to discourage the couple from marrying, but his face showed concern, not triumph. "What should I do for her?"

"I'm not sure. Missing is better than confirmed dead, but I think they feel like the same thing to Claire just now. I'll go see if I can comfort her."

"Give her a minute," Mr. Donovan said. "Let her get a few tears out. My wife always said it was healthy for a woman to cry from time to time."

Evette obediently waited. Maybe the late Mrs. Donovan was right.

As Evette wondered how to help Claire with her problem, an idea for fixing one of her own formed. "Mr. Donovan, I would like to ask a favor of you."

"I would be inclined to grant it, especially on Christmas."

"I'm trying to find a traitor, and I've narrowed the investigation down to three men. They all have accounts at the Caisse des Dépôts et Consignations. I need to know if any of them made a large deposit in June. If I can confirm one of them received bribe money when a German agent was in Paris, I'll have the evidence I need to take the matter to someone who can prevent them from doing any more damage."

"I know the manager. I shall have a chat with him as soon as he is back at work."

"Thank you, sir."

"With Russia out of the war, the Germans will have the advantage. Maybe this will help even things out. Run along after Claire now. I'm not the best person to comfort her about Captain Flynn, given what happened this fall. But I love my daughter more than anything. If you think I can help her, tell me how."

Evette spent the rest of the night letting Claire cry on her shoulder. She ached for Claire and for herself. If neither Captain Flynn nor Lieutenant McDougall had returned, it probably meant they were dead, and Spider along with them. Spider's death was bitter—with him gone, Evette lost a dream, an ideal. But it was worse for Claire. If Captain Flynn was dead, Claire was losing something much more tangible than a dream.

\* \* \*

Mr. Donovan was true to his word. He somehow convinced the bank's manager to let Evette read through the deposit histories for Captain Peter Broxton, Major Kent Halliday, and Lieutenant Colonel T. Horatio Walsh. In both May and November, Major Halliday had made abnormally large deposits. It was enough of a red flag for Evette to take the information to Lieutenant Colonel Walsh.

He worked in the same building as McDougall, and he seemed to recognize her when she came up to him. "Sir, may I have a moment of your time?"

He glanced at his watch and nodded curtly before leading her into his private office.

She explained how she'd overheard Lohr telling Simon about his source in British Intelligence, someone who had known why Simon was released and of the spies in Essen and Munich.

"Several of my men knew those facts, including me," Walsh said.

"Yes, sir. Lohr also said the man was expensive. I have a friend who is on good terms with the manager of the Caisse des Dépôts et Consignations. Your Major Halliday deposited a large sum into his account in May, when Lohr was here, and again in November, when Lohr may have been here again."

Walsh studied her for a moment, and she knew she'd convinced him.

The next day she heard the news. Lohr's source, Major Kent Halliday, would spend New Year's behind bars. She breathed a little easier knowing he couldn't betray any more intelligence. But Halliday confessed to selling out the spies in Munich and Essen. Lohr knew about Spider, and Evette had sent both McDougall and Flynn into a trap.

# Chapter 41

JULIAN'S EYES NO LONGER STUNG, and his throat no longer burned, but each breath seemed to draw insufficient air. He could move his arms and legs, but he felt weak and empty, as hollow as the center of a mortar, and he doubted he'd recover much strength on the pitiful prison meals. Warren had suggested the Germans might kill them by starvation instead of a more traditional execution, back when he was joking. But he didn't joke anymore, hadn't said anything remotely funny for over a week.

They took turns sleeping on the wooden bench. Warren often paced when it was Julian's turn. Julian was getting used to falling asleep to the pilot's shuffling feet. While Warren slept, Julian sat on the floor, debating whether he looked forward to the German lieutenant's return because it would mean an end to their limbo or whether he dreaded it because execution would shortly follow.

Few things encouraged talk of religion the way impending death did. Julian had told Warren he believed in God but wasn't sure if God was merciful or vengeful. When he saw Dorothea Kallweit speaking with the jailer one morning, his suspicion tipped toward vengeful.

She held a basket in her hands and looked much the same as she had the day Julian was arrested. Her clothes were too big, and her face was still etched with a permanent melancholy. A feeling of horror came over him as he thought of all the lies he'd told her. What would she say? Was she here for revenge? To demand justice?

The sergeant waved Dorothea back. There were other cells with prisoners, but she walked straight to Julian's. He stood, still wobbly on his feet, and held the bars for support. He waited for her to lash out, to call him names and curse him for lying to her family. Instead, she reached into her basket and brought out a loaf of bread.

"Here." She handed it to him.

Astonished, he reached for it. "Thank you." It wasn't the fine bread Herr Sauer occasionally brought from Berlin, but it was far superior to their typical prison fare.

"You look ill. Did they beat you when they arrested you?"

"No. I was exposed to something at the testing range. I've not been well since."

"Is that why your voice is changed?"

Julian nodded. He hadn't noticed a difference in his voice but assumed any change Dorothea heard was from the gas.

"I should have come sooner." Her lips pursed together. "But it took me this long to forgive you."

"You have reason to be angry. I'm sorry I lied to your family."

"Yes, you did lie to us." Dorothea's gaze dropped to the floor. "But you also shared your rations with us, planted a garden so we wouldn't starve, and gathered wood so we wouldn't freeze. You stayed up all night with my children when they were sick. And you encouraged Willi when I had no idea how to help him. You are our enemy, but you've been good to us."

Julian looked away and cleared his throat to keep his emotions in check. He almost winced—clearing his throat was now a painful ordeal. "How is Willi? I've worried about him."

"Willi is adjusting. He was too proud to come today, but he understands."

"And Franz?"

"Franz is confused. He looked up to you a great deal, but you're his enemy. It's given him something to talk to his brother about, and perhaps that's a good thing. Those two boys need each other."

"And your father?"

Dorothea frowned. "My father is ashamed he was fooled so completely for so long. He has said more than once that he hopes you are shot."

"He will probably get his wish."

Dorothea glanced at the guard. "Yes, he probably will." She turned back to Julian. "I'm not sure if I'll come again. My father wouldn't approve. But I thought you would like to know that Frau Von Hayek disappeared before anyone could question her. And most of all, I wanted to say thank you."

"You're a good woman, Frau Kallweit. Thank you for the bread. And for the forgiveness."

"I will pray they show you mercy," she said. "And if they do not, I will put flowers on your grave in the spring."

* * *

Leave ended for the German lieutenant, and on his first day back, he scheduled a trial for Julian and Warren. Julian had two days, and then he would be condemned. Maybe Warren would get off with a lighter punishment, but no one liked spies or those who assisted them. The future looked bleak and short.

The afternoon before their trial, Julian sat with his back against a wall while Warren slept. Despite Julian's best efforts, each breath seemed unable to satiate his body's needs. Someone walked into the front of the prison, but Julian couldn't see who without moving, and he was tired, so he stayed where he was. He could hear the sound of a conversation but not the words, until they came closer.

"Knew him in the factory. Never figured him for a spy. I owe him a bit of money—he bought me a few beers one night when I was broke. So I thought this would make up the difference. Spy or not, I don't like being indebted to anyone, even someone who will be dead by the end of the week."

Julian wondered who they were talking about. The man in the next cell was charged with desertion, not espionage, and the third cell held a pair of petty thieves. No one from the factory owed him money, but as the men came into view, it took all Julian's willpower to hide his shock. With the guard was the Dutchman who had smuggled McDougall in and out of Germany so often.

The Dutchman stood slightly behind the guard. He met Julian's eyes and winked. "Becker, or whatever your real name is, I know I owe you a beer, but I thought this might be more appreciated under the circumstances." The Dutchman's perfect German echoed around the cell.

Julian pushed himself to his feet and walked to the bars, where the man handed him a heavy loaf of black bread.

"We're even now?"

"Yes," Julian said for the guard's benefit. "Have a few rounds in my memory, will you?" Julian had no idea if that was a normal tradition in Germany, but he hoped it would give the right impression.

The Dutchman nodded and turned to leave.

"Thank you," Julian called after him.

With another wink, the man strode off and was soon gone.

Julian suspected there was something special about the bread, but he waited, not wanting the guard to see. Staring at it, he could make out a tear along one edge, like someone had ripped the bread apart and pasted it together again. Julian would eat it regardless of the paste and knew Warren would too. The bread the guards gave them was often moldy, usually dry, and always given in meager quantities. The occasional soup was mostly water, sometimes with a few pieces of cabbage or turnips floating inside.

When Warren woke, Julian motioned for him to sit between Julian and the front of the cell. With Warren blocking the guard's view, Julian gently tugged at the end of the bread. It came off in one chunk, confirming Julian's guess that it had been cut before. Shoved inside the loaf was a tiny revolver with a piece of paper wrapped around the grip. The weapon was so small that Julian could hide it under his hand. He met Warren's eyes and saw something there that had long been absent for both of them—hope.

Julian passed the revolver to Warren, who checked to see that it was loaded, then slipped it in his pocket. Slowly, so the paper would make no noise, Julian unfolded it and read the message, then showed it to Warren.

*Uniforms, ammunition, cash in the Essen safe house. Sorry I can't do more for you. Good luck. HM*

"Thank you, Howard McDougall," Warren whispered.

Julian slowly tore the paper into shreds and hid the pieces in the latrine bucket in the cell's corner. It wasn't much—a weapon and the promise of more supplies if they could sneak into the right apartment—but it was something.

# Chapter 42

THEY DISCUSSED THEIR OPTIONS IN hushed voices long into the night. Shooting anyone before the cell was unlocked wouldn't free them, so they waited. Their best chance would come when they were taken to trial.

Warren kept the revolver. He didn't want to shoot anyone point-blank, but he was worried about Julian's stamina. Better for him to shoot than to have the injured Frenchman disarmed in front of him, ruining their only chance to escape the firing squad.

They completed their plans several hours before dawn, but Warren didn't sleep. He prayed, not sure if it was appropriate to ask for help when he was trying to escape justice. Over the weeks since his arrest, he'd come to think that maybe there really was a God, but even if He existed, would He help someone like Warren?

The German lieutenant went to explain the case to the tribunal early, so the guard would take them to trial by himself. The sergeant's face was set as he came to their cell. He walked stiffly, a man resigned to an unpleasant task. Warren positioned himself closest to the door. It was only with difficulty that he kept his hands from shaking.

The guard motioned to him as he unlocked the cell and slid it open. He said something in German and motioned Warren forward as he pulled out a set of handcuffs. Warren pretended to obey, but as he stepped from the cell, he pulled the revolver from his pocket. The guard's jaw dropped, and he raised his hands as he took a step back.

Julian slipped from the cell, took the handcuffs, and fastened them around the guard's wrists. He also took the man's pistol and keys. "Thank you," he said in German.

Warren motioned the sergeant into the dank cell and locked him inside. He kept his handgun aimed at the guard until Julian called to him. "I've got the car keys."

Warren tossed the prison keys to the deserter in the next cell and followed Julian outside to a black Horch. The sun was brighter than Warren remembered, as if eager to draw attention to the two fugitives. He hoped the imprisoned guard wouldn't make too much noise. They needed a head start before someone discovered their escape and organized a manhunt.

"I've never driven before," Julian said.

Warren took the offered keys, and the two of them climbed in, ready to leave the prison behind them. "You know the house McDougall mentioned?"

"Yes."

Following Julian's directions, Warren drove from Essen's outskirts to its center. He clutched the steering wheel a little too firmly and had to fight the instinct to duck each time they passed someone along the road.

"It's just ahead." Julian pointed to a row of apartments.

Warren pulled the car over and parked in front of another building just to be safe. He waited until a woman walked by, heading the opposite direction. Then they backtracked. Warren matched his pace to Julian's painfully slow stride. At least the Frenchman was walking. That was an improvement, but Warren wondered if his recovery would ever be complete. He still wasn't sure they'd live long enough to find out.

Julian led him into the building and through the third door on the left. The front room was bare, but in the second room, spread on the bed, were two German infantry uniforms. On the desk lay a roll of bandages and a bottle of brown-red liquid. A pair of crutches leaned against the wall, and the top drawer of the desk contained a fistful of cash, ammunition for the revolver, and a pile of maps and train schedules.

Warren studied the timetables, wondering how difficult it was to sneak across the border—if they could get there. The one item McDougall had neglected to leave them was official paperwork. If train stations in Germany were anything like train stations in France, they'd be asked to show papers. "I wonder if my plane is still where I left it."

"Going back will be dangerous."

Warren picked up one of the garrison caps lying on the bed and put it on Julian's head. There was no peak to pull down over the man's face.

"Put a bandage around my forehead so it covers most of one eye," Julian said. "I'll look at the ground and perhaps no one will recognize me. You'll get a bandage around your jaw, I think. So no one expects you to have a conversation in German."

Warren nodded and put the German uniform on over his clothing. It was a good fit. "Thank you, McDougall," he whispered. *And thank you, God.*

After they changed, Warren handed Julian the crutches to help explain his slow gait. "What are you doing?" Warren asked as the Frenchman spread liquid from the jar along a folded piece of paper. Footsteps sounded in the hallway, and both men tensed until the sound faded.

When it was quiet again, Julian offered the papers to Warren. "Someone will ask us for papers. I'm hoping no one will want to handle them if they're covered in what looks like blood."

Warren accepted the painted mess. They split the money and bandaged each other's heads, and Warren pocketed the extra ammunition. He was hesitant to leave the relative protection of the apartment, but their shelter gave only the illusion of safety. Time was working against them. Even if no one had stumbled on the guard they'd locked up, they were late for their trial, so he assumed the search had begun.

They were back in their stolen Horch within fifteen minutes of leaving it. "Getting to where you left your plane will require a bit of a trek," Julian said after Warren started the engine. Their walk had been brief, but he sounded out of breath.

"Are you up to it?" Warren asked.

"I hope so. One hike, then a nice, easy flight to freedom. I'll have good motivation for making it."

They drove past the Sauer estate and parked the car to the side of the road. They left the extra bandages and the crutches in the car, thinking they wouldn't need them. The sensation of being hunted dimmed as they entered the shade and obscurity of the trees. But after tromping through the woods and reaching the field, Warren's plane was nowhere to be seen.

# Chapter 43

WARREN SEEMED CRESTFALLEN AT HIS plane's disappearance. They searched for a fruitless half hour in case the weeks had marred their memory.

"We can take the train out," Julian suggested. His lungs burned from the day's exertion, and the thought of sitting on a train, even a German train, was appealing.

"Were I in charge of the manhunt, the train station would be the first place I'd look."

"How much petrol is in the car?"

Warren frowned. "Not much."

"Enough to make it to a different station?" Perhaps taking the train from a smaller station would be safer.

Warren shook his head. "We may have to walk partway to the station as it is. Unless we can buy more."

"Fuel is rationed, and we don't have cards."

"Black market?"

Julian tried to think of where they could get illegal fuel. Herr Sauer wasn't above using the black market, and Julian knew some of his sources, but he didn't think it would work. "Most of the local dealers would recognize me. Earning an illegal profit is one thing; aiding a spy is a little more serious. If we went farther from Essen, it might work, but—"

"But we don't have the fuel for that. I guess we'll take the train."

Julian pulled together a strategy as they started back. "They'll expect us to go north to the closest border. We can go to Cologne and then Aachen instead. Less direct, less suspicious. I've never crossed the border on foot, but there's got to be a way."

"We have plenty of money for bribery," Warren said. "That should help a little."

They hiked back to the Horch. Julian moved more slowly now, wheezing as much as breathing, and Warren was using his left leg only gingerly. Neither of them was completely healed, and three weeks in jail had eroded their physical endurance.

As they neared the edge of the woods, Julian held his hand out. "Slowly. We've been gone a while." He peered around a tree, and his stomach dropped. The guard they had left handcuffed in jail was strolling around the car. Julian spotted a second policeman a few paces away.

Julian motioned Warren back. They could shoot the guards, but he wasn't sure that was the best strategy. Once they were in the thicker trees, he whispered, "We can go around."

\* \* \*

The sun was slipping beyond the western horizon when they reached the station. Smoke and steam filled the air, a sign that most mechanics had gone away to war and German trains were no longer running at their efficient best. In the mist-filled twilight, Julian picked out numerous military policemen checking passes. He gulped, then winced at the pain in his throat and glanced at Warren. Some of the Canadian's bandages had fallen out of position, so Julian tugged them back into place around his jaw. "I'll buy tickets to Bonn."

"I thought you said we'd go as far as Cologne, then head for Aachen."

"We'll pay the extra. If anyone asks, the clerk will give them the wrong destination."

While he waited in line to purchase tickets, Julian looked back. He could tell Warren was nervous. The uniform helped him blend in, but not being able to understand what was said all around him had to be nerve-racking. In front of the trains, a line had formed, and prospective passengers were being thoroughly questioned. With his bandages, no one would expect Warren to speak, but they would expect him to follow directions.

"This way," Julian whispered, pulling on Warren's elbow and leading him away from the crowd. He hailed a pair of soldiers at a broken train window. German soldiers weren't so different from French ones, and he had an idea. "Comrades, will you make a pair of men on their way home for convalescence leave stand in line in the cold? I've been gassed, and the cold is bad for my lungs. And my friend's leg isn't completely healed. If we stop to rest, we might miss the train, and then my friend will miss the birth of his first child."

Almost instantly, the window was pushed open to its widest, and the men hoisted first Warren and then Julian into their car. Julian caught the bewilderment on Warren's face, but the pilot quickly hid his surprise.

"Thank you," Julian told the soldiers. McDougall had been thoughtful enough to put cigarettes in his uniform pocket, so Julian handed them around as thanks to the men.

It wasn't until after the train left and most of the soldiers had finished their cigarettes that Warren leaned next to Julian. In a voice barely audible over the noise of the train, he asked, "What did you tell them?"

"I said we were too weak to wait in line, and if we missed the train, you would miss the birth of your first child."

The corners of Warren's lips crept up. "I wonder what Claire would think were she to hear rumors that I'm fathering German babies."

"Claire?"

"My girl." Then Warren frowned. "Or at least she was."

The boxcar they sat in was crowded with other soldiers, but Julian hadn't slept well the night before, and their series of escapes had worn him out. He drifted off to sleep as soon as he closed his eyes.

When he woke, it was light outside. Had they slept through their stop? One of the real German soldiers was awake too. "Where are we?" Julian asked.

"A few minutes from Cologne."

"Why did it take all night?"

The soldier shrugged. "Mechanical problems. And they searched the train a few times. Probably looking for deserters."

Julian wondered if they had also been looking for escaped spies. He shook Warren awake when the crowded Cologne station came into view. As they pulled to a stop, a conductor came through and told everyone to stay where they were. The policemen needed to see everyone's papers.

"Not again," one of the soldiers grumbled. "At this rate, I'll spend all my leave on the train."

A policeman yawned as he came into their section. "Papers, please."

The passengers groaned collectively, then reached into their pockets for identification, leave passes, and travel papers. The policeman reached Julian midway through his search of the car and cringed at the blood-stained paper and Julian's apologetic explanation. He glanced at the document but didn't touch it with his fingers. He did the same with Warren's.

Only after all compartments on the train from Essen had been checked were the passengers allowed off. Julian bought tickets to Aachen. He slipped a lean, elderly conductor a wad of bills and managed to avoid another paperwork inspection.

"I'm not sure how much longer we can do this," Julian admitted to Warren. "We're bound to run into someone who isn't timid about dirty papers and who doesn't accept bribes." The train rolled out, but the smooth hum of the wheels meeting the track failed to soothe Julian's anxiety. Frost crystals formed on the windows of the insufficiently heated train car, blocking his view of the land they passed, but even if he couldn't see it, he was still in enemy territory. Freedom was far, far away.

# Chapter 44

WHEN THEY PULLED INTO A small village train station, it looked as though there would be another inspection.

"Let's get off," Warren said. He couldn't take another brush with the police. "Find somewhere to hide for a few days. Maybe the search will die down."

Julian seemed uncertain, but as another group of policemen boarded the train, he stood. They left through the boxcar's front door as the police entered from the back. They trudged along a wet dirt road surrounded by fields full of the frost-tipped remnants of last fall's harvest. The sharp air, the absence of people, and the lack of sounds other than the crunch of their feet made Warren feel like he was finally free. If his three weeks in prison had taught him nothing else, it was that the Germans loathed the British, and he didn't think they would ease their hatred at all for a Canadian. Being away from the crowds lifted a huge weight from his shoulders.

But as the morning passed, Warren started limping. Julian's breaths had long been coming in short gasps. Now his breaths were interrupted by coughing fits. Warren had suggested they rest before, and Julian had said he wanted to press on. This time Warren didn't ask. "We're stopping for a bit."

Julian was coughing too hard to argue.

It was a long way to the border. They wouldn't make it on foot, not in their current state. The deserted nature of their surroundings that had filled Warren with hope just hours before now made him face the harsh truth. They needed a place to hide, somewhere sheltered from the barren landscape and icy wind.

They rested for a while. Julian's coughing didn't stop. As the cold crept under his skin and sank into his bones, Warren wondered if they should go back to the village for food and warmth. A rumbling in his stomach told him food couldn't come too soon. Perhaps half a mile away, a rise hid the rest of the road. "I'm going to see where the road goes from there." Warren pointed. "If I don't see anything promising, we may have to turn back."

Julian nodded his agreement.

Warren's pace was slow. The morning's trek had lasted about three hours. It was barely noon, but he suspected it would take them until nightfall to get back to the village. He worried about Julian. He had improved in prison, but he was still weak. Warren was too, but not in the same way. Though Julian never complained, Warren could tell each bit of their journey was wearing him down more and more. The blisters from that first terrible night might be gone, but the gasping for breath and coughing were worse than they'd been in weeks.

From the hill's crest, Warren could make out a small scattering of homes. Perhaps they could hide in one of the barns. But for how long? Eventually they would have to go back to the train station.

"Father in Heaven," Warren whispered as he walked back to his friend. "I came to Germany to rescue Julian. I didn't count on getting shot or getting arrested. And now I've gotten us into a mess. If you're real, and if you care, I would appreciate a little help. A little guidance. Something."

Nothing happened. Warren wasn't sure what he'd expected. Perhaps a cart to come by that would take them to the village or a peal of church bells announcing the end of the war. Maybe Warren's desperation was forcing him to hope for miracles when they no longer existed.

Julian's breathing had quieted by the time Warren returned. It wasn't a miracle, but at least it was positive.

"There are half a dozen houses beyond the hill. We can hide there."

"They'll think we're deserters."

Warren hadn't thought of that, but Julian was right.

"Don't look so gloomy. They may think we're deserters, but that doesn't mean they'll turn us in."

Warren pulled Julian to his feet. Before they reached the hill, Julian's cough returned.

"We can tell them you're on your way home but that you need to rest before you can continue," Warren said.

Julian paused for a while, catching his breath. "Except the only village around here whose name I know is the one where we left the train."

"Can we swing around and approach from the other direction? Pretend we're on our way to the station we just left?"

"They'll wonder where we got off." Julian coughed again and winced. "We'll figure something out. Let's go."

Approaching the set of homes in the bright afternoon sun gave them no way to hide. They were in the open, highlighted against the snow for all the residents to see. Warren spotted a plume of smoke coming from the nearest home's chimney. Julian too stared at the inviting cottage. They shared a look, then turned off the road.

An elderly woman answered their knock. Julian handled the conversation. Warren wasn't sure what was said, but the woman soon ushered them in and chatted happily with Julian while she sliced pieces of bread for them. Julian gave her some of their money, and she brought out a jar of preserved pears. Next she took four eggs from a basket and fried them for the men.

It had been at least a month since Warren had eaten so well. He hoped Julian was thanking the woman profusely. Warren knew how to say *danke* but didn't want the woman to think he could talk, so he kept silent while Julian and the woman spoke.

After the meal, the woman bundled up and headed outside.

"Chores," Julian explained.

Warren walked to the window. Several logs were piled next to a dwindling stack of firewood near the back door. Maybe he could help repay the woman's kindness. "Will you ask if I can chop some wood for her?"

Julian stood. "Yes."

"You rest."

Julian seemed about to protest.

"Your lungs finally calmed down. We may have more walking to do soon."

"She said we can stay the night. There's a convent not far away. The nuns turned it into a hospital a few years ago. She assumes we came from there. Sounds like she's seen several soldiers released for convalescence leave who thought they could walk to the train station rather than waiting for the weekly carriage ride. She assumes we did the same."

Warren nodded. Maybe miracles were real after all.

Julian went outside with Warren to talk to the woman about the firewood. He had to stay close since the woman would occasionally ask a question and look to Warren as if expecting him to answer. When the woman went back inside, Warren gestured for Julian to follow her. The man needed rest.

Warren had a feeling he would be sore the next day. He hadn't chopped wood since he was a teenager in Canada. But his rhythm soon improved, even if it never felt as smooth as it had when he was doing it regularly. He had tripled the woman's supply of firewood when a familiar sound caught his ear. He couldn't quite pinpoint the type, but an airplane engine rumbled nearby. He walked from the woodpile, his eyes on the sky until he spotted it. A little biwing two-seater trainer plane. Something was leaking, and the plane was headed for a nearby field.

As Warren watched it land, the old woman and Julian came outside. Warren motioned toward the plane, and the three of them trudged to the field. He picked out the angry tone of one of the men, probably the instructor, berating the other man, probably the student. Warren was drawn to the machine. A tree branch jutted from the side of the fuselage; the student must have flown too close to the treetops. He examined the hole in the radiator. It would be easy enough to give it a temporary patch.

The instructor saw him touch the plane and turned his anger on Warren. He had to remind himself not to react, not to show his expertise. His current uniform, after all, proclaimed he was an infantryman, not a pilot or an officer. He took a few steps back, which was enough to satisfy the instructor, who was undoubtedly used to the attention airplanes generated.

First the instructor shooed Warren, Julian, and the old woman away. Then, as more civilians crowded in for a closer look, he motioned to Julian and spoke to him earnestly for a few minutes. Julian nodded, seeming to agree to something, then took up a guard stance and motioned for Warren to join him.

With a wave of his hands and a shout like artillery fire, the instructor made the civilians step back. Then he jerked a finger at the student, and the two of them stomped off. Warren watched them confiscate a car from one of the local inhabitants and drive away.

It was a few minutes before a combination of the cold and the memory of the instructor's threats drove part of the crowd away and Julian came close enough to Warren to whisper in French. "We're guarding the plane. Do you suppose we can steal it after they repair it?"

"Why wait?"

Julian eyed the gash in the radiator.

"It's minor. Find me some soap, and I'll fix it." He checked the fuel levels. "Find me some petrol, and I'll fly us home." He looked at the sun, shading his eyes with his hand. "We shouldn't leave until almost dark. There isn't a plane stationed near the front line that can't shoot this thing down if they see us."

"Soap is rationed just like the petrol. Good thing McDougall left us with a small fortune."

Julian waited until only a handful of boys from the village still watched the plane. Then he slogged from door to door, offering money for fuel or soap. Warren saw him collect a can of something, most likely petrol, at the house where the instructor had borrowed the car, but he had to stop at several other homes before he came back. A satisfied smile brightened his face despite the wheeze coming from his lungs.

Warren grinned back. "Well done." He topped off the fuel tank. Were he flying a plane he planned to use again, he would be far pickier about the type of petrol he poured inside. But he felt this would be the trainer's last flight. As long as it ran all the way to France, Warren didn't care about the engine's longevity.

He shoved the soap into the radiator's hole. It wasn't an ideal, permanent fix, but he knew other pilots who had done the same thing with holes in their radiators. He left Julian with the plane while he fetched more water for the radiator from the old woman's well. The bright sunlight reflecting up from the snow would help slow the freezing process, but on his way back to the plane, he had an idea. It wouldn't be unusual for a pair of soldiers on guard duty to build a fire.

Warren wished, not for the first time, that he spoke flawless German. He glanced at Julian when he returned to the plane.

"What?"

"I hate to ask, but can you see if the woman will sell us some firewood? I don't want the parts to freeze up. We may have to take off in a hurry if the instructor returns before evening. And it will be cold up there, especially at night. I doubt this goes very high, but I'll want to take it to its ceiling so we're less vulnerable to ground fire. If she has any hats, gloves—even socks—it will make the trip better."

Julian tried to hide a cough and headed back to the cottage.

"I'll carry the firewood—don't you try to drag it out here."

Julian turned back. "I thought your leg was injured."

"It's not bad," Warren lied. *Not as bad as your lungs.*

# Chapter 45

TROUBLE DROVE INTO TOWN MIDAFTERNOON in the form of the returning instructor and a pair of mechanics. Warren had hoped they'd have another two hours before they had to take off, but maybe they could fly to another field and wait there until dark. He didn't overanalyze his options. He had to start the engine immediately.

He threw some green branches on the bonfire, hoping the added smoke would give them an advantage. "Time to go," he told Julian. As Julian climbed into the rear seat, Warren clicked the ignition switch and strode to the propeller. Usually someone else spun the propeller so the pilot could control the plane from the second it had power. Warren hoped his legs would be agile enough to clamber into the plane in time despite the cold and the lack of chocks.

He spun the propeller once, twice. Nothing happened, but that wasn't unusual. He had built the fire between the road and the plane, so he got in a few more spins before the instructor and his mechanics noticed.

The shouts in German barely reached him. Spin. Silence. Spin. Silence. Spin. A slight whir that quickly died out. Spin. More German shouts. Spin. The engine almost catching. Spin. A German rifle shot. Warren spun again and hoped Julian was ducking in his seat.

The engine finally caught on the fifteenth try. Warren ducked under the whirling propeller and climbed onto the moving plane, sliding into his seat without bothering to strap himself in. Straps were useful but only during stunts and landings. He doubted this plane would do many stunts, and he would worry about landing after he'd managed takeoff.

Rifle shots came with increasing frequency as Warren tried to pick up momentum. The car sped toward them, moving as quickly as the plane.

Warren heard a cry from the back seat. "Julian?"

"Just my arm. It's not bad."

"Come on!" Warren said to the plane. He had seen phenomenal Hun aircraft in action, but apparently they saved their good engines for something other than trainer planes.

He could count three rifle holes in the wings without even turning his head before the plane was fast enough to try for takeoff. The first time he failed, the front wheels plowing back into the snowy field, the plane losing momentum in the process. He checked over his shoulder. The car was gaining on him, its wheels better designed for travel through uneven snow.

*Why couldn't they have been training on a Fokker?*

Warren tried again, and the gutless plane finally lifted from the ground. Another pair of rifle shots hit the fuselage, but now that he was airborne, he was certain those shots would be the last. Had the plane been armed, he would have been tempted to turn around and strafe the car, but perhaps it was just as well that he didn't have that option. Strafing with a damaged plane was risky.

The trainer's engine was almost as unimpressive in the air as it was on the ground. He had to struggle for each foot of altitude. He was high enough that he didn't have to worry about trees, but what would happen when they flew over a battery of field guns? He kept looking for potential landing strips, somewhere to hide the plane until nearly dark, but nothing turned up. In the snow, he didn't want to risk landing on anything questionable. He might get stuck on the ground and thus stuck in Germany.

"Julian," he shouted over the engine.

"Yes?"

"If we land, I'm not sure we'll be able to take off again."

"Then don't land until we're in France."

"We'll hit the lines during daylight."

"Do what you think is best."

German pilots would have trained on a similar plane, so they would recognize it as theirs and hopefully hold their fire. The Allied airmen, on the other hand, wouldn't immediately realize the plane was German. Would they show caution before attacking? The plane had no identifying marks, no clear sign to the uninitiated that it was German. Most of the pilots he knew would come in for a closer look before shooting it from the sky, close enough to see the plane was unarmed. If Warren signaled his intention to land in their territory, perhaps they would escort him down. The men on the front line and in the supporting trenches were less predictable, which was another reason to keep flying. Maybe by the time he reached the churned-up landscape of the trenches, he would be high enough to avoid small-arms fire. If he landed again and took off too close to the lines, he'd never regain the altitude he'd fought so hard for.

The plane flew on, sluggishly cooperating with Warren's directions. Higher, faster, westward. The cold wind bit into Warren's nose and cheeks, made his fingers ache with pain. He alternated putting them inside his jacket to keep the blood moving. On occasion he looked back. Julian was huddled in his seat, a pair of knitted socks over his hands and a wool cap over his head.

"How's your arm?" Warren yelled.

"Numb. Too cold to bleed much."

Warren glanced back at Julian's arm, tied with a handkerchief. Another hour and they would be home. Another hour and they'd have medical care. Another hour and they would be free. Warren remembered to fasten his safety strap. He checked over his shoulder again; Julian had already buckled himself in.

The landscape passed below them in a white, brown, and gray patchwork broken occasionally by evergreen groves. Finally, the familiar sights of battle appeared. The stockpiles of supplies, the artillery teams. And then a long series of trenches. Warren wasn't sure which section they were flying into. Would French poilus or British Tommies greet them when they landed? There were other possibilities too, but it didn't matter much as long as they weren't German.

The sun was low, making shadows long, but also highlighting the little two-seater. As he passed over the last of the trenches, now safely over friendly territory, he let out a holler of joy. They had made it. They had escaped.

His relief ended abruptly when an artillery shell exploded not more than fifty yards off. He saw another streak and identified the culprit—friendly Archie aimed at him. "Stupid devils," he muttered under his breath. Rather foolish thing that, wasting shells on a slow-moving, unarmed plane. Warren dove under the next series of white explosions, cursing the artillery.

They managed to dodge at least a dozen bursts, reducing their altitude as they went. Then the world to his right erupted in a shower of light and shell fragments. He heard them ripping through the plane's wing, and an instant later, a piece of shrapnel slammed into his face. Warren screamed in pain. He lifted a hand to his face, feeling the damage.

"Are you all right?" Julian called.

Warren's hand came away red with blood. He could no longer see with his right eye, and he had to wipe away gore to see with his left one. He'd never felt such agony before. The plane had been shaken by the explosion, but it still flew. And like the mangled plane, Warren had to ignore the pain and carry on a while longer.

"Warren?"

"I'm taking her down." Originally Warren had hoped to find a nice, flat place to land. He no longer cared about that. He just wanted to be on the ground again. The landing didn't have to be pretty. They just had to survive it.

The fading light and the loss of vision in his right eye made it difficult for him to tell how close he was to the trees, to the ground, to the blur of men running underneath them, probably with rifles. He would have to land more by feel than by sight. He knew to slow down by cutting the engine off for intervals, knew he wanted to hit the ground at the shallowest of angles. Having never flown the plane before, he had no idea how long it would take to stop, but he touched down roughly and hoped the field ahead was clear.

It wasn't. The edge of his eyesight was fading, so he never saw the tree, just felt it tear off the right wing. The plane twisted and skidded to a stop.

"Warren?"

Warren swallowed. He'd never run into a tree before, but he'd never had to land with such piercing pain in his face before either. He meant to answer Julian but never got around to it. A group of men approached. Dazed from the crash, he couldn't even pick out which uniform they wore.

"They're Aussies," Julian said.

Warren nodded, but that made him dizzy. "Not one of my better landings," he mumbled. A few minutes ago, he had been eager to be on solid ground again, but now he simply sat until some of the men released his straps and plucked him from the wrecked plane.

"Warren. Your face!" Julian broke off in a choking sound, either from shock or a relapse of his lung problems. Warren was in too much pain and was too exhausted to care which. He collapsed in the mud. While he waited for the stretcher, the world around him turned gray, then black.

# Chapter 46

*March 1918, Beaufort War Hospital, Bristol, England*

WARREN AND JULIAN WERE SENT to a British hospital in Southern England and shared a room with a handful of other patients. The room had no mirrors, for which Warren was grateful. Seven weeks had passed since the crash. Six and a half weeks had passed since Warren had come out of a morphine-induced haze and the doctor had told him he hadn't been able to save his eye. Gone was his right eye and, with it, his flying career.

He tried to keep it in perspective. Better to be permanently injured than executed by the firing squad, and he shared the hospital with patients who had lost far bigger pieces of themselves. Some days were easier than others, but the nights . . . the nights were always bad.

McDougall came to see them that afternoon. He'd come before, but Warren had still been dealing with the pain at its worst, so he barely remembered the visit. Most of the information McDougall needed was from Julian anyway, so they hadn't talked much back in February.

The three of them went out to the hospital's garden. It was a pleasant March day, the sun shining brightly, the wind cold but weak. "I hear the Germans are driving us back," Warren said. He no longer limped, but sometimes his leg still hurt. A black patch covered his injured eye.

McDougall frowned. "Like 1914 all over again. They don't have to worry about the Russians anymore, so they can transfer men west. Even with help from the Americans, our men are being overwhelmed."

"It will work out," Julian said.

McDougall scoffed. "Paris is being shelled. That's how far they've come."

"This is their last effort." Julian looked south, toward France. "Like a wave washing up on the sand just before the tide turns."

"If the tide turns," McDougall said.

"The Yanks are coming, remember? The Germans have no new allies. I read Sauer's diary. The territories Germany took from Russia will take more men to control than originally thought. If they shift too many men west, they'll appear weak, and their allies in the east might demand part of the spoils."

"I hope you and Herr Sauer are right."

"You said Paris is being bombarded?" Warren broke in.

McDougall turned to him. "Yes."

"Is Claire all right?"

"Why don't you write to the bonnie lass and ask?"

Warren didn't answer. He'd received a handful of letters from her, forwarded from his old aerodrome, but hadn't answered them. If he wrote back, she'd know where he was. What if she came to visit? He wasn't ready for her to see him like this. He supposed he would have to face the world outside the hospital eventually, but he needed more time. He hadn't even written to his grandmother, knowing how quickly news would spread from her to Claire. It wasn't right to keep his loved ones in the dark, but every time he grabbed a sheet of paper, he felt sick to his stomach.

"Any word on when either of you will be released?" McDougall asked.

Julian glanced at Warren. When he didn't answer, Julian did. "The doctors think my lungs have scarred over. I might not make any more progress."

"When they release you, write to me. I have connections in the French Army. We can find something that doesn't require much physical exertion. Translation, liaison duty. Things of that sort."

"Thank you, sir."

"Flynn, when will they release you?"

He wasn't sure. The scar running from his eyebrow to his cheekbone had healed in a permanent sentence of mutilation. "Soon." The word was terrifying.

* * *

Several weeks later, a dark-haired nurse looked up from a file of papers and turned first to Julian, then to Warren. "Why isn't your friend in the gas ward?"

Panic welled up inside Warren's chest. In Germany he'd learned to distinguish Julian's waking breath from his sleeping breath. When Warren was having a bad night, knowing Julian was awake brought comfort, even when no words were exchanged. He didn't want Julian transferred. "This is where he was assigned when we came."

"Hmm. Strange that they shipped a Frenchman all the way to England." The nurse moved to the next patient, but that didn't mean the matter was settled.

"Maybe I should go back to France," Julian said after Warren translated the conversation.

"You still have coughing fits."

"And they aren't getting any better. I'd rather take a few weeks of convalescence leave with my father. I haven't seen him in years . . ." Julian's words
trailed off, tinged with melancholy.

Warren knew why. Julian's mother had died during his first winter in
Germany. Julian, unlike Warren, had written to his family immediately after
their escape. Warren had finally posted a letter to his grandmother last week,
four months after his disappearance.

"This is a nice hospital," Julian continued. "I didn't know hospitals could
be so nice . . . but it isn't home."

"Weren't you in hospital before?" Warren thought back to the first time
they'd met, the day he'd crashed his old B.E.2.

"They called it a hospital. It felt more like a butcher shop. It was filthy and
crowded, and the staff would only help the men they could send back to the
front."

That explained why McDougall had sent Julian to England. "I'm sorry.
If I'd known more about French hospitals, I would have had you sent to a
British one with Boyle."

"That probably would have been against regulations. But maybe I should
see about being discharged before that nurse asks too many questions and gets
me kicked out. It's probably still against regulations."

Warren knew he too should see about leaving. He glanced at the eye patch
on the bedside table. It wasn't so horrible, was it? Just a bit of black fabric.

"Warren?"

He recognized the soft voice instantly. How did Claire get in here? How did
she even know where he was? He reached for the patch and yanked it on before
turning. Even with only one eye to see her, she was beautiful. Her red curls were
pinned up, giving him a clear view of her creamy skin dotted with freckles and her
blue eyes currently fixed on him. She stepped forward cautiously, as if unsure she
was welcome.

"How did you know I was here?"

"Your grandmother told me."

That didn't surprise him. Claire probably wrote to his grandmother more
than he did, especially lately. "So news from the single letter I wrote her made
it all the way to Paris, did it?"

"You aren't angry that I've come, are you?" Her lips turned down but not
in the exaggerated pout he was used to seeing. This was a more subdued sign, one
of unconscious worry rather than of purposely displayed displeasure.

Warren stood. If he was going to have a conversation with Claire, he didn't want to do it in front of five other men, even if they were pretending to start a card game. "No. I'm not upset. I just wasn't expecting you, and I suppose I've gotten out of the habit of smiling. Let me show you the garden."

She nodded her agreement, and they walked silently through the hall and down the stairs to the ground floor. Stairs still made his leg twinge, so he took them slowly. Claire noticed. "Your grandmother didn't say what happened."

"I didn't tell her."

"Will you tell me?"

Warren studied her face. He wasn't used to Claire being timid, but it had been a while since they'd seen each other. He waited until they were outside. "I was shot in the leg. And took some shrapnel to my eye. It's gone now." He let out a huff. "The shrapnel and the eye."

He sat on a bench, and she sat next to him. "I'm sorry, Warren." She hesitated, then slipped her arm through his.

He watched her as the seconds ticked by, unsure what to say. It was good to see her, but this wouldn't change the past, couldn't change his dismal future.

"I was so worried," she said. "At first I thought you were ignoring my letters because you were angry. You had every right to be, but I still hoped for forgiveness. Then I heard you had disappeared. You have no idea how relieved I was to find out you were alive. I came to England as soon as I got your grandmother's message." She smiled through a few tears. "Papa must have been so confused. He's been trying to send me to London since the Germans started shelling Paris, and I kept saying I wasn't going to run away. I didn't tell him the real reason I finally came."

"Is the shelling bad?"

"It's . . . it's scary more than deadly. They're firing from behind the front lines, so we never hear any warning. At first everyone suspected bombs from an airplane or a zeppelin, but the skies were clear. Evette and Lieutenant McDougall were running ragged those first days, thinking it might be sabotage."

After McDougall's visit, Warren had found newspaper accounts of the Paris bombardment. He didn't want Claire to go back while the huge gun was in range. "Will you stay in London?"

"I'm not sure. I don't like the idea of being here where it's safe while my father and Evette and Franke are all suffering through the barrage." She glanced up at him, her eyes seeming to memorize every detail of his changed face. "But if I was wanted here, I might could prolong my visit."

Warren didn't answer.

"Will you be released soon?" Claire pulled her hands into her lap and stared at them. "If you were to recover for a while at your grandmother's house, I had thought . . . I had hoped we could see more of each other. Maybe start again where we left off." She peeked up at him. "I know things didn't work out like you were hoping last year, but I didn't see that as an end to our future, just a delay. I was scared, but I never stopped caring for you, Warren. When your grandmother wrote to me, I knew it didn't matter how badly you were injured—I would still love you."

"My face is destroyed, Claire. It's not the type of face you want to look at over tea or have escort you to the theater."

"It's the face of a hero."

Warren shook his head. "No, all the real heroes are dead."

Slowly, hesitantly Claire lifted the patch on his eye. He didn't stop her. She would see it eventually, and it was better to get it out of the way before he let his hopes build more than they already had the second she appeared again. He expected her to gasp, to recoil, to show some sign of distaste, but instead she stood and kissed his empty eye socket. "I'm not so sure. I think I'm sitting with a hero. One who I hope will forgive me."

"Claire, I—" He broke off, still at a loss for what to say. He still cared for her as much as he had when he'd proposed. "Claire, I love you more than airplanes."

She gazed down on him, a smile pulling at her lips. "Is that the best thing you can come up with?"

He was speechless. Didn't she realize what he was saying?

"It's the most romantic thing I've ever heard."

He took her hand and pulled her toward him until she was balanced on his knees. Then, despite the string of patients, doctors, orderlies, and nurses passing the bench, he wrapped an arm around her, ran a hand along the back of her neck, and kissed her.

\* \* \*

Warren spent two weeks with his grandmother, wondering why he hadn't left the hospital earlier. His Grandma Beatrice and Claire's Grandma Huntley spoiled him completely, and the kisses he stole from Claire whenever they were alone helped convince him that a lost eye wasn't the end of the world.

She caught him rubbing his good eye early one morning while he read the paper. "You might shouldn't read three newspapers every day. You're straining your eye."

Warren turned the page. "Two, not three. And after sitting in a German jail without access to any news at all, I want to read all I can."

"Any good news?"

"No." Warren folded the paper. Claire was easier on his eye than the newsprint was anyway.

"You were in a German jail?"

It wasn't the first time Claire had asked about Germany, and as usual, Warren tried to change the subject. "I'm not supposed to talk about it."

"But what about the man you went to rescue?"

Warren hadn't thought Claire knew his purpose in going to Germany, but he supposed Evette had told her. "It turns out I'm not very good at rescuing people. The man I went after ended up in jail with me, both of us injured. Then he got shot when we finally escaped."

Claire hung her head as if mourning Julian's hardships. Warren was about to ask her how much she had learned of Spider when his grandmother's butler interrupted them.

"Sir, an officer is here to see you."

Warren followed the butler into his grandmother's sun room, where a Royal Flying Corps lieutenant waited.

"I have orders for you, sir."

Warren nodded and motioned for the man to be seated. "Thank you for coming."

The man remained on his feet. "First, I am to inform you that you are no longer a member of the Royal Flying Corps."

"What?" Ousting him from the corps completely? They might as well tell him he couldn't eat. "I can still fly. My eyesight might not be sharp enough for dogfights, but I could train new men or pilot reconnaissance flights or—"

"The Royal Flying Corps and the Royal Naval Air Service are now the Royal Air Force. You've been transferred, but you're no longer a captain."

"Oh." Warren wondered if the merger had created too many midlevel officers.

"You are now a major. Congratulations on your promotion, sir. You are expected at your new squadron in three days." The lieutenant handed him some papers. Warren had been promoted out of routine flying duty, but he would still be on the front lines, still breathing the scent of castor oil, still hearing the buzz of engines and feeling the blast of propellers. And plenty of squadron leaders still flew from time to time.

The young lieutenant saluted, turned sharply, and walked from the room.

It was probably the best Warren could have hoped for, given his handicap. He'd always known he wouldn't be able to fly every day for the rest of his life, especially when the war ended. Claire came into the room, and he wondered how Mr. Donovan would react to his new situation. He was permanently mutilated, but his new job would be less risky, and with the promotion would come a pay increase. Would it be enough to win Donovan's approval?

# Chapter 47

*May 1918, Calais, France*

THE DAIRY OUTSIDE CALAIS HAD changed during the war. With Julian's mother gone, the place felt empty, older, less cheerful, but Julian did what he could to repair the roof, the barn, and the stairs from the kitchen to the garden. His father seemed to have aged in decades rather than years since the war began. He had kept the cows alive and fed, had planted the garden and the fields, and was still making cheese. But there was too much for one sixty-year-old man to do by himself. Like most children, Julian had grown up thinking his father was old, but it wasn't until now that his papa seemed elderly.

As the end of his convalescence approached, Julian looked around the familiar home and wished he could have done more. He still had trouble breathing when he exerted himself and still felt weak when it came time to draw water or rid a field of weeds. His father caught him staring out the window at the grass invading the garden. "I'll get it out before I go," Julian promised. He still had three days of leave.

"I can do it eventually. You're supposed to be resting, remember?"

"I've been resting all spring."

His father chuckled. "If you call fixing the roof and milking the cows resting." Then he sighed. "I wanted to leave you a nice dairy, not a rundown wreck."

"We'll make it good again when the war ends."

"Did the doctors say if you'll recover any more?"

Julian shrugged. "They aren't sure."

"So many gas cases. You would think they'd have a better idea."

Julian hadn't told his father where he'd been, what he'd been doing, and he couldn't tell him that he still wasn't sure which gas or gases he'd been exposed to. He tried to change the subject. "Do you think they'll stop the German advance?" Julian believed Sauer's genuine worry that German manpower was at its end, but waiting for the tide to turn took patience.

"Eventually. Then maybe they'll come to a settlement, and when the army releases you, the two of us can muddle through, get this dairy up and running again so you'll have something worthwhile to offer a pretty girl."

Julian frowned.

"What's that look for?" his father asked.

"I'm not sure I have much to offer a woman. The dairy will improve, but I might not."

His father huffed. "You still have both arms, both legs. So you can't run a marathon—"

"I can't even run a kilometer."

"I've seen the casualty estimates, Julian. When this war is finally done, a smart woman will know she's lucky to get a man at all, extremely fortunate to get one with land and a willingness to work hard."

"A willingness, but not the ability."

"Give it some time." His father patted him on the back. "Whatever happened to that girl you wrote to me about, the one you met when you went to Maximo's village on your last leave?"

He thought of the delicate woman with brown hair, green eyes, and a hidden fear. "I never learned her name. And that was three years ago."

"But you know where she lives."

"She's not there anymore. She was going to Paris."

"Perfect. The Scotsman found an assignment for you in Paris. If her family is still in the village, you can stop by and get her address."

Julian was glad the war hadn't crushed his father's optimism, but he shook his head. "That's a long way to travel on a maybe. Besides, I don't think the war will be over before harvest. I planned to use my money to hire help for you."

"A train ticket isn't that expensive, and I can manage harvest without help. I think you should go."

\* \* \*

Julian's father talked him into it. If the woman was married, he would turn around and head right back for the train station. But if not, maybe it was worth pursuing a memory that still affected him three years later.

He doubted she was at her half brother's house, doubted she even wrote to him. But he easily found the home he had helped move the mother's things to. Everyone wrote to their mother, didn't they?

The woman who answered vaguely resembled the woman of his memory but had brown eyes instead of green and skin lined with wrinkles rather than the smooth complexion he remembered. The sister, he assumed. Her eyes widened when she noticed his uniform. "Oh no. It's Phillipe, isn't it?" Her hands shot to her mouth. Behind the fingers, Julian could see her lips tremble.

"Who's Phillipe?"

"My husband. Did you serve with him? Is he all right? I haven't heard from him in three weeks."

"I don't know your husband."

"Oh." He watched her shoulders relax. A child came to the doorway, and she shooed her away.

"I was actually trying to find your sister. I met her briefly when she moved your mother here."

The woman's eyes narrowed. "So now the army's looking for her? You leave Evette alone. I don't care what Gaspard says. If she threw hot soup on him, it's because he was threatening her. I don't know why you and the gendarmes and the mayor can't let it go—it was three years ago. Gaspard's face barely scarred."

"Your sister threw hot soup at your half brother?"

The woman didn't answer. Her glare continued.

"I'm not trying to punish your sister. I'm glad she got away. I just . . . I just wanted to see her again. I don't wish her any ill."

The woman's face softened slightly. "Even if you don't mean her harm, I don't know where she is."

"She doesn't write to you?"

"No. She was afraid Gaspard would come searching for her, and he knows everyone at the post office. She wrote to our brother, but he died last year, and I've not heard any news of her since. She sent a package for the children at Christmastime, from somewhere in Paris, but there was no street address."

Knowing the meek woman had fought back against Gaspard only increased Julian's admiration for her. That was the type of spunk she'd need to thrive in Paris. But Paris was a very large place. "Do you know which factory she works for?"

"No, monsieur. If you mean her well, good luck. I hope you find her. If you mean her harm, I hope the zeppelins get you." One of the children came to the door again. "Excuse me, monsieur."

"Wait." Julian had to ask one final question. "Is she married?"

"Not that I've heard."

He walked slowly back to the train station. He had a long wait to think about the woman, Evette. He pictured meeting her again, planned what he would say. Paris was enormous, but Julian knew how to be persistent.

She stayed in his mind the entire train ride to Paris. During his first days in the capital, he made lists of factories to check. When he wasn't working, he was searching. He settled into the job McDougall had found for him, sifting through German newspapers and intercepting transmissions for French Intelligence. It was a safe, clean job, the type of easy duty he'd envied while in the trenches. He quickly grew proficient with his assignments, but Evette proved elusive. He spent hours seeking her, walking through crowds of shoppers until his lungs burned, then sitting on benches to watch factory workers arrive for their shift. Months went by, and he didn't stop, but finding one woman in Paris without knowing where she lived or worked was like combing Flanders in search of a misplaced helmet.

# Chapter 48

*October 1918, Paris, France*

EVETTE SAT ACROSS FROM McDOUGALL and gave him her analysis. "He's interested in higher wages for factory workers, which we already knew. I don't think he's eager to disrupt the war effort for political reasons, but the army comes second to his workers in his eyes."

McDougall took a few notes. "So you don't think it necessary to arrest him?"

"No. But if negotiations with the factory owners break down, we should watch him. Or maybe you could find a way to put pressure on the owners. If he's right about how well the factory is doing, there's room for better wages or fewer hours—some concession to keep the workers happy."

"Anything to stave off revolution?"

"It just seems like the right thing to do under the circumstances."

"Hmm." McDougall studied her face. "Perhaps I have had you tail a few too many Communists. Their ideology is starting to sink in."

"I'm not a Communist, sir. But I've heard some of the things Mr. Donovan does for his factory workers in America. He treats them well and claims he gets better work from them in return."

"Speaking of Communists, what do you think of Monsieur Martin?"

Evette frowned and bit her lip. She'd been following Martin for nearly two weeks because he'd once met with a member of the League. "I'm not sure. He hasn't done anything suspicious, but he's very careful, and that makes me think he has something to hide. Checks his back often, doesn't go to the same café more than once or twice."

McDougall considered it for a while. "Keep an eye on him. But not tonight. Tonight I want to do something I should have done a few years ago."

"Oh? What's that?"

"Tonight I am taking you to supper." He glanced at his watch. "May I pick you up in an hour?"

Evette's face grew warm. "Yes, that would be lovely."

As she walked back to the Donovan's to get ready, she wondered how she felt about McDougall's invitation. Claire had long predicted something like this—a social invitation, some hint that Howard was ready to advance their relationship beyond employer and employee. Of all Evette's postwar options, a secure marriage to someone like McDougall was the most promising, but she wasn't sure she was ready for courtship. She saw how Claire glowed whenever she received a letter from Major Flynn. Seeing or hearing from Howard caused no such reaction in Evette. Would that come with time? Maybe she and Howard simply had different temperaments from Claire and Warren. Or was something missing?

Once she had met someone who made her feel lit up inside. McDougall wouldn't talk about what happened with his agent in Essen. But Claire had passed on the news from Warren: Spider had been shot when they'd tried to escape Germany. Warren disfigured, Spider killed. She wished she could go back in time and somehow change things. It was partially her fault—Spider may have died anyway, but if she hadn't told Warren about the danger, he would never have gone to Germany.

Evette was distracted from thoughts of romance and regret when someone came up behind her, jerked her arm into a painful hold, and pushed her into an alley. She would have screamed, but a large hand clamped over her mouth before the sound made it out of her throat.

"Who are you, and why have you been following me?" a gruff voice whispered in her ear. She only saw the speaker when he released her arm and slammed her into the side of a building. Monsieur Martin. He had always reminded her a little of Gaspard, minus the limp. Close up, the resemblance, especially in size and strength, was terrifying. He moved his hand from her mouth to her neck. "If you scream, I'll kill you. Why are you following me?"

"I'm not following you."

His grip on her neck tightened, making it difficult for her to breathe. "Don't lie."

Evette took a few moments to think. Martin obviously knew someone was on to him. Dying to keep her assignment a secret wouldn't make him any less suspicious. "Orders."

"From who?"

She almost said British Intelligence, but then she had a better idea. "The League."

Martin's face recoiled in shock. "Why is the League watching me?"

So he knew what the League was. "Lohr is concerned about traitors."

He frowned and squeezed her neck. "I met with Lohr last week. He trusts me completely. Who are you really working for?" His face was close to hers, his warm breath brushing her face.

"Let her go!"

Evette and Martin turned to the source of the warning: McDougall, with his pistol out, aimed at Martin.

"I'm working for him," Evette said as Martin released her neck.

He raised one hand, the one McDougall could see. His other hand slid into a pocket. As he slowly drew it out, Evette recognized the shape of a handgun. She kicked him in the knee. "He's armed!"

McDougall barreled down the alley and forced Martin to the ground before he could get a shot off. "Go back to the office and get help."

Evette obeyed, looking back as she turned onto the main street. Martin lay prone, and McDougall stood over him, his pistol aimed at the man's head. It was only a block and a half back to McDougall's office, but by the time she got there, she felt ill. Her hands shook, and her throat hurt.

Lieutenant Colonel Walsh was leaving as she arrived. She explained what had happened and let him take things from there. He ordered someone to come with him and someone else to contact the Paris police. She followed Walsh and a young corporal back to McDougall. The men in the alley were exactly as she'd left them.

She leaned against a wall while the corporal handcuffed Martin's wrists and Walsh and McDougall spoke in rapid English. When he finished, McDougall came over and placed a hand on each of Evette's shoulders. "Are you all right?"

She nodded, but the tightness in her throat told her she was about to cry. McDougall pulled her into an embrace, and she stayed in his arms for several long moments.

"It's all over now."

She swallowed back her tears but couldn't shake the knowledge that it wasn't all over. Lohr had been in Paris as recently as last week. And if Martin had tracked her, could someone else track her too?

"Let me walk you home," McDougall said as he relaxed his arms. "Walsh and the corporal can handle Martin."

"Thank you." She didn't want to be alone after what had just happened. The ordeal had been quick but terrifying.

"Are you hungry?" he asked when they reached the Donovans' gate.

Evette shook her head. She'd lost her appetite completely. "Could we try another night?"

"Take tomorrow off. I'll pick you up in the evening." He ran his fingers gently over her hair and looked at her lips as if contemplating a kiss. Evette held her breath in surprise, but a pair of pedestrians came into view, and McDougall pulled back. "Let me know if you need anything before then."

As she closed the Donovans' door, she knew what she needed. She needed Lohr behind bars or in a coffin.

Mr. Franke waited outside the parlor, listening. She wondered how often he did that and how many of her conversations he'd overheard. She'd always trusted him, but what if his loyalties still lay with the country of his birth rather than with France?

"Papa, he rarely flies now." Claire's voice came from inside the room.

"Aside from the danger of his profession, there is the fact that he is socially your inferior," Mr. Donovan said.

"He was his grandmother's only heir. He has more money than you did when you married Mama."

"I'm not so sure about that." Mr. Donovan sighed audibly. "But I do think you're emotionally exhausted. Now isn't the time to discuss your marriage prospects."

Claire's voice was closer to the door when she spoke again. "Fine. But I've felt this way about Warren for a long time now."

Mr. Franke slipped away, but Evette waited. Claire might as well know what Evette had heard. When Claire turned the corner, it was obvious she'd been crying.

"Claire?"

She took Evette's hand and led her to her room.

When they were inside, Evette spoke again. "Claire, are you all right?"

Claire slumped into a chair. "Warren's grandmother died. Influenza followed by pneumonia."

"Oh no. I'm so sorry."

Claire stared out the window. "There was no funeral, just a graveside service. So many people have been getting sick that public gatherings are discouraged. Warren came by this afternoon to let me know in person. Papa was rude to him. Warren didn't need that. He's just lost his closest family member." Claire's face pinched in anger. "Papa and I argued. I've never been so upset with him before. If Warren didn't have to report back, I think I would have run off with him and eloped." Claire smiled faintly. "Maybe over his next furlough."

"When will that be?"

"Not soon enough." Claire turned to Evette and gasped. "What happened to your neck?"

"One of Lohr's friends."

Claire's eyes widened. "The League again? Are you hurt?"

Her neck was sore, but that didn't worry her. "I'm fine. Disappointed in myself. Somehow he saw me tailing him, and then he tailed me, and I didn't notice. I guess I'm not very good at this sort of thing after all."

"No, you're brilliant. He just got lucky."

"I'm not brilliant. But I am ready to be done with the war and with espionage."

# Chapter 49

*November 1918, Paris, France*

As AUTUMN PASSED, THE FRONT line moved farther and farther from Paris. Evette watched Mr. Franke more carefully, wondering if there was anything sinister to his eavesdropping habit. Nothing came of her quiet surveillance, so she questioned the other staff.

She found the housekeeper alone in the kitchen and gradually worked in her question. "Have you ever noticed Mr. Franke listening to conversations from the hallway?"

"Naturally he checks in from time to time. We all like Major Flynn, and we're eager to see what happens."

"Of course."

The maid had said something similar. Evette still wasn't sure Franke's interest was only curiosity, but he had the other servants convinced.

The housekeeper patted Evette's arm. "We like Lieutenant McDougall as well. Is he taking you to supper again tonight?"

Evette nodded. He took her to supper every Wednesday. Their conversations were pleasant but tended to revolve around the League. Lohr and his men were still busy, and though Evette and McDougall had arrested two of them that fall, others remained free and active, and the identity of the League's financial benefactor was still a mystery.

Five days later, on November 11, Paris came alive like Evette had never seen it before. The bells pealed, huge crowds thronged the streets, and the air seemed to taste different. She knew what she wanted the change to mean but kept herself from celebrating until it was certain.

"Is it really over?" she asked when Claire joined her on the balcony.

"They signed the Armistice this morning. The cease-fire began at eleven."

Evette felt a choking sensation in her throat. So much suffering, so many lives lost over four long years. She was crying—no, sobbing—with a hundred different emotions: relief, sorrow, hope, shame. She wished Emile could have lived to see the end, to see a victory pulled from all his suffering. Claire drew her into an embrace, and Evette realized Claire was sobbing too.

"I don't know why we're crying." Claire sniffed. "I'm so relieved it's over, but it's been awful."

They wept together for a while, then their tears turned to the laughter of joy.

"Miss Donovan?" Mr. Franke interrupted them.

"Yes?"

"Major Flynn is asking for you."

Claire glanced at Evette as if asking for permission to leave their private celebration.

"Go." Evette emphasized her opinion with a wave of her hand.

Claire gave Evette a hug, then turned away. Suddenly she stopped. "How swollen are my eyes? Do I look awful?"

Evette laughed. "You look as though you've been crying, but I think that's expected on Armistice Day. You still look lovely."

Evette followed Claire from a distance and watched her rush into Major Flynn's arms. He swung her around in jubilation. Evette studied them for a moment, wondering if Mr. Donovan would finally drop his objections to their marriage. Claire was radiant whenever Major Flynn was near. His right eye, covered in a black patch, reminded Evette of a pirate from the cover of one of the adventure novels in the Donovan library. It added a hint of mystery that paired well with his dashing silk scarf.

She walked into the garden, thinking, hoping, praying. She didn't know what would come next, and she didn't care. All that mattered was the war was finally over.

\* \* \*

A few days after the Armistice, Claire decided they should have a celebration. Mr. Donovan resisted at first, as did Evette. Was it proper to throw a social gathering after a devastating war and an influenza pandemic?

Claire brought the subject up over supper for the third night in a row. "In America, we have a tradition of Thanksgiving. I think we have much to be grateful for, and I want to celebrate the good with others."

"So we'll have a Thanksgiving feast," Mr. Donovan answered. "With a few guests."

Claire smiled the smile she used when she was thinking of Major Flynn. "I want dancing too, Papa. Something informal."

He finally relented. "You plan it. I'll pay for it."

Claire beamed. Evette wasn't sure what to think, not at first, but as the days passed, Claire's excitement began to rub off on her. Evette didn't have any more spies to tail, so she would soon need to find a new career. Claire asked her to stay through the end of the year at least, and Evette agreed, trading counterintelligence for coordinating all the duties of a hostess.

The night of the party, Claire arranged Evette's hair in a fancy coiffure. Evette wore one of Claire's evening gowns from when she was a teenager, before her figure had filled out. The alterations had seemed less daunting on it than on any of the others Claire had offered, and the classic lines of the black silk dress would never go completely out of fashion. Claire wore a damask gown that matched her blue eyes.

"You look beautiful," Claire said as they walked to the parlor.

"So do you."

"Thank you. Warren said he liked me in blue."

"He's coming, isn't he?"

"Yes, and Papa promised to behave."

"Is he still in mourning?" Evette asked. It had been seven weeks since his grandmother's death.

"No. Besides, this would make his grandmother happy."

Evette peeked out a window that faced the road, wondering if she'd be able to pick out the RAF uniform under the street lights. She watched a few people walk past. Based on the knocks that followed about a minute later, most of them were coming to the house. They were all strangers to her. McDougall was coming, but he, Major Flynn, and the Donovans would be the only people she knew, unless McDougall brought some of the men he worked with, as Claire had suggested, but those men were only acquaintances.

Claire went to greet the guests, but Evette stayed by the window a little longer, wondering what Emile would think of her, of the party. Would he be happy for her? Or would he consider her a traitor to her class? Insensitive to the suffering of so many? Claire wanted the evening to be one of gratitude, but the chatter coming from the other rooms sounded more festive than solemn.

She turned from the window, but the dog barked and made her look back. She stood, frozen, focused on the top hat, the tall frame, and the coat falling across broad, powerful shoulders illuminated in the lamplight. Not long after, the figure came back, as if he had decided there was too much traffic in front of the Donovan home and was thus returning the way he'd come. What was Lohr doing in Paris?

Evette slipped out the servants' door and ran after him. The November air bit into the exposed skin on her arms and back, but she didn't have time to return for a coat. Lohr came into view again as she reached an intersection a block from the Donovan house. She turned to follow, changing her pace from a run—as much as one could run in an evening gown—to a quick walk. The darkness would help, but Evette's dress was anything but inconspicuous. She wished McDougall had arrived early. He would have known whom to call and could have set up a manhunt for the spymaster from Lorraine.

She followed Lohr for perhaps twenty minutes from a distance of forty meters, ignoring the glances people gave her when she passed other pedestrians. She suspected he was aware of her when he took four left turns in succession, circling a block. She hadn't seen him look over his shoulder, but perhaps he had checked behind him while in shadow. A horse-drawn taxi came toward Lohr, and he hailed it, then hopped aboard. The taxi turned around and sped off. Evette ran a block, trying to follow it, but she couldn't keep up, and the streets were deserted, so she couldn't hire her own taxi. She knocked on the doors of a few nearby shops, hoping one of them would have a phone so she could call the gendarmes, but they were all closed for the night.

Lohr had escaped. Again.

Her arms felt like ice, and the wind had pulled her hair apart a tendril at a time during the pursuit. She was cold, disheveled, and scared. Why was Lohr in Paris—outside the home where she lived? The war was over . . . wasn't it?

Evette went back to the party; maybe McDougall would know what to do. Her teeth chattered by the time she walked into the kitchen.

"What happened to you?" the cook asked.

She shook her head and stood by the stove to warm herself, pulling out the pins in her hair and twisting it into a simple bun. When her skin returned to a normal color, she left the kitchen in search of McDougall. The meal was finished, and a group of four musicians was tuning their instruments for the dance.

"Evette!" Claire rushed up to her. "You disappeared! What happened?" She stared at Evette's redone hair and her arms, still covered in goose bumps.

Major Flynn waited behind Claire. Evette knew Claire wanted to dance with him more than anything, so she forced a smile. "I'm sorry I left. Go ahead and dance. I'm fine—we can talk later."

Claire's eyebrows drew together.

"Go dance," Evette whispered as she took Claire's elbow and turned her toward the major.

McDougall found her as the music started. "I was hoping to see you tonight."

"Lohr's back. I saw him outside on the street just before supper. I followed him a good twenty minutes, but he jumped on a coach and got away. What should we do?"

Surprised etched itself onto McDougall's face. Surprise and skepticism. "Are you sure it was him? It is rather dark outside for confirming identities."

"He passed under lamp lights. And why would anyone else try to evade me? I'm sure it's him. I'm sick thinking about what he might have planned. What are we going to do?"

McDougall was quiet for a while. "We are going to enjoy Miss Donovan's party. We'll worry about Lohr tomorrow."

Evette wanted to argue, but she was at a loss for words. An armistice didn't make Lohr any less of a danger. Didn't McDougall believe her? How could he enjoy a party when a saboteur was still loose?

"Will you dance with me?"

Evette looked at her feet. She'd scuffed her delicate shoes, and she wanted a minute to herself. "I need to change my shoes. I'll be down again soon."

# Chapter 50

EVETTE TOOK HER TIME SWITCHING shoes and checking her hair. She hadn't eaten yet, so rather than going directly back to McDougall, she stopped by the kitchen and grabbed a roll. There were hors d'oeuvres in the grand hall, but she wasn't ready to face McDougall. Eating in the kitchen gave her a few extra minutes to herself. Didn't he trust her judgment? Didn't he want to stop Lohr? Hurt, disappointment, and worry left her chest in almost as much upheaval as the ground around Gallipoli.

She finally worked up a combination of stoicism and courage and went to dance, stopping to study Claire's face as she gazed up at Major Flynn. That was real love. But when it came to Evette and Howard, something was missing. A few short years ago, she would have accepted McDougall anyway. He wouldn't hit her, and he would see she was sheltered and fed—expecting any more than that from a husband had been unrealistic. But now a marriage without love seemed pointless. She could find another way to get by—a factory job again, or perhaps enough of Claire's refinement had rubbed off on her that she could find work as a lady's maid. Marriage was no longer her only option.

She found McDougall and inhaled sharply when she saw him from across the room. Standing next to him was the French soldier who had helped her move her mother and given her money for a train ticket to Paris. She had been sure he was dead, but he was too handsome to be a ghost. He seemed to have aged since their last meeting, and she had the impression that life had been unkind to him in the intervening years. The stiff resignation she'd seen when he had spoken of returning to war was still on his face, but his eyes were different—weary but unafraid. And very much alive.

McDougall was trying to introduce the man to one of the other guests, but the French soldier glanced up and met Evette's gaze. His mouth opened slightly in surprise, then pulled into a smile as he stared at her for several long seconds.

Ignoring the other guests, he walked toward her. She met him halfway across the room.

"Hello, mademoiselle."

McDougall strode toward them and eyed them suspiciously. "Have you two met?"

The soldier's eyes didn't leave her face. "We've not been introduced."

McDougall pursed his lips before speaking. "Julian Olivier, may I present Mademoiselle Evette Touny."

Julian bowed slightly. "Pleased to meet you, Evette Touny." He said her name differently than McDougall or Claire did. It was different even than how her parents or Emile said it—better, like it was poetry.

"I'm glad to meet you, monsieur."

"Would you care to dance?" For the first time since seeing her, he glanced away, toward the dancing couples.

Evette nodded, but she didn't miss the stern set of McDougall's face as they walked away from him. She chose to ignore it, just as he had ignored her warning about Lohr. A waltz played as Julian gently took her hand in his and placed his other hand on her back.

"I'm afraid I'm not very good at this," he admitted partway through the song. She hadn't noticed—maybe because she wasn't very good at it either. "You don't know how many times I've kicked myself for not learning your name that day and for not doing more for you, angry sergeant to deal with or not."

"I regretted the same thing—that I didn't even ask you your name. I never even thanked you."

"You didn't have to. I could see it in your face."

The waltz ended, and Evette spied McDougall on the opposite side of the ballroom. She suspected he was going to ask her to dance, but she wasn't ready to lose Julian again. "Will you come with me to the garden?"

He agreed, and she kept hold of his hand, grateful for the other couples between them and the Scotsman.

She almost regretted going outdoors when the chill hit her skin, but Julian took his jacket off and arranged it across her shoulders, and then she wasn't cold anymore. "And what have you been up to for the past few years? No more falls?" Julian brushed his fingers along her temple where Gaspard had left a bruise prior to their last meeting.

Evette savored his touch. "No. No more falls."

"I see you made it to Paris. You've been well, I hope." His eyes seemed to drink her in like a thirsty man being offered clean water after a long stay in the trenches.

She almost said Paris had been safer than living with Gaspard, but that wasn't entirely true. "Have you been well?"

He hesitated before answering, and she wished she knew more about what he'd done in Germany and since—and how he'd managed to escape alive when she'd been so sure he was dead. "Off and on. But I am well tonight, especially after seeing you."

Warmth spread across Evette's cheeks. "Only well some of the time, yet you've still managed to save the world?"

He grew quiet, watching her with a sober expression. "I've done nothing extraordinary, and I certainly haven't saved the world."

He backed away, and she reached out to hold his arm so he wouldn't disappear. "You're Spider, aren't you?"

He didn't answer, but his face suddenly looked haunted, and he took another step away.

"Please don't rush off again. I don't want to wait another three years for our next meeting."

He kept his feet in the same place, but his eyes were no longer drawn to her face. "When we met, there were things you didn't want to talk about, and I didn't press you. Tonight I ask you to return the favor. There are things I'm not allowed to speak of."

"But I know what you did in Essen. And I got your letter."

He drew his lips into a thin line, wary. "My letter?"

"It was written to me, wasn't it? Or have you helped other green-eyed women escape abusive family members?"

"No, you were the one in mind when I wrote it," he whispered.

"Did you mean it, all the things you said?" He had spoken of love at first sight, said he hadn't believed in it before, and Evette hadn't either, but now she wasn't so sure.

"I meant every word." He smiled. "But I never would have been bold enough to write them if I thought there was any chance you'd read them." He folded his arms across his chest, each breath visible in the cold. "How in the world did you get that letter?"

"I'm Sparrow."

"You're Sparrow?"

"Yes."

He stared at her. "I thought you were coming to Paris to work in a factory."

"I was. I did. Until I caught someone trying to sabotage the munitions plant. Monsieur McDougall had been looking for the same person. He offered me a job." She paused, willing herself to have the courage to say what she wanted to say. "I'm sorry I lied to you about my bruises back when we met. It's just, unless you've been caught in a trap like that, you can't understand how scary it is to talk about it, especially with a stranger—even a kind and handsome stranger. But I didn't lie to you about anything else. And I'll never lie to you again."

A smile crept across his lips. "I searched for you when I got back. All summer, whenever I had time, I'd watch the shifts change at factories."

"And I didn't know where to look for you. When Major Flynn disappeared last year, I assumed you were dead."

"Of course. Warren said a sparrow sent him." As she stepped toward him, Julian wrapped his arms around her and pulled her into an embrace. Then he brushed his lips across her temple. "Thank you for sending help, my little sparrow. You saved my life."

She beamed at his soft kiss and at the way he'd called her *his* sparrow. She realized she wanted to be his. She belonged with Julian on the dairy he'd written to his father about, in France, not across the sea in Great Britain with a Scotsman who didn't listen to her. Julian's arms were strong and warm, and she felt completely safe with him. She didn't want him to ever let go, but eventually he did. He gently took her hand in his and raised her fingers to his lips. "I'm sorry if I've been too forward," he whispered.

Evette shook her head. "No, you've not been too forward. Thank you, Julian—for being alive, and for making me believe in love, and for somehow finding me again."

# Chapter 51

JULIAN HAD FINALLY FOUND EVETTE. He spent the rest of the party talking with her, learning more about her childhood, her time in Paris, and her most recent sighting of Lohr. She began to shiver as the clock struck ten, and he caught himself yawning. "Let me take you inside." He offered her his arm and led the way. "Tomorrow we'll figure out what to do about Lohr."

Most of the other guests had already left. Evette looked around at the staff diligently cleaning up the leftover food and tidying the furniture. She squeezed his hand. "I should excuse myself, but don't disappear again."

"I'll call on you tomorrow evening."

Her eyes were drawn briefly to his lips, and her cheeks colored in a way that made her even more beautiful. She brushed her hand along his arm. "Good-bye, Julian. I look forward to seeing you again." She handed him his jacket, and he held it briefly to his nose, capturing her scent and warmth.

He was worried about Lohr. The man had beaten him before, but maybe here in Paris Julian would have the advantage. And it was hard to be concerned about a saboteur when he'd just found the woman he'd been seeking for so long. Finding Evette—and knowing he could find her again—seemed like a divine reward for everything he'd been through. Julian planned to court her a respectable amount of time, but he didn't doubt the outcome. So often he had rolled his eyes when other men had told him they knew they were going to marry a woman after seeing her only once, but now he found himself in a similar situation, and it didn't feel ludicrous.

"I see you met McDougall's girl."

Julian recognized Warren's voice and turned. "Evette? She's McDougall's girl?"

"He hasn't proposed yet, but he's thought about it for at least two years. When he heads back to Scotland, I think he hopes to bring her with him."

Julian felt a knot form in the pit of his stomach. "You're sure?"

"I don't know how attached she is. She's quiet. But a few days ago, he asked me if I knew any good jewelry shops in Paris."

Julian guessed there were hundreds of jewelry shops in Paris, but he recognized the meaning behind Warren's words. Evette wasn't available. And yet, if she was in love with McDougall, why hadn't she said something? Her laugh and the way she'd touched him suggested Julian had a chance, a good one. Were it anyone other than McDougall, Julian would do what he could to win Evette, no matter how serious her other relationship. But how could he rob a man who had saved his life?

* * *

Julian spent the next morning reading everything he could on how the Lothair League operated in Paris. Why was Lohr back? The war was over, so what did he hope to achieve? Julian searched for patterns in Lohr's spy networks and sabotage rings. There were no longer French battle plans for him to learn, and most of his sources had been arrested, but perhaps Lohr was back for destruction. He normally worked through a middleman who then hired the actual saboteur. Would anyone help him now, or would he act on his own?

During his meal break, Julian went to a nearby church and asked to speak with the priest. "May I ask your advice, Father?"

The tall man nodded his gray head. "Of course, my son."

"There is a woman I met very briefly in 1915. I've never been able to forget her, and I saw her again yesterday. I wish to court her."

"Is she a religious woman?"

"Yes. She's wonderful. She's everything I've ever wanted in a wife. Somehow I think I realized that the first time I saw her."

The priest led Julian outside. "So court her. Marry her. Enjoy the peace. We've all of us seen enough misery to last a lifetime, haven't we? Find joy in holy matrimony."

"There's one complication." The chill weather bit his nose, and Julian pulled his scarf more tightly around his neck. "I have a friend. We worked together during the war. I wouldn't be alive if it wasn't for his help, and he's in love with her too."

The priest was quiet for a time, moving along at his calm, steady pace.

Into the silence Julian spoke again. "The more I learn of her, the more I want to spend the rest of my life with her. But how can I steal her from a friend, from someone I owe my life to?"

The priest paused and looked Julian in the eye. "Perhaps you should let the lady decide."

# Chapter 52

EVETTE CLEANED HOUSE MOST OF the afternoon, then washed and spent longer than normal arranging her hair in anticipation of Julian's visit. She chastised herself for being so concerned about romance while Lohr was in Paris, but war and counterintelligence had consumed her for more than four years. For once, she wanted to think about pleasant things.

When the night grew dark, she couldn't wait any longer and headed to the front parlor to keep vigil by the window. On her way, she heard a raised voice in Mr. Donovan's office. Curious and concerned because she'd never heard Mr. Donovan raise his voice before, she paused near the office entrance.

"I don't want you coming here again," Mr. Donovan said.

"I waited until dark."

"The war is over. So is my role in it."

A soft chuckle, vaguely familiar to her, crept from the office. "An armistice may have been signed, and the battle of the trenches may be over, but the battle of negotiations has yet to begin. It's not too late to get what I want."

Mr. Donovan huffed. "I'm done."

"I don't think so. You'll cooperate, or I'll make sure your past work becomes public. And you'll cooperate because you have a daughter and you don't want her to get hurt."

"How dare you threaten my daughter! And how dare you threaten to blackmail me! After all I've done for you—"

"I need more. If you don't want to meet here, we can meet at my home. I'll leave now. You come in fifteen minutes. But come, or you'll regret it."

Evette slid around the corner so she was out of sight. She didn't need to see who was talking with Mr. Donovan. She'd heard that voice before. Lohr hadn't found her. Simon hadn't found her. They'd been coming to Mr. Donovan.

Evette slipped a hand to her forehead and brushed away the slick sweat of panic as she waited for the front door to close. She wouldn't follow Lohr. He was too good at detecting her. She would wait and follow Mr. Donovan. She grabbed a coat and went outside via the servants' entrance. When Mr. Donovan left, she would be outside with her bicycle, hiding in the shadows near the gate.

How could someone like Mr. Donovan be mixed up with the League? She felt sick to her stomach. She liked Mr. Donovan. He'd helped her find Lohr's other agent, so why was he cooperating with Lohr now? And what would it do to Claire when she found out?

Footsteps along the sidewalk startled her from her thoughts. Major Flynn strode toward the Donovan home, a set of papers in one hand.

"Major Flynn?" She stepped out from the bushes.

"Miss Touny. I was hoping to have a few words with you before I surprise Claire." He stopped beside her on the sidewalk. "McDougall arranged Julian's current assignment and is on good terms with his superior. I think they gave Julian extra work today, so he might be late. And I'm not sure what your preferences are when it comes to Howard McDougall and Julian Olivier, but they're both very fond of you. You're in a position to make one of my friends incredibly happy . . . and the other absolutely miserable."

"Major Flynn, I need your help."

"I won't help you break either man's heart."

"No, not that. That will have to wait. But I overheard something this evening, and I think Mr. Donovan is involved with the League."

"What?" Of all people, Major Flynn had the most reason to dislike Mr. Donovan, but Mr. Donovan had hidden his treachery so well that even Flynn looked shocked. "Are you sure? Mr. Donovan has profited from the war, but I have a difficult time believing he's aided the enemy."

"He's going to meet Lohr tonight. He's leaving in a few minutes, and I plan to follow him."

"Does Claire know?"

"No."

Flynn studied her carefully. "I don't want to believe it, but I trust your judgment. What do you want me to do?"

The door to the Donovan home opened, and Evette pulled Major Flynn into the bushes so they'd both be out of sight. She watched Mr. Donovan head the opposite direction.

"Just be here for Claire," she whispered. Then she followed Mr. Donovan into the night.

\* \* \*

Partway through Mr. Donovan's journey, he took a cab. Evette had to pedal her fastest, but she managed to keep the taxi in sight as it slowly twisted through a series of residential areas. When Mr. Donovan got out and paid the driver, he waited for the car to leave, then backtracked a block. He obviously knew a few security precautions, but it was dark, and Evette kept her bicycle well oiled for just such occasions.

He went into the end unit of a long row of townhomes. Evette hesitated outside. Should she go for the police or make sure Lohr was inside first?

Remembering McDougall's skepticism of the day before, she crept closer. He wouldn't believe her unless she saw Lohr and Donovan together. The side window was closed, locked, and obscured from the inside with a curtain. The other windows were equally blocked, so she went to the back. The door was locked, but in her pocket she had the set of skeleton keys McDougall had given her. The second key unlocked the door. She gently pushed it open, wincing as it squeaked, but no one raised an alarm. She left her shoes by the door, then sneaked along the hallway until she could make out male voices.

"The German Army was still on French and Belgian territory when the Armistice was arranged," Lohr said. "We didn't lose the war, not on the battle-field."

"The German Army was being rolled up. Had the war continued, you would have been pushed back across the Rhine."

"No, we'll put the right pressure on the right people, convince them to return to the prewar boundaries. We can even give up our colonies, but Alsace and Lorraine must remain part of Germany. We only lost because of traitors at home and weak civilians. The Kaiser's gone—he's the one who started the war. Germany has a democracy now. The democratic nations have to deal with us kindly."

Mr. Donovan's voice was quiet but piercing. "Just as you dealt with the Russians kindly?"

"That was different. That was the Kaiser's government."

"The war is over, and Germany lost. I'm sorry, but I don't see any way Alsace and Lorraine will remain part of Germany when all is said and done."

"That's why I need you." Evette could hear the sneer in Lohr's voice. "Bribery will convince the delegates to give up Alsace and Lorraine."

"My entire fortune won't be enough for that type of bribery."

"Your entire fortune was achieved because of the war."

"I was wealthy before the war."

"You hid it well, but you had debts equal to your assets. Why do you think I insisted on prepayment whenever I sold you information about Krupp's competitors? I don't care if you have to sell all your factories and drain all your bank accounts. You'll give me what I ask, or I'll turn you in. If you want your daughter safe, you'll do as I say."

Evette had heard enough. She didn't need to hear what Mr. Donovan had done for Lohr during the war because, regardless of the past, he would do anything to protect Claire. She should have told Major Flynn to take Claire somewhere safe, away from Paris.

She slipped her shoes on again. The back door had opened easily enough, but it screeched as she closed it. Alarmed, she rushed away. After being inside the well-lit home, she could barely see anything, so she felt along the house. Partway to the street, she stumbled into a rubbish bin, and it tipped over. She prayed the men inside hadn't heard.

Before she could reach the street, the front door flew open, and someone shouted at her. She sprinted for the nearest lamppost, but someone barreled into her from behind and knocked her to the sidewalk. Pain shot through her shoulder, and she screamed. A hand slapped over her mouth, and she was hauled to her feet and dragged into the house.

In the light, she recognized Mr. Donovan staring at her. That meant Lohr was holding her.

"Go check the front. See if anyone heard her scream," Lohr said.

While Mr. Donovan was gone, Lohr tied her to a chair at the kitchen table. When Mr. Donovan came back, Lohr glanced from her to Mr. Donovan. "You recognize her, I assume? She tried to follow me yesterday."

Mr. Donovan nodded. "Yes. She lives with me. I told you about her."

"Yes, and you thought you were so brilliant to listen in on her conversations with that fool McDougall, but now you've let her follow you. Not so clever after all, are you?"

"What should we do with her?"

"Kill her, obviously. She's seen our faces, and the French will execute traitors, regardless of the Armistice."

"I didn't hear anything," Evette lied. "I followed Mr. Donovan, but I couldn't get in."

"Then why did I hear the back door close?" Mr. Donovan asked.

As Lohr circled her, Evette tried to pull her hands free, but they were bound too tightly. Lohr disappeared behind her and gagged her. Then he tugged on the handkerchief as if he wanted to make sure it would hold. "What I'm wondering is if there's a way to make her death ruin the Armistice."

"The war is over. Kill her if you must, but perhaps it's time to end your work and let things be. I can set you up as a rich banker in Switzerland, whatever you want."

Anger shot across Lohr's face. "You think I care about money? I want Alsace and Lorraine, not a payout!"

"The momentum is against the League. It's over," Donovan repeated.

"No." Lohr was thoughtful for a moment. "Perhaps I need to change my strategy. We don't need to bribe delegates to change the negotiations. We just need time to get our new weapons into production and to the army. We won't make the same mistake we made with the gas or that the British made with their tanks. We'll give them a surprise and exploit it before they can react. We'll break through their lines and annihilate their army—what should have happened with the Schlieffen plan in 1914. We'll take Paris and have a complete victory, just like 1871."

"The world is different than it was in 1871, and the German Army doesn't have the manpower it had in 1914."

"Neither do the Allies." Lohr held his hand up. "Picture this. We take her to the Eiffel Tower and mutilate her body. Using her own blood, we write a message: *All of France will be treated thus if Germany loses Alsace and Lorraine.*"

Evette hoped they planned to desecrate her body after they'd already killed her.

Mr. Donovan grimaced. "A public that has lived through newspaper reports on Verdun and the Somme will be little moved by one woman's death."

"That's why it has to be brutal and public."

"Just slit her throat and be done with it. No one will restart the war just because you kill one woman, no matter how gruesome you make it."

Lohr strode into Evette's line of sight again. "Not me. Us. And you've heard of the Trojan War? Helen wasn't even killed, just kidnapped."

Mr. Donovan walked to Evette and reached for her cheek. She pulled away and nearly unbalanced the chair she was tied to. "This is hardly a face that will launch a thousand ships."

Evette glared at him.

"We don't need anyone to launch ships. We just need to delay a settlement until our factory in Essen completes its latest project." Lohr grabbed Evette's chin, and she jerked back. "Major Halliday didn't think McDougall was talented enough to place someone in the Krupp factory. And you underestimated this one's ability to connect the dots about you. Maybe you're underestimating the potential fallout of a few well-placed, highly public murders. Tonight, we take her to the Eiffel Tower. Tomorrow, we find another woman and kill her at the Arc de Triomphe. If you fail to cooperate, I'll use your daughter."

Mr. Donovan's face turned white, but he didn't speak.

Lohr crossed his arms, satisfaction on his face. "A murder a day ought to keep the delegates from coming to any easy agreement. We don't have to reignite the war; we just have to postpone the peace."

# Chapter 53

GUILT WAS A FUNNY THING. Warren felt it as he searched through Mr. Donovan's office, but he also would have felt it had he ignored Evette's conviction that something was off about Mr. Donovan—something other than his refusal to allow Warren and Claire to marry.

He had waited on the sidewalk for ten minutes of indecision, long enough to spot Julian coming to court Evette. He caught him and explained the turn of events. Julian had set off to enlist McDougall's aid so they'd be ready to act when Evette reported Lohr's location.

The piano music Warren had bought for Claire lay on the chair across from Mr. Donovan's desk. Warren had spent hours in that chair discussing the war with Mr. Donovan before he'd asked to marry Claire.

He was jeopardizing his future with her now. With the war ended, perhaps Mr. Donovan would reconsider and give his blessing to their union. But if Claire or Mr. Donovan found Warren going through Mr. Donovan's things, suspecting him of treason, Warren would never be welcome in the house again. Piano concertos drifted from the library. Claire could play the piano for hours, and he hoped that was what she would do that night. At the party she'd said the servants were being given a day off after the extra work, so she was probably the only one home.

He wasn't sure what he was looking for, but he found a ledger and read it. Mr. Donovan was too smart to put an entry like *the League* in his book, but there was one mystery entry marked as LO, and it always represented money out. Recalling how Mr. Donovan would pull papers from his desk and put them in a drawer when Warren came into the office, he searched the desk drawers. If there were incriminating letters or notes, Mr. Donovan had already hidden them.

Warren turned to the coal stove in the corner of the office. It would be easy for Donovan to destroy anything he didn't want seen. On the chance that there were papers inside waiting to be burned, Warren leaned over and opened the front. He found nothing but coal, as one would expect in late November.

Warren heard a slight sound and felt a hint of rushing air—more than what could be attributed to opening the stove—but before he could turn around, something whacked him in the back of the head, and the world went black.

\* \* \*

When Warren regained consciousness, he felt a sharp pain in his neck that spread into his skull. He lay on a cold, hard surface. He tried to change positions in the darkness, but his arms were fastened to something above his head. The back of his hands scraped against the roughness until he recognized it as a wooden board. Why had someone stretched his arms out and tied them to a plank? He lifted his feet. They were tied to each other but not to anything else.

"Hello?"

No one answered, and not so much as a star gave its light to his prison.

He tried to lift himself off the ground, but the wood was too heavy. He swung his legs up and flexed his abdomen; the momentum lifted the board off the ground an inch or two. That was progress. He rested his muscles before attempting the same thing again. This time he got the board off the ground a foot or two, but between the beam's weight and the awkward position of his arms, he was unable to hold it up. He crashed back onto the hard floor, knocking his head and feeling a pull of agony that extended from his chest out to his wrists.

*Just when I thought the war was finished . . .*

A key sounded in a lock, and Warren turned toward it. A crack of light appeared, and a silhouette with a lantern thrust the door open. It wasn't until the shadow hung the lantern on a hook that Warren recognized Mr. Donovan.

"Be a good chap and untie me, will you?" Warren didn't think Mr. Donovan would, but he wanted to be wrong about the American.

Mr. Donovan navigated around the wooden boxes filling part of the room and folded his arms across his chest. Unlike Warren, he came directly to the point. "Why were you snooping around my office?"

"I was hoping to find proof that you're innocent."

"Innocent of what?"

"Helping Lohr."

"Humph. And what did you find in my ledger?"

Warren didn't answer. The ledger hadn't seemed like much, but perhaps in the hands of a competent accountant, it would be more significant.

"Never mind. I know what you found. And despite my intense dislike for you, I realize you're smart enough to come to the correct conclusion or find an expert who will. But never mind that. Tell me who else is suspicious of me."

"I'm afraid I can't do that, sir."

Mr. Donovan began pacing. He appeared taller than Warren remembered, but perhaps that was only because Warren was stuck on the floor. "I suppose it started with that little French girl, Mademoiselle Touny."

Warren did his best to keep his face as phlegmatic as an empty gas mask. "She's no longer a threat."

Warren couldn't help himself. His face jerked toward the American. Had they killed her?

Donovan shrugged. "She's not dead yet. But Lohr will take care of her as soon as the crowds have gone to bed. Actually, Major, I find myself being overly grateful that I discovered you in my office. You have given me the opportunity to take care of two problems at once."

"Oh?"

"Yes. First of all, I want to get rid of you. Since the Armistice, Claire has been pestering me daily about giving the two of you my blessing to marry. She doesn't want to choose between us, but it's only a matter of time before she chooses you. I never should have welcomed you here. Yet your stories provided a pulse for how the air war was going, and I needed that inside information."

Warren felt his jaw drop. Had he given information to the enemy through Mr. Donovan? He tried to think of everything the two of them had discussed over the years—who had the better planes, which tactics were working. Warren squeezed his eye shut against the painful realization. He had spoken far too much, to a traitor.

"I won't lose my daughter to you."

"And what of her happiness?"

"She'll be heartbroken for a while, but she'll recover."

"But you helped Mademoiselle Touny arrest McDougall's superior, the one who was working with Lohr. I don't understand."

Mr. Donovan slowed his pacing. "I've never wanted a German victory. All my business has been with the Allies."

"Then why this?"

"A prolonged war is the most profitable kind for me. The Armistice isn't good for business, and the peace will be even worse. Which is where you come in. Lohr and I have our differences, but he's convinced me to help him scuttle the peace talks."

"You and Lohr are the only people on the continent who wish for more war. You won't get it."

Mr. Donovan smiled. "Maybe. Maybe not. But we have multiple goals. I want you and Mademoiselle Touny out of my life. Mademoiselle Touny, because she suspects me, and you, because you'll take Claire from me. So early tomorrow morning, Mademoiselle Touny's mutilated body will be found near the Eiffel Tower. A brutal murder with a warning that Germany will deal thus with all French civilians should Alsace and Lorraine pass from German hands. Lohr thinks the murder will delay a settlement until their new wonder weapon can be produced. Even if it doesn't, I get rid of a dangerous woman and have the chance of continued profits."

"The need for peace is too great. No one will call off the peace talks over the death of one woman. And the German Army is practically in revolt. They won't last, even with new weapons. Let her go."

"That's what I thought at first. One more death won't reignite a war. But the more I think about it, the more I see Lohr's side of things. This war began with an assassination. Perhaps a series of murders can keep it going. Which is where you come in. Are you familiar with the rumor that early in the war the Germans captured a Canadian soldier, fastened his body to the side of a barn with bayonets, and crucified him?"

"It was never proven. Just guff from the trenches."

"Just a rumor, perhaps, but a persistent and powerful one that's about to come true. As soon as Lohr arrives, he'll help me hoist your body. I expect you'll be dead by the time we need your corpse placed near the Arc de Triomphe. If not, we'll gas you. It wasn't my first choice of how to get rid of you, but Lohr is persuasive."

Warren looked along the board to where rope bound his wrists and hands, finally understanding why he'd been tied that way.

"You aren't a Canadian infantryman, but you are one of their highest-scoring fighter aces, among the top in the Royal Air Force. Your death ought to inflame both Canada and Britain."

Warren didn't want to talk about Mr. Donovan's plans any longer. He doubted they would provoke another outbreak of war, but that wouldn't make him any less dead. "Where am I?"

"A private section of the mansion's basement. The only entrance is through my sitting room. No one will find you or hear you. You can scream all you like, although something tells me you'll suffer in silence."

As if to contradict Mr. Donovan's statement, Warren heard the bark of Claire's dog, and then Claire's voice. "Papa?" Her call sounded as if it was echoing down a staircase.

Mr. Donovan turned on Warren. "One word from you, and she's dead."

With plans for a double murder, Warren was beginning to think Mr. Donovan capable of anything, but surely he wouldn't kill his own daughter. Yet Warren recognized a hint of fear in Mr. Donovan's eyes, and his one-word explanation made everything clear. "Lohr."

Mr. Donovan wouldn't hurt his daughter, but his accomplice would. Or was Lohr in charge? Either way, Warren bit his tongue rather than calling for help.

"Claire, dear." Mr. Donovan went through the door and closed it almost completely behind him. "Whatever are you doing down here? It's damp and dirty. No place for a lady."

"Why are you down here? I've never seen this staircase before. It's like a secret passageway from an adventure novel."

"Yes, a grand adventure, with monstrous spiders lurking around every corner."

"Spiders?"

Warren could guess exactly how Claire's face would tense with nervousness, how her eyes would scan everything in sight. His contempt for Mr. Donovan grew. Depriving Claire of her betrothed wasn't enough. He also had to deliberately scare her.

"Papa, I found Warren's hat in your office. Did he come talk to you?"

"The hat looks common enough."

"It's Warren's. He keeps a bracelet I gave him inside the band for good luck. And there was a new ragtime piece on your chair. You certainly didn't buy it for me. What did you say to make him leave without his hat and without saying hello to me?"

"Claire, he's not right for you. Trust me."

"I've trusted you my entire life, Papa, but you're wrong about this. I don't want to choose between the two of you, but if you force the decision, I'll choose Warren. I love him, and with the war over, there's no reason for us not to marry."

"I can think of several million reasons, all of them sitting in bank vaults." The voices and the light began fading.

"Maybe I don't care about wealth as much as you do—besides, Warren is an officer, not a pauper. He has all his grandmother's money now, and he's brilliant. He'll do well, Papa."

"Let's talk about it in the morning, Claire." It was the last part of the conversation Warren heard before he was left in thick, dark silence.

# Chapter 54

WARREN LOST TRACK OF TIME in the dark basement. The waiting was awful—a countdown to crucifixion. Maybe Julian would rescue Evette and McDougall would arrest Donovan and Lohr, preventing two horrific murders. But what if they didn't? McDougall hadn't believed Evette the day before. Would he believe a message from her today, one delivered by a romantic rival? Would everyone but Julian assume nothing was wrong, that peace on the battlefield meant peace in Paris?

Warren knew better, and so would Evette. He wondered if Lohr and Donovan had told her their plans, wondered if she, like Warren, waited, knowing what horrors lay ahead.

He'd begun praying again in the German prison, and he prayed now in the basement. He believed in God, and he believed he would continue to exist in some way after death. But he didn't *know*, and he wished he did. He thought there was an afterlife, thought there was a place where Captain Prior and Flight Sergeant Boyle had gone, a place where all the dead infantrymen now lived, a place to where he would soon journey to see his mother and grandmother again. But the doubt was there, and it ate at him the way trench foot ate away at a weakened soldier's flesh.

Eventually a light appeared from the stairwell where Donovan had left the door slightly ajar, and Donovan returned with Lohr and a lantern. Donovan wouldn't meet Warren's eyes, and Lohr looked at him as if he was a package to be moved.

"The hooks are up there."

Warren followed Donovan's finger to a pair of jagged metal prongs sticking out of the gray brick wall. Lohr moved some of the crates to either side of the hooks.

"Donovan, don't do this." Warren wouldn't beg, but he had to ask for mercy one more time.

"Sorry, Major. That's war."

Donovan bent down and picked up one end of the wooden plank. Lohr grabbed the other, and the two of them dragged Warren backward, eventually lifting him up against the wall, stepping onto the crates to suspend him from the hooks. They left him dangling there, his feet too high to touch the ground. Warren immediately noticed how hard it was to breathe. He could inhale, but he could only fully exhale if he pulled himself up, and that made the rope bite into his wrists.

"Nothing for his feet?" Donovan asked.

"We want him dead by this time tomorrow. No support will finish him off faster. I'm not so much interested in prolonging his suffering as I am in the shock this type of death will evoke in the papers."

Donovan glanced at Warren and shuddered. "Have you dealt with that French girl yet?"

"No. I don't want a trail of blood from my home to the tower. I'll take care of her there. Better to have fresh blood for our message." Lohr led the way out.

Donovan stopped in the doorway and turned back to Warren. "Pity you didn't die in your plane." Then he slammed the door, leaving Warren in darkness again.

Warren found himself agreeing with the Yankee traitor. He had watched men burn in their airplanes, seen them tumble in a free fall from twelve thousand feet when their damaged planes had fallen to pieces around them. He would have preferred that death over his current torture.

The weight of his body pulled at his arms and made it feel as if they would tear from their sockets. Far worse was the pressure on his chest. He could get some traction from the wall behind him, but not enough, and he knew he wasn't getting sufficient oxygen. It was different from altitude sickness, and the end result would be more permanent, but he recognized the symptoms as his body was starved of air.

There was an extra agony in this type of death, a strange mix of wanting death to come to end the pain and the fight for each breath, each second of life. Being in the dark alone with his doubts made it even worse.

* * *

Warren wasn't sure how much time passed as he was slowly asphyxiated in the basement. Torture manipulated time; it stretched out the seconds and made the minutes seem like millennia. Each breath took more effort, and each tremor of pain was a little harder to control. A dozen times he heard a slight sound, probably a rat, and his hopes soared. Would Mr. Franke discover him? The cook? But they both had the day off, and so did the housekeeper and the maid. Even if they didn't have time off, they were unlikely to come to the basement.

Nothing changed. No one came. Why had he survived four years of war only to be murdered now? He wasn't sure how much longer he could last. At one point, he decided to get it over with, but his body's natural urge to breathe wouldn't let him end his agony until every last effort was spent.

Hundreds, maybe thousands of people had been crucified before, but Warren's mind turned to the most famous, the most perfect, and after a time, his doubts started to fade. Death came to all, but it wasn't the end. Despite the external agony, Warren felt a peace that he couldn't explain. He finally knew. His death would be painful, but it wouldn't be final.

After all the other sounds, Warren didn't think much of the soft scraping noise when he heard it. His ears were probably playing tricks on him in the dark, or the rodents were growing more bold. He paid more attention when a sliver of light appeared, then widened near the stairs. Was that what happened when one died? Was his mother or some other heavenly being coming for him? He tried to call out, but he couldn't talk.

The light became brighter and drew closer until he recognized it as a candle on a candlestick. It trembled because Claire held it, and her hand shook. "Warren? What have they done to you?"

He had thought an angel was coming to end his misery. He hadn't been far off. She put the candlestick on the floor and shoved a pallet against the wall. She dragged another one over and stacked it on top so it was high enough for her to reach the ropes around his right wrist. "Are you going to be all right, Warren?"

He hadn't a clue but wasn't capable of speaking right then.

"Say something, Warren. I've never been so scared."

He managed a strangled grunt.

"I can't get the knots out. I'll have to get scissors or a knife, but I'll be back." She reached out to touch his cheek. "Hold on a bit longer."

She scrambled down from her makeshift tower, and to Warren's everlasting gratitude, she pushed the pile of boxes under his feet before she ran to the stairs. The change was immediate. It was still uncomfortable, but it was further from the grave. After a few breaths, he realized he hadn't warned her about Lohr or her father. *Don't let them hurt her*, he prayed in his head, hoping the men were gone. If they were, Claire was safe and Warren saved.

She came back not long after, a butcher knife in her hand. She climbed up next to him and attacked the ropes on his right wrist. Soon he was partially free. As his hand dropped, he felt a new type of agony and groaned.

"Are you all right?"

"Better." His voice was raspy and quiet.

Claire moved to his left wrist. "It was my father, wasn't it?"

Warren wanted to say no, but he couldn't do that. Claire would know he was lying, and if the truth didn't get out, Evette wouldn't survive until morning. "Yes."

Claire's body shuddered with a sob. "I thought he might try to bribe you, threaten you with a scandal or something to get rid of you. I never thought he'd torture you and try to kill you. I'm so sorry, Warren. I should have married you a year ago."

She finished sawing through the last of the ropes, and he slid down the wall. He was too weak to stand, but sitting on the pallet was a pleasant change.

"What time is it?" he croaked.

"I'm not sure. After midnight."

"Then there's not much time to explain. Your father is working with the League. Lohr is holding your safety over him, so your father will do anything Lohr asks. They've caught Evette, and they're planning to kill her at the Eiffel Tower sometime before daylight. Do you know where McDougall works?"

"Yes."

"He and Julian should be there. Tell them what's about to happen. Then find the gendarmes. Then a doctor for me."

"Let me get the doctor first."

"No. You have to go now. It might already be too late. And be careful."

Claire set down the knife so it was next to his hand. "In case you need to defend yourself." She put both hands on his face and kissed his forehead, sealing Warren's newfound belief in miracles. "You'd better still be alive when I get back."

# Chapter 55

EVETTE STRUGGLED AGAINST LOHR WHEN he told her it was time to go. He leveled his gun at her head, but that didn't make her behave because he was going to kill her anyway. A quick death was better than what he had in store, but she suspected he wanted a body that wasn't marred by a bullet. He had other plans for its defacement.

Her struggle didn't gain her much time. Perhaps an extra five minutes of life. Lohr added more ropes around her already-bound body, pulled the gag tighter, and threw her over his shoulder. Sometimes she hated being so small.

The ride in a horse-drawn carriage—the same carriage she'd taken with Claire to restaurants and plays—felt long. And it felt like riding in a hearse. Terror and resignation competed inside her. She was going to die just when it seemed like everything in her life was finally perfect. She had a good friend in Claire, a good man in Julian, and peace—finally, peace. Or so she had thought.

When they arrived, Lohr picked her up again. He grunted under her weight after a few meters, which made her wish she weighed three times as much. Mr. Donovan went ahead of them, probably to ensure they were alone. He carried with him a bucket, a paintbrush, a knife, and a hatchet.

Mr. Donovan's voice came back in a whisper. "Here's a good spot. Close but hidden until we're ready."

A few seconds later, Lohr dumped her on the ground among some bushes. She didn't think the drop broke any bones, but it was the kind of fall that left bruises. Lohr pulled her left arm from the tangle of ropes. She did her best to pull it back toward her body, but he quickly overpowered her.

"I'm sorry, Mademoiselle Touny," Mr. Donovan said. "I always liked you. And Claire—poor Claire will lose her best friend and her intended all in the same night." Her gag prevented her from asking what he meant, but he continued as if sensing her question. "Major Flynn will provide tomorrow night's body." He nodded at Lohr. "I'll keep lookout."

*What wicked men,* she thought as Lohr forced her to her knees and held her wrist over the pail. With no hesitation, he sliced his knife into her skin. The pain was sharp, and her body immediately reacted. The panic was enough for her to free her arm from Lohr's grip, but he caught it again within seconds.

As the blood drained from her wrist, she began to lose her peripheral vision. It was dark anyway, but now all was gray, and then black. Evette collapsed to the hard ground, thinking at least she wouldn't be aware of whatever came next.

# Chapter 56

JULIAN SEARCHED THE PLAZA AROUND the Eiffel Tower, wishing it wasn't so dark, hoping he could find Evette or Lohr or Mr. Donovan. He would never forget Claire's face as she'd told him her father was part of the League. Pain could show in multiple ways, but Claire's expression portrayed a broken heart so clearly that Julian had feared Warren was dead. Claire had said enough for Julian to know that wasn't far from the truth, but right now he had to focus on Evette. McDougall had wanted to come instead, but he didn't know Lohr like Julian did, and Julian lacked McDougall's pull with the police.

He caught a hint of movement near a clump of bushes and quietly moved to investigate. As he approached, he saw moonlight reflecting on a bucket. A wrist was held over the pail, and the wrist was attached to a woman. Most of her body was hidden from sight, but Julian didn't have to see details to sense who it was.

He barreled into the man huddled over the woman with the force of a 75mm shell. As he collided with the shadow, he recognized Lohr. The man from Lorraine was stronger than Julian—he remembered that all too clearly. But Lohr was also slower, and Julian had caught him by surprise.

As Julian shoved Lohr to the ground, the bigger man began fighting back, but Julian quickly landed an elbow in the murderer's throat and three jabs to his nose.

Lohr stopped struggling, so Julian scrambled back to Evette. The liquid inside the bucket gleamed dark in the moonlight. A trail of blood from the bucket to Evette's wrist showed she still bled. Julian yanked out his handkerchief to bind the wound and had just tied it when he felt Lohr rushing toward him. Julian turned to meet him, but this time their struggle was more matched.

Lohr reached for Julian's neck. Julian dodged his grip and rammed into his assailant with more strength than he thought he had after the gas in Essen. Lohr grunted but had enough dexterity to throw them into a roll across the grass. Lohr's fist connected with Julian's jaw and momentarily stunned him.

Julian gasped for air with aching lungs. A glance at Evette's prone form was sufficient motivation for him to strike back, attacking Lohr's neck again and pinning him to the ground on his stomach. Julian twisted Lohr's arm around behind his back and yanked. The bone cracked loudly, and Lohr's grunt turned into a cry. Julian felt no remorse. The League was, after all, trying to butcher the woman he wanted to marry. Julian was about to bash the man's head into the ground, preferably hard enough to knock him unconscious so he could care for Evette properly, when a mechanical click sounded in his ears.

"That will be enough, Monsieur Olivier."

Julian looked up to see Mr. Donovan holding a Lebel revolver. Julian slowly raised his hands, letting Lohr slip from his grip.

Mr. Donovan motioned toward Evette. "Perhaps we should take her elsewhere. There's been too much of a disturbance here, and we wouldn't want anyone else to interrupt us."

Lohr stood and winced. He cradled his broken arm as he stepped away from Julian.

"You know the thing about spiders?" Mr. Donovan asked. "I've never felt guilty for crushing one."

Julian thought Mr. Donovan would pull the trigger then, but instead he handed the weapon to Lohr. "Should we incorporate his body into our scheme?"

Lohr grunted. "France has seen a million dead poilus in this war. One more won't make a difference unless he's famous."

"If he's found dead, they might release details of what he did in Essen. A murdered spy could be worthwhile."

"He's dangerous. I'd rather have him dead now."

"Fine. I'll get the girl. Give me time to take her to the carriage before you fire in case someone hears. Bring the bucket of blood with you when you've taken care of the pest."

Julian watched Mr. Donovan drag Evette's unconscious body away. Despite years of dreading death, he felt strangely detached about Lohr's upcoming shot. But he'd come so close to saving Evette, and his failure to help her stung.

As the sound of Donovan's footsteps faded, the only noise was the rattle of Julian's breath. His lungs still weren't up to fistfights. Lohr was a silent guard. Quiet, wary, and focused. Julian thought that perhaps by changing one of those conditions, he could impact the others.

"I'm sure Herr Sauer would be proud of your scheme to punish France," Julian wheezed.

"What?" Lohr stepped closer to hear, just as Julian had hoped.

"I said Herr Sauer would be proud of your scheme to punish France."

"We aren't simply punishing France. We're going to reignite the war."

"Continuing the war will hurt Germany as much as it hurts France."

Lohr smirked. "No. We have new weapons. Give us time to implement them, and we'll have not only Alsace and Lorraine but Paris and the north coast under our control too."

Julian forced a laugh. "New weapons? Just like your gas or your flame throwers? They gained you a few kilometers, nothing more. Germany is worn out. Everyone is exhausted except the Americans, and they're on our side."

"Our new weapon will take the Americans out of the war."

"How? What is this miracle weapon?"

"Herr Sauer promised it will be ready early next year."

"You don't know what it is, do you?" When Lohr didn't answer, Julian continued. "Sauer is many things, chiefly a survivor. In the peace that will come, no matter what you try or what you do, you're a liability to Herr Sauer, a connection that proves he's complicit in sabotage. Did you ever think he might have sent you off on a mission like this to get rid of you?"

Julian was exaggerating, twisting the truth, but he could tell he'd struck home. Lohr's shoulders and his grip slackened ever so slightly.

Knowing he would die if he did nothing, Julian took a gamble. Lohr was less than a meter away. Julian jumped to his feet and rushed him. Lohr pulled the trigger, but Julian anticipated the move, and the bullet missed him. He gripped Lohr's wrists and kneed the man in the groin. Chivalry had long ago died in a storm of shells in a muddy trench, the Queensberry rules along with it. As Julian twisted, Lohr cried out in pain and released the pistol. Julian snatched it. He raised it and shot the man from Lorraine in the forehead.

As Lohr fell, Julian ran in the direction he'd seen Mr. Donovan drag Evette. It took a few minutes of searching, but eventually he saw the tall American standing next to a horse-drawn carriage, fastening the door.

When Julian's footsteps drew near, Mr. Donovan spoke. "Why did it take two bullets? You made twice as much noise as needed. Bring the bucket, and let's get out of here."

"It took two bullets because Lohr missed the first time."

Mr. Donovan turned around slowly. When he noticed the handgun Julian now held, he raised his arms. "Lohr's dead?"

"Yes."

Mr. Donovan seemed more relieved than anything. "Look, Olivier, this plan wasn't my idea. Lohr threatened to harm Claire if I didn't do everything he asked. He's gone now, and we can let the whole problem disappear. I know you're fond of this girl. She's still alive, and we can save her. Forget this whole mess happened and I'll make it worth your while. Set you up like a bourgeois. Keep my secret and you'll never have to work another day of your life."

"It's too late for that. You broke your daughter's heart. She found Major Flynn, and she knows who crucified him."

"None of this was my idea! You don't know what it's like to have someone threaten your daughter. Come, put the gun down. Save Evette."

Julian could barely see Evette. He kept his weapon aimed at Mr. Donovan and reached through the window. When he grasped her unwounded wrist, he felt a slight pulse. The bandage on the other wrist seemed to have staunched the bleeding. Julian motioned with the revolver toward the front of the cab. "Climb up and drive to the nearest hospital."

Mr. Donovan hauled himself into the driver's seat.

Julian studied Evette until the sound of fast footsteps jerked him back from the window. Mr. Donovan was running away, but Julian didn't shoot. There were few places he could hide, and enough people knew the truth that he was ruined.

"Halt!" a French voice cried in the distance.

The footsteps continued, and the warning was repeated. But perhaps Mr. Donovan knew he couldn't escape. Several guns fired, and only then did the footsteps fall silent. Julian led the horse toward the commotion to verify his suspicions. McDougall had called the gendarmes, and rather than face justice, Mr. Donovan had run into their bullets.

# Chapter 57

Evette woke in her own bed at the Donovan mansion.

Claire sat in a nearby chair and quickly filled her in on all that had happened. "We brought you here because most civilian hospitals are full of influenza cases. You should rest. I'm going to visit Warren. He's in a military hospital." Claire reached for Evette's good hand. "I'll check on you when I get back."

Evette nodded, surprised Claire had waited the night with her when Warren was also injured. But perhaps the military hospital had restricted visiting hours.

Mr. Franke and the arthritic housekeeper came to check on her often. Evette didn't feel like eating, but they convinced her to drink some juice, then to nibble on some rolls. By midafternoon, she felt well enough to walk into the garden. When she got there, she realized she should have rested longer. Going back now would take too much effort, so she wrapped the blanket she'd brought from her room around her shoulders and sat on the bench. Within minutes she was smiling as she recalled the last time she had been in the garden and the man she'd been with. She felt her temple where he'd kissed her. Julian's lips were absolutely perfect, and according to Claire, he had risked his life to save her.

Yet soon the thoughts that had haunted her all morning returned. Mr. Donovan was a traitor. Claire had put on a brave face, but Evette could tell she was crushed. Major Flynn was seriously injured. And though the war was over, she wasn't sure it would ever really leave her.

She took a deep breath, closed her eyes, and did her best to seal her mind to all the bad memories. It was the warmest part of the day, and despite the season, the sun shone clearly, pouring into the garden like a promise of something good to come.

"Evette?"

She recognized Julian's voice and turned.

"May I sit with you?"

"Please." She slid along the bench to make room for him.

"How are you?" He brought a hand up to touch her cheek. "You were so pale last night. Like you were about to slip into the grave."

"I almost did. Thank you for saving me."

"I'm glad I made it in time."

Evette glanced at the bandage wrapped around her wrist and recalled the way she'd felt when she'd regained consciousness. It had been close.

"Evette?"

"Hmm?"

"You haven't answered my question. How do you feel?"

"Better than I did this morning."

"And how did you feel this morning? Remember, you promised you'd never lie to me."

Evette felt a smile form on her lips. She wanted to be more open with Julian than she felt was proper, and he had just given her a reason. "This morning I felt horrible. Weak. Dizzy. Nauseated." She paused, the joy of being with Julian smothered by her recollection of what had been the worst part of waking up. "And I feel awful about everything that's happened. I would give anything for Lohr's contact to have been someone other than Mr. Donovan. If I hadn't seen it myself, I don't know that I'd believe it. He was always so kind to me before."

"That's what Warren said. But he also said Mr. Donovan was using him as a source."

"How is Major Flynn? I heard bits and pieces about what happened in the basement."

Julian didn't answer right away. "His shoulders are sore. When I saw him last night, it looked like every breath was an effort. I saw him again this morning in the hospital. Most movement makes him wince, but he could breathe without pain."

"Will he be all right?"

"The doctor thinks he'll have mostly normal function eventually. His shoulders may always be a little fragile, but there shouldn't be any reason he can't still fly once he's feeling up to it."

"I'm glad."

"And you, will you be all right?"

Evette held up her wrist. "Just a little scar is all, here on my wrist. And I suppose a larger one on my heart." Warm tears formed, and she tried to blink them away.

Julian rested his hand on her back. His simple touch radiated sympathy and support.

"I'm sorry," she said. "I don't mean to cry. It's just . . . I thought the war was bad enough, thought it had hurt me all it could when the Armistice came. I wasn't prepared for this. It seems so small compared to everything else that's happened, but it hurt me more. Not my wrist—it's painful, but the skin will heal—but I was ready for good things, not betrayal and more tragedy."

"We've all seen enough tragedy, haven't we?"

Evette sniffed, and Julian held her hand in his.

"I feel like that sometimes," he said. "Like the war has stolen everything from me. For a long time, I thought it would strip me of my future—my chance to work on the dairy, the hope of a family. When I was in Germany, I'd sometimes let myself think about what might have happened if the war hadn't come. And I thought maybe I would have gone to visit Maximo, not just his widow. And maybe I would have met you because you both lived in the same village. And maybe I would have asked your name instead of rushing off to the train station, and come back the next day to ask if I could take you on a walk. I could have found an excuse to stay longer, and maybe I would have courted you, and maybe we would have fallen in love and gotten married. The war stole that from me. It stole a lot of other things from me too, took my friends and my health. But you . . . you were the missed opportunity I thought about the most."

Julian turned her hand over and traced the lines of her palm. "Then I saw you at that party, and I thought maybe God was giving me another chance. The war had taken so much, but God was giving me something back, something worth living for." He withdrew his hand slowly. "I had every intention of courting you, but then I found out McDougall too is pursuing you."

"I've made no promise to Howard."

"He saved my life, you know, over in Germany." Julian leaned forward, resting his forearms on his knees and staring into the garden. "Anyone else, and I wouldn't care what his claims on you were . . . but with him it's different." Julian glanced back at her. "I thought long and hard about it, and ultimately it's your decision, your happiness. You know where my heart lies because I laid it bare in that letter. I still feel every word I wrote. You're ill today, and you may need time, but let me know when your heart decides."

He stood, and she reached out a hand to him. "Please don't go yet."

"All right." He stayed, but he did not sit.

"I think I've already made my decision."

"Do you love McDougall?"

Evette inhaled and exhaled deeply. Why was it so hard to breathe? She'd promised Julian she would never lie to him, so she answered as honestly as she could. "I respect him, and I admire him. I know he's fond of me. He would never hit me and would always see that my needs were met. Life with him would be secure, and yet I dream of more. He didn't trust I'd seen Lohr again. It hurt, and that's not the first time he's shrugged off my opinion. I can understand why—I've received only a basic education, and I'm a woman. But as his wife, I would never be his equal."

Evette pulled the blanket more tightly around her shoulders. "According to Claire, at least the old Claire, I should hold out for someone who's wealthy, someone who will worship me, sweep me off my feet. But I don't think I want to be worshiped, and in any case, I don't think men like that are real." She glanced at Julian. "I could be content with Howard. But somewhere between settling for someone safe and searching for someone who isn't real, I think there's another option. Happiness and joy and you, Julian."

He turned toward her, a wistful look on his face. "I am poor, I will never fully recover my health, and the war has left me a little broken."

Evette stood and stepped closer to him, stumbling as a wave of dizziness flowed from her feet up to her head. Julian was at her side in an instant, supporting her with one hand on her elbow and the other on the small of her back.

"You should be resting. Let me help you sit down again."

"Only if you sit with me."

He nodded. Evette purposely sat near the middle of the bench so he would be forced to sit right beside her.

"Julian, what I mean to say is that life doesn't have to be perfect in order to be good. I think I could find real happiness with you, and that's what I want—more than anything."

Julian cupped her face in his hand. "You choose me?"

"Yes." Evette leaned into his hand and closed her eyes as he brought his face toward hers. The kiss that followed began gently. One second, two seconds, maybe three passed. Time no longer mattered. His kiss was almost shy, but it somehow resonated all the way to her heart. Maybe this was what Claire had meant when she'd spoken of being swept off her feet. Evette didn't want her time with Julian to ever end.

\* \* \*

Julian stayed with Evette until she was ready to retire for the night. She slept in the next day, and when she woke, she did little other than rest and wait for news.

McDougall came to see her at noon. He held a bouquet of flowers in one hand and wore an uncertain smile when Mr. Franke showed him into the parlor.

"These are for you."

She took the bouquet, inhaling the scent of lavender. The weather had turned cold, so he must have paid a premium for them at the flower shop. "Thank you. They're beautiful."

They chatted for a while about the weather, about the Armistice. Then the conversation turned to espionage. "I am sorry I didn't do more to track down Lohr the night of the party."

She nodded, accepting his apology but not knowing how to reply to it.

"Can you forgive me?"

He had been quick to forgive her when she'd stolen his files, so she returned the favor. "Of course."

He hesitated, looking at the floor for a few moments before turning back to her. "I've been planning for the end of the war a long while now. And some time ago I decided that I wanted you to be a part of my life when everything was over. Will you marry me, Evette?"

She hated how much she was going to hurt him but knew she couldn't delay any longer. "I've considered it. You're a good man, Howard. You're smarter and braver than Major Halliday or your father ever gave you credit for. But I'm not in love with you."

"Not everyone marries for love. Pleasant marriages often grow passionate with time."

"It's not just that. I'm in love with Julian."

McDougall's eyes narrowed into angry slits, but he glared at a spot on the wall rather than at her. "Julian Olivier is poor, and his lungs are scarred. He can only give you a fraction of what I can give you."

"I know, but I love him anyway. I'm sorry. I never wanted to hurt you." She reached for his hand, but he pulled it away.

He inhaled deeply, then looked up at her. "Is there anything I can do to change your mind?"

She shook her head, not trusting her voice.

"I shall always regret the day I met Julian. But I shall never regret the day I met you. I shall just regret not asking you sooner." He sat there for a few moments, his mouth tense as his hands gripped the upholstery. "I shall be on my way. But my offer stands if you're ever willing to give me a chance instead."

He walked out the door, his shoulders slumped and his eyes on the floor. Evette felt a mix of emotions. She didn't doubt she'd made the right choice, but she wished her decision hadn't created pain for anyone else.

Claire returned from the hospital a few hours later and sat next to Evette on the sofa.

"How is Major Flynn?" Evette asked.

"It will take time, and he's still in a great deal of pain, but he's improving."

"And how are you?"

Claire was quiet for a while. "I'm so ashamed, Evette. How could my father do what he did? And how could I never suspect him? And how can I abhor someone and love them at the same time? I've told Warren I'm sorry, begged for his forgiveness. He says there's nothing to forgive, but . . . how could I be so blind?"

"You aren't the only one he fooled. I'm sorry, Claire."

Claire reached out and grasped her hand. "I know it's going to be awful for a while, but I also know it will get better. I have Warren, and I have you. Love and friendship. That will help."

Claire's wisdom struck a chord with Evette. Love and friendship. No matter how dark the world was, no matter how uncertain the peace was, those two things could make it better.

# Epilogue

*April 1919, London, England*

IT WAS ONE OF THOSE sunny but cool spring days when Warren went to visit McDougall in London. They sat in McDougall's library and exchanged the usual pleasantries, then McDougall asked about Warren's arms.

"Don't ask me to spin a rusty propeller or lift anything heavier than my flight jacket above my shoulders. Other than that, I'm back to normal." It had been a long, painful recovery, and despite Warren's words, he had frequent reminders that he wasn't the same. He hoped that, as with Julian's lung injury, slow improvement might come with time, but he didn't think it wise to mention Julian or Evette. McDougall's mind, however, must have been on the same track.

"Did I ever tell you why I picked Sparrow for Evette's code name?"

"No."

"In ancient Greek mythology, sparrows were associated with the goddess of love, Aphrodite."

"I'm sorry, Howard. I, um . . ." Warren trailed off. He'd almost lost Claire, but that had been different. There had always been the hope that it would work out later. McDougall's loss was final. Warren was happy for Evette and Julian. The two of them together made better sense than Evette and McDougall did, but saying so out loud was unlikely to help the Scotsman feel better.

"In my better moments, I know she'll be happier with him. Maybe that's why it took me so long to seriously pursue her—I knew we were an unusual fit. But in my weaker moods . . ." He grabbed a file from his desk and caressed the ends of it with his fingers. "In one of my lesser moments, I created my most brilliant operation yet. Nemesis, named after a Greek goddess who represented revenge personified."

Warren felt the hairs on the back of his neck stand on end. McDougall might be his older friend, but he wouldn't hesitate to step in if he was planning revenge on Julian and Evette.

McDougall stood and walked to the fire. "Growing up, I felt in constant competition with my brother, felt I would never measure up. I finally stopped competing with Henry, but to lose a lass like Evette to a French peasant . . ." He stared at the flames, then at the papers in his hands. After a few long seconds, he tossed the file into the fireplace and watched it burn. "There. I have decided to act on my better feelings. I suppose the two of us are committed bachelors for the time being."

Warren cleared this throat, not sure if he should bring up his own news.

"What?"

"Claire has agreed to marry me. So I won't be a bachelor for much longer, actually."

"Her father nearly killed you."

"That's not Claire's fault."

"Hmm." McDougall returned to his seat. "Congratulations. When is the happy occasion?"

"We haven't set a date. There's the estate to settle, and Claire's still in mourning."

"Mourning for a murderer?"

Warren sighed. "Mourning for the loss of her father and the loss of her innocence and the loss of an image she'd believed in for twenty-some years. It hasn't been an easy time for her. Especially not with the story all over the papers."

"No, I don't imagine it has been."

"She'll pull through. Soon, I hope." Warren leaned forward. "And you? What will you do when you're demobilized?"

For the first time in years, Warren witnessed a genuine grin spread across his friend's face. "Yesterday someone from the Secret Service asked to meet me. During the war, before it too, they had success sending agents along with university archaeological expeditions. Mostly in the Ottoman Empire. They got to know the area, the people, and noted military installations and learned travel routes."

"Lawrence of Arabia?"

"He's the most famous."

"And they want to try it again, I suppose."

"Yes. In Greece."

Warren laughed out loud. "Your dream job. Congratulations."

"I wonder if Evette would have liked Greece."

Warren had no idea. He gave what seemed like the wisest response. "Probably not. Are you leaving soon?"

"In a month. But I am off to Oxford in the morning for preliminary training. Life is strange, isn't it? One day you're dying of a broken heart, and the next day you're planning the adventure of a lifetime. Funny, I think my new assignment is something my father might actually be proud of me for, only I've stopped caring what he thinks."

McDougall explained more about the type of training he would receive and what the expedition would entail. As the conversation lulled, Warren stood, not wanting to miss teatime with Claire. The two men shook hands. "I'm happy for you. Good luck, and God bless."

McDougall raised an eyebrow. "God bless? I thought you left your religion in Canada."

"I changed my mind." It felt natural to pick up the habits of his youth again, and he was pleasantly surprised by how quickly his faith had returned and, with a little effort, grown stronger than before.

"Well, I hope that works out for you. Religion and marriage." McDougall cocked his head to the side and shook it slightly.

Warren just smiled. He had a feeling that both were going to work out well.

* * *

Warren hadn't seen Claire in weeks. She'd been in Paris settling her father's affairs, and he'd been helping the Royal Air Force demobilize. He found her in her grandmother's drawing room setting a plate of biscuits on a low table next to a glass pitcher and a china teapot.

"Hello, Claire." He held out his arms, and she slipped into them. "I missed you." He kissed her forehead. She looked up, and he decided to kiss her lips too. Her mouth was soft, responsive, enticing. He only ended the kiss when he heard one of the servants rattling something in the kitchen.

Claire's cheeks were flushed when he finished. "I missed you too. And your kisses." She leaned her head against his chest. "How was your friend?"

"He's lost the girl of his dreams but gained the career of his dreams. He's managing well enough. How have you been?"

"Each day gets a little easier. It helps to have everything in Paris settled. And being with you, I can almost forget the war and my father's role in it. How long can you stay?" She glanced up from his chest to meet his eyes.

"It depends. I'd like to stay with the RAF, and they've only given me a few days of leave. I won't get to fly as often in peacetime, but I want to be involved." He ran his fingers along one of her stray curls. "Even more, I want you to be happy, and if you prefer to live somewhere other than England, I'll resign."

"You? Sitting behind a desk in an office somewhere? I can't imagine you being happy with a conventional career like that." Claire went to the table. "Tea or lemonade?"

"Lemonade. If I stay with the Air Force, I'll probably be sitting behind a desk most of the time. But as long as I can come home to you, I'll be happy."

Claire handed him a teacup of lemonade and sat in one of the armchairs. The china was the same pattern as the one he'd broken when the war had begun. He looked closely and could see a slight line along the handle.

"You might should hold that by the cup instead of the handle. I pasted it, and I'm not sure how well it will stay. I know lemonade would be better in a glass than a cup, but I liked the symbolism. That's the cup you broke when the war started. When the world fell apart. Now the world and the cup seem to have been glued back together."

"You saved the handle? I thought you were going to toss it out."

Claire blushed. "I, um . . . well, it would have been a shame to throw it away after you'd kept it, especially since you'd kept it to remember me. So I put it in my jewelry box . . . I guess so I could remember you."

Warren studied the teacup, then his fiancée. A lot of things had been torn apart the last four and a half years—Europe, the teacup, himself, and Claire. He supposed now was the time to mend what was left.

* * *

*Calais, France*

The sky rained water, ordinary water, through the calm, misty morning. It fell on everything, turning the grass an emerald green with its moisture and bowing the new buds in the garden with its weight. Occasionally a rumble sounded, but it was thunder, not artillery fire, and thus troubled Julian little.

Julian gazed around the dairy as he walked from the barn to the house. The garden was weeded, the roof was mended, and last week he'd put a fresh coat of paint on the barn. He thought he would have everything fixed the way he wanted by the end of the summer.

Four years of war . . . four years of thinking he would never take over the dairy as planned. The rain soaked his shirt as he inhaled the smell of rich, damp earth. He felt a lump in his throat. So many people had died, but for some reason, God had seen fit to let him live a little longer.

He shifted his gaze and caught sight of something even better than the dairy. Evette opened the kitchen door and called out to him. "Your shoes will take hours to dry if you don't come inside soon."

"Hmm. Then I'll have to spend hours inside alone with you until they dry." Julian's father had gone into town and was unlikely to return until the rain stopped.

"Sounds miserable. Perhaps on your way in, you should step there." She pointed to a puddle. "Then you'll be stuck with me all day."

He strolled over to her and took her hand, pulling her out into the rain. Her shoulders rose in surprise as the cool water hit the back of her neck. "You are positively wicked, Julian."

"I'm just making sure you'll be stuck inside too."

She laughed. "In that case, I have the rest of today all planned out. First you will ooh and ahh over my completed knitting project. Then we'll see about getting out of our wet clothing. And after that . . ." She shrugged, then gave him that smile of hers he loved, the one that made her whole face light up.

He leaned in and met her lips, kissing her long and deep. She seemed to melt into him, and one of her hands reached up to play with his wet hair. He held her waist and paused for an instant, watching her as she caught her breath. There was so much in the depths of her eyes—pain from the past, joy for the present, and hope for the future. "What are you thinking about, Evette?"

She sighed as Julian moved his lips to her neck. "I'm not thinking; I'm feeling."

"And what do you feel?" He pulled his mouth from her skin, wanting to focus only on her words.

Evette snuggled closer. "I feel safe and loved. And eager for your undivided attention over the next hour or so."

Julian ran his finger along her jaw, guiding her mouth to his for a kiss full of passion. His bride of three months draped her arms around his neck, and he scooped her up to take her inside, fully prepared to make the appropriate compliments about the infant-sized socks she'd been working on. Evette now carried his child—the child and the future Julian had almost given up on. He folded his arms more securely around her back and carried her into their home. She would have his attention not only for the next hour but for the rest of their lives together.

# Notes and Acknowledgments

SINCE COMPLETING MY FIRST NOVEL, *Espionage*, I've wanted to go back and write about Julian Olivier's spy work during the Great War. I was nervous to jump into a new time period, but the more I researched, the more interested I became in WWI. Like WWII, WWI spanned a wide range of experiences, and I hope I've given readers a glimpse of them in this novel.

By the May 1915 Artois offensive, only a portion of the French Army had received the new Adrian helmet, so I've chosen to depict Julian, Maximo, and their unit in kepis. All events shown or referred to on the battlefield are based on fact, as was the declining morale of the French Army in 1917. Oddly enough, most sources report that Germany didn't find out about the mutinies until they were long quelled. Though every soldier who fought would have had a slightly different view on the war, opinions shown or expressed by Julian, Warren, Emile, and Willi were created to mirror the fears, frustrations, and hopes of real soldiers of the Great War.

The story of a German embassy worker falling asleep on the subway and losing his briefcase to the U.S. Secret Service is true, but the newspaper article was created for this novel. The incidents of sabotage, including a proposed invasion of Canada, really were considered during the war, but some of them came from a source other than the briefcase.

The Lothair League and its members are all fictional, but there were German saboteurs trying to disrupt Allied production and German spies trying to stir up labor unrest. The Renault factory in Boulogne-Billancourt existed during the war, but during my research, I didn't come across any examples of attempted or successful sabotage there. German agents were in Marseilles during the war, and they gathered information on shipping for U-boats, but Lohr wasn't involved. Lohr's postwar plot to disturb the peace settlement is wholly fiction.

Sauer wasn't real, but his background as head of Krupp's industrial espionage department is based on Krupp's sometimes questionable business practices in the prewar years. General information about the Krupp Factory complex, its products, and the Essen testing range are based on history. Some details, such as the building near the testing range and the chemical weapons held there, are based on conjecture, plausibility, and the needs of the story rather than on research. Information about Mr. and Mrs. Faber is true. The Paris Gun did exist and really did hit Paris. Mention of its development is adjusted to fit the plot.

The story of French officers telling their men to take off their rain coats because they were khaki rather than blue comes from *Poilu* by Louis Barthas.

The story of fixing a plane's radiator with soap comes from the writings of James McCudden (*Flying Fury: Five Years in the Royal Flying Corps*), one of Britain's most successful WWI aces.

Wages for factory workers and soldiers changed during the war and the inflation that accompanied it. The figures Evette and Julian discuss during their first meeting are admittedly from a few months later than early autumn 1915 but are included to show the discrepancy in pay between the groups.

During this era, a white feather was often given to men not in uniform to suggest they were cowards.

I have come across examples of counterintelligence officials walking dogs in the hope that the dog would identify an arrested spy's friends. In my research, however, these examples came from WWII rather than WWI and were planned by the Gestapo rather than British Intelligence.

The fictional Kallweit family had perhaps an easier war experience than the average German family during the war but a more difficult experience than was normal for members of their class.

Kaiser Wilhelm's paternal grandfather, Wilhelm I, won military victories over Denmark, Austria, and France, and successfully unified Germany. Kaiser Wilhelm's maternal grandmother was Queen Victoria of Great Britain.

The story of a Canadian soldier being crucified by the Germans is unconfirmed, but different versions of the event appeared in newspapers all over the world in 1915. Fact or fiction, it was used as propaganda throughout the war.

As with all my projects, I received vital help from others. Thanks goes to my test readers: Melanie Grant for letting me know I was on the right track with the history; Linda White, who always pushes me to write my best; Brad Grant for pointing out several significant ways to improve the plot and the characters; and author Rebecca Belliston for boosting my confidence in the story and pointing out several things that needed to be corrected. An extra-special thanks goes to Lilo Huhle-Poelzl for reviewing the manuscript with an eye for catching errors about everyday life in Germany. And to Ron Machado for doing the same thing with a pilot's eye. Naturally, any mistakes about

German culture or WWI-era aviation are mine. Thank you to Sacha for her help with Claire's Southern use of the double modal. If I got it right, it is thanks to her. If I got it wrong, it's my fault. And thank you to members of my writing group and fellow Covenant authors Kathi Oram Peterson and Jeanette Miller for their help and insight.

Thanks also goes to my long-suffering editor, Sam, and the rest of the team at Covenant. And to my mapmaker, Briana Shawcroft.

I would like to express love and appreciation for my family. This book took longer than usual to complete, and my husband and children were patient as I worked to finish it during a busy time for our family. I am also extremely grateful to my Father in Heaven for the mix of blessings and challenges He has given me throughout my life. To paraphrase some of my characters, life isn't perfect, but it is good.

* * *

Readers who wish to know more about Julian and Evette's children may want to read my WWII trilogy: *Espionage*, *Sworn Enemy*, and *Deadly Alliance*.

# About the Author

WHEN SHE WAS A CHILD, A. L. Sowards knew she someday wanted to be a mom and an author. Some of her other wishes, like making the U.S. Olympic swim team, didn't work out, but you could say she's living her dream by squeezing writing time in between naptime, stroller rides, and homework sessions. She enjoys reading, writing, learning about history, and eating chocolate, sometimes all at once.

Previous to this book, Sowards wrote four novels set during the Second World War, including two Whitney Award finalists. This is her first novel set during the Great War, but she doubts it will be her last. Find A. L. Sowards online at her website, ALSowards.com, and on Facebook, Twitter, and Goodreads.